LAST SPY OUT

Robert Andrews

BANTAM BOOKS

NEW YORK · TORONTO · LONDON · SYDNEY · AUCKLAND

LAST SPY OUT
A Bantam Falcon Book / June 1991

*FALCON and the portrayal of a boxed "f" are trademarks of
Bantam Books, a division of Bantam Doubleday Dell
Publishing Group, Inc.*

ISBN 0-553-29126-2

Published simultaneously in the United States and Canada

---

*Bantam Books are published by Bantam Books, a division of
Bantam Doubleday Dell Publishing Group, Inc. Its trademark,
consisting of the words "Bantam Books" and the portrayal of a
rooster, is Registered in U.S. Patent and Trademark Office and in
other countries. Marca Registrada. Bantam Books, 666 Fifth
Avenue, New York, New York 10103.*

PRINTED IN THE UNITED STATES OF AMERICA

RAD   0 9 8 7 6 5 4 3 2 1

This is for B.J.,
and for Bandit, who has gone to the Heaviside
Layer.

This book is fiction, as are its characters, except for those who have chosen to stand in the light of public scrutiny, and even their thoughts and actions are creations of the author's imagination.

The Central Intelligence Agency does exist, thank God, and the descriptions of its analytic and operational sources and methods are as accurate as the law and common sense allow.

Author's Note

Old habits linger on. Even after leaving the intelligence business, one continues to feed bulging and ill-kempt files. The excerpts below are from those files and are the seeds of this story.

Whatever direction Gorbachev follows, we believe that . . . tension within society and the leadership will increase. Bureaucrats will become increasingly frustrated by loss of privileges and status and by demands that they show greater initiative. Military leaders are likely to become more and more uneasy if benefits from the industrial modernization fail to materialize. Soviet citizens will need to see some improvement in living standards if the regime is to achieve necessary gains in worker productivity and avoid widespread discontent.

[Gorbachev's] failure to head off these tensions would, at a minimum, make it more difficult to pursue his economic program vigorously and could, ultimately, call

into question his strong political position at home. [Emphasis added.]

—*Gorbachev's Economic Program: Problems Emerge* Central Intelligence Agency report to Congress. 13 April 1988.

Revolutionary changes are sweeping what we once called the Soviet bloc of nations. Communist parties and Marxist doctrines are collapsing or already lie in ruins. . . . As these upheavals continue to gain momentum, they will be progressively more difficult to suppress. In fact, the changes are probably already irreversible in several critical respects: perhaps most important, there is little chance that Soviet hegemony could be restored in Eastern Europe.

. . . *even a major reversal of leadership and policies in Moscow would be unlikely to restore an international order resembling the one that existed until only a few years ago.* [Emphasis added.]

—Statement of the Director of Central Intelligence before the Armed Services Committee, House of Representatives. 1 March 1990.

Prologue

Bremen, Germany

The gigantic plaza was packed. Gas and battery lanterns lit the beer- and sausage-sellers' tents set up against the buildings rimming the Markplatz. Steam from breath and body heat hung in the frosty air over the crowd. Everywhere torches held high flickered in the night.

The chant began by the Schütting, the sixteenth-century guild hall. At first only a few voices, it was picked up by more as it rolled off the front of the building around the periphery of the square. Then, having circled back on itself, the chant gathered strength as it was taken up by those in the middle of the mob.

The thousands shouted: the students, the dockworkers, the housewives, the pensioners. It was a rasping, demanding roar. A traditional German band picked up the harsh beat with a Prussian marching song. The crowd became a live thing, pulsating, swaying, closing ever tighter around the heart of the square. *"Dietrich! Dietrich! Wo ist Dietrich?* DIETRICH! DIETRICH! WO IST DIETRICH?"* Dietrich! Dietrich! Where is Dietrich?

* * *

"It's no use." She tried to put it lightly. There was something about this one that was frightening. "Perhaps later . . ."

Neuhaus's massive open hand caught her left cheek, rocking her head back. He was now out of the overstuffed chair, standing above the woman cowering on the floor before him.

"Slut," he spat. Zipping his trousers, he slapped her again. She whimpered for mercy. Neuhaus reveled in the power of it. It was exhilarating.

Opening the door of the hotel room, he heard her start to cry. He allowed himself a caress of his now tumescent cock as he stepped out into the corridor. His bodyguards, three on each side, fell in with him as he made his way to the elevator and to the crowds below.

Suddenly, massive banks of floodlights sent shafts of light stabbing down from the balustrade of the town hall. The light focused on a giant statue of the fifteenth-century Teutonic knight, Roland. Towering over thirty feet above the center of the Markplatz, Roland grasped a great two-handed sword. The eagle of Imperial Germany glared from his shield.

The speaker's platform, festooned in blood red bunting, was at the base of the statue, still well above the crowd. At each end of the platform, two young women came forward to light massive torches. As the torches flared, the crowd gave a guttural moan of appreciation and surged even closer. The chant began again.

DIETRICH! DIETRICH! WO IST DIETRICH?

As suddenly as the floodlights had come on, they turned off. Instantly the crowd fell silent. The lights came on again. Alone, at the center of the platform, stood Neuhaus. Dressed in a factory worker's blue cotton jacket, he raised his right arm, fist clenched. A bright spotlight below him cast his shadow over the statue behind him. He shouted to the crowd, pumping his right arm, his words made into a thunderous pronouncement by a hidden sound system.

ICH BIN DIETRICH! DIETRICH IST HIER!

Then Dietrich Neuhaus addressed the television cameras and repeated in English,

I AM DIETRICH! DIETRICH IS HERE!

Massive cheering exploded and reverberated in the Markplatz. Neuhaus turned slowly on the platform, the lights transforming his blond hair into a golden crown. All the time he held his clenched fist aloft, saluting his followers, urging them on. As he offered himself to a new part of the crowd, those he faced clamored for him. The Markplatz became a frenzied orgy. Neuhaus aroused men as well as women, projecting himself to them. Each lusted to touch Neuhaus, to feel his flesh, to see if he was real.

Completing his circuit, Neuhaus dropped his arm. The crowd fell dead silent. He stood without moving, then became a lover making a pledge, filling the square with a hoarse, amplified whisper: *"Ein Deutschland."*

The crowd-animal erupted with a primal roar. *"Ja, Ja, Ein Deutschland."* One Germany.

Neuhaus raised his voice to a trembling shout.

"There are those who say Germany should not have been united."

From the crowd there was a savage restlessness. It was the wakening of a beast.

"There are those who say we should still be divided, East and West."

Now a hail of curses.

"We know!" his voice roared. "We know, don't we, who they are?"

"Yes, yes," roared back the crowd.

"There are the British," Neuhaus taunted the beast, curling his words with contempt, holding up the first of his store of villains, "whose idea of a united Europe is one in which Germany is reduced to a servant." Neuhaus paused. "We will not eat scraps from England's table," he swore to the accompaniment of applause and shouting. Neuhaus raised both arms toward the sky, hands closed into fists. "Shall we entrust Germany's future to the British?"

Again, louder, the shouts, the curses, the *no*s.

Neuhaus dropped his arms. Hands now on the railing of the platform, he leaned forward and, in a conspiratorial working-class voice, told the crowd, "There are the Americans." A wave of murmuring discontent swept the crowd. "And there are the Russians." Another wave, louder, more angry than the first. "Their troops are still on our soil." The crowd was now seething, a bubbling caldron of anger. "Shall we let them stay?"

"No, no. Don't let them." In the crowd Neuhaus's female agitators began. "Send them home, send them home." Soon the crowd picked it up. The sound waves battered against the walls enclosing the square.

Sensing the peak, Neuhaus raised his hands. "And the special money interests." As he said it, the crowd fell silent, slavering to exorcise another demon. "They have manipulated our economy! They have made the German mark useless! They have stolen the milk from our children! They have taken jobs from good German men and women!"

On cue Neuhaus's male agitators started. "Kill them, kill them."

For long minutes the crowd vented its bloodlust. As if in time with a great metronome, thousands of voices echoed, "Kill them, kill them." Again, at the peak of the tumult, Neuhaus raised his hands. The wall of noise cut abruptly, though the silence still seemed to pulse with the massive beat of the crowd's heart.

Neuhaus began his tirade. His voice was more than a rich baritone. It was a fine tool, synchronized with every gesture of his hands, arms, and head. Voice rising, then falling, Neuhaus paced the long platform. Now he looked down into the front ranks of the crowd. Now he extended his arms to those at the very back. Now he raised his face to the sky, seeming to implore some very special German god.

It was a voice that was being heard across Germany—a harsh voice that harangued growing crowds from the Rhine to the borders of Poland. It was a voice that evoked forgotten histories and rediscovered destinies. It was a voice in whose wake hundreds of thousands of Germany's newly disillusioned raised the old flags, sang the old anthems.

This night Neuhaus began with the defeat of the First World War, and how the German people had been stabbed in the back. He led the crowd through the thirties, when Hitler betrayed national socialism by selling out to Krupp and his gang of belly-worshiping industrialists. He carried them through the postwar years, when Germany was parceled out and raped for the profit and enjoyment of the Russians and the Americans and their hangers-on. He reminded them again how the two Germanys had been set against each other, armed clients of Moscow and Washington.

Neuhaus's face was now flushed and, despite the cold, covered with a fine sheen of sweat. He was coming to the climax. The crowd sensed it in the changing rhythm of his words and his quickening arm motions.

"Even after the Wall, even since reunification," he raged, "Germany has been ravaged by *der Auslanders*—the foreigners!" He strode to one end of the platform and looked down on the crowd there. "Inflation! Unemployment! We know the cause! You and I! We know!"

The crowd, quiet, listened with the rapt attention of students. "It is the special money interests! They have captured our government! Gerhard Heinemann," Neuhaus shouted with contempt. "He is not our leader! He is the footman of the Rothschild bankers!"

From the sound system came the first, almost tentative, notes of music. The audio specialist below the platform gradually began turning up the volume as Neuhaus's voice rose in pitch.

"We Germans vote next week! What is it that Germany needs?" Neuhaus asked.

From the back of the crowd, the agitators took their cue. "Dietrich," they shouted.

Neuhaus repeated more stridently: "We vote next week! What is it that Germany needs?"

This time the answer came back louder, thousands of voices louder. "Dietrich, Dietrich, *Dietrich!*"

Within seconds the crowd took up the cry. Neuhaus stood in the center of the blue white fire of the floodlights. He saluted the crowd again with the clenched right fist, turning slowly. When he came around full circle, the lights went out, and Neuhaus disappeared into the blackness. Now the music swelled and the crowd, recognizing it, joined in singing. *"Deutschland, Deutschland, über Alles."* Germany, Germany, over all.

One

The flight attendant checked the small cabin. It was less than half-full. Still, the passenger in One-F had two first-class tickets, one just to keep the adjacent seat vacant—tickets that had been delivered by a Marine officer from the American embassy. One-F had barely made the connection from Nairobi, and the captain had gotten word by wireless that One-F would be met by the Secret Service when they touched down in the States.

"C. Ford," as he was carried on the manifest, would have drawn the flight attendant's interest without the travel arrangements. She had been struck by the lean, angular face, clear blue eyes, and a promising smile that had come and gone all too quickly. He was a slender six feet, give or take a fraction; black hair, slightly graying, with a snow white streak running from just over his right ear toward the back of his head. Late forties, early fifties. Tanned. Probably that from Africa. He moved easily. A skier, perhaps? No jewelry. No wedding band, though that meant nothing. Meant damned little either way, she amended.

Telford awoke. Feeling a grittiness, he closed his eyes, massaged the eyelids, then opened them again.

Here and there in the darkened cabin, a few reading lamps funneled light down from the ceiling. He shifted in his seat. Outside the window bright stars pinpricked the sky down to an inky black horizon; they were still over the Atlantic. He found Betelgeuse, the red giant, near Orion's shoulder and judged the angle to the horizon—they would fly with the darkness almost into Washington.

He looked at his watch. Still on Kenya time. Groggily he wrestled with the time zones, then subtracted eight hours. They would be landing at Dulles just after six in the morning. He didn't sleep well on airplanes, and he wouldn't ordinarily have taken the late-evening flight out of London's Heathrow. Not his preference, but, given the urgency of the message, there had been no other choice.

Coffee would be good. He fumbled to find the call button. Then, seeing he was the only passenger awake, he got up and padded down the aisle. The flight attendant sat in the last seat, asleep with paperwork in her lap. He looked at her for a moment, feeling a quick sexual warmth in his stomach. Pretty woman. Classic British complexion. Lips in a sensual pout. Blouse hinting of full breasts. Cautiously, gently, he touched her shoulder.

She woke with a start, eyes round, mouth slightly open. He whispered his request for coffee.

She gathered herself; then, having gotten her bearings, she prepared her best smile for him. But he'd already turned to go back to his seat. Chiding herself for her disappointment, she made more noise than necessary in the galley. Abrupt, that one.

Cup in hand, Telford looked out again to the stars. It wasn't often you knew that a different, entirely different, chapter was about to begin. Rarely were changes so clean-cut.

He had seen too many men pitch their lives away in eight-hour pieces, working in someone else's office for wages others declared they were worth. He shrank from them—from the shelter seekers. They drove him, as now, to pit himself against new challenges.

This was a good place to be, he thought, this vault between heaven and earth. A place to sort through the colored chips, the mosaic of his life. Like the marriage that had gone bad so imperceptibly.

They had married for all the wrong reasons that the times threw up to them: that was what couples were *supposed* to do. The successive hoops became ever less satisfying. Their sex, once white hot and all-consuming, had been the first to go. Then communication. With greater fury they slashed at each other with the weapons forged from betrayed trust.

After the divorce he had sought refuge in his work. Riding the booming tide of California's burgeoning aerospace industry, Telford had built a third-tier electronics laboratory into a broad-based company that mixed it up as an equal with the likes of Rockwell, Lockheed, and Hughes.

Astronetics International soon dominated the black world of espionage. It was Telford who made the cover of *Newsweek* and fortunes for stockholders on secret contracts for the most advanced space technology. And it was Telford who put together the design teams for the spy satellites and the high-flying airplanes that formed the backbone of America's far-flung intelligence empire.

There was more to it than Telford's drive and engineering genius. Unlike most of the industry mullahs who took great pains to avoid Washington, Telford frequently flew east to learn about the bureaucratic rivalries of the often-feuding, always-competing fiefdoms inside the American intelligence community. He got to know the faceless men who formed the shifting alliances in the vicious Washington trench warfare for political power and for a fatter share of next year's budget.

Telford had slowly gained access to the celebrities of the espionage establishment: CIA, the signal-snooping National Security Agency, and the Defense Intelligence Agency at the Pentagon. He was even welcome at the smaller and more secretive Exoatmospheric Surveillance Center, which directed clandestine missions into outer space. There were also the bland offices with titles made up from a pool of sterile words such as *joint, studies,* and *observations.* And he became known in still others that had no names at all.

They were good years, years when Telford had walked with an easy confidence. As he savored past triumphs, Telford felt the cold, familiar pull of a darker memory, of a January morning—of aiming the remote at the screen and thumbing the buttons. The recorder would rewind. Knowing what would happen, yet unable to stop, he would watch again: cobalt blue suddenly furrowed by white arching plumes as the space shuttle *Challenger* eviscerated itself in the skies over Florida.

From the very beginning, when the shuttle design was unveiled, Telford had questioned the solid-fuel boosters. All other manned missions had relied on better-known liquid fuels. Astronetics had nothing to do with the boosters, however—only with the shuttle vehicle itself.

And so Telford had said nothing. But as the pieces of *Challenger* hurtled into the Atlantic, he knew. It had been the boosters.

The trauma was endless. There were the agonizing technical postmortems of the disaster. And the press: the network superstar anchor who drunkenly bragged at a Beverly Hills party that he would boost his ratings by turning *Challenger* "into the space program's Three Mile Island."

Through his window Telford saw that Betelgeuse had dipped closer to the black horizon. He willed himself to stop thinking about *Challenger*. The sun, having chased the plane across thousands of miles, finally splashed its gold on the wings.

Telford closed his eyes. No. It wasn't often you knew you had a choice. If he wanted, he could fly on. End up half a world away. Singapore, even. Or Bangkok. No matter. He could find something to put a hand to. God knows, money wasn't a problem.

But he'd get off in Washington. And answer George Bush's summons.

Two

Lvov, the Ukraine

The large blue truck stood in the center of a dim pool of light cast by a single bulb high in the dusty rafters of the warehouse. To one side a slight young man, no more than twenty, pulled back the truck's heavy canvas tarpaulin. Konstantin Tarapov frowned at the numbers stenciled on the sacks stacked on the truck bed, then checked his calculations. The book had called for a different fertilizer. This stuff was similar, but not the same. He glanced again at the small black notebook.

Frayed and mildewed, the notebook had been passed down from one survivor to the next, through the Ukrayinska Viyskova Organizatsiya, the fighting arm of the Ukrainian independence movement. Along with the notebook came the legends of the UVO. Of Stefan Bandera and Yaroslav Stetsko, leaders of a bloody war against the Russians, a war for Ukrainian freedom that raged throughout two decades after World War II. Of Bandera's assassination by the KGB in West Germany. Men die, Konstantin thought grimly. Legends do not.

Almost seven hundred miles southwest of Moscow, Lvov is a proud center of Ukrainian culture.

Its university was founded in 1661, nearly a century before Moscow University opened its doors. Founded by a Ukrainian prince in 1256, Lvov had been governed by Poles, Austrians, and Germans. Over the long centuries Lvov was ruled by Ukrainians but once. In 1917 the short-lived but long-remembered Ukrainian Peoples' Republic flickered into life only to be crushed by the Russians in 1923.

Konstantin snugged down the tarp and patted the truck's flanks much as he might pet a large, friendly animal. I hope we don't need you tomorrow, old friend. But you're ready if we do.

The student occupation of Lvov began at first light the next morning. Konstantin's classmates filled the streets in disciplined groups. Student commanders led their battalions, armed only with banners, to meticulously chosen objectives. One group to the train station, to block the tracks with their bodies; another to the airport, to spread across the runways. Still others fanned out to surround government offices and police headquarters and to block key intersections in the city.

"They're going for the transmitter site!" Captain Boris Krestov shouted into his microphone. Behind his command car straggled four armored personnel carriers. Surprised by the students, Krestov barely managed to scrape together a pickup force of clerks and cooks, certainly nothing like his handpicked riot squads in which he'd had such confidence.

Lvov's television and radio transmitters were at the south of the city, protected by a high reinforced concrete wall. There was but one gate to the compound, and it was closed. Krestov saw the guard towers were unmanned. He also saw a massive crowd of students approaching the gate along the avenue to his right. His small convoy and the crowd were equidistant from the gate, perhaps two hundred yards away.

Like a giant amoeba, the crowd's rudimentary neural circuits only slowly became aware of Krestov's little convoy. The students at the fringe reacted first, then as word of the convoy penetrated the crowd, more turned their attention from the closed gate to the dark olive troop carriers.

"Block the gate," Krestov ordered over his radio. Not waiting for an acknowledgment from the carriers behind him, he nodded to his driver. Krestov's armored car lurched ahead.

The students began racing for the gate. From its depths came angry shouts and a growing hail of stones. Through his command periscope Krestov saw the personnel carriers were close behind him. Seconds ahead of the crowd's advance guard, Krestov made it to the gate, his car and the personnel carriers forming a ragged cordon. He spun the dials of his radio to the headquarters command frequency. He would button up and sit this out. Relief forces surely would reach him in minutes.

But Lvov was gridlocked. Hasty barriers of overturned trucks and felled trees blocked every approach to the transmitters. The students formed a semicircle perhaps twenty yards from Krestov and his personnel carriers.

Paving-stone barrages pelted Krestov's car, the din making it nearly impossible to think. Krestov tried his radio, his throat tightening from fear and his hand sweaty on the transmit button. Nothing—

no response from headquarters. More stones rang on the armor. Krestov tried to swallow a growing feeling of claustrophobia and desperation.

In the second ranks of the crowd, a student knelt beside a backpack, pulled out a vodka bottle whose bottom was covered with rags. Soaking the rags from a small can of lighter fluid, he carefully elbowed his way to the front. Grasping the bottle by its long neck, he lit the rags and in a smooth underhand toss lofted the burning bottle toward the nearest personnel carrier.

The carrier's gunner, a frightened private that Krestov had pulled from a supply room, saw the flaming bottle arching toward him. Unfamiliar with his controls, he traversed the turret around in jerky stops, hysterically firing long uncontrolled bursts first into the sky, then into the ground, and, finally, into the crowd.

By the time Krestov got the shooting stopped, dozens of bodies were sprawled on the street. As if by some dark power, the crowd had vanished, though Krestov knew they were huddled in doorways and hidden in side streets just out of his line of sight. The silence was as frightening as the tumult had been.

Krestov was startled by a grinding roar, distant at first, then rapidly louder. He pressed his face to the rubber mask of the periscope. He saw a large blue truck hurtling down the avenue toward him. Toward him and the gate. It was the last thing Boris Krestov would see.

The massive collision of the truck and Krestov's armored car drove Konstantin Tarapov through the windshield. The dead-man switch he'd rigged worked flawlessly. The moment his hands left the steering wheel, a spring closed a circuit. The electrical blasting caps set off the half sticks of dynamite stolen from the quarry. In turn, these provided the heat and shock necessary to detonate the five tons of ammonium nitrate fertilizer tightly packed in concrete sewer pipe.

Seconds later the students poured into the transmitter site and raised the blue-and-yellow flag of the Ukraine Republic. Their first broadcast announced the birth of an independent Ukraine and paid homage to the Ukraine's newest legend, Konstantin Tarapov.

The Washington Post

UKRAINE VIOLENCE ROCKS THE KREMLIN
Gorbachev Orders Army to Suppress Uprising
by Kathy Babcock

Moscow—Reacting quickly to what sources here call a "general uprising," President Mikhail Gorbachev has ordered the Soviet army to restore order in the Ukraine.

Although the Ukraine has been closed to Western journalists, persistent reports from the troubled region describe the violence as the result of a well-organized struggle for Ukrainian independence, rather than spontaneous demonstrations against unpopular policies or consumer shortages.

The epicenter of yesterday's political upheaval appears to have been in the ancient city of Lvov, where, after forcing entry to state facilities, students broadcast radio and television declarations of a "Free Ukraine Republic," and appealed for recognition and assistance from the United Nations.

Caught by surprise, the Bush administration . . .

Moscow

Gregori Romanov thought for a moment, then looked at the shorter of the two men before him. Through the thick stone walls, he could hear the faint pealing of the bells of Saint Basil's. He chose his words carefully, Mikhail Gorbachev was not one for verbosity.

"Their intentions were clear. They were out to spark a political struggle." The bells ceased. Romanov leaned forward ever so slightly. "They want an independent Ukraine—a Ukraine free of the Soviet Union."

Romanov's words fell into the thick silence of the Kremlin room. Morning sun through the high-set windows warmed the air chilled by a night of Moscow winter. Gorbachev and Eduard Shevardnadze, the foreign minister, sat expressionless, waiting for him to continue.

"The UVO—the Ukrainian rebels," Romanov continued, "have rebuilt the networks Stalin believed he'd destroyed. Apparently Stalin wasn't as successful as we had thought. Obviously the UVO went deeply underground. They hid weapons and communications equipment the Americans and

British sent them in the forties. They have maintained clandestine training schools. The explosion in Lvov was a textbook example of expedient demolitions." Romanov drew a finger across his throat. "They weren't posturing. They were playing for keeps."

A grim-faced Gorbachev interrupted. "The leadership. Have we identified them?"

Romanov shook his head and made a helpless gesture with his hands. "They made it through . . ." It would do no good to finish, to say that the Ukrainian underground that survived Stalin could easily hide in the time of *glasnost.*

Gorbachev studied the younger man before him. Gregori Stepanovich Romanov, like Gorbachev and Yuri Andropov, had grown up in the Stavropol region. And one's roots still meant much, even after seventy years of socialist internationalism. Because of those roots the slender dark-haired man had been a trusted confidant of Andropov in the perilous months when Andropov, as head of the KGB, battled Brezhnev and his cronies to become Brezhnev's successor. It had been Romanov who turned aside Brezhnev's last and most threatening attempt to destroy Andropov.

As the new Soviet leader, Yuri Andropov's first act had been to put Romanov in control of the most critical directorates of the KGB. Andropov wanted to be certain that Moscow Center was truly the sword and shield of the Party and remained under his control now that he was general secretary.

The Brezhnev clique had enjoyed momentary success after Andropov's unexpected death. Konstantin Chernenko, a Brezhnev toady, managed to vault into Andropov's chair. But Chernenko lived

only a few months after becoming general secretary.
And so, Mikhail Gorbachev.

There had been whispers at Chernenko's funeral. Whispers that Romanov had had a hand in
Chernenko's sudden demise. They were useful rumors, strengthening the perception that the KGB
was solidly in support of Gorbachev.

Gorbachev himself had moments of curiosity
about Romanov, but there were questions even Gorbachev left unasked.

Unsmiling, Gorbachev stood. Shevardnadze remained seated, his face impassive, staring at the
notepad before him. Romanov knew it was time to
go. He closed the file folder. As he left the room, he
glanced back. It was as if he were looking down a
hall of years to an older, aged Gorbachev. The Soviet
leader stood, shoulders slumped, his vitality drained.

Gorbachev waited until the door was completely shut. He turned to face a distraught Shevardnadze. Gorbachev laughed bitterly. "Well, Eduard
Amvrosiyevich, I imagine there are those who will
attempt to take advantage of this in quick order."

With a wry smile Gorbachev put a hand on the
seated Shevardnadze's shoulder. "The Ukrainians!
They've always had their own way of causing trouble. Now they put us in the role of the counterrevo-
lutionaries. One must admire them. Their spirit,
their flair. What is the French for it? *Panache?*"

Bonn

Helmut Kohl, chancellor of the German Federal Republic, stood looking from his window, across
the Rhine, toward the darkening east. Winter rains

had set in three days ago, and now even Kohl's office echoed the damp chill outside. Now well into his sixties, Kohl was still an erect, solidly built man. He drummed the windowsill lightly with his fingertips, stared another moment into the gathering mist, then turned to his visitor.

"Another dreary day in Bonn. There've been so many lately, it seems." The leering face of Dietrich Neuhaus haunted Kohl. "At any rate, it's my last. What is so galling is that that bastard Neuhaus won't ever have to put up with this place." He smiled ruefully. "I leave Bonn, and the next chancellor of Germany gets Berlin." It had been only a year ago, Kohl reflected, when the final act of reunification had been to declare that Berlin, once again, would be the capital of Germany. He remembered the somber mix of pride and sadness with which he'd signed the legislation.

Moving slowly because of the lower back pain that had come calling during the early morning hours, Kohl eased himself onto a straight wooden chair opposite the sofa and Erwin Pordzik.

Pordzik, a brilliant political analyst, the enfant terrible of Kohl's Christian Democratic Union, had brought the official results of yesterday's elections. There had never been any doubt that Neuhaus would win. The only question was the margin. And it was considerable.

Kohl had listened stonily.

"We have lost our bearings, Erwin." Unable to sit, Kohl heaved himself off the chair, wincing from the sudden pain. "It was my responsibility to point the way. To provide those bearings."

"It wasn't a matter of bearings," Pordzik disagreed gently. "There were things beyond your control."

Most observers agreed that Kohl's downfall began with the problem of absorbing East Germany after reunification. Although East Germany was by far the most prosperous of Moscow's former satellites, it was an impoverished relation compared to West Germany. Its roads and railways were run-down. Industrial pollution was staggering, and after the Wall thousands of East Germans daily fled their homes and jobs to resettle in the West.

The problem was to keep the East Germans in place. Bonn—Kohl—had first tried currency reform, exchanging the East German mark on a par with the stronger West German mark. Bundles of East German marks appeared for conversion. And still the refugees came west, albeit richer. Inflation mounted. Finally the tottering East German economy collapsed, a resounding implosion that created millions of unemployed.

"And then there were the Americans," Pordzik began a suggestion.

"Yes," interrupted Kohl with the air of a man weary of trading in used arguments. "Always the Americans. A convenient excuse for our troubles."

"Meddlers," sniffed Pordzik.

"Saviors," countered Kohl. "They wouldn't have come here except for Hitler, and they wouldn't have stayed except for the Russians. They can be stupid at times. Occasionally even more arrogant than we or the French. But never malevolent, never malicious."

Kohl returned to the window. Off to his right he could see the lights burning in a boxy high-rise office building. The Bundestag was still in session. The last session in Bonn. On the Rhine a tug was nosing a barge of coal north toward Düsseldorf.

He turned to face Pordzik. "Whatever their strengths and weaknesses, we have gotten used to the Americans—to our accidental guests. For over half a century, they've been major players in Europe. Much of the time we knew where they stood. And more important, so did the Russians. We've all cursed American stubbornness. But that stubbornness convinced Moscow that any adventures in Europe would be met with all-out war. With the atomic weapons. There would be no sanctuaries. We would all be in the stew together."

"Until now," Pordzik prompted. The German analyst had been an observer in Washington, watching the Senate debate on stationing Americans in Europe. Even before Neuhaus the winds of freedom sweeping through Eastern Europe and the continuing uneasiness in the Middle East oil fields made it more difficult each day to justify keeping hundreds of thousands of American troops in Europe.

Kohl shook his head. "The debate in Washington was a warning of growing American weariness. They grew tired of risking nuclear war to protect an increasingly wealthy and arrogant Europe."

"But if they remove their troops precipitously, they will only make matters worse," Pordzik protested. "They should learn. They took their nuclear missiles out and made us vulnerable to extortion by the Soviet tanks."

Kohl considered this, then nodded in agreement. "But Herrchancellor Neuhaus has pledged to make just that happen. The Americans go home. The Russians go home," he said with a touch of irony. "It seems like an equitable solution. Equitable

solutions find eager acceptance on both sides of the
Atlantic. The problem is that the Russians at home
are still very close to us, but the Americans will be an
ocean away. It would take another war for them to
return. And then it would be too late."

Kohl shook his head wearily. "Ah, Erwin, it was
not just the Americans. We can thank ourselves as
well." He chuckled. "Blame finding ranks above
football and sex as our favorite pastime. What matters is that we have to begin to fend for ourselves.

"For decades we complained about the Americans underfoot. But we knew we owed our freedom
and our Mercedeses to them. That ate at us. American uniforms on German soil were an affront to our
pride. Neuhaus played to that. He played quite well.
He created a situation in which our own demands
for the Americans to leave caused us to fear the
future. And when we fear for the future, we turn to
someone who shouts loudest that he has the answers."

Pordzik frowned. "Certainly you can't believe
this is something the average person understands.
Do you really believe that the office worker or car
salesman worries much about the Americans and
their role in the European balance of power?"

"Live long enough, Erwin, and you will learn
things those cannot measure." Kohl pointed to the
spill of election printouts on the low coffee table. "It
is not just the pollsters and politicians who can sense
the tide of events on the continent. The nose for a
shifting wind belongs to all Europeans. We have
taken it in with our mothers' milk. We constantly
measure the balance between war and peace, order
and chaos. We all give thought to burying a bit of

gold in the back garden, to moving our loved ones to safety in Sweden or Switzerland."

Pordzik knew it was over: the meeting and much more. He would undoubtedly see Kohl again, but not as chancellor, and never again in Bonn.

"I'm sorry." It was all he could say.

Kohl looked at the distraught Pordzik. "Thank you, Erwin," he said softly with an old-world courtliness. "To tell you the truth, I feel sorry for myself at times. And, to be even more honest, angry at the people for turning me out."

The older man raised his eyebrows and pursed his lips. "But then, perhaps in self-protection, I tell myself that no matter who sat here when unification came, it would have been the same. Our new Germany is no longer a junior partner to the Russians or Americans. The people wanted a different face, not the same old tired politicians of the Cold War."

"But Neuhaus . . ." Pordzik began the protest.

"Yes, Neuhaus. Or someone like him. Someone who wasn't tainted by association with a divided Germany. A man for the future."

"And Neuhaus is Germany's future?" Pordzik asked, not expecting an answer.

"For now he is," Kohl said philosophically. His eyes switched to the opening door. "And now for the constant in my life—Frau Weber and my supper." A middle-aged woman, hair in a bun on the back of her head, carried a small tray that she put on Kohl's desk. Lentil soup, dark bread, and a pot of herbal tea. Pordzik saw there was but one cup, and that Frau Weber gave him a severe look as she was leaving. He gathered his papers and stood.

Kohl came to Pordzik's side to walk him to the door. He gripped the younger man's shoulder. "We

Germans will always live in the jaws of a nutcracker. It is the price we pay for living in the heartland of Europe. Every so often our adversaries change. You are living in a time when such a change is taking place." Kohl pulled the young man around to face him. Pordzik was surprised at the old man's strength. "It will be an interesting time, Erwin. A very interesting time."

Helmut Kohl returned to his office. Frau Weber gave him a moment, then stuck her head through the doorway. Wordlessly Kohl waved her off, pointing to the tray on his desk. Satisfied he would be going about his supper, the old woman shut the door. She would hold all calls and give him an hour alone. He lifted the spoon, addressed the soup, then put the spoon down and swiveled his chair around toward the bust of Adenauer. The hatchet-faced old man seemed to stare reprovingly at him. Not for the first time, he addressed *"der Alte."*

"Who would have thought that Reagan, of all people, would have brought all this about? He, who started out trashing the Soviet Union? Brave words —good words. It truly is an 'evil empire.' But in the end he embraced Gorbachev. Reagan mistook the man for the machine. In so doing he destroyed the threat that united us in the West." Kohl realized he was almost shouting. Frau Weber couldn't possibly hear him, nonetheless. . . .

Kohl paused expectantly, waiting for some glint of understanding from the bronze bust. Disappointed by Adenauer's silent, icy stare, Kohl rubbed his hands together to wring out the cold. "Well, the Americans will no doubt have an opportunity to rid themselves of their burden in Europe. But it may not be exactly what they had in mind."

* * *

A week later and six hundred kilometers to the northeast, a buzzer hummed insistently in an office far larger and more ornate than Helmut Kohl's. Recognizing the signal, Dietrich Neuhaus pressed a button concealed under the edge of his desk. Behind him a wood panel opened in the wall. Neuhaus set a number in the cipher lock, opened the armored box, and lifted a white telephone handset. The conversation was brief, a conversation in German interspersed with an occasional Russian phrase. Hanging up, he closed the box and pushed the concealed button. The wall panel closed with oiled precision.

Neuhaus sat for a moment, thinking; then he operated a switch and spoke into an old-fashioned intercom box. Within minutes there was a deferential knock.

Ehren was in his forties, of a Prussian family that had dropped the *von* with the founding of East Germany. A stocky, unsmiling man, Ehren had a square, regular face, brown eyes, and thick black hair that he combed straight back from a high forehead.

Neuhaus waved Ehren to a deskside chair. Ehren sat, hands folded in his lap. The moment he sat, all motion ceased, yet Ehren seemed vibrant, charged. For nearly twenty years Neuhaus had marveled at Ehren. Neuhaus had kept up with the rapid advance of computers. But none of them could match Ehren. He'd die without mental challenge, Neuhaus thought, like a caged gazelle unable to run.

Neuhaus looked at the waiting Ehren. "I have just talked with Letnikov. He believes the Ukraine provides an adequate pretext. He has begun."

Even at this Ehren said nothing. He took in Neuhaus's report, nodded, then waited.

"We are ready, Felix?" asked Neuhaus.

Ehren nodded again. "Yes," he answered in a low, modulated baritone. "There are details to be worked out. Intermediate steps to be taken." Ehren got up from the chair. "If all goes well with our friend in Moscow, we shall be ready."

Minutes later Neuhaus sat alone once more. He savored Ehren's smile, taking delight in the man's brashness, feeling a trill of excitement. It was a goal worthy of a thousand lifetimes. Bismarck had begun the creation of the German state. Then that bastard, that incompetent Austrian, Adolf Hitler, had nearly wrecked everything.

Neuhaus got up and walked to the large window. The large square below used to be called Marx-Engels-Platz. Marx and Engels. Two Germans— their philosophy pirated by the barbarians in the Kremlin. Communism in Russia! Idiots! Russia—a nation in name only. A crazy-quilt assortment of mongrel races and outlandish religions.

The Russians had failed to make a success of communism. They stole Marx and Engels and gave us *glasnost* and *perestroika* in exchange, Neuhaus reflected bitterly. Gorbachev's spineless "reforms" had given away Eastern Europe and destroyed the East German party.

Thanks to Gorbachev the Wall was gone, and the massive street demonstrations in Leipzig and Dresden had gutted the will of the party and destroyed its ability to control the population. No, Neuhaus thought, we do not have much time left. This is the last chance to bring about the Germany that Marx and Engels had in mind. At least, he told himself with some satisfaction, if we succeed, we will do so on our own, not because it was handed to us by the Russians.

Neuhaus gazed down at the statue of Marx and Engels. Who might be standing with them a hundred years from now, he wondered. Perhaps, just perhaps, there might one day be a small German monument to Letnikov. Neuhaus enjoyed the irony of it. Yes. That would be fitting. A small German monument for Yegor Letnikov.

"I called for this special meeting, Comrade Gorbachev."

Yegor Letnikov rose from his seat and walked confidently, even arrogantly, down along the long length of the table. Every few paces he paused to search each face before him, silently demanding allegiance. Eyes would meet, and Letnikov would move on.

Vlasov, a junior member of the Politburo, obviously ill at ease, sat staring at the tabletop. Letnikov came to a full stop, glaring until Vlasov looked up, gave an almost imperceptible nod, then hung his head again.

With a chill of apprehension, Mikhail Gorbachev watched Letnikov's procession. He felt a reassuring nudge on his arm. From the corner of his eye, he caught a small smile from Shevardnadze, sitting to his right.

"We are here, Comrade Letnikov," Gorbachev said, trying to manage an even tone, hoping his voice wouldn't betray him. "What is it you wish us to consider?"

"Your expulsion from the Party."

Ah, yes, thought Gorbachev, fighting a wave of anger. I often wondered how it would be. How the balancing act might fail. It could have happened anytime. Anytime from the start. It was always that precarious.

The silence held until it was unbearable, a thread stretched until it was finally snapped by an escaping breath.

"I assume there are grounds?" Gorbachev's anger was receding, and he was surprised to find himself feeling a sense of relief—a heavy burden being lifted.

"Endangering the security of the state and betrayal of the socialist revolution."

The charges came harshly and, to Gorbachev's ear, well rehearsed. He holds all the cards, Gorbachev reasoned. He'd never have called the meeting if he didn't have the votes. Still, one did not acquiesce quietly in one's own destruction.

"Serious accusations, Comrade Letnikov. I assume you will expand on them?"

Letnikov made a face of theatrical surprise. "Why, the Ukraine, of course. The Soviet Union is near disintegration." Letnikov threw his arm in a sweeping gesture to include the table. "The loss of the Ukraine would be a dagger aimed at us here."

"And I let it happen," Gorbachev said with heavy sarcasm.

"It is but one of many mistakes. East Germany. The loss of Eastern Europe . . ."

"The people who live there, their leaders—they are to blame for what happened. They will have to live with it."

". . . and the foolish disarmament treaties!" Letnikov overrode him. "By destroying our SS-20 missiles, you have reduced the leverage we formerly exerted on Paris, London, and Bonn."

"On the contrary," Gorbachev shot back, "we drove a wedge between the Europeans and the Americans. When the Americans had the Pershings and cruises in Europe, they could strike Moscow and Leningrad. But with those missiles gone, the only nuclear missiles that can hit Russia must be launched from American soil. Few Europeans believe the Americans will risk Chicago or New York in revenge for Munich or Amsterdam."

Letnikov gave a wave of dismissal. "Destroying our missiles was a sign of softness. The same softness that led to our defeat in Afghanistan."

"Afghanistan!" Gorbachev erupted. "A misbegotten bastard of Brezhnev's stupid adventurism. I heard none of you counseling to stay there. I saw none of you sending your sons. . . ."

"Nonetheless," Letnikov insisted, boring in, "a defeat for the Red Army. It has all been downhill for us. No one trusts us since we left the Afghan party to the tender mercies of the religious rabble."

"Leaving Afghanistan was merely a tactical retreat," Gorbachev protested, despairing of getting such a sophisticated point across. "It was necessary to advance our strategic objectives. Leaving Afghanistan permitted us to exploit the divisions within the West."

"Yes," Letnikov said with silky irony, "we certainly exploited the West. Especially in Nicaragua. What a wonderful surprise we gave Washington! And you talk of divisions within the West! What of the divisions in the Soviet Union?" Letnikov asked. "*Perestroika* and *glasnost* have accomplished nothing except to erode the discipline of the Soviet peoples. There has been unrest from the Baltic to Armenia. Now it is the Ukraine. Where will it stop?"

Gorbachev stopped himself from a cutting retort. It was important to him that those around this table hear words of reason from him. Last words, perhaps, but words that would come back to haunt this fool Letnikov. "You do not understand, Comrade Letnikov. The people will not go back. . . ."

"I am not talking about going back," Letnikov broke in. "I am talking about regaining a sense of direction under firm leadership."

Gorbachev finally lost control of his temper. "Firm leadership," he snapped. "*Your* leadership, I take it?"

Giving Gorbachev an insolent look, Letnikov strode to the large double doors, flinging them open. In the large anteroom a command was shouted, and there was a crashing of feet and weapons as the platoon came to attention. Gone was the Kremlin *kommandantura*, the special guard of the KGB; these troops wore the scarlet berets of paratroopers of the Red Army.

So he has the army on his side, Gorbachev thought. In spite of his situation, he found himself admiring Letnikov's cunning and thorough planning.

"I ask for a vote," demanded Yegor Letnikov.

London

"And just how did we come about this information, Sir Rodgers?"

Rodgers Mooreman started; anyone poking around about sources and methods set off an instantaneous protective reflex. I ought to be used to it, he reproved himself. Prime Minister Eric Hill had the professional's habit of asking about the provenance of a report before getting into its substance.

"From a Most Sensitive Source, sir," casting in capitals the appellation for a highly placed human agent. In this case, the fellow was a member of the Politburo, a treasure the identity of which was one of British intelligence's most closely held secrets. Had the prime minister pressed for details, Mooreman would have given way only with the greatest reluctance.

But Eric Hill did not probe further. He poured Mooreman's tea, then his own and waited for Mooreman to get to the matter that had got them up two hours before dawn.

Mooreman consulted a pocket watch he pulled from his vest. "In six hours, Yegor Letnikov will make a special address over Europe-wide television. He will announce that Mikhail Gorbachev has stepped down."

Mooreman, the head of MI-6, the nearest British equivalent to the American CIA, watched as the prime minister took that in.

Hill, sandy-haired and younger looking than his years, had learned his politics as a Protestant in Northern Ireland's Cranmore Park. Those lessons he carried with him into Parliament as one of Margaret Thatcher's bare-knuckled backbenchers. He'd done well at requisite posts in defence and the Foreign Office, and it came as a surprise to no one that Hill gained the leadership of his party after the Iron Lady stepped down. A hand went up to the back of his neck. "I can't say it's a surprise. Even so, it is a shock." He rubbed his neck, lost in thought. "The Germans," he finally spoke, "I warned them about the unification—that it could unsettle all Europe."

Then, addressing Mooreman: "This Letnikov. I've met him before. He was the commissar, wasn't he?"

Mooreman suppressed a smile. "One might say that, sir. He was the second secretary of the Party secretariat. Responsible for ideology and personnel. Early opponent of Gorbachev. Gorbachev demoted him to Agriculture in 1988."

Tilting his chin ever so slightly upward in victory, Hill bent Mooreman's explanation into full agreement. "Ah, yes. The commissar. Sour man. Older than Gorbachev. How did it come about?"

"It was a classic Kremlin power struggle, an alignment of cliques. Gorbachev had the KGB. Letnikov apparently lined up the GRU—their military intelligence—and the army. Letnikov and his crowd exploited Eastern Europe, of course. And the unrest about the Russian economy. The slow pace of *perestroika* and fears the German problems are contagious. There are the cave-dwellers as well, who were never happy about *glasnost.*

"The final straw was the Ukraine," Mooreman continued. "Letnikov used it as a club to beat Gorbachev. Said it was proof that Gorbachev has not managed affairs properly. That he is presiding over the demise of the Soviet empire. That sort of thing."

"Is that the analysis of MI-6?"

Mooreman felt his ears redden. Hill preferred to make his own judgments without the inferences of his intelligence or Foreign Ministry staff. As prime minister, he'd insisted on separating hard facts from conjecture. It was a trait he shared with many world leaders. A trait that frustrated cabinet officers, but one with which they'd learned to live.

"It is from our source, Sir."

Hill thought for a moment. "So the opposition has an excuse to do what they've wanted. Gorbachev's reforms were too much for them. I imagine many of them saw their own little empires being swept away. Their precious privileges disappearing." He took on a note of regret. "Mikhail Gorbachev was a product of their system. Perhaps more dangerous to us than any before him. Nonetheless, I thought him one with whom I might deal on a rational basis."

Hill's blue eyes made a worried survey of Mooreman. "Will he be shot, do you think?"

"No. No, he was too powerful for that. He retains too many followers, especially in the KGB, although I should think they will be lying low for now. He'll be given some minor post. Somewhere outside Moscow."

Eric Hill studied his lanky intelligence chief. Mooreman sat stiffly upright behind the pointed knees of his long legs. One of the middle sons in a sprawling family of textile laborers, Rodgers Mooreman stood out from an unremarkable line of Lancashire yeomen by his ability to run the low hurdles—which got him into Oxford—and by a keenly probing intellect—which got him into the clandestine service. Hill trusted him. Unlike many, he was not constantly out to prove himself. Though shy of cameras, he willingly marched toward the sound of the guns.

Elizabeth II had given Mooreman the ivory ten years before, while Margaret Thatcher was prime minister. The small plaque was the token of an office that Her Majesty's government still refused to acknowledge existed, even after centuries of faithful service to the Crown. As the head of the Secret Intelligence Service, Mooreman, as those before him, was referred to only as "C," and then but in whispers.

"Prime Minister, 'C.' We must inform Washington at once." The plummy voice, with a slight but petulant lisp, came from a deep chair slightly to Hill's left. Its owner was of an age made indeterminate by gross rolls of fat. Sir Charles Lister was Hill's new foreign minister. More precisely, he was Hill's cross. The price he'd had to pay for the support of a noisy claque of "moderates" in the Conservative party, who'd threatened to bolt to the left if their man was not named to the Whitehall post.

Capturing a frown, Hill glanced toward Lister. This vulgar pudding was born pompous, he thought. A master of the banal. "In good time, Sir Charles."

Then, as he was turning toward Mooreman for another question, Lister again sallied forth. "But Prime Minister! The Americans are determined to reach a new relationship with Moscow. We should be more accommodating." Lister nodded toward Mooreman. "Information such as C's should be provided Washington at once. I shall prepare the necessary telegrams. . . ."

"We've been at this before, Sir Charles. In the first instance, you know I do not agree with your assessment of the Americans. They are not of one mind about abandoning Europe."

"But now! Now even the Germans want them out. Neuhaus. . . ," protested the fat man, one hand on a well-shaved jowl, the other waggling a bunch of pudgy fingers.

"The Americans," Hill continued, relentlessly, determined to have his way over Lister, "are still uncertain. Nothing is settled in Washington."

Hill flushed as Lister persisted. "But sir, their Congress wishes to withdraw all American troops from Europe."

"The American Congress, Sir Charles, are like naughty children who play with matches. One hopes that adults will keep them from burning down the premises."

"But. . . ."

Hill would have no more. "The White House is firm in its commitment to stand with us against such precipitate action. Your approach would undercut President Bush and leave Europe to the Germans and the Russians. The Americans who count are not ready to see that. Neither am I."

Lister recoiled as one lashed. His eyes opened round and his full red lips made a flabby O.

Mooreman sat transfixed, watching Hill, the stonemason's son. Oh, good. Give it to the pretentious bastard. Mooreman considered excusing himself, but the notion winked out as quickly as it'd come. He wanted to see Lister, the fat wreckage, get what he'd asked for.

Lister got his bulk onto its feet. He stood looking at Hill with incredulity. Then he shifted his eyes, seemingly remembering Mooreman. He made a pathetic play to his only witness. Drawing himself up in wounded dignity, he thrust his lower jaw forward. Instead of resolution, he achieved the sullen caricature of a petulant child in full pout. "This, sir, is intolerable. I cannot continue. . . ."

"I quite agree, Sir Charles," interjected Hill. "I regret it had to come to this."

Lister had the stricken look of a man who'd just kicked a pebble and realized it had become an avalanche, one that would carry him away.

Eric Hill stood and gave a small but imperative gesture toward the doorway. "I will see you out. I shall inform the cabinet secretary to expect your resignation."

Certain that he was finished with him, Mooreman was shouldering into his coat when Eric Hill returned. He had no air about him of victory won. No bravado flush on the cheeks. Rather, there was the aplomb of one who'd taken care of an unremarkable chore. They walked to the door in silence. To Mooreman's surprise, he stepped outside onto Downing Street to bid him good-bye. A constable in his domed Robert Peel helmet moved discreetly aside.

Eric Hill looked at him, reflective, sad. Coatless against the morning cold, he rubbed his hands to warm them. "We are in danger of coming apart, Rodgers. The Continent—Britain, too—we are in an awful state. This man Neuhaus," he frowned, deeply worried, "is a throwback to the worst of Germany. We have other Listers—far too many of them. And the Americans are on the verge of washing their hands of us all." He dropped his head, looked momentarily at his feet, then looked up again.

"It was Grey," he softly said to himself, obviously retrieving a scrap from his memory.

"I'm sorry, Prime Minister?"

He took Mooreman's arm. "Edward Grey, the foreign minister." Hill pointed toward the Foreign Office near St. James Park. "The evening before

First World War, he saw the lamplighters at work in the park. He knew war was coming, that things would be forever changed. It struck me so powerfully when I read about it as a young boy in school. I wondered how Grey felt." There was ever so slight a tremor in his voice. "I *used* to wonder how he felt," he amended. "I'm afraid I've found out."

Walking away into the dawn mists, Mooreman remembered Grey's words. "The lamps are going out all over Europe; we shall not see them lit again in our lifetime."

Three

Confusion wrinkled across Chernov's face. The new master of Soviet intelligence, Letnikov sighed to himself, is a dullard. From the start Letnikov knew he'd have to neutralize the awesome power of the KGB, which solidly supported Gorbachev. So he'd gone to the KGB's intramural enemy, the GRU. There he found a willing if not very bright accomplice in Boris Chernov, the chief of Soviet military intelligence.

"I repeat, Comrade Chernov: we are going to push the Americans out of Europe. Is that difficult to comprehend?"

"Yes . . . I mean, no. It is perfectly understandable," Chernov answered stiffly, trying to patch his dignity. "But that has been our goal since Stalin."

"Mikhail Gorbachev lost sight of it," Letnikov menaced. "And that's why he's admiring the shores of Lake Baykal."

Chernov recoiled, instantly meeker. "So, the Americans. But what is new? How will you—we—succeed where others have failed? How do we get the Americans to quit the field?"

Letnikov sighed. Chernov's stupidity was trying. It was too bad that he didn't have someone of the caliber of, say, the long-dead Yuri Andropov to handle this. But someone with Andropov's brains would have found out about Neuhaus. No, better to have an idiot like Chernov than for it to be known that the Germans had played such a pivotal role in Party maneuverings.

"Because, Boris Mikhaylovich," he began slowly, using Chernov's patronymic, "this time we will have the help of our newest good friends—the Germans."

The Times (London)

SOVIETS CALL FOR MUTUAL SECURITY PACT WITH GERMANY
American Troops to Leave Germany

President Letnikov today proposed a summit meeting with German chancellor Dietrich Neuhaus to discuss a "mutual security agreement" between Moscow and Berlin.

The Soviet leader, appearing before a committee of the Supreme Soviet, said that such an agreement could "strengthen stability and security in Central Europe."

Although Letnikov is not reported to have discussed American troops in Germany, that issue was discussed at length several hours later on *Vremya,* a popular Russian national television news program. American forces, the commentator stated, would be expected to leave Germany as a precondition for any agreement.

German chancellor Neuhaus was not

available for comment. German Foreign Ministry sources, however, described Neuhaus as viewing a pact with Moscow "with great caution."

Neuhaus's caution, the sources say, stems from the German leader's reluctance to align Germany with the Soviet Union. "But Neuhaus may have no choice," one senior official observed. "He sees Germany being pushed into a corner by the French and the British."

The Washington Post

LETNIKOV PROPOSAL STUNS WHITE HOUSE
Russian Scheme under "Intense Study"
by Alan Ptak

A high official today characterized the White House as "stunned" by Yegor Letnikov's proposal for a mutual security arrangement with Germany. While a spokesman for President Bush claims the matter is under "the most intense study," knowledgeable insiders say that the unexpected initiative by the new Soviet leader has caused confusion and disarray among the president's closest policy advisers.

Caught by surprise, government spokesmen in London and Paris refused to comment. In Berlin . . .

In Berlin, Chancellor Dietrich Neuhaus contemptuously tossed the photocopied clippings onto his desk. "Thank you for informing me of world events," sarcasm souring his voice.

Hoare, the British ambassador, reddened. Clearly uneasy, he shifted from one foot to the other. Beside him Laval, the French ambassador, stood glumly, a small man whose most un-Gallic ill-fitting suit and slumping posture made him a tragicomic Chaplinesque figure.

Hoare had been rocketed by Whitehall and Laval by the Quai d'Orsay to find out what the hell was going on ("Informal inquiries, Your Excellency"). Together they went to Wilhelmstrasse, having asked for a joint appointment with the foreign minister. But at the Foreign Ministry, they were shuffled directly and somewhat rudely next door to the chancellery and into Dietrich Neuhaus's ornate office.

"The clippings were but inclusions in our agenda to your foreign minister," Hoare said in an understated manner he calculated to be soothing.

Neuhaus, if anything, became even angrier. In a sweeping motion he scooped the offending clippings from his desk, crumpling them in his closed fist. He raised the fist in front of him, looked contemptuously at the tail ends of the clippings, then to Hoare and Laval.

"The press! Will they ever get anything accurate?"

Fear began to subside in Hoare's breast. Perhaps the rage was at the newspaper account. He gave a sidelong glance at Laval. The Frenchman's dour expression hadn't changed.

"So Dietrich Neuhaus 'sees Germany being pushed into a corner by the French and the British,'" he quoted the London account.

That's it, Hoare thought. He's angry at the paper. Not us. Relief flooded him. He prepared an amiable smile of sympathy for Neuhaus and searched for a bon mot to suggest that putting up with the media was a common cross for all those engaged in serious matters of state.

"I don't 'see' Germany pushed into a corner!" Neuhaus raged, his face turning dark. "Germany *is* being pushed into a corner!"

It took a full second, a seeming eternity, for Hoare to register, to forget the smile and the hunt for the droll comment. The impact of Neuhaus's statement buffeted him, and the German's obviously growing anger and agitation caused Hoare's stomach to knot and the back of his throat to taste sour. Laval remained expressionless, a wax-museum figure.

"Germany *is* being pushed into a corner!" Neuhaus repeated ever more loudly. He stood, his chair rolling violently back from the desk. "Both France and England have taken advantage of Germany. You have raped us in the European Community. Our economy is in a shambles, thanks to your clever manipulations in Brussels."

"Sir . . ." Hoare feebly began a protest.

"Silence!" screamed Neuhaus, his eyes widening and bulging. He pounded his clenched fist on the desk before him, the offending clippings still in a death grip. "And if your sabotage of our economy isn't enough, Germany has to live each day knowing it is a target of your nuclear weapons."

Hoare again tried to speak. He was barely able to get his mouth open.

"I did not call you here to *listen* to you!" Neuhaus drew himself up, a blond giant, his chin thrust out. "You are here to listen *to me!*" Suddenly Neuhaus bent forward, planting both hands wide apart on his desk, bringing his face down to within inches of the two ambassadors.

"You are going to carry a message back to Prime Minister Hill"—he glared at Hoare, then shifted to Laval—"and to whoever it is who pretends to run France today. The message is this: I will bring Germany to one of two tables. I will discuss with the French and the English how they will get rid of their nuclear weapons. Or," Neuhaus paused, "or I will sit down with Yegor Letnikov and discuss how Germany can find its own place in the sun."

Hoare was to recall later his point of greatest fear. It wasn't at Neuhaus's anger. That was bad enough. But worse was when Neuhaus straightened up from his crouch over the desk. The anger was completely gone. The German chancellor was icy, his face composed, and Hoare thought he could detect the slight curling hints of a humorless smile under Neuhaus's glittering reptile eyes.

"That's my message to London and Paris. Good day, gentlemen."

Later, too, Hoare was to remember Laval's silence through the ordeal. He remembered wondering what the French had up their sleeves.

The black cone entered the thin outer fringes of the earth's atmosphere at over seventeen thousand miles an hour. As it plunged deeper, increasing friction from the air slowed the seven-hundred-pound projectile to just under six thousand miles an hour, heating its carbon-carbon compound skin to over thirteen hundred degrees Fahrenheit.

At two hundred sixty-four thousand feet, a retro

rocket fired briefly, then fell away. The cone, now white hot; had been slowed to nine hundred miles an hour, and its angle of entry modified by a few critical degrees.

Inside the cone a two-inch diameter rod of depleted uranium extended from the nose tip to the back one-third of the projectile. There the rod flared into a protective cage, enfolding diamond-hard fingers around the fusing assembly and body of a half-megaton hydrogen bomb.

Three minutes later the cone smashed into the ground, and two separate sequences began, parallel events that had been precisely measured up to now only in the laboratories. The first involved the dense uranium rod. Its incredible kinetic energy literally vaporized the earth at its tip. As it did so, a shock wave raced up the rod. It would pulverize the fusing components in seven-millionths of a second.

It was within the threatened electronics that the second sequence raced against the first. Timers, two of them for redundancy, counted down. As they did so, the weapon burrowed ever deeper into the earth. Exactly seventeen nanoseconds—seventeen-billionths of a second—before the shock wave reached the payload, the timers commanded the weapon to detonate.

Except there was no explosion this day in New Caledonia. Instead every detail of the warhead test was broadcast by coded telemetry to monitors of the French Ministry of Defense, a network of manned and automated stations strung across the South Central Pacific. The tapes would be gathered, analyzed, and ultimately used to perfect the new warhead for the Hades III mobile ballistic missile.

The warhead telemetry was also captured by

Cosmos 6534, a Soviet signals-intercept satellite whose great elliptical orbit had been shifted six degrees at apogee to allow it to monitor the test from atmospheric reentry to splashdown. It took little time to decrypt the now-familiar French code. The KGB specialists needn't have bothered.

The Washington Post

FRENCH DETAIL RESULTS OF
NUCLEAR TEST
Triggers Immediate German Protest
by Alan Ptak

In an unprecedented news conference, France unveiled a new earth-penetrating nuclear weapon designed specifically to destroy deep underground shelters.

Although French nuclear programs are normally shrouded in deepest secrecy, defense officials described the Hades missile in uncharacteristic candor and detail.

The news conference today is seen by many specialists as a response to German demands for a nuclear-free zone in Europe. French and British nuclear weapons have been an increasingly contentious issue for German chancellor Dietrich Neuhaus.

The angry mob surged through the Brandenburg Gate and into the Pariser-platz. Torches illuminated the protest banners and placards and cast flickering shadows across the front of the French

embassy. The German government later claimed its
riot police had been dispatched. Whatever the case,
a surprisingly disciplined and masked group of perhaps fifteen toughs easily forced their way into the
embassy.

They came upon little Laval in his office, standing quietly, facing the door as if waiting for them.

Felix Ehren watched as Dietrich Neuhaus
clapped his hands with glee. The big man's face was
wreathed in a bright, cheerful smile. Neuhaus
turned to Ehren.

"How did they do it?"

"The window," Ehren said with economy. They
had brought him the photographs of Laval's crumpled body sprawled on the paving stones wet with
his blood.

Neuhaus laughed again. "He was such a little
shit. He probably didn't bounce more than once."

The Washington Post

NEUHAUS ANNOUNCES MISSION TO
MOSCOW
German Leader Blames 'French Provocations'

Four

Sam Rubel groaned softly in pleasure as he rolled his shoulders forward, stretching a back too long bent over a desk. Standing under the massive portico of CIA headquarters, he watched the drizzle.

Crachin. French for spitting rain. He'd learned that in Laos—what?—thirty years ago. Yes, thirty years ago. He might have worn his overcoat, he thought. But after the cloying warmth of the office, he welcomed the prickliness of the damp cold. The air smelled sharp, clean. He looked at his watch. The puckered skin on the back of his hand was bluish purple. He thought again about the chill. No. He would have felt swaddled in the heavy coat. And anyway, he would not have long to wait.

He glanced to his left. Fifty feet away stood a dark bronze life-sized statue of Nathan Hale. Hands bound behind his back and waiting for hanging, America's First Spy looked toward glory just above Rubel's head.

Somewhere in his childhood Rubel had gotten it in mind that Hale had regretted that he had but one life *to give* for his country. On coming to the Agency, he'd been disappointed to find that Hale had been sorry that he had but one life *to lose* for his country.

The Hale quote was so *wrong*. Losing turned Hale from a hero to a poor schlemiel who had bumbled willy-nilly into a British noose.

Rubel gave up perfecting Hale's farewell, looked at his watch again, then scanned the still-empty drive to his front. Dirty clumps of snow survived by huddling along the curbs and around the pines that ran almost to the road.

Webster had been an adequate director. Nothing like Bill Casey, of course. But adequate. At least he'd kept the Agency from being put through the wringer up on Capitol Hill after the Iran-Contra fiasco. Then Webster'd had to resign. Rubel shook his head. Good health was a blessing. And for some a fleeting one at that.

Security had sent the complete file, not just an executive summary. But files couldn't tell how a man would shake out as DCI. Sam had the government careerist's jaundiced view of political appointees. The idea of a DCI from outside struck Rubel in much the same way as had the Nathan Hale quote. In the natural order of Sam's universe, the head spy should be someone who'd come up through the ranks—learned the business from the ground up.

The military was that way. Sam had known his share of cretinous generals. But at least they'd all once been second lieutenants. At least they had a shared experience with the men they might send out to fight, and perhaps to die.

So now Sam Rubel, CIA's deputy director, waited for Steven Carey Telford, who, if the Senate confirmed him, would become the fifteenth director of Central Intelligence.

*   *   *

Earlier that day Telford had been ushered into the Oval Office. It was smaller than he'd expected, and George Bush was taller than he'd remembered. They'd first met in Beijing—he there on business, Bush there as the American representative. When Bush showed up at CIA, the two renewed their acquaintance as Telford's Astronetics took on an increasing number of the Agency's satellite programs.

Bush was well briefed. He apologized for interrupting Telford's African trip, and the two got off onto Purdy shotguns, causing the note takers to shift in their chairs with impatience.

Reluctantly, almost grudgingly, Bush yielded to the note takers. He outlined the relationship he wanted with Telford, granting a no-knock access enjoyed by few others in the government, then got into personalities. "Your number two's your choice. Sam Rubel is that now. He's been working on getting you ready for confirmation. Almost burned to death in Laos," Bush continued. "Plane crash. They were still doing grafts on him when I was out there." He paused. "When I was DCI."

Telford noticed Bush said it in a wistful, almost proprietary way. As the Duke of Windsor might have said, "When I was king."

Bush hesitated, remembering other times; then, in a slight apologetic way, he picked up. "A good man. But of course," he repeated, "number two's your choice."

One of the note takers cleared his throat. Bush glanced at his watch. "I want to thank you for taking this on. I don't suppose there's ever an easy time for these kinds of things. I wish it could have been better for you."

"Interesting times in Europe, Mr. President."

Bush got a worried look. "First Neuhaus, then Letnikov. It's all happened too quickly. If we'd had more time to work on the German unification thing . . ." Bush shook his head. "Well, we didn't have the time. It's done. My concern now is to keep us from being thrown out of Germany completely."

"Neuhaus ran for chancellor promising to do just that."

Bush's lips pressed into a thin line. "He did. But after he was elected, I thought there was some maneuver room. That we could reason with him."

"You were talking to him?"

Bush nodded. "There were all kinds of talks. Everywhere. In Berlin. At NATO. I thought we had the guy convinced that American troops could be a reassurance—a stabilizing element." He shrugged. "But now he seems to be hell-bent to link up with the Russians—with Letnikov. We're still talking, still hoping to keep some skeleton force in Germany, but . . ." Bush did not seem optimistic.

"We're going to leave, Mr. President? Pull them all out?"

"As I said, we're still talking. Perhaps we might be able to move into France if Neuhaus kicks us out."

"And Neuhaus himself?"

"A frightening man," Bush said grimly. "Untrustworthy. We have no proof, but I *know*, I just *know*, he prodded the French—absolutely *prodded* them—into that nuclear test. I suspect he knew they had the test planned, and so he timed that tirade of his to corner them. He knew how stiff-necked they can be. They went ahead with it. They had no other choice."

"He seems to have made a match in the Kremlin."

Bush recalled the Kremlin coup. "Gorbachev had other priorities—restructure their economy, catch up on technology. He was causing some mischief in Germany for us—calls for denuclearization and that garbage about a 'common European home.' But he wasn't willing to sacrifice Russia's future to drive us out of Europe."

"And now, Mr. President?" Telford asked.

"And now?" Bush worked to keep desperation out of his voice. "Now, I . . . I just don't know."

"Your office." Rubel opened the door. The CIA director's office was small. Certainly not as grand as that of the secretary of defense, or even the commissioner of internal revenue. But Allen Dulles had personally designed it, and it had remained unchanged since 1961, when the Agency had moved from downtown Washington to Langley, Virginia, nine miles up the Potomac valley.

Like a captain's cabin on some gargantuan starship, the DCI's office sat squarely atop a huge seven-story building whose glass-and-white concrete wings swept back into the rolling hills of northern Virginia. Because Allen Dulles had usually been at his desk at sunrise, he indulged himself by facing the entire office east wall with tempered glass. Furniture consisted of Dulles's ornate walnut desk, several sparsely upholstered armchairs, two small sofas arranged in an *L,* and a thoroughly decadent and literally priceless silk carpet from Azerbaijan. This last was a token of appreciation to the Agency from the shah of Iran, who owed his seat on the Peacock Throne to an earlier—and less restrained—generation of CIA field officers.

Sam Rubel watched as Telford slowly circled the office, pausing to inspect the signed Monet prints (a gift of DGSE, the French intelligence service), an exquisite Sui dynasty vase (bequeathed by Madame Chiang Kai Shek), finally stopping at the glass wall to look out over an uninterrupted expanse of forest along the banks of the Potomac. Telford had surprised him outside. Sam had expected a small convoy. But Telford came to CIA in a nondescript White House pool car, sitting up front with the driver.

To Telford's left a door led into Rubel's office. Outside the door they'd entered were the secretarial and executive assistants that tended to the needs of the DCI and his deputy. There was a small dining room that shared the same glass wall and panoramic view. A private elevator operated by an armed security officer stood ready to take the director down into the underground garage or, with a twist of a special key, to drop an ear-popping eight hundred feet deeper into the operations center, where teams of specialists kept a twenty-four-hour watch on the world. A third door from the DCI's office opened to the conference room.

In that conference room an hour earlier, the Agency's top management had sat around the large oval table. They were like the big cats in the circus, Rubel thought. Restless, watchful, dangerous; gathered to measure the nerves of a new trainer.

Telford had thrown them off balance. Instead of going directly to his chair, he had walked around the table, meeting each person, pausing, cocking his head as if concentrating on getting each name just so. All got a smile, some a handshake held for an extra second, others a squeeze of a shoulder or elbow. Telford was open and friendly without being effusive.

The names tended to, the rest of the hour was spent explaining duties and responsibilities. There were the inevitable budget and logistics executives —the green-eyeshade types. Then came the Trinity —the deputy directors for Science and Technology, Intelligence, and Operations. The three senior officers took care of such matters as designing spy satellites, winkling out the crucial details and implications of the latest Kremlin intrigue, and raising secret armies for wars in back-of-beyond corners of the world.

Rubel saw that Telford took notes and asked detailed questions of the administrative officers. But when the Trinity began, Telford sat back, totally absorbed, his pen on the table.

"They call you Sam?" Telford turned from the window.

Rubel nodded. Taking a nearby chair, Telford gestured toward one of the sofas.

They went through the small talk of explaining their lives to each other. For both it was more than a social ritual. Each knew he would have to depend on the other without the confidence born of years of familiarity. Rubel had the advantage, having had access to Telford's files. Even so, he worked at the conversation, using it to explore Telford's texture, his character.

Telford's recital squared with the file. The facts, that is. But it was the emphasis, the nuances, that intrigued Sam. Telford dismissed his military service with a single sentence. Sam knew it had been four years in military intelligence, three of which a young Steven Telford spent working with the Agency's

Berlin Station. Telford's description of Astronetics was similarly scanty, limited to the work the company had done for CIA, and nothing about the shuttle or NASA.

"Confirmation's in ten days. I've put together an agenda for your orientation." Rubel took a single page from a government-issue manila file folder.

Rubel was, Telford reckoned, in his early fifties. It had been Rubel's ordinariness that had helped him in fieldwork. Medium height, brown hair and eyes, and the slightest Mediterranean cast to his complexion. "A good gray man," his training officer at the Farm had noted in Rubel's 201 file. A small, wiry man with a slight paunch, Sam Rubel could have been anyone's tax accountant. The kind of face you'd forget five minutes after meeting him. But that had been before Laos.

The face that Telford saw was now very memorable. The right side was slack, evidence of destroyed nerves and muscle. Telford took the paper Rubel extended to him. Hairless scar tissue crisscrossed the knuckles and twisted the fingers into purplish claws with thick yellowed nails.

Telford studied the paper. He looked up. "I-S-O?"

Rubel answered in a flat, almost bored, tone. "Short for isolation. One of our training areas. We call it the Farm. Run you through some of the tradecraft. Weapons familiarization, that kind of thing."

Sensing a watchfulness about Rubel, Telford asked, "You think this is important." Telford made it a question by waiting.

Sam Rubel ticked off another item on his mental

checklist. Telford had caught on. A good hunch player. Trusts his intuition. Another test passed.

"It is," Rubel answered. "Substance is our lifeblood. But it isn't everything. It's important to get a feel for the physical side of the business. The Farm's a good place to start."

Telford changed the subject. "The president joked about the Russians being the least of our problems. He didn't go into details. But he seemed to think we've got our hands full in Washington."

Rubel laughed. "Bush is the first president to know the Agency firsthand." He thought for a moment, a frown of concentration on his face. "The others—Kennedy, Carter, Reagan, the rest—they didn't understand the difference between intelligence and the policymakers—between us and the people at State and Defense."

Telford encouraged him with a look of interest.

"The textbooks have neat, clinical descriptions. We feed analysis to an eager audience at State and the Pentagon. They use our picture of the world to crank out foreign policy or to build their submarines or airplanes a certain way."

"And it doesn't happen like that," prompted Telford.

"No. It's like a supermarket. State and DOD selectively pick over our stuff to support decisions they've already made. If we put out anything that goes against their preconceived notions, they cry foul. Claim we're cooking the books to fit our own agenda."

"And of course, we don't do that." Telford gave it a bantering touch.

Rubel flushed, lowered his eyes, then looked up. "I suppose there've been times when we've gone overboard. God knows, it's tempting to show those snotty Foreign Service bastards they aren't all-knowing."

"It's good to be on the side of the angels," Telford gently needled him.

Rubel's eyes widened, then wrinkled in a smile. "Okay. Score one for you. We're not perfect, either. One of my predecessors used to say that CIA can describe in excruciating detail how foreign policy is made in every country in the world except the United States."

Telford laughed, then looked at the paper again. "The briefings, Sam. What are they going to tell me?"

Rubel pursed his lips. "The big thing, of course, is Moscow and Berlin—this thing's turned over a hornets' nest. But you can't get sucked into ignoring everything else. The word'll get around that the DCI"—Rubel pointed to Telford—"that you aren't minding the store. Then the people who watch the out-of-the-way places slack off. Lose their motivation. Morale slumps. And," Rubel warned, "then we get blindsided. Surprised by some coup that unhinges the world.

"Everybody in the Agency worries about something," Rubel continued. "Or pretends to worry. It's a status symbol. You're nobody unless you have a crisis. Middle East is still a mess. Nicaragua's likely to flare up again. There's the nerve-gas operation in Zimbabwe, the China hands are watching for a new cultural revolution, and the Japanese seem to be gearing up for a secret space launch.

"You'll get more of that in all the detail you can handle. Most of those briefings will be done here. At Langley."

"Most?" asked Telford.

Rubel carefully chose his words. "There're some things we have to talk about at the Farm." Noticing Telford's quizzical look, Rubel waved his hand around the office. "Oh. This place is safe. It's got more security than the Oval Office. But we have some of our people under deep cover. We can't risk exposing them by bringing them out here. There's someone coming to talk to you. From Germany. The plane'll land him at the Farm."

Five

Telford got up at dawn, had coffee, and took a slow run down the sandy paths that wound for miles through the pine forests and open fields. The Farm, tens of thousands of acres along Virginia's James River, was known officially as Camp Peary. Along the well-guarded perimeter, signs told the public that Camp Peary was an experimental training facility of the Department of Defense.

Telford and Rubel had flown down the evening before, landing at one of the Farm's two airfields. Today Telford would make a whirlwind tour of the place. Paramilitary trainees lived in barracks, while individual cabins and turn-of-the-century Tidewater homes housed transient high-level officers and permanent party. There were the expected demolitions and small-arms ranges along with parachute training towers and infiltration courses.

Telford was particularly intrigued with the Surrogate Environmental Control Center. Set behind double-apron razor-wire fence, the four-story windowless building covered more than six football fields. Sam Rubel called it "the world's most realistic stage set." Technicians at SECC (an acronym that instantly was absorbed into the Agency's patois as "sexy"), aided with computer-driven fabrication devices, could quickly replicate any man-made feature on earth.

SECC was a theater of deadly business. Delta teams could hone their hostage rescue drills in an Airbus, then minutes later blow open a particular safe in a specific apartment in East Beirut. Elsewhere in SECC, case officers practiced filling dead drops along Moscow's Kutuzovskiy Prospekt or brushed up on surreptitious entry of a certain friendly nation's embassy on Washington's Massachusetts Avenue.

After SECC, Sam Rubel drove them in a battered van to what was once a large stable. Through a steel-reinforced door, they stepped into the Agency's armaments showroom. Glass-fronted cabinets covered the walls.

Engrossed, Telford wandered from one display to the next. Hand weapons were arranged in neat categories. Here the silent killers: garrotes; straight and folding knives; saps and bludgeons; gas and poison injectors. Then the pistols: a nine-millimeter Russian Makarov; a rare (and clumsy) British Webley Mark One; a Japanese Type Ninety-Four eight-millimeter "suicide pistol." He stopped in front of a richly blued weapon with a needlelike barrel and canted checkered grips.

"That there is a fine piece," came a soft burred voice behind him.

Telford turned. A wizened bald-headed man stood a foot or so away. Dressed in a rough blue work shirt and gray trousers, his front was covered with a three-quarter canvas shop apron. Like the tack room, he carried the crisp, pleasant odor of gun oil and nitro cleaner. His blue eyes measured Telford in a frank, businesslike way.

Sam Rubel introduced Bodnant, the Agency's chief armorer for nearly forty years.

Telford took Bodnant's callus-ridged hand, then pointed to the pistol. "A Luger?"

Bodnant let a small, condescending smile play at the corners of his mouth. "No." Then, mercifully, "But most think it is. It's a Finnish Lahti. Nine millimeter. Model thirty-five." Bodnant opened the cabinet and took the gun to a nearby worktable. He disassembled the weapon with a sorcerer's motion. "See. It has a reciprocating bolt. Luger doesn't." He held up the bolt. "Also has an accelerator. Keeps the weapon from jamming in cold weather."

Bodnant reassembled the Lahti with the same swift magic, wiped it with an oily rag, and put it back in the cabinet. Closing the door, he gave Telford another appraising look. "You'll not be wantin' a weapon, Mr. Director. If the likes of you need one, we're all in deep trouble."

He smiled at his joke. He moved to another similar table nearby. From a small cardboard box, he produced a man's belt and held it out to Telford. "I hope you're still a thirty-four."

Telford took the belt, a rich burgundy cordovan leather with a sterling silver buckle. Telford's monogram was let into the silver. The buckle, with a patina of minute scratches and dents, could have been a family heirloom.

Bodnant and Rubel watched as Telford tried to puzzle out the meaning of the belt. Bodnant took an extra second after Telford looked up. "It's a homing device."

Taking the belt, Bodnant showed how the buckle studs could be connected by touching them to a common metal conductor. This done, he ex plained, the miniaturized electronics in the buckle would send a coded pulse to an antenna that ran through the belt.

"It's good for eight hours of continuous transmission. If you have to use it, though, you should transmit for only ten minutes at a time. That's long enough for us to get a fix, and short enough so you won't run the batteries down too quickly."

Seeing Telford was still nonplussed, Sam Rubel interjected, "For likely targets. It's difficult to find hostages. This could give you an edge."

Telford's first impulse was to refuse the belt; that by accepting it, he was joining with them in their melodramatic posturing.

Then he remembered the videotape he'd seen the day before. Of an Agency officer held for two years in a hidden terrorist camp in the Bekaa Valley.

Of his graphic torture and slow death.

Of his captors sadistically leering into the camera while doing unspeakable things to the helpless man strapped in the chair between them.

Telford looked again at Bodnant and Rubel. Wordlessly he exchanged his belt for the one Bodnant held out to him.

That evening Telford and Sam Rubel ate dinner with a training class. After, Telford stood for drinks in the club bar, where he made a point of talking to each of the trainees. At eight Sam appeared at his elbow and made a gesture toward his watch. Telford said his good-byes, and the two men left for their cabin.

Cabins at the Farm were named after trees. Aspen had been the director's cabin since Hoyt Vandenberg, the Agency's second director, chose it in 1947. Dulles mischievously renamed it Hemlock shortly after the debacle at the Bay of Pigs, but his patrician successor, John McCone, frowned on such levity, and the place became Aspen again. The living room was paneled in butter gold knotty pine. Exposed beams and rafters were dark oak, and one wall was taken up with a fieldstone fireplace centered between overflowing bookcases. Four deep armchairs upholstered in double-strength sailcloth formed a *U* with the open end toward the hearth.

At a bar built into an antique armoir, Sam Rubel poured two balloons of cognac. Handing Telford's glass to him, Rubel settled in a chair opposite.

"Another acronym you should know: D-E-C. Deck. For deep cover. Most of our operations people overseas are under what we call official cover. They're identified as U.S. government employees, and they work out of our embassy or consulate. There're advantages to it: it lets us work a pretty straightforward logistics system—pay, travel, housing, schools for their kids—all that.

"The problem is"—Rubel sniffed at the cognac, then took an experimental sip—"official cover gives the other side a head start. Each new arrival in the embassy's put under surveillance by every counterintelligence operative in town. And certainly by the Soviets."

"And sooner or later they turn us?"

Rubel thought for a moment, searching for an answer. "Not always," he began. "Sometimes we have people under official cover who never get blown. Or at least we think they haven't. But working out of an embassy increases the odds that eventually the opposition will tumble to them. And there're some operations so sensitive we can't take that chance."

Telford felt a flash of impatience at yet another tutorial from Rubel. He'd thought he knew something about intelligence. In the past few days, however, Rubel had shown him how little that was. Even now, even on the inside—from the *top* on the inside, he amended sourly—he was constantly finding that much was still hidden from him.

This was not the engineer's world to which he'd become so accustomed. A world neatly divided between things that were already known and things that with certainty (and enough money) would be known.

No, intelligence was a bog of qualifications. A sucking mire of "Yes, but . . ." and "No, yet . . ." It was a land of shifting shadows where one could forever chase fleeting images of "Might . . . ?" and "Might not . . . ?" It was a place where one could find insanity in a twisted infinity that constantly reversed right and wrong, enemy and friend.

"And so we have DEC?" he asked Rubel.

Detecting a tightness in Telford's tone, Sam Rubel hesitated, then continued more warily. "Yes. We give our man—or woman—an identity and job that's got nothing to do with the government. When we were running the Bay of Pigs, we built an organization called the Gibraltar Steamship Company." Sam smiled ruefully. "Then all the cars going in and out started drawing attention. So, to explain *that*, we had to set up a branch office of a car-rental agency next to the steamship operation. Then we had an awful time turning away salesmen who wanted to rent cars."

As Rubel hoped, the Gibraltar Steamship Company struck a ludicrous note. "I don't suppose the fellow we're meeting tonight works for Hertz or Avis," said Telford.

"No. As a matter of fact, he's . . ."

Telford held up a hand. "No need, Sam. There're some things I don't need to know. Just tell me why this meeting."

"Because of a special source. An East German— former East German. ZG-SKEAN is the cryptonym. We recruited SKEAN fifteen years ago. At the time he was a young officer in the HVA. . . ."

Telford nodded. It was suddenly important that Rubel not explain this acronym to him. It came back quickly: "Hauptverwaltung Aufklaerung," Telford gave it in German. The Main Administration for Intelligence of the Ministry for State Security.

Rubel noticed Telford's obvious pleasure in remembering. "We kept SKEAN pretty much inactive. Oh, we'd pulse him once in a while. Give him something to do. Some small thing. But safe. Just to make certain he knew we still had a hook in him. But we never pushed for anything difficult. Anyway, SKEAN moved up in the HVA."

"How high?" asked Telford.

"High enough—he was head of HVA's counterintelligence."

Telford gave a low whistle of admiration. "Not bad. Not bad at all. Now?"

"Now he's doing the same thing for Neuhaus."

Telford started. "An East German? Working in the BND?" Telford used the acronym for German intelligence, Bundesnachrichtendienst.

Rubel gave a matter-of-fact nod. "It's happened before. Remember, the BND itself was formed after World War II by Gehlen. He'd been Hitler's top spy. After reunification there were some damned good intelligence officers in the old HVA. The BND took them in."

Telford shook his head, amazed. "A BND-HVA merger. It's hard to believe. And the fellow we're meeting tonight still handles SKEAN?"

Before Rubel could reply, both men heard the closing of car doors outside, a mutter of conversation, and footsteps on the cabin porch. Rubel glanced at his watch as he rose and headed for the door.

Rubel was suddenly tense. He hurried to the door, where he dimmed the living-room lights while switching off the outside light. Opening the door with his right hand, he did not, as most might, step back and toward the rear of the door. Rather, he moved to his left, blocking the opening. Rubel, satisfied, then stood aside.

The man came into the room. Hatless, dark hair neither ratty nor noticeably well styled, he wore a dark boxy European topcoat. Slender, he was of medium height. He had a certain confidence, the physical sureness of cats and fighter pilots. A man who'd never bump against the furniture or hesitate in doorways.

A chill began in the middle of Telford's back and rippled to his arms. He stood abruptly. He gasped, short of breath. A flood of memories burst the barriers of years long gone.

Rubel, surprised, attempted an introduction, then gave up.

Ignoring Rubel, the man moved swiftly to face Telford. "Hullo, Steven. You're looking well." His baritone carried a slightly Europeanized American accent.

As the man's smile began, Telford knew its final

shape, the wrinkles about the mouth and eyes. "Paul. Paul." Telford whispered, taking the hand now extended to him. "I thought . . . They told me you . . ."

He had met Paul Brandt in Berlin, thirty years before. Then a lieutenant in the Army's 66th Military Intelligence Group, Telford had been seconded to CIA's Berlin Task Force. The two had become fast friends, a friendship cemented in the hours of boredom waiting in seedy safe houses and in the moments of terror in missions into East Berlin. Off duty they'd gone on monumental tears through the bars and *tanzclubs* along the Kurfürstendamm, bringing laughing women back to the huge old apartment they'd leased in the Charlottenburg district.

The mission had gone wrong, as such things do, with a flickering suddenness. Telford had been the case officer for a particularly productive source, a Soviet payroll clerk in Pankow, where the KGB ran a school for the intelligence services of the Warsaw Pact and other clients. The clerk, a boozer, had about run out his string and was demanding safe haven.

Telford had set up a meeting with the Russian in East Berlin, on an S-Bahn platform. Brandt went early, to put the elevated tram station under surveillance and to provide backup security. Telford arrived two minutes before the meeting time and, getting an all clear from Brandt, stood on the platform reading a tattered propaganda pamphlet.

The Russian showed, unable to control his shaking hands. As soon as he recognized Telford, he shouted. Three men bolted from inside the station. Instantly Telford turned and sprinted toward the shadows where Brandt was concealed. He remembered the first shot tearing through his coat, then, nothing.

He awakened the next day in a small military clinic. A grim Agency officer was at his bedside. Tersely he explained what had happened. Brandt, himself wounded, had carried Telford off the platform and had crashed their car through the barriers at one of the more lightly guarded checkpoints.

He'd been lucky—a grazing shot had creased his skull. Brandt hadn't been so fortunate. At least that's what the Agency man had told him with a reproach that became a damning accusation to Telford over the years. The body would be cremated. There would, of course, be a memorial ceremony in the chapel the following day.

Three weeks later Nikita Khrushchev put up the Wall. Steven Telford, by then at Fort Irwin, California, gave up any notions of a military career. He resigned from the army to take up engineering.

A seething rage gripped Telford. He had changed his life because of a lie. "Goddamnit, Paul." His voice was thick with anger. "Why . . ."

Brandt made a gesture of futility. The corners of his mouth sagged tiredly. He shook his head. "Someone saw it as an opportunity to drop me off the rolls. Put me under deep cover." Brandt paused, then spoke again, pleading for understanding. "They made the decision when I was out, Steven. Unconscious. When I came around, they told me. By that time the army had you back in the States."

Telford, still staring at his old friend, dug into a pocket and brought out a closed hand that he offered to Brandt. He opened his fingers. In his palm was half of a small silvery coin, a West German fifty-pfennig piece.

"Our recognition signal. Remember?"

Brandt gave a perplexed look.

Telford, suddenly feeling vulnerable, tried to trivialize the keeping of the coin. "Silly, what you hang on to. Pack-rat instinct." Then, clumsily, he took Brandt's shoulder, and the two men moved to the fireside chairs. Telford, now seated, looked at Rubel, still standing—a man clearly bewildered.

Quickly Telford told Rubel the story.

Rubel, intrigued, listened intently, then sighed. "It's the way we operate." He nodded toward Brandt. "Hell, if we hadn't had to pull this guy back to brief you, you could have spent a lifetime as DCI without . . ."

"Without knowing," Telford finished with a trace of bitterness. "Without knowing."

Telford welcomed the thin first light. He had slept fitfully, memories twisting into dreams and nightmares. Each time he awoke, he relived the shock of seeing Brandt again and the shame he'd carried since the night on the S-Bahn platform.

His life had changed because of that night. Because he blamed himself for Brandt's death. Then, in the moment Brandt stepped through the door, the foundation of the last thirty years vanished. Oddly, the realization that he had not been responsible for Brandt's death brought no relief. Instead he felt adrift. An anchor of guilt, he thought, was better than no anchor at all.

He lay for a moment in a tangle of blankets, then got up to shower in the small bathroom. Finished shaving, he listened. The cabin was quiet. He dressed quickly in heavy wool field trousers, flannel shirt, and boots. Going out the door, he plucked his shooting jacket off a nearby rack.

It was a dawn of cold grays. The James, its dark waters yet untouched by the sky, lapped at the docks nearby. Telford's breath-frost rose in the still air. Before him the white sand path cut through dark pines.

He had taken only a few steps when he heard the sound of the cabin door opening. "Steven, wait." Turning, he saw Brandt pulling on an overcoat.

Telford, having looked forward to a walk alone, was surprised to find that he welcomed Brandt's company. The two walked in silence for a distance, quickly falling into an easy stride that fit them both.

They continued, their footsteps grating the frozen sand. Slowing his pace, Telford turned to Brandt. "Sam—my first day at the Agency—Sam warned me about ignoring what he called the out-of-the-way places."

"Good advice," Brandt made a neutral return.

Telford continued. "Bush seems to blame it on unification. That it happened too quickly."

Brandt covertly searched Telford's face while dissecting the statement, searching for the trace of Potomac hubris that usually came with recitals including "the president says." Finding none, he felt reassured and closer to Telford. "I suppose he's right. If West Germany'd gotten integrated into the European Community first, it'd made things easier all around."

"How?"

"West Germany's energies would've been aimed at building ties with France, Britain, the Low Countries. Once that was done, the community could've absorbed East Germany quite easily. As it happened, East Germany got up for grabs before the community got going. The West Germans couldn't resist. When the Wall fell, it marked a rebirth of German nationalism. Having been split for nearly half a century, the Germans aren't about to pay homage to the European Community in Brussels."

"And Letnikov? Can he turn things back? Everyone seemed to think Gorbachev's reforms were . . ."

"Irreversible?" Brandt supplied. "Ah, yes, our Mr. Gorbachev. A master at putting a friendly face on the bear." Brandt smiled wryly. "Never underestimate the power of a Communist in an Italian-tailored suit. Irreversible changes? Some things stay the same. Remember, the Russians always considered East Germany their crown jewel. Gorbachev didn't let it go out of the goodness of his heart. He lost control."

"You can't believe Letnikov's out to put the bloc back together." Telford's tone made it apparent he believed that was precisely where Brandt was leading.

"No," Brandt demurred. "At least not in the same way. The old Warsaw Pact is gone. But NATO's next to go. And we're going to find that European balance of power politics can be as cutthroat as the Cold War kind. A Russian-German partnership would put Poland in a vise, and the rest of Eastern Europe would have to go along."

"Particularly if we pulled all our troops out."

"Bingo." Brandt gave a mirthless laugh. "Letnikov's proposal encourages the Germans to go it alone. Anything that does that automatically weakens the chances for a solid European Community. It's a zero-sum game."

"And a Germany unrestrained by the community . . ." Telford felt no need to finish.

The two walked, lost in their own thoughts. Rounding a bend in the path, they came onto a small deer. The animal, stock still, watched them until it made their scent, then bolted into the woods.

"They drive them in Germany," Brandt offered, talking to himself and thinking of more than deer. Then, seeing Telford's quizzical expression, explained, "The beaters drive the deer. The hunters wait in a blind."

The two walked, listening to the sound of the deer crashing through the underbrush.

"And where do you come into this?"

"SKEAN. Neuhaus's BND is critical. It's become a crucial link between Moscow and Berlin."

"So SKEAN cuts us in on the traffic between Berlin and Moscow?" Telford asked.

"There's more to it than that. It was SKEAN who put me onto Neuhaus. Before he became a household name. A lot of money was going to Neuhaus. Russian money. He was beating the drum for a reunited Germany before the Wall came down. The money and reunification gave him quite a head start."

Telford shook off a feeling of suffocation. There was no transition, no thread from yesterday. Little more than two weeks before, he'd been in the heat of Kenya, concerned only with an outraged cape buffalo. Only six days ago Yegor Letnikov had tilted Europe on its ear.

Telford remembered how Bush had put it. How Letnikov's proposal had gotten almost immediate support from much of the leadership of the Senate and House of Representatives. "No more American troops in Europe. That's the cry. They're hailing it as the arrival of the millennium," the president had remarked. "The House has already started beating the swords into welfare grants. The Senate Armed Services Committee is talking about cutting next year's defense budget by almost a third."

Telford and Brandt were now deep into the forest. Brandt finally spoke. "I'm leaving this afternoon. For Berlin. Sam told me you'll be coming to Germany after your confirmation. We won't be able to meet there. It'd be too dangerous."

"How do we communicate?" asked Telford.

"It depends. We have a secure satellite link for emergencies, though I don't like broadcasting. There're mail drops for routine reports. Tech services has developed some very good secret inks since you and I . . ." Brandt let the sentence hang, then picked up. "There're the usual trouble numbers, of course." Here Brandt was referring to telephones in CIA operations centers that were monitored day and night, telephones used only for incoming calls. Brandt was assigned certain numbers that were periodically changed to reduce the vulnerability to eavesdropping.

The two reached a branch in the path and, in unspoken agreement, turned and began the walk back to the cabin. Gusts had now joined into a steady wind, which carried with it light flurries of snow.

Brandt glanced at his old friend. Telford was striding, hands jammed deep into coat pockets, collar closed against the cold.

"Why did you come back, Steven?" The question came just above the noise of the wind.

Telford was silent for a moment or two. "Why?" he repeated, as if thinking about it the first time. "I don't really know. I mean," he struggled for the words, "I hadn't thought about it before. But suddenly, when they called, I knew I wanted it. Why did I want it? I guess it was that I'd gotten to where everything coming my way was nothing more than a tired version of what'd come before."

"No missionary zeal? No crusades?" Brandt asked in mock astonishment, immediately ashamed of his small joke at the enthusiasm he and Telford had once shared.

Telford shook his head. "No crusades," he echoed sadly with an awareness of loss. "And you?" he asked in self-defense. "Why're you still with it?"

Another pause.

"Curiosity, mostly."

"About?"

"About how it will all end up."

"Germany?" Telford asked. "Us—the Russians?"

"That, certainly. But, me—how I . . ." He sought the words. "Don't you see? There's a progression to things. All my life's been spent, at least since college, in the Cold War." Brandt smiled, thinking of a long-ago history professor. "They'll probably look back and call it the Fifty Years War. It really began in 1940, you know. I have this feeling that it's not quite over. And I won't—can't—quit until it's time."

"When is that?"

"I don't know. But I'll know it when it comes."

"So here we are. And where from here?"

Brandt stopped and turned to face Telford. The snow was falling more heavily now, flakes dusting his hair. "Yes. Where from here." He brought his face closer to Telford and took his arm. "We're in this, you and me. Neither of us wanted it. All we know is that there's something that's yet to be played out."

Telford felt the sudden desperation of a man forced to grasp beyond his reach. This hadn't been in the bargain. Everyone had declared the Cold War over. Director of Central Intelligence was to have been a comfortable Potomac peerage, where he would brush elbows with the famous and become one of them himself. It was to have been a trophy, another addition to the string of scalps that showed what a man had done with a lifetime.

Instead he'd been cheated, taken in by his own gullibility into a deadly bait and switch. There'd been the scarred Sam Rubel, Bodnant and the belt, and finally, Paul Brandt and Yegor Letnikov and Dietrich Neuhaus Lives, perhaps many other lives, would depend on him. He found himself angry with Brandt for coming back from the dead, for bringing him to this lonely place in a winter wood.

The DeHavilland Twin Otter engines idled as the plane waited for Brandt. In three hours he'd be at New York's Kennedy airport, where he would connect with a Lufthansa flight. On boarding the Otter, he'd resume his other identity, an expatriate American businessman returning to Germany.

He and Telford had had lunch with Sam Rubel. It was a desultory conversation. It fell to Rubel to punctuate long silences, and he was relieved to be able to announce it was time to leave for the airstrip.

Telford and Brandt left the warm waiting room and walked to the Otter. A crewman on board swung the passenger door open. The snow was falling steadily now. Telford saw that the Otter bore the logo of a small commuter airline, an Agency proprietary company that hid its secret missions behind a profit-making business. The two stopped short of the frigid propeller blast and shook hands. Telford stood on the snow-covered tarmac and watched Brandt climb aboard.

Brandt paused in the door to wave. Before he could turn, Telford started forward. Brandt stepped down the small ladder. The two met, standing close to be heard over the whine of the turbine engines.

Telford bent, bringing his lips close to Brandt's ear. "I didn't want you to go without knowing." Telford searched for the words. "It's good—it's good to know you didn't—that you're alive."

Brandt smiled, reached across to clasp Telford's shoulder, then pulled him into a hug. He stood back, the smile still on his face, and got into the plane.

Six

Telford was surrounded, trapped by the glare. He could barely pierce the magnesium blaze of the overhead lights. The heat was suffocating, and the smell of scorched metal and charred electrical insulation filled the room. He kept his hands folded on the plain table in front of him, hoping the slight tremors couldn't be detected. All morning the questions had been coming at him from behind the lights. His throat was parched. A pitcher of water and glass, inches away from his right hand, beckoned him.

Don't start drinking, they'd told him at Langley. You could drop the glass. You might spill something. Or you'll have to urinate, and start squirming. Even the staff psychologist had weighed in: "Keep your hand away from your mouth. Some take that as a sign you're lying." And Rubel: "Don't be imaginative. Don't try to make friends. Or hope they'll understand. Keep to the book. They're after your balls."

"So you won't run an operation without a Finding?"

It was the second day of Telford's confirmation hearing in the Senate. That was the follow-up from Joseph Cantabile, chairman of the Intelligence

Committee—a senator from New Mexico. Cantabile was running true to form. At Langley they'd predicted he would zero in on "Findings," the official notification CIA gave Congress of a pending secret operation. The senator had been badly mauled by Oliver North in the Iran-Contra hearings. Since then he attacked every witness with a determination seen only in the politician who'd been publicly diddled.

Sam Rubel had devoted hours to the history of CIA's often stormy relations with the Hill. Congress wants an ironclad guarantee that we'll always give them a heads-up, Sam had explained. But the White House wants to keep some wiggle room. In case there's something so goddamn sensitive they can't risk a leak.

Cantabile kept on. "Now, Senator McCary earlier posed a situation in which you recommended that the president notify the Congress, but the president told you not to notify the Congress. Your answer to Senator McCary conflicts with other testimony before this committee. I want to clear up what may just be a little bit of ambivalence or contradiction in your testimony, Mr. Telford."

The lights that pinioned Telford were kinder to the Senate's Select Committee on Intelligence. Members and staff sat behind an elevated horseshoe table, surrounding and looking down on the solitary figure of Telford at the witness table. The lights, so necessary for television, hung from the ceiling of the hearing room, focused over the shoulders of the senators and their aides. Telford squinted, trying to follow Cantabile's voice back to its origin. But he could only make out dark silhouettes clustered around the table.

"You told us yesterday," continued Cantabile, "that if this occurred, you would contemplate resigning. You and I had an exchange in which you said that Congress should be brought in at the very beginning of plans for a covert operation."

There was a rustle of paper in the darkness behind the lights.

"Yet," Cantabile's voice was now rich with the certainty of the hunter with his quarry cornered, "in questioning from Senator McCary yesterday, you said, well, of course, there might be situations where the president should be allowed the maximum flexibility. I think you cited as an example CIA's planning to rescue hostages. You said that you might not notify Congress before embarking on something so sensitive, an operation where human lives are clearly in jeopardy."

Telford felt his heart begin a thunderous pounding that ran from his chest up into his throat. Don't get trapped into specifics on hypothetical situations, Rubel had warned. They'll save the answer and hang it around your neck somewhere down the line.

Yesterday's answer had seemed so reasonable. American lives were at stake, as McCary, his first questioner, had graphically put it. The slightest leak of CIA's plans could mean a slow and painful death of the hostages. In that case mightn't Telford opt to tell Congress later? After the rescue operation had gotten under way? Or perhaps when the hostages were in safe hands? What were human lives against a bureaucratic requirement to entrust the details of a plan to Congress—to those who would play no part in the mission, who would run no risks?

But that was yesterday's answer. Today was different.

Today informing Congress was a crucial matter. One that went straight to the very foundation of America's democratic institutions. Americans had died for the Constitution. His oath of office—if he ever took it—would bind him to "protect the Constitution of the United States, against all enemies, foreign and domestic." Wasn't keeping Congress informed—keeping the sanctity of constitutional obligations—a matter so serious that it transcended the fate of a few hostages?

"If I might interrupt my colleague from New Mexico," came a soft but insistent voice from Telford's left. "The hostage predicament was of my making. I put Mr. Telford into it, and I feel a certain obligation to get him out of it."

The knots in Telford's stomach loosened ever so slightly. Although younger than many of the other members of the committee, Frank McCary was well into his second six-year Senate term. The Agency briefing book described McCary as a moderately conservative Democrat, often voting with the Republicans on foreign policy and defense issues, but opposing them on domestic topics such as taxes and voter registration. Clippings in the briefing book repeatedly portrayed McCary as one of the bright hopefuls in the Democratic party.

"I have reviewed the transcript of Mr. Telford's testimony yesterday," McCary told Cantabile. "What he told me specifically was that the key for him would be the point at which he thought the relationship of trust between this committee and CIA would be jeopardized by a delay in notification. Now, that leaves a judgment call in Mr. Telford's hands. But I believe that's the best we can hope for in a less-than-perfect world." McCary paused. "And, Mr. Chairman, I'm satisfied with that."

Clearly unhappy, a disarmed Cantabile took another tack.

"President Letnikov—Mr. Telford—how do you see his proposal for a mutual security agreement with Germany?"

At the prospect of gaining firmer ground, Telford breathed easier. He tossed a fuzz-ball response that had come out of hours of rehearsals. "From the viewpoint of national intelligence, Senator, our task is to explore futures—to lay out for the president and his policymakers the consequences of various courses of action."

Cantabile wasn't having any. "Mr. Telford," he interrupted, "that's a boilerplate answer to just about any question on foreign policy."

"But Senator, the director of Central Intelligence doesn't make foreign policy—he shouldn't get into that game," Telford parried.

"Very well, then, Mr. Telford. I won't violate your neat concepts of turf with questions about American foreign policy." Cantabile's sarcasm cut across the lights. "No one's here to make you judge American policy. But surely you must have some thoughts on the Letnikov proposal. What kind of Europe do you see after American troops come home?"

Telford still dodged. "I'm unaware that the troops are coming home, Senator. I do know that we're still discussing that with the Germans and in NATO."

"Well, then, Mr. Telford, what kind of Europe might we see *if* the troops come home?"

They'd gone over this, too. But there hadn't

been the lights, the atmosphere of confrontation. The neat answers in the bound book before him seemed painfully inadequate now. Telford cleared his throat and leaned forward to make certain his answer carried into the microphone. "It could be a very dangerous Europe, Senator."

There was more rustling of papers, and the sensual sound of ice in a glass. Then Cantabile asked, "Bringing our boys home—you see *that* as dangerous?"

"I see an unstable Europe as dangerous, Senator."

"Well, now, Mr. Telford." The voice had a hectoring, belligerent tone to it. "Look at this from President Letnikov's perspective. If Germany is less threatening because of a treaty, and the American troops are out of Europe, then wouldn't Moscow feel more secure in further reducing its military?"

"You're asking me to read intentions, Senator. My job as DCI is to look at capabilities. I see nothing in Soviet behavior to indicate that they are—or would—significantly reduce their military capabilities."

"But Mr. Telford, don't you believe that Moscow's massive military comes from the fact that the Russians have historically felt encircled? Surrounded by a hostile world?"

"Their military forces, Senator, and their actions around the world point to something more than a concern for self-defense."

"What about Gorbachev's 'new thinking'? Didn't that result in a less militaristic Russia? There was the pullout from Afghanistan. . . ."

"Do you think, Senator," Telford interrupted, "that the Red Army would have left Afghanistan if we hadn't given Stingers to the *mujaheddin*? And Mr. Gorbachev's new thinking disappeared as quickly as it came—as quickly as he was replaced. CIA sees no evidence that the basic structure of the Soviet government has changed. The USSR isn't a nation of law, Senator. It is a nation of men—a nation run by a very few men. That's where change is needed."

There was a momentary silence, then Cantabile spoke, at once unctuous and faintly contemptuous. "It is obvious, Mr. Telford, that there's no new thinking in this administration. I had hoped that at least there might be a breath of fresh air in your appointment. I see that I am going to be disappointed. My time is up for now, Mr. Telford. But we will have other chances to talk."

At seven-fifteen that evening, the Intelligence Committee approved Telford's nomination, fourteen in favor, none opposed. Senator Cantabile voted "present." For the first time in the hearing, the television lights were turned off. Telford saw that Joseph Cantabile was a senator straight from a Hollywood central-casting office. Over six feet, wavy silver hair, square jaw, and a rich, ruddy complexion. As Cantabile brushed by without speaking, Telford noticed a puffiness under the eyes and a trailing trace of gin in his wake.

Leaving the hearing room, Telford was handed a note by a staffer. Telford glanced at it, whispered a few words to Sam Rubel, then nodded to the staffer. Telford followed the staffer first onto the small subway to the Capitol, where they wound through a narrow labyrinth of damp basement corridors with dusty heating pipes hiding the ceiling overhead.

The staffer stopped before a door painted in institutional cream enamel. He knocked once, opened the door, then left the way he'd come as Telford entered.

The contrast between the seediness of the Capitol corridor and Frank McCary's hideaway office startled Telford. The plastered walls were painted an off-white, and he sank into a lush light blue carpet. He was drawn immediately to the room's large Palladian window, which was made up of two quarter circular panes of old glass that rippled the outside light. The room's long axis opened on the Capitol's West Front. Centered in the window was the Washington Monument. Floodlights on the flags at its base caused shadows to flicker across the granite needle in the winter night.

"Bar's limited. But we do have some vintage Budweiser." Frank McCary, off to Telford's left, crouched peering into a small refrigerator. Popping the cold cans open, McCary handed one to Telford and, with the hand freed, steered him toward two leather easy chairs facing the huge window. "We can talk better here. And it's a good view of the mall."

McCary raised his beer in a toast. "To the fifteenth director of Central Intelligence." McCary had a perfect oval face and an infectious little-boy grin. A thick shock of sandy hair was brushed into a moderate truce with orderliness. Telford and McCary traded small talk, gradually coming to focus on Washington and its personalities. McCary steered around to Joseph Cantabile.

"You gotta understand Joe. He represents New Mexico. But he isn't a real westerner." McCary frowned in concentration, searching for the ultimate, irrefutable proof of Cantabile's alienism. Then, triumphantly, he announced, "Hell, the guy went to Harvard *and* Yale!"

"How does he keep his seat?" Telford asked. "New Mexico's not exactly a liberal state."

McCary laughed scornfully. "Ah, shit. Most of New Mexico doesn't know what Cantabile does in Washington. Matter of fact, none of our constituents know what any of us do.

"Think about it," he asked Telford. "When's the last time you saw a newspaper story on how *your* senator voted?" McCary scratched the back of his head. "Long's we don't jump in the Tidal Basin with a big-titted bimbo, we're safe. The hometown media depends on us for press releases—they can't afford a reporter in Washington. You can vote any way you damn well please, long as you're good with the press release."

McCary's eyes narrowed. "Joe's taken over the isolationist movement. Close down our overseas bases. Junk our deep-water navy. Don't build long-range bombers or troop transports. He's after a toothless America. One that can't reach past our borders."

Frank McCary looked past Steven Telford's shoulder to a picture on the wall. A Yankee minié ball had mangled great granddaddy McCary's elbow at Second Manassas. Three years later an itinerant photographer captured granddaddy sitting on a rickety parlor chair. Behind him was the dark underground dugout cut in the Anadarko prairie— home to nine human beings and assorted dogs. A shapeless wide-brimmed hat covered his head. Hard eyes looked out over a massive mustache and a stern frown. Across his lap was a shotgun, and his right hand rested lightly over the trigger.

"He's after your ass, you know." Waving the beer can, McCary gave a lazy grin. "Nothing personal, mind you. Just that Br'er Cantabile is aiming for the White House. An' he's going to do it by jumping into the briar patch Mr. Letnikov's made."

Telford took a sip of his beer. "You'll have to explain. I didn't take too many lessons in good-ol'-boy English."

McCary laughed. "Cantabile intends to ride that troop pullout business right into the White House." Gone was McCary's soft southern accent. "On the way he's going to smear the Agency. I just thought you were entitled to a heads-up."

Beside granddaddy was another picture: Frank McCary at a dusty firebase in the Central Highlands. McCary sitting on a wooden chair, scowling at the camera with granddaddy's hard eyes and handlebar mustache, a scope-mounted M-14 rifle lying across his lap, his hand resting over the trigger.

McCary squinted at Telford. With a slow, looping hook, he lofted the beer can toward a wastebasket in the corner. It dropped straight in. Telford saw scars on the plaster from earlier pitches. McCary snapped a finger in victory.

"Come on." He jerked a thumb toward the door. "Unless you left a trail of bread crumbs, you'll never find your way out."

Seven

On the final approach into Berlin's Tegel airport, Brandt made out the district of Spandau, where the high criminals of Hitler's vanquished Third Reich had been imprisoned. The victors had set up a costly and regulation-laden rotating guard of the grim place. Over the years some of the Nuremberg defendants died in Spandau. Others were released. When Albert Speer got out, there was but one left—Rudolf Hess, Hitler's deputy.

For Brandt, Spandau was an allegory of the Cold War. The Americans and the Russians had found themselves captives of their own monstrous creation. Unable to reach any other accord, they had been forced to keep their lockstep routine for twenty more years, just to cage Hess—a senile old man who, toward the end, had taken to baying at the moon.

He gave the cab driver an address just north of the Tiergarten. Arriving home, he instinctively jabbed the button on the panel set into the entryway. For the smallest part of a second, he waited for the answering buzz to unlock the door. Then a clutching emptiness swept over him as he remembered that Elise had left. He cursed under his breath as he dug for his keys. The empty feeling persisted.

He'd tried to keep a certain distance and thought he'd succeeded. But on letting himself in, he was saddened to smell her perfume, trapped in the still air of the apartment.

The Bauhaus building was a product of the Berlin of the late twenties. It was an expensive place. If the Agency wouldn't pay him the wages of a senior vice president at Barclay's, they were at least forced to house him as one. The annual renewal caused set jaws back at Langley, and Brandt imagined that some faceless auditor would count it among his life's greater victories to close out the lease.

Brandt's apartment was on the fourth floor. From the French doors connecting the living room to the balcony, he could look down on a small park. In the near distance stood the six Doric columns of the Brandenburg Gate.

Brandt put his bags in the guest room. He would unpack later. Bone weary from the overnight flight, he stripped off his clothes and stood for long minutes under the needle spray of the shower. He dried himself and, towel around him, rummaged through the kitchen, coming up with a quarter loaf of black bread, a wedge of Liederkranz, and a glass of chilled Riesling. He savored the pungent cheese and tart wine, thought about going to the office, then gave it up. Instead he padded into the bedroom, stretched out on the bed, and was instantly asleep.

The next morning Brandt put an ad in the lost-and-found columns of the *Berliner Zeitung,* paying cash at a walk-up window. Tugging his scarf round him against the damp cold, he walked to the Berlin offices of Barclay's, where he was in charge of industrial loan assessments.

Like many intelligence officers under deep

cover, maintaining cover was itself a full-time job.
Brandt had to carry his weight at the bank, ren-
dering risk analyses of loans to potential industrial
borrowers This left his espionage to off-hours, vaca-
tions, or time cribbed from the job. None in the
Berlin office knew of his connection with CIA. That
was a matter between an Agency alumnus high in
Barclay's New York branch and a special-liaison section that operated out of a nondescript office in
downtown Washington, far away from CIA at Langley.

Industrial assessments was an excellent cover. It
not only gave Brandt a reason to travel throughout
Europe, it insured a hospitable reception by government officials, especially those in the east, who were
always on the lookout for Western capital to bail
them out of the mess left behind by the Russians.

Brandt was good at both jobs—banking and spying. According to the secret arrangements, he got
only his CIA salary—a sum far less than he would
have been paid as a bona fide Barclay executive. As
the years went on, Brandt increasingly gave thought
to chucking the Agency job for the one at Barclay's.

An hour after the evening edition of the
Zeitung came out, Brandt's private line rang. A
wrong number; someone asking for the utilities
complaints desk. Brandt hung up, then consulted a
small calendar. The afternoon phone booth for today was in the lobby of the Schweizerhof, a hotel
near the zoo. He would take the call from SKEAN,
then perhaps drop by the bar.

The call came on time. Brandt had barely got
into a chair before the bellhop paged a Herr Bancroft. Slipping into the designated booth, Brandt
picked up the phone and, in German, identified

himself as Richard Bancroft. The call was brief. Through a query about stocks on the London Exchange, SKEAN gave him the short numerical code necessary for the date, time, and place of the meeting. Halfway to the bar Brandt turned and left the hotel. He and Elise had come to the Schweizerhof at the close of evenings together, and he had no desire to relive those memories tonight.

Brandt drove his small Opel across the vastness of the Potsdamerplatz, made a series of left turns to Wilhemstrasse, then turned north onto Friedrichstrasse. It was here that for thirty years Checkpoint Charlie had been freedom's end of a barricade-choked passage barely wide enough for two passenger cars. Nearby, decaying buildings, gray and rust red shells, abutted the ruins of the Wall, their upper windows bricked up, their rooftops still covered by tangled remnants of rusted barbed wire.

Brandt had made an appointment with Belker, the commercial attaché in the American embassy. There was a nice touch to that: Belker was also an Agency officer, but under official cover. Brandt knew this. Belker, on the other hand, didn't know about Brandt and so assumed Brandt was, indeed, who he said he was. Brandt would make the usual business inquiries and pass along a bit of salacious gossip making the rounds in the American community. Then he'd say his good-bye in time to join the lunchtime pedestrian traffic and make his meet with SKEAN.

The appointment with Belker went well. There were no pressing commercial issues, and so after no more than fifteen minutes, Brandt left, leaving be-

hind a small gift of Colombian coffee he'd gotten in
New York. Throughout he was preoccupied with his
meeting with SKEAN, surreptitiously glancing at his
watch every few minutes.

He'd parked the Opel on the street across from
the American embassy. He let the car warm up
while he scrubbed the mist from inside the windshield. Then, pulling away from the curb, he saw a
gray Trabant fall in behind him. The tiny Trabant,
two men hunched absurdly in it, stayed back several
hundred meters.

Throwing off a tail was not difficult. The trick
was to do so without appearing to do so. Standard
evasion tradecraft would tell even the goons behind
him that this American, one Richard Bancroft,
might have a job with Barclay's, but that his profession definitely was not banking.

Brandt turned onto Unter den Linden and
headed east, away from the Brandenburg Gate. He
checked his watch again, then looked in the rearview mirror. The Trabant was still there. Crossing
the Spree River, he continued to Alexanderplatz, a
hub of stores and restaurants. There the automobile
traffic suddenly thickened, with trucks, taxis, and
buses jamming the square and boulevards.

At a nearby underground parking garage,
Brandt suddenly wheeled onto a down ramp. The
Trabant, by now separated by a large van, missed
the maneuver. In his mirror Brandt saw the little car
pass the garage. He gunned the Opel down successive levels, parking on the bottom floor, which had
only a few scattered cars.

Above him he could hear the squeal of tires.
Smiling to himself, he locked the car and took the
dingy elevator that carried him up to Alexander-

platz. There, precisely on time, the German Information Bureau was herding together hundreds of foreigners for the afternoon tour of Berlin and Potsdam. Brandt quickly joined a throng of British tourists milling about, looking at guidebooks and taking snapshots.

From his coat pocket he pulled an Irish walking hat, turned up his collar, and worked his way through the jostling crowd. Coming out the other side, he continued across the square and joined the stream of shoppers and lunch crush on Karl-Marx-Allee.

Brandt paused to examine a display of Czech leather goods in the windows of a large department store and continued on. Then, as if he'd reconsidered, he stopped and doubled back to the store entrance. He saw nothing resembling a tail. Once in the store he wandered through the aisles, occasionally pausing or reversing his path. Again, nothing.

He needed an excuse for his excursion after the American embassy. Spending several minutes in contemplation, he selected a pair of Dresden figurines and had them wrapped. His purchase under his arm, he found the toilet, ducked in for a minute, then came out. Scanning the shoppers, he could see no one watching the door. He left the store through a side-street exit.

The meeting would be at the Metropol, a hotel that catered to foreigners. He paid for a newspaper and took a chair in the lobby where he could watch the door. He had five minutes. It would have been better to have watched longer, but the department store moves had taken more time than he'd planned. With three minutes left he got up, folded his newspaper, and walked back to the bank of elevators. His pulse pounded in his neck, and he felt a huge weight on his chest, making each breath a conscious effort. Getting off on the seventh floor, he took a stairway down two flights.

Coming off the stairs, Brandt found himself face-to-face with an elderly chambermaid vigorously pushing a wheezing vacuum cleaner. The woman was humming to herself over the noise of the machine. Startled by Brandt, she fastened on him with round eyes. Her vacuuming was forgotten. As if on automatic her arm pushed the machine back and forth over the same patch of worn carpeting.

Brandt squeezed by. Ten feet away was the room. The edge of a matchbook jutted out beneath the door—SKEAN's all-clear signal. SKEAN would have put it there just two minutes before their meeting. Brandt could feel the maid's eyes following him. Another pace or two and he'd be at the room. He couldn't continue on and come back when she'd gone—SKEAN would have left as well. Yet knocking at the door with her watching him would add yet another grain on the scale that could any moment tip against him.

Brandt imperceptibly slowed his pace. Just as he was about to pass by SKEAN's door, the humming resumed. Glancing over his shoulder, he saw the woman's broad backside. He tapped, and the door opened instantly.

Rudolf Wolf, deputy minister of state security, motioned Brandt into the room with a curt jerk of his head. Brandt's first reaction was surprise that Wolf hadn't changed in the four years since their last meeting. The German had then been the commander of East Germany's elite uniformed guard, the Wachtregiment Felix Dzierzynski.

Tall, with a parade-ground arrogance, Wolf still kept a tight complexion and flat belly. Brandt searched around the near black eyes but found no trace of crow's feet. Erect in a gray vested suit, snow white shirt, and a precisely knotted British regimental tie, Wolf stood unsmiling at the closed door, then gestured into the room, to two heavy, overstuffed chairs.

Same overbearing bastard, Brandt noted. Instead of going directly to the chairs, Brandt walked over to the large bed. Putting the boxed Dresden figurines on the night table, he shucked his coat, tossed it onto the bed, then nodded to the chairs. "After you, General," he offered in English.

Wolf stood at the door, eyes locked with Brandt. Brandt gave a small smile, then slowly extended his hand toward the chairs. Wolf's eyes narrowed. Then, affecting the manner of one used to having doors opened for him, he muttered a perfunctory *"Danke schön,"* and settled in the nearest chair, carefully adjusting his trousers so as not to wrinkle the knife-edge creases. Brandt saw that Wolf's shoes were delicate hand-sewn Italian tasseled slip-ons in a soft, glowing black. Probably has them bone-polished, Brandt thought.

Wolf cocked his head at a slight angle and touched his fingertips together, making a tent of his hands. His black eyes darted over Brandt. Brandt remained standing to wrest some small advantage. His face an impassive mask, he stolidly permitted Wolf his inspection.

Wolf uncrossed his legs, then crossed them again. From a professional repertoire, he drew up an ironic smile. "The years have treated you well, Bancroft." He paused. "I assume your name remains the same."

Brandt did not acknowledge Wolf but moved to the opposite chair, first glancing at the curtained window. Brandt saw an attaché case on the dresser. Although closed, a small power cord snaked from one side to a wall outlet.

The German general had certainly swept for microphones on entering the room. Inside the case, Brandt suspected, was some sort of monitor to detect transmissions in case the sweep had missed a miniature transmitter. The heavy drapes and street noise below eliminated the possibility of a laser window pickup. Lasers were overrated, anyway.

The cavity transmitter was the KGB bug of choice. A metal capsule about three-quarters of an inch in diameter, it could be put anywhere, even embedded in plaster or in wooden furniture. It needed no power and was nearly undetectable. To activate it, you squirted a high-powered radio beam at it from outside the building. The bug responded with an electronic echo that carried the conversation in the room. The Russians had buried so many in the new American embassy in Moscow that the place would have been made into a huge microwave oven if the KGB ever turned on all its radio beams at once.

Brandt settled in his chair as if he were finally—and only grudgingly—satisfied with the room and its security. He sat expectantly, looking at Wolf. The German rewarded him with a grimace of impatience.

"See here, Bancroft." Wolf waved a hand to encompass the room. "We are both very vulnerable here. You called this meeting. What is it you want?"

Brandt judged the normal response time the autocratic Wolf expected, then hesitated a second or two longer. "The relationship between Letnikov and Dietrich Neuhaus," he began. "Discussions about the mutual security treaty. We want detailed reporting on . . ."

"We want?" Wolf echoed Brandt. *"We want?"* The German's face was flushed. He sat forward in his chair, fists clenching the armrests. "You say those words so easily! My God, why not ask me to turn over the keys of the BND to you? Do you know what you're asking? Do you think the BND is populated by fools? What you ask of me is impossible. Things have changed in Germany, Bancroft. The East may no longer see you as an enemy, but what used to be the West no longer considers you a friend."

Brandt had expected the outburst. Much of it had to do with how Wolf had come to them, years ago, a talented young man in the Free German Youth, Wolf had been spotted by an Agency officer who had not met his agent-recruiting quota in many months.

Berlin Station ran a simple false-flag operation. An American case officer of German extraction posed as an HVA internal-security inspector. In this guise he found the enthusiastic Wolf easy pickings. He inducted Wolf into what Wolf believed to be an undercover cell of the Ministry of Security.

Wolf, thinking he was serving East German intelligence, eagerly took on minor chores such as surveillance of foreigners and, later, of East German officials "suspected of corruption." Wolf was painstaking about his reports. They were prompt and extremely detailed.

Berlin Station played Wolf well. They kept his

reports on file. In that file as well were receipts young Wolf had signed for the small sums he'd reluctantly accepted for "personal expenses while serving the state."

Wolf's case officer then steered the young German toward formally applying for service in the HVA. Wolf did well in his basic training at Karlshorst. There he caught the eye of a KGB liaison officer who sent him to an advanced training course at a nondescript but well-guarded camp north of Moscow.

It was on Wolf's return from Russia that the Agency had moved. Wolf's case officer confronted him with the voluminous evidence of his earlier work. Laid out were copies of reports, receipts, even glossy photos of Wolf with a man now identified as an Agency officer well-known to the HVA. That afternoon the Agency set its hook. Wolf's first assignment was insignificant. A job easily done. But in the doing of it, Wolf crossed a line over which he could never again step back. In Wolf's world, as in Brandt's, there was no such thing as a small treason.

However incriminating the Agency's evidence, Brandt had to struggle to maintain control over the strong-willed German. Wolf had been snared by his own youthful patriotism; forced to work against his country by a file tucked away somewhere by the Americans. Over the years Brandt tried to fathom the forces that tore at Wolf. In part Brandt's attempt at understanding was a natural human curiosity, one rooted in sympathy. But there was a professional side as well. The better he understood Wolf, the more easily the German could be manipulated.

Brandt came to know and appreciate Wolf's intricate balancing act. While Wolf feared exposure, he knew that American threats to do so were total and irreversible. The German general knew the CIA would not casually burn him simply because he did not immediately bend to its every demand. The trick was to use his value to the Americans to gain as much leeway as possible without bringing the roof down on himself. And so he tested Brandt's limits, continually probing their elasticity, putting off the Americans with protests about his security.

Brandt relented, taking care that he not be seen as giving in to Wolf. "Those are the larger requirements, General," Brandt replied, using Wolf's rank as an ever-so-slight concession. "You are a professional. You know that small bits of information can be assembled to answer the cosmic questions. Those small bits are what we are after." Then, to reassert himself over Wolf, he tossed a slip of paper onto the small table between them.

Wolf, curious, picked it up, looked at it, then at Brandt with questioning eyes.

Brandt pointed to the paper with a rehearsed casualness. "Your account at Credit Suisse in Basel," he explained, voice heavy with meaning. "A respectable balance. Another deposit is being made today."

Wolf, suddenly aware of the implications, quickly pitched the statement back onto the table. His eyes remained on the pale blue paper, hypnotized by it.

Brandt, knowing he would be the first to leave, ignored the bank statement. Wolf would have to dispose of it. Brandt thought of the after-action report he would have to write this evening. There would be, of course, the standard boilerplate: Brandt's assessment of Wolf's access and reliability, and the requirements Brandt had put on Wolf. But Langley always appreciated a tidbit or two in addition. Something the analysts could give Telford to take to the White House.

"Neuhaus—what's been the reaction to Letnikov?"

Wolf was still distracted by the latest shackle the Americans had put on him. Then he looked up at Brandt, Brandt's question finally overcoming Wolf's horror and fascination with the damning bank statement. The American had had his way; now Wolf would assert himself. Regain a measure of control.

"*Reaction?*" asked Wolf, sneering. "Why do you assume, Bancroft, that we are always *responding* to Moscow? It is beyond you to comprehend a situation in which we are partners with Moscow? That the mighty Russian leaders can treat us as equals?"

"What do you mean, General? That Neuhaus was somehow involved in Letnikov's proposal?"

Wolf's face drained of color. For a moment Brandt feared the German might be on the verge of a stroke. Wolf passed his hand wearily over his mouth. His eyes, formerly flashing at Brandt, now shifted to an invisible spot on the floor.

"It is nothing," Wolf protested weakly. "An outburst of pride on my part, Herr Bancroft."

Brandt noted that Wolf for the first time had adopted a shred of good manners, using the mild honorific *Herr.* What was it Churchill had said? About Hitler either being at your feet or at your throat? Time to push, Brandt thought. Before he gets to my throat again.

Brandt stood and moved to the seated Wolf. He bent forward, so that his face was but inches from the German. "Your pride has nothing to do with it, Wolf," he spat with a cold fury.

The German stared, hostile and menacing. "No? What is it then?" he challenged.

"There is something you know. Something you're keeping from me."

Wolf was looking up at Brandt standing over him.

"You think you have us pegged, don't you?" Brandt demanded. "That we won't turn you over because you're too valuable." Brandt leaned even closer.

Wolf's face was loose around the mouth, his pupils dilated.

"Let me tell you this, Rudolf Wolf. If I leave this room and find out later that something—*anything!* —has gone on between Berlin and Moscow that even hints that you could have known of it . . ." Brandt straightened up. His voice took on a quiet deadliness. "You can stall us on the trivial stuff. We're used to that. But Letnikov's out to change the face of Europe." Brandt bent closer to the stock-still Wolf, his voice menacing. "And your continued service to us doesn't mean a goddamn thing in comparison to that."

Brandt straightened up and asked softly, "Do you understand?"

Wolf studied the backs of his hands, which were resting in his lap. Then he looked up at Brandt. "It is nothing concrete. A matter of conjecture." Wolf shrugged, visibly subdued.

Brandt sat down with an air of a weary but triumphant negotiator who expects no further arguments. "Let's talk about Dietrich Neuhaus and our good friend Letnikov."

Much later Brandt looked at his watch. They'd been at it for almost an hour. The analysts back at

Langley could have grilled Wolf for days. They'd howl at his report. Too brief, they'd scream. But the soft ones weren't sitting in a Berlin hotel room with the deputy minister of the BND, either. Old spies and bold spies. But no old, bold spies.

Still, there was enough here for Langley. For decades the professors had pronounced the relationship between Moscow and East Berlin with the rigid certainty of a catechism.

Clients, they said of the East Germans. Puppets, they said.

But now? Now that along with everything else was changed. And that change would shake the very foundations of American security. In the entire web of American intelligence, he was the only person to know of it.

He looked at Wolf. More had to be learned. Much more. Wolf was the only guide into that unknown—the one slim thread that, carefully worked, could reveal the entire tapestry. Brandt recalled Penkovskiy, an Agency legend. In the sixties the well-placed Soviet colonel had funneled a treasure house of military secrets to CIA and MI-6. But Wolf could get something much more valuable than plans for intercontinental ballistic missiles. Suddenly, of all the Agency's treasures, Wolf was easily the most important. The bastard.

It was time to go. Wolf sensed it, too. Both men rose as if by accord. Brandt shouldered on his overcoat, feeling the pockets for his gloves and walking hat. He moved toward the door. He would leave first, followed by Wolf a few minutes later. Brandt was giving thought to his parting words when a key grated in the lock.

Wolf's eyes opened wide in dismay. The German general froze in place as the door swung open.

A man had one hand on the key, the other on the doorknob. He was talking to someone over his shoulder, facing away from the open door. Stocky, and judging from the smooth neck and thick brown hair, fairly young. A taller blond woman looked over his shoulder, mascaraed eyes taking in first Brandt, then Wolf.

The man turned toward the room. His smile vanished into perplexity at seeing the two men. He slammed the door shut. Brandt heard him say something in the corridor, then the woman's reply.

"My God," cried Wolf. "He was one of our people. He recognized me."

The realization knifed through Brandt. Wolf had set up the meeting in a BND safe house! The BND, like most intelligence services, kept a number of apartments and hotel rooms for agent meetings. Obviously Wolf wouldn't have reserved the room through the BND's support office. Just as obviously Wolf couldn't answer the inevitable questions as to why he was here. Or whom he was with.

"Get out," Brandt ordered Wolf. "Get back to your office." With the German general still frozen in shock, Brandt opened the door and dashed out. To his right he saw the man, followed by the blond in a leather miniskirt. They were at the stairwell at the far end of the long corridor. The man had run because he, too, had no legitimate business in the hotel. Safe houses were not only for meeting agents, they were also handy for a quick fuck over lunch hour.

The blond saw Brandt running toward them. She tugged at the man's sleeve, then followed him through the stairwell door.

Seconds later Brandt pushed through the door. He heard the clatter of rushing footsteps. He began taking the concrete steps three and four at a time in a controlled fall, balancing himself on the round iron handrail. Judging from the sounds beneath him, he hadn't gained on his quarry.

He heard a crash of metal and a woman's shrill voice. Coming down the flight of stairs to the next landing, he saw the cleaning woman in a sprawl.

The old woman, bleeding from a badly scraped forehead, was trying to right herself from a tangle of pail, mops, and vacuum cleaner. With the dazed stare of a victim, she saw Brandt leaping down the stairs at her and gave a cry of supplication. Behind her the door onto the landing was closing shut. Heavier footsteps echoed below him. The hooker had left, the man had stayed on the stairs. Brandt jumped over the old woman and took the next flight down.

At the bottom of the stairwell, a heavy steel door slammed. Seconds later Brandt wrenched it open. He found himself in the hotel basement, dimly lit, thick with the heavy, musty smell of detergent and coal dust. To his left, through a forest of gray concrete support columns, he heard running steps.

Keeping close to the wall, Brandt ran toward the footsteps. His breath was coming in ragged heaves. His right knee, which had taken more than one jolt on the crash down the stairs, was now throbbing. Without breaking stride he stooped and snatched up a heavy steel crowbar near a jumble of tools kept for servicing the furnaces. Rounding a row of columns, he came abruptly on the man, frantically tugging at a door that appeared to open onto the alley.

Within striking range of the man, Brandt raised the crowbar. At the same time the man turned. Brandt was momentarily stunned by the man's youth. Twenty, twenty-five at the most, Brandt judged. No field man, this one. A kid, a headquarters clerk, out for some ass on a workday afternoon.

Brandt hesitated, and the man simpered, throwing his arm up to protect himself. He's seen me, Brandt thought. He's seen Wolf and me together.

Brandt brought the steel bar down with all his strength. He felt the grating of breaking bones. The man's gathering cry choked off into a grunting belch as the bar smashed the forearm, then crushed the skull. The man fell heavily to the floor, lifeless. Blood and brain fluid spread, darkening the dusty floor.

Brandt, exhausted from the chase, stood gasping, trying to catch his breath. From some hidden corner deep within, a cramping spasm of pain doubled him over. He dropped the bloodstained crowbar, his hands clutching at his stomach. Falling to his knees beside the corpse, his body was racked with massive shudders. He vomited, heaving till nothing came except bile. The basement was silent save for the hum of the heating fans.

Shaking his head to clear it, Brandt found his face wet with tears. He rested for another second or two. Then, lurching to his feet, he picked up the crowbar, wiped it on the dead man's coat, and flung it into a dark corner. He took off the man's coat and wrapped it around the corpse's head, tying the sleeves in a hard knot. Flexing his knees, he managed with difficulty to get the dead man up into a fireman's carry. He staggered to a large metal trash container.

Resting his burden against the wall, he freed his left hand to tug at the container's door. It finally swung open on creaking, rusted hinges. From inside came the sour odor of garbage. Brandt glanced up. A chute connected the container to the floors above. To Brandt's left there was a large overhead door that would be raised to permit a truck to pick up the container and replace it with an empty one.

Still laboring for breath, Brandt boosted the body off his shoulder and into the door of the garbage bin. As if it had some grotesque will of its own, the corpse resisted him. It hung, half in, feet sticking out at a crazy angle. Brandt noticed that one shoe had a hole worn in the sole. Brandt pulled the feet together and folded the legs into the bin. He carefully latched the door and struck out across the basement. He looked at his watch. Five minutes ago he'd jumped over the cleaning woman on the stairwell.

Brandt found the shelter of a doorway and inspected himself. He dusted his knees, then checked his tie and shirt for bloodstains. He carefully examined his reflection in the glass pane set in the door. Nothing. He made his way to the lobby, then through a cold mist to Alexanderplatz and the parking garage.

As soon as he got to the apartment, Brandt showered and threw himself into the report. Drafting, editing, and encrypting required his fullest concentration. After, there was the intricate preparation of the letter itself, with its secret inks and telltales. All to keep at bay for an hour or so the snarling beasts of guilt and self-reproach.

Gathering his notes, he took them to the kitchen, where, in the sink, he separately burned each sheet of rumpled foolscap, crumbling the ashes, then washing them down the drain.

Brandt, one hand on the rushing faucet, stared into the sink long after the last ashes had been carried away. He'd thought he'd never make it back to the apartment. His hands were trembling like a drunk's. He knew he'd fumble the simplest question. Thank God he hadn't been stopped. Brandt shuddered at what might have been.

Back in the hotel room: Had Wolf lied? No—it had happened too quickly. Wolf had recognized the intruder, and the intruder had clearly recognized Wolf. If the stranger had gotten away, Wolf would have been done for. Where did that leave everything?

Brandt cupped his hands under the running water, leaned over, and drank deeply, greedily.

Yes, where did it leave everything? Langley, then State, the Pentagon, and the White House would explode as the implications of his report sank in. There would be a storm of questions coming out of that. And the only person who could answer them —at least for now—was Wolf. A real shit who was still alive while a kid who only wanted a piece of ass was now beginning to rot in a fucking dumpster in a hotel basement.

The killing was in the report. There were the usual operational reasons for it, of course. But there was also Brandt's hope that this might cause Langley to put an end to it all. He could request early retirement, and who knows, maybe talk Elise into leaving with him. If Langley wouldn't buy that, screw them.

There were things he could do, places he could go without the damned pension.

He ran the water again, splashed a handful over his face, then dried with a rough towel. From a cabinet he took a bottle of gin, filled a bowl with ice, and walked to the living room. Time to face the beasts.

Eight

PRIORITY PRIORITY PRIORITY PRIORITY
PRIORITY PRIORITY PRIORITY
TOP SECRET/NILDIS/PERMANENTLY
EXCLUDED FROM AUTOMATIC
DOWNGRADING
FM: TABARD 003

Steven Telford looked up. "TABARD?"

At first Sam Rubel gave no sign he'd heard. Then: "Brandt's cable crypt," he explained listlessly. "The number after it means this is the third cable this year."

Telford, suddenly impatient with Rubel, rattled the paper in his hand. "How did Brandt get it to us?"

Sam Rubel stood looking out the glass wall in Telford's office. Outside, snow was beginning to fall. He glanced at his watch. Rush hour's gonna be a bitch, he thought grimly. And his wife, Sarah, had tucked a grocery list in his coat pocket as she kissed him good-bye that morning. He turned away from the winter afternoon and pointed to the cable.

"Brandt does the report in SW—secret writing. The new inks can't be developed by the opposition without destroying the whole message. Then he simply mails what looks like an innocuous business let-

ter to a commercial mail drop in Berlin. Berlin
Station develops the thing and transcribes it to
that." Rubel gestured again to the cable.

"Does Berlin know Brandt's identity?"

Rubel shook his head. "Only you and I know
him as TABARD. He encrypts the message using a
cipher system hidden in a word-processor program.
You and I are the only ones on this end who can
decrypt stuff he sends as 'Eyes Only.'"

Telford considered this, then returned to the
cable.

TO: DIRECTOR VIA DDCI [EYES
ONLY]
SUBJECT: NEUHAUS RELATIONS W/
LETNIKOV FACTION (TS)
SOURCE: (TS) SKEAN

SUMMARY: (TS) SOURCE MAINTAINS
THAT GERMAN LEADER DIETRICH
NEUHAUS ACTIVELY SUPPORTED
YEGOR LETNIKOV IN OUSTER OF
GORBACHEV. SOURCE BELIEVES
THAT, UNKNOWN TO GORBACHEV,
LETNIKOV RECIPROCATED BY PRO-
VIDING COVERT POLITICAL FUNDS
AND/OR MILITARY ASSISTANCE.

1. (TS) FOLLOWING HIS ELECTION
TO CHANCELLOR, DIETRICH NEU-
HAUS ORDERED BND TO ESTABLISH
SPECIAL-ACCESS COMMUNICATIONS
BETWEEN BERLIN AND MOSCOW.
GENERAL ERICH (NMN) MIELKE,
THEN BND DIRECTOR, WAS PER-
SONALLY RESPONSIBLE FOR THE

OPERATION. SKEAN DISCOVERED EXISTENCE OF COMM LINK DURING INVESTIGATION OF CORRUPTION CHARGES AGAINST SIGNALS TECH DIRECTOR OF PROJECT. IN SUBSEQUENT FORCIBLE INTERROGATION, SIGNALS TECH RECOUNTED MEETING DURING WHICH SOVIET REPRESENTATIVE REFERENCED INSTRUCTIONS FROM BELIAKOV (FNU). MIELKE HIMSELF CAUTIONED SOURCE, WARNING THAT LINK WAS MATTER OF GRAVE IMPORTANCE TO NEUHAUS.

2. (TS) SKEAN REPORTS THAT SHORTLY AFTER ESTABLISHING COMMUNICATIONS LINK, NEW SECURITY CLEARANCES WERE ORDERED FOR A SPECIAL MILITARY-UNIT OF APPROXIMATELY 100 PERSONNEL. THE CONTINGENT, CODE-NAMED OSTGRUPPE RABE (ENGLISH: EAST GROUP RAVEN), DEPARTED FOR THE USSR UNDER COMMAND OF COLONEL JOACHIM (MNU) GOLDBACH. GOLDBACH WAS RECENTLY REPLACED BY COLONEL KLAUS (NMN) GAEBLER. GROUP HAS BEEN EXPANDED TO APPROX. 300 PERSONNEL. SOURCE BELIEVES THIS IS RELATED TO PARA 1 ABOVE, BUT HAS NO EVIDENCE OF CONNECTION.

3. (TS) SOURCE CONJECTURE: RELATIONS BETWEEN LETNIKOV AND NEUHAUS PRECEDED NEUHAUS'S POLITICAL RISE AND ELEC-

TION. SOURCE CONVINCED THAT
NEUHAUS DOMINATES LETNIKOV RE-
LATIONSHIP TO GREAT EXTENT AND
MAY HAVE PLAYED MAJOR ROLE IN
GORBACHEV OVERTHROW.

TABARD

TOP SECRET/NILDIS/PERMANENTLY
EXCLUDED FROM AUTOMATIC
DOWNGRADING
PRIORITY PRIORITY PRIORITY PRI-
ORITY PRIORITY PRIORITY PRIORITY

Telford turned to Sam Rubel, who was glumly
watching the snowfall intensify. Telford cleared his
throat to get Rubel's attention. "My God, Sam.
Brandt's suggesting that Neuhaus is pulling the
strings. That the Soviets could be the ones being
manipulated."

"It's a lot of reading between the lines," Rubel
cautioned. "It could be a lot. It could be nothing.
SKEAN's suppositions. Guesses. Rumors."

Rubel regarded Telford for a moment, as if mea-
suring him anew. "Whatever, we have to work on
the assumption that it's a lot. It's a better start than
we normally get. I checked with DI's Soviet and
Western Europe desks. There is a Beliakov who fits
in the context of SKEAN's story. Oleg S. He's one of
Letnikov's boys. He's an engineer, like Letnikov.
They met in Novosibirsk in the late forties. He was
head of the defense industry department of the Central Committee. Letnikov's just named him a full
member of the Politburo. Moscow Station says that
Beliakov and Mielke—Neuhaus's new ambassador—
are quite an item. Apparently Beliakov has the unof-

ficial portfolio to see to Letnikov's interests with the Germans."

"What about the reference to Raven?" asked Telford.

"Nothing about that. But the two names—Goldbach and Gaebler—check out in BRD."

Biographic Reference Division had been one of the first analysis sections to be completely computerized. In its huge memory banks, the Agency stored the lives of millions of men and women: corporals who in one violent moment might become emperors; enemies who might become friends, if only for an hour or so.

BRD's unique feature was that its computers tracked and recorded the activities of its inhabitants automatically, without human supervision. Twenty-four hours a day unblinking optical scanners combed media reports in hundreds of languages from thousands of newspapers and television and radio stations around the world. The scanners sent their take to the computers. The computers also sifted through the massive flow of secret State, Pentagon, and Agency cables. Each time a name popped up, the paragraph and reference source was automatically copied into the memory banks and the place where a certain Chilean colonel or Nigerian economist had last been seen was updated.

"Both are former East German officers. Goldbach was a Party man. He was one of the senior staff in the Ministry for National Defense. Later chief of a bureau for technology and weapon development. BRD says he dropped out of sight about the time that SKEAN has him taking over Raven. Gaebler, who took his place, hasn't been seen since that time."

"This Gaebler," asked Telford. "What do we know about him?"

"Nothing," Rubel answered quietly, "which could mean he was a nonpolitical. Professional soldier. Even the East had a few. We've got a priority search on for him."

Telford looked steadily at his deputy. Brandt's message, significant as it was, did not account for Rubel's manner. Telford had gotten used to a Sam Rubel who was alert, incisive. Today Sam was vague, distracted.

"What is it, Sam? What's bothering you?"

Rubel pursed his lips, hesitating. He felt his pulse throb in his neck. Rubel pointed to the cable. "There was more to it. I didn't print it out."

Later Telford would remember glancing to the door to make certain it was fully shut.

"Brandt had to kill someone. A BND officer who came onto SKEAN and him." Rubel tersely recited the details of Brandt's last paragraph, the physical description of the dead man, where and when the killing had taken place, and how Brandt had disposed of the body.

Telford listened with special care, not wanting to have to ask Rubel to repeat anything. Not wanting to hear it again. Brandt could have let the killing go unreported. But Brandt had always been a good field man.

Brandt told Langley because Langley had to know. It was as simple as that. Brandt knew that, unreported, his act could in some unforeseen way affect operations he knew nothing about, operations seemingly isolated in time and space from that dark basement in Berlin.

Rubel's news had been a bludgeoning shock. It

was yet another brutal lesson about a dangerous and violent world—a place of ragged edges, a place of meager light and deep shadows. Telford found himself having a hard time accepting it.

The logic of Brandt's response was inexorable. Had the man lived, SKEAN would have been compromised. Whatever was up between Berlin and Moscow would have to wait for a public unveiling. That unveiling might mean oppression and death for millions. Brandt had seen it that way, Telford was certain of that. But what now? Could Brandt hold together? See this thing through? For that matter, Telford wondered, can I?

Rubel was still waiting. What to do? The obvious course—and the safest—was to pass it on. Buck it up. Toss the hot potato right into the White House. An officer of the American government had killed an officer of the German government. A nation with which Washington was at peace. That's how the lawyers would see it.

Notify the White House. Report to the Senate and House intelligence committees. Obvious? Certainly. That's what the moralists would say. Moralists not plagued by responsibility.

Responsibility, his responsibility, dictated differently. Rubel knew that, too. That's what Rubel was telling him when he didn't print out that part of Brandt's message.

What would happen if this was reported—as legally required—to Capitol Hill? It would be in the next morning's *Post*. SKEAN would be rolled up before dinnertime in Berlin. The tantalizing crumbs of Brandt's report? The earlier the Kremlin and Berlin could get to work, the more effectively they could control the damage SKEAN had caused. In Washington, Cantabile would turn it into a circus—it would be grandstanding unlimited. Cantabile and his friends wouldn't let an opportunity like that pass by.

How about telling just the White House? Impossible. The lawyers would insist on notifying the Hill. Even if they didn't, Cantabile probably had his sources among the president's staff.

He could go to Bush privately. But if Bush agreed with Telford that notifying Congress would put SKEAN at risk, Bush would become vulnerable himself. Telford, fresh from his own hearing, imagined Cantabile sanctimoniously holding forth about high crimes and misdemeanors—the delicious stuff of impeachments. The last thing the world needed now was to have an American president in the dock.

Telford put his pencil down. On the cable he wrote, "Set up a special-access compartment to support Brandt. Call it"—here Brandt's cable crypt caught his eye—"call it CHAUCER."

Rubel's eyes glinted. He'd already scented the excitement of embarking on an operation. Sam Rubel had resigned himself to another two years as DDCI—two more humdrum years dealing with budgets and settling turf squabbles—before retiring.

Now, suddenly, it was like Laos again. Laos at the beginning, when victory was a goal, not a delusion. Laos before the betrayals and the compromises. The snow outside and Sarah's grocery list were forgotten.

"Keep it small," Telford continued, "but get the best people we have. I want it self-contained. It's got to be airtight. No going to the rest of the Agency for analysis or logistics support."

Sam Rubel walked to the door. Hand on the knob, he turned. Years had dropped from his face.

He stood straighter, taller. "I take it I'm in charge?" He asked it only partly hiding his eagerness.

Telford instantly realized how this was for Rubel and how his answer wasn't just an answer, but a commitment as well. A commitment to see this through. He nodded to Rubel. "Yes," he said softly with trepidation. "You're in charge."

Telford turned off the lights in his office and walked to the window where Rubel had stood. Night was approaching, and the thickly falling snow formed a cotton white blanket. To his right the lights of Washington painted the horizon a pewter rose.

He remembered another such night in Berlin. A slightly drunk and much younger Paul Brandt had looked owlishly at him over a *steinhager* late at night at the Corsican's. He had quoted a World War I poet. Something about having to kill a man who—in other times, in other places—would have been a good companion. He wondered if Brandt still remembered.

Fräulein Gruhl frowned at the list. It was noon, and all names had been scratched off except Weihs. Yes, Manfred Weihs. She consulted a directory, then dialed Weihs's supervisor. After a question she listened, then hung up. Weihs still hadn't called in.

BND procedure was clear. At eight each workday morning, the names of absentees were forwarded to Fräulein Gruhl. Department heads reported their latecomers as they arrived. In before ten, the penalty was one point. After ten, two points. At noon the names of those who still hadn't come to work had to be reported to security.

Gruhl fetched up Weihs's file on her computer.

Excellent work record, save for a point he'd been docked almost a year ago. No matter. She had no leeway. She called Weihs's name into security.

There were other unexplained absences that day. And with admirable efficiency, security took them in alphabetical order. One by one they were resolved. Vacation slips had been improperly filed, supervisors hadn't known of illnesses, and there'd been one case of an individual who'd been transferred to another department without his old boss's knowledge.

Security got around to Fräulein Gruhl's report in the late afternoon. Weihs was a category seven, which meant that he had access only to the most routine files. Tomorrow would be soon enough to send someone by his apartment.

Nine

Frances Helen Watkins was a short, plump woman with silver hair, rimless glasses, and a round, cherubic face. Within the embassy family she was everyone's favorite aunt. It was Frances who would round up the smaller children for a springtime jaunt to the zoo. And at Christmas it was Frances who cooked dinner for the Marine guards, many of them youngsters away from home for the first time.

Her overwrought title was Deputy Economic Attaché (Agriculture). Coming from northern Missouri farm stock, the job fit her perfectly. She crisscrossed Germany in a battered Volkswagen, a pair of rubber Wellington boots in the backseat for trudging across farm fields to inspect sugar beets or dairy cattle.

Those who knew Frances best, however, remembered her for penetrating Fidel Castro's DGI with such thoroughness that the Cuban intelligence service, for all practical purposes, became a subsidiary of Frances Watkins's Miami base. Which is why Telford's predecessor had sent Frances to Germany, to be chief of station, Berlin.

Berlin Station was barricaded behind steel doors and cipher locks on the embassy's third floor.

A veritable warren at one end of the main corridor housed an armory, darkroom, and communications center. Midway down the corridor was the registry, and next to that, the tank.

Used for particularly sensitive discussions, the tank was a room within a room. The inner room, insulated from the original walls, floor, and ceiling by large sound-deadening fiber blocks, was sheathed in copper plate. The copper was electrically charged in such a way as to make bugging impossible. Inside, the furniture was of clear plastic, to insure that listening devices hadn't been implanted in a chair arm or a table leg.

The tank was miserable. Body heat, plus poor ventilation, quickly turned it into an oppressive cell. This afternoon Frances sat in the tank, dabbing a tissue at her forehead as she read from a sheaf of yellow flimsies.

Letnikov had caused a monstrous flap at Langley. In one discipline or another, there were literally thousands of analysts who dealt with the Soviet Union. Economists, geographers, agronomists, even theologians and psychologists joined with the usual battalions of military and political experts. Now this vast army had shaken off its lethargy and lurched into a frenzied cranking out of torrents of collection requirements.

What outsiders (and far too many insiders, Frances added) didn't appreciate was that good intelligence hinged on good questions. Even in a closed society like the USSR, the amount of raw information was almost infinite. And collection resources were definitely finite, Frances reflected grumpily, remembering the latest reduction Langley's ac-

countants had levied in the name of the great god of
cost-effectiveness.

Langley management justified itself by claim-
ing it made order of chaos. Langley set priorities on
requirements. But Frances never saw it that way.
Watkins's Law, formulated over years of field experience, said that the bureaucratics of espionage
worked better in slow times, when they weren't
needed, than in times of crisis, when they were.

So it always came down to the chief of station to
cut through Langley's confusing and often contradictory demands. And that was a no-win proposition.
The people you put at the top of the list were never
satisfied with what you sent them. And then, of
course, you'd always get rockets from everyone you
put lower than first place. Oh well, Frances Helen,
she reminded herself, that's why they pay you top
dollar.

The address block showed that the cable had
been distributed only to Berlin Station for action
with an information copy to the DDCI—Sam Rubel.
Sam had been an instructor when Frances was a
junior officer trainee at the Farm. He'd persuaded
her to turn down an assignment with DI—the Directorate of Intelligence—and apply instead to Operations. Their paths had crossed over the years. It had
been Sam who'd recommended her for chief of station—a plum for any DO officer, and especially so for
a woman.

The cable was a hodgepodge; the new requirements had merely been stacked on top of the old
ones. Langley needed a good fire, Frances thought,
not for the first time. Make the ribbon clerks start
over again. On this, her third time through the
cable, she made notes on a lined pad, translating the

requirements into assignments for specific station officers.

Finished, she looked at the cable. Something about it nagged at her. With growing curiosity she scanned the cable again, then her notes. The waters parted: the jackstraws sorted themselves into two neat piles. The Russian questions were what one might expect, given the upheaval in the Kremlin. They could have been written by a third-grader—tell us what you know about anything in the USSR. A collection of general mush.

The German questions were different. She made tiny ticks down the message. KGB funds to West German political groups before reunification. KGB ties to current political parties and individuals. KGB penetration of the Neuhaus government. German military missions to the USSR since reunification. These requirements weren't generated by one of the professors at headquarters, she thought. They were follow-ups, follow-ups based on some very specific information. Judging from the nature of the questions, the initiating report had probably come from a human source or perhaps a signals intercept.

She frowned, angered over Langley's blunder. What she could deduce from the cable, others could, also. And that's how you lost good sources. She stripped out the German requirements. Those she'd discuss only with the station case officers who were working German targets. At the same time she made a mental note to send a scorcher "eyes only" to Sam Rubel, citing the offending cable as a perfect example of how Langley's contempt for field officers could result in a serious security breach. Frances made certain she'd transferred all assignments to her lined pad, then consigned the offending cable to the burn bag.

SAM 43E was that year's forty-third special air mission to Europe. Lifting off from Andrews Air Force Base in the Maryland suburbs of Washington, SAM Four-Three was flown by a C-20A, the military version of the sleek Gulfstream III, a long-range corporate jet. The Gulfstream bypassed Tegel and landed at a smaller military airfield in what used to be West Berlin.

The runways were still. The sun would not be up for nearly two hours. Here and there an isolated floodlight caught errant flurries of snow. The Gulfstream, sniffing behind a black-and-yellow "follow-me" truck, taxied directly to a darkened hangar distant from the modest terminal. As the truck cut away, the hangar doors opened. A solitary figure in orange coveralls stood in the center of the huge floor and, a flashlight in each hand, directed the jet as it nosed into the dimly lit building.

The massive hangar doors were still rolling shut when a dark gray Mercedes cautiously approached the halted jet. At the plane a fuselage door opened, and steps reached downward from a hatch. Two men, each armed with stubby Steyr submachine guns, hurried down the steps. One stood back as the other identified the occupants of the Mercedes. When he returned to join his comrade, the pair mounted the steps and disappeared into the airplane. Seconds later they reappeared, a man in overcoat and hat between them, his face partially obscured by a scarf and a pair of thick-lensed glasses. The man got into the rear of the car. One of his companions took the front passenger seat, the other returned to the Gulfstream.

"You're Frances Watkins," Telford smiled as he took off his hat and the cheater glasses. In spite of a thorough reading of her file, Telford nonetheless marveled at the woman who looked anything but what she was—one of the Agency's best chiefs of station.

For her part Frances Watkins welcomed the opportunity to inspect the new director. She had seen DCIs come and go over the years. Admittedly her own changing perspectives might have something to do with it, but it seemed that each was more political than his predecessor. As each president after Kennedy had insisted on naming his own man, the qualifications appeared to include hewing to the prevailing Democratic or Republican view of the world. Ideological loyalty was to be expected, even encouraged, elsewhere in the president's list of appointments, but was it wise to do so at Langley? Was a president well-served with a yes-man (there were also yes-women, Frances reminded herself) as his chief intelligence officer?

This Telford had been a hotshot entrepreneur of exotic technologies. Someone to be reckoned with when it came to technical intelligence. And there had been Telford's stint in human intelligence, working with Berlin Station. But that'd been thirty years ago. That was then, Frances thought. This is now. How will this one measure up? You only find out when it hits the fan. And if it turns out you've got a bad one, there are no exchanges or refunds.

She sketched Telford's busy schedule during the short drive into the center of Berlin. A few minutes later she saw Telford to the guest suite in the ambassador's residence and made arrangements for the morning's briefings.

Two hours later a showered and shaved Telford toured the station with Watkins, meeting her deputy, the operations officers, communications specialists, and support technicians. Telford noticed large red metal boxes on communications equipment and on the armored safes. These were connected to each other by a parallel set of steel mesh-covered cables. "Central destruct system," Frances explained. "They put them in all the stations after Tehran."

Telford nodded. A classic case of government barn-door closing. When the Iranian "students" took over the American embassy in 1979, they also inherited intact the contents of the Agency's Tehran Station. The KGB was still living well off the proceeds of an American auditor's pinchpenny wisdom.

The station briefing began in the conference room. Around the table were assembled the staff, whom Frances introduced. Following this she escorted Telford to the tank. One by one the principal station officers detailed their responsibilities and gave Telford a summary of their critical issues. Frances had structured the presentations along station organizational lines. First came the operations officers who were responsible for espionage against the targets assigned to Berlin Station.

Target assignments frequently had little to do with a station's location. It was safe to assume that Berlin Station was targeted against Germany, Eastern Europe, and the Soviet Union. And indeed, most of the station's resources were so devoted.

But the devil—and many of Frances Watkins's headaches—was in the exceptions. One of the

Agency's best windows into Chinese economic planning happened to be a diplomat presently assigned to Beijing's embassy in Berlin. Similarly a Finnish World Bank official, also in Berlin, had very good connections in Pyongyang. And so, Frances Watkins's stable had to contend with collecting information on China and North Korea, and had to serve the headquarters Asia desk requirements with the same dispatch expected by the European desk.

Individual station officers briefed Telford and left. Finally, as Frances Watkins put it, the dog-and-pony show was over. Telford glanced at the three small green lights by the doorway that signaled that the monitoring devices were working. He'd agreed with Sam Rubel that Frances Watkins had to be briefed into the CHAUCER compartment. But Telford insisted that she be the only person in the station to be put on the BIGOT list, and that he personally would do the briefing.

Without preamble he launched into CHAUCER. Over the next few minutes Telford confirmed Frances's earlier suspicion—that a deep-cover Agency officer was working a high-level human source in Neuhaus's government. Telford gave her the gist of Brandt's report and described the special operation Sam Rubel was setting up at Langley. Then the two of them discussed appropriate tasks for the station. These were general in nature. Frances knew that she and Sam Rubel would work out the details.

Things seemed at an end. Telford wearily rubbed the back of his neck. He looked at the clock. And only midmorning in Washington. He was beginning to fade. He pushed his chair back. Frances Watkins gave no sign the session was over.

"A question, Steven," she began, using his given name for the first time. She leaned forward. "Who is the German source?"

Telford was taken aback. He'd seen no need to tell Frances Watkins. Only he, Sam Rubel, and Brandt knew SKEAN's identity. "I don't believe you need to know that, Frances," he answered.

"On the contrary," she countered emphatically, "I believe I do. One of our station standing directives is the penetration of the German government. If I don't know who we already have on the hook, we could cross wires somewhere. I have to know if only to protect him."

Telford considered this for a moment. Her face was set, stern and unyielding. He was startled by the sudden hard warning he saw in her eyes.

"You're a difficult woman," he said, only half-jokingly.

"That's the only kind to have around." She smiled, knowing she'd won.

He told her.

She clucked her tongue in professional admiration. "Once in a while something like this comes along and restores my faith in the Agency."

Telford paid no attention. He was puzzling out another aspect he and Sam Rubel hadn't considered when discussing what Frances Watkins would and would not be told.

She saw Telford was preoccupied, so she sat and said nothing.

"You also have to know," he began slowly, reluctantly, "that our man had to kill a BND officer who stumbled on the meeting. He did it to protect Wolf."

Frances searched Telford's face. He's emotionally involved in this in some way, she thought. And

that probably made him even more reluctant to tell
me about it.

"We'll watch for any discovery of the body. In-
vestigations."

Telford's agonizing disclosure struck a note of
foreboding within her. She recalled Miami and a
promising young officer she'd been particularly fond
of. She still remembered his downhill slide after having to kill a Cuban militiaman who caught him slipping ashore on a deserted beach near Caibarién.
"I'm sorry for whoever has to live with it."

Waking, Telford struggled with time and place.
Outside, street lights had already begun their futile
attempt to hold off the darkness of a late winter
afternoon. The bed, Telford recalled, was in the
guest suite of the residence. The buzzing noise was
the alarm. He had decided on a nap after the station
briefing. The ambassador's driver and bodyguard,
Crothers, would be picking him up in half an hour
for drinks and dinner with Heinrich Langguth, director of the BND. Telford wondered if Langguth
knew he had a dead officer on his hands, or if Langguth might somehow read it on his face.

Frances Watkins would not be going. CIA directors, unlike "C" in the British MI-6, are public figures. And while Telford's presence in Berlin was not
publicized, Frances could not accompany him to see
Langguth without risking her thin cover.

As Telford left the residence, Jack Crothers
opened the rear curbside door of the black sedan.
He was bigger than Telford remembered from their
brief meeting in the embassy that morning, a beefy
man with blond eyelashes and thinning red hair. A

man who moved with the ponderous grace of a football lineman. At the car Telford pointed to the front.
"If you don't mind, Mr. Crothers. I'm more comfortable up here."

Crothers moved easily to accommodate Telford. In the car he pushed a button, locking the
doors. Telford noted there were no buttons or
cranks by which to lower the thick windows. "I
watched them do the job," Crothers offered in a
rumbling, authoritative bass. "Small Pennsylvania
shop. Two brothers. Added over seven thousand
pounds. Laminated glass, Kevlar door panels,
double-steel armor bottom. Won't win any fuel-
economy runs. But then, can't have everything."

Reaching into the backseat, he brought up a
heavy canvas bag, securely fastened with a combination lock. Carefully twisting the knobs, he gently
opened the latch. "Force it open, and a small charge
burns the stuff inside. Also sprays red dye and tear
gas on the guy who's tryin' to get into it."

Crothers handed Telford a sheaf of papers, then
started the car. Adjusting the small map light, Telford sorted through the briefing papers. As Crothers
drove smoothly through the short residential streets
of Charlottenburg, Telford got deeply into a biographic sketch of Langguth. Seconds later the car
shuddered violently, and he was thrown against the
seat belt.

A black limousine had swerved in front of them
from a side street to their left. Crothers cursed
softly. Telford glanced up, noticed the limousine had
American diplomatic license plates, then returned
to the life and times of Heinrich Langguth.

Telford was only half-aware of Crothers responding to a radio call.

"Embassy," Crothers grunted, latching the handset back into the dashboard clip. "Another demonstration by Neuhaus's goons at the French embassy. Big one. Traffic might be snarled."

"Is it on our way to BND?"

Crothers nodded. "We can bypass." He turned to look at Telford. "Or we can turn back." He flicked his eyes to the front, then back to Telford, waiting for an answer.

Telford glanced down the long boulevard. The evening traffic seemed ordinary enough. "Turn back? No. Let's go on." And he returned yet again to Heinrich Langguth.

Two miles away the crowd, a thousand strong, had ended its demonstration. The unpredictable chemistry of mobs had somehow deprived the raucous throng of an appropriately significant but safe victim. The French had taken to heavily arming their embassy security staff. Unhappy, the mob spilled out onto the broad avenue of the Strasse Des 17. Juni, where fate delivered them a long black limousine bearing American diplomatic plates.

The jeering and insults came first, and then, in the near dark, bottles and stones followed. It would be minutes before the well-trained riot police were notified, and more minutes before they mobilized their armored cars and water cannon.

Crothers first saw isolated figures in his headlights. Then pairs, clusters, walking and running alongside the roadway, then more ahead, crossing in front of him. Flicking his beams on high, he saw a thickening crowd ahead, blocking the northbound lanes.

Telford looked up from his reading. Crothers had slowed and was talking calmly into the car phone. He replaced the transceiver in its cradle and peered ahead, trying to appraise the situation. "Looks like a big one. Embassy doesn't have any details. So what else is new?" he asked with contempt for the disembodied voices safely tucked away in the station comm room.

Telford twisted around. Crowds had spilled across the boulevard. "It's cut off behind us."

Crothers grunted his acknowledgment. Flames burst out ahead. Crothers wheeled left. The heavy car mushed across the grassy divider, bumping heavily as it dragged across the curbing, then fishtailing slightly before Crothers brought it under control. Reaching the other side, Crothers continued east, toward the Brandenburg Gate. The crowd ahead was now gathered off to their right, around the growing fire. The lanes ahead were open.

"That's the embassy car," Telford shouted. Out his window, perhaps fifty feet away, he saw the black limousine with the diplomatic plates. It was on its side. Four, perhaps five, men were rocking it, attempting to turn it completely over. The rest of the mob—the wary, the followers—stood back, watching. Flames from the engine compartment were shooting skyward, engulfing the right front tire.

"Stop!" Telford pounded the dashboard, remembering the sound of voices trapped in flame. "Stop, goddamnit."

Stopping had been Crother's first reaction. That had lasted less than half a second. Then he'd thought of his passenger. Four days ago in Hanover, a mob had damn near beaten the American consul to death. What would this bunch do with the head of the CIA? But the insistence, the demand, in Telford's voice gave Crothers the leeway to do what he wanted in the first place. He was already wheeling the car to the side of the road, switching off its lights.

"Put that stuff back in the bag." He saw with approval that Telford was already spinning the combination lock closed.

Telford swung the massive door open and was out and running toward the burning car.

"Wait!"

Telford impatiently turned around. Crothers was moving swiftly. He came up to Telford.

"We stay together. There's too many of them."

Telford saw Crothers's eyes were wide with excitement, his nostrils flared.

Crothers thrust something at him resembling a sawed-off shotgun. "Riot gun," gasped Crothers as they sprinted together to the car. "If you shoot, keep it low."

In one hand Crothers carried what looked to be two police billy clubs joined end to end with a short length of chain. Telford remembered the armory at the Farm. The weapon was a Japanese ninja's nunchaku. In Crothers's other hand, Telford saw what resembled a grenade.

The naked belly of the car faced Telford and Crothers. Five men, their backs to the Americans, were pushing and pulling on the car, setting up a rocking motion that would soon turn the car on its top. Crothers hesitated, head up as if sniffing the air. Satisfied, he pulled the pin on the grenade and heaved it in a looping parabola over the car. The wind would carry the CS gas into the crowd, keeping them away from the far side of the car.

"I'll take right," grunted Telford, now only a

few steps from the unsuspecting men rocking the car.

Crothers raced forward, as if to make certain Telford wouldn't cheat him out of his share of the fighting.

Telford heard the fluttering hum of the nunchaku. Out of the corner of one eye, he saw a rioter crumble and Crothers move toward another.

Telford's own target saw nothing. The man was straining, arms extended overhead, hands gripping the automobile frame, trying to push it over. Telford swung the riot gun like a baseball bat, catching the man in the ribs, just below the armpit. The man didn't fall so much as he seemed to dissolve into a heap on the ground. The flames suddenly flared; Telford felt the heat scorch his face and hands.

"The car," shouted Crothers. "In the car."

Telford saw the big man stagger under the concerted attack of two of the rioters. Then one went down, howling and clutching his mangled testicles. Telford rounded the back of the car. The smell of spilled gasoline was overpowering.

He swung the stock of the stubby gun against the rear window. The laminated glass held.

From the other side of the car, he heard Crothers curse. Then again the sound of the nunchaku. He could see hands inside the car, waving in supplication.

In growing desperation he swung again at the window. The wood stock of the riot gun splintered. Nothing. Telford's breath was coming in deep, sobbing gasps.

"Get outta here. This fucker's gonna blow!" Crothers's disembodied voice came in his ear. "Nothin' you can do."

He turned toward the big man. Blood streamed from a massive wound above Crothers's right eye, his clothing was in shreds, but he still clutched the deadly wand in his hand. With his other hand Crothers grabbed Telford's shoulder and began to pull him away from the growing inferno.

Telford twisted out of Crothers's grip and turned back to the car. The heat was fierce, carrying with it choking clouds of burning rubber. Above the roaring of the flames and shouts of the mob came the harsh falling and rising bray of police Klaxons. He jammed the muzzle of the stubby gun against the window and pulled the trigger. The recoil was massive, a thundering hammer blow to his arms.

Crothers was bellowing something about the gas tank. The back window was gone, blown into countless thousands of rounded plastic shards.

Telford found the hands, then, reaching farther, got a grip on the elbows. The body came suddenly through the opening, and Telford tumbled backward. Before he could scramble to his feet, Crothers was dragging them both away from the car as it exploded in a searing fireball of heat and flames.

Frances Watkins shook Telford's hand. Behind him the Gulfstream's auxiliary power supply whined softly, impatient to start the engines that would carry the plane on to France. Telford's left hand was wrapped in gauze, burn unguent adding its medicinal odor to the hangar's smell of fuel and hydraulic fluid. The riot, the attack on an American embassy car, and the death of its driver unleashed a torrent of press inquiry. Telford's role in the matter hadn't been uncovered. Telford obviously preferred that it remain that way. His itinerary had been quickly adjusted; he would arrive at Paris Station a day early.

Crothers, ignoring the embassy doctor stitching his face, had given Frances the details of the incident. The big man's terse recital brought the fear and urgency of those minutes into the sterile clinic room.

She looked now at Telford. There were still questions, but as far as Frances was concerned, the basics had been established. Steven Carey Telford hadn't let his side down.

The Gulfstream's pilot was motioning through the cockpit window. Special mission or not, landing slots were tough to come by at Charles de Gaulle. Frances smiled at Telford as she released his hand. She waved to the pilot. The starboard engine began to start up. Telford nodded in understanding and moved toward the steps leading into the plane. Frances stayed at his side. At the steps he turned to her. "The woman we got out . . ."

"They took her to Rhein-Main by helicopter. To the air force hospital there. Mild concussion. Nothing too serious."

Telford smiled. "I doubt she'll remember much."

"That's something you don't forget," Frances shook her head in disagreement. "I imagine you'll have some questions to answer. The ambassador wasn't happy. Said the German police could have handled everything. He called the president to complain."

"He did?" Telford laughed. It was a laugh of satisfaction. Of having been shot at without effect. "Why, I'll just tell the president we had to kick a little ass. He'll understand."

Ten

The distribution clerk dropped the day's mail into Fräulein Gruhl's in basket. On top she saw the lemon yellow copy of a personnel action. It had originated in security.

Yes, the Weihs matter. "Manfred Weihs," she read, "to be dropped from rolls." She sighed. DFRs mercifully happened only occasionally. It would take up most of her morning. Payroll, of course, must be notified. Then insurance and medical offices would have to be informed. Weihs's housing certification had to be canceled. And there were even the BND athletic and social offices.

Fräulein Gruhl had known this was coming. The day following her report on Weihs, two Security investigators had taken Weihs's personnel records (with proper authorization papers, of course). They had then inventoried everything in Weihs's desk and all documents in the registry to which he'd had access.

She became fixed on Weihs's photograph. He was good-looking—a year or two younger than she. Perhaps he tired of the grim sameness, she imagined, with a thrill of excitement. Perhaps he ran off for the bright lights. Just to have a good time, she thought wistfully, just to have a good time. She found herself wanting to believe that—and wishing him luck. Fräulein Gruhl looked furtively about, frustration and guilt suddenly at her elbow, then began the tedious process of dropping Manfred Weihs from the rolls.

Constance Gomez Hayden Higby neither clawed her way to the top of Washington's intensely political society nor burst upon it. Rather, with the aid of thirty-nine million dollars, she simply carved out a niche among the peaks, then claimed it as hers alone. Overnight, it seemed, there was the requisite gushing article in the *Washington Post* style section. The reporter breathlessly detailed how Constance and a flock of brightly plumed decorators had redone a huge house in Washington's exclusive Kalorama section. Immediately Constance began a swirl of parties to raise campaign funds for those she judged to be the best and the brightest of America's political stars.

Constance was a passionate woman of the left. She'd come by her politics early as a red-diaper baby —a child of dedicated American Marxists. Her parents left the Party disillusioned with Stalin but still obsessed with Lenin and convinced of the social perfectability of man. At Radcliffe, where the great terror and Communist collusion with the Nazis were nonevents, Constance's revolutionary fervor was stoked anew and found flame during her year abroad in Leningrad.

After college she embarked on a series of successively wealthier marriages. Death (from old age, it was said) and divorce (from promiscuity, it was rumored) built Constance's fortune. The latest remunerative event was an avalanche on a ski slope in Gstaad that claimed but one victim: her most recent husband, Sam Higby.

Samuel Ryan Higby's grandfather had made the first family millions exploiting cheap Chinese labor for California's railroads. The next generation Higbys multiplied those millions many times over on the sweat of Hispanic migrant workers in the San Joaquin valley.

All this had given Sam Higby the wherewithal to rage about the unfairness of America. Young Sam energetically funded progressive politicians, supported lettuce boycotts, and—in well-publicized outings—bivouacked on heating grates with muttering schizophrenics and primping Hollywood stars. Two weeks after the beloved Sam's demise in Gstaad, Constance took his money and her politics to Washington.

Constance knew about money and politics. Not that money *bought* politicians—though gossip had it that some could be rented at reasonable rates. No. Constance knew that election costs had risen so much that politicians increasingly were spending more time raising campaign funds than seeing to the nation's government.

And that's where Constance shone. Because of federal law she could only give dribbles and drabs of her own money directly to any one candidate. But she could use her money to support tax-free foundations and special-interest groups that got around the Federal Election Commission's picayune restrictions. And she could use her California connections to make certain that the exotica of Hollywood would be at her Kalorama bashes, adding their glitter to their own thousand-dollar-a-head campaign contributions.

Political power followed Constance's successes in fundraising. Few senators or congressmen dared cross her. Increasingly the major players had to consider Constance and her views before they proposed or opposed this legislation or that policy. All Washington knew Constance had truly arrived when the *Post* carried under her name a sophomoric article on foreign policy ghostwritten by two Harvard professors over beers one Friday afternoon in the Boathouse Bar.

Constance, in addition to being wealthy, was a handsome woman. Forty-six, her deep auburn hair needed no dyes or rinses. She had a high-cheeked, fine-drawn beauty, accented by green gray eyes and a wide, sensuous mouth. Her body needed only modest attention from Beverly Hills's best plastic surgeons: her breasts, though not overly large, were angled so as to be enticingly prominent, and thanks to the latest in silicone implants, they did not disappear when she lay back naked. Which at this moment she was doing.

Poised over her on the verge of orgasm was Joseph Cantabile. She felt him quicken. She raised her legs higher, scissor-gripping him tightly around the waist. Cupping her hands over his pumping buttocks, she pulled him ever more deeply into her.

Seconds later, and spent, the smell of their sex was a musky haze around them, touching and mingling with the sweat on their bodies.

From a tangle of clothes on a nearby chair came a sudden, insistent electronic beeping. Cantabile started from his postcoital drowsiness. "Shit," he mumbled. "Goddamn roll-call vote."

Constance gave a grumbling moan. "I thought we'd have the whole afternoon, Joe. We see each other little enough now."

Cantabile, now out of bed, leaned over, caressed a breast, then lightly tweaked its nipple. Constance did the lowered-eyelid, tip-of-tongue number that generally convinced her men she wanted still more of them.

But when she opened her eyes, she saw only Cantabile's hairy ass, inches away, as he bent to step into his underwear.

"Can't miss this one," he grunted. "Promised Hawkins I'd vote for the corn research center in Iowa. Don't give a shit about corn research, but I'm going to need him later."

Constance sat up, swinging her perfectly waxed legs over the edge of the bed. She made her voice husky. "When will I see you again?"

"Soon." Cantabile finished knotting his tie, gave it a final adjustment, and turned away from the mirror. "Pat's going up to New York next week. Be gone two, three days. We can slip over to Eastern Shore. Like that?"

Two hours later Constance was again lying back naked, and from the groaning, bucking, and gasping going on, one would judge that she was enjoying the proceedings far more than she had with the senior senator from New Mexico.

Both finally quiet, they lay close, legs still entwined, sharing a cigarette.

"And so our senator friend advances."

Constance breathed out a plume of smoke. "I don't know if he's getting anywhere. But he damn sure works at it. He's got the Intelligence Committee pretty well wrapped up. Everybody owes him something."

"The Intelligence Committee's magnificent. But we can't ignore Foreign Relations."

"Don't worry," Constance smiled. "Joe'll get them in his pocket, too. He's a regular power piranha. He doesn't give a shit about ideology. The socialist revolution or economic democracy is just garbage to him. He only wants one thing, and that's the White House."

The man stubbed out the cigarette, then turned back to Constance, leaning across to nibble at the same sculpted breast Cantabile had played with earlier. "And you, Constance Higby. What do you want?" asked Vladimir Krotov.

"Me?" Constance smiled lasciviously, fondling the GRU *rezident*. "All I want right now is some more of that darling little Marxist-Leninist pee-pee of yours."

Some five hundred miles east of Moscow, a small command car skittered along the ice-encrusted road. Now and again it would break free of the frozen ruts that threatened to steer it head-on into ungainly monsters that suddenly came at it out of the night's blackness—huge broken-backed beasts with dim yellow blackout lights and snarling diesel engines.

Inside, the car's driver hunched over the wheel, nervously absorbed in keeping the vehicle out of the ditch or from being crushed under the approaching vehicles. The defroster was inadequate, and the man kept up a steady stream of curses as he wiped the windshield with a dirty rag. Beside the driver another figure sat, bundled in down parka, scarf, and heavy fur hat.

Klaus Gaebler fumbled inside the parka to come up with a cigarette. He briefly considered one for Fischer, but his driver had enough on his hands tonight. He found the hard plastic case, pulled out one of his last Marlboros, and fired it up with a butane lighter. Fischer, still cursing the winter and the defroster, paid no attention.

Today, of all days, they'd had to go into town. Two of his men were being held by the local police. Hooliganism was the charge; drunkenness and breaking up a whorehouse were the specifics. The militia commandant told him the damage had been considerable, and it had taken a personal visit from Gaebler to get his two corporals out of the stinking jail

Once out of the jail and out of earshot of any Russians, he'd chewed the miscreant's asses. Gaebler savored the rich earthy smoke and smiled to himself as he relived the dressing-down. It didn't take much to chasten a good soldier. A few sentences and a frown. Shamefaced, the corporals had stared at their feet. He really couldn't blame the two. It was a wonder there hadn't been more of it. They'd been in Russia too long. But they never could have gone through such training in Germany without everyone knowing about it.

First, there'd been the technical training. Weeks learning nomenclature, functioning, and maintenance. The pace had picked up even more toward the end of the time at Plesetsk, five hundred freezing miles north of Moscow. Gaebler assumed that had something to do with the fall of Mikhail Gorbachev, but no one talked about it, and Gaebler, a professional soldier, was not given to thinking much about politics or politicians.

After their graduation they'd moved southwest some six hundred miles by rail to Kazan, for field tactical training. Gaebler liked that better, in spite of the bitter Russian winter. Siting exercises to avoid surveillance satellites. Establishing secure communications. It had been good hard work. Soldiers' work. Tomorrow the camouflaged carriers, communications vans, and support equipment would load at the Kazan railhead and move west.

Gaebler winced as Fischer careened toward the ditch to dodge another lumbering vehicle. As it passed, Gaebler ripped off a long incendiary curse. In spite of his strictest orders, his troops insisted on stenciling the unofficial symbol of their unit on the big carriers. Time and again he'd raised hell about it, yet there it was again! On the vehicle that had nearly run them over!

He took another drag on the cigarette and, calmer, allowed himself to chuckle. Spirited men were proud men, Gaebler reflected. The political officers could prattle about socialist solidarity all they wanted to, but it would do no good—these were Germans in Russia. Their insignia reflected their national pride: a fierce black bird, wings back, diving in attack. The insignia of Ostgruppe Rabe— East Group Raven.

Eleven

Back in his car Telford searched his coat pockets for the pale blue index card. Ruth Donohue made certain he always got two copies of his day's schedule: one for his desk, the other to carry with him. He'd stayed an extra half hour at the Pentagon over his Wednesday breakfast with Jim Blair, the secretary of defense, to discuss the search for Ostgruppe Rabe. After, he had dropped by Senator Frank McCary's office to get a feel for Congress's growing unrest about Germany.

Now he was running late for his next appointment. For too many in Washington, intentional lateness was a pecking-order gambit to imply that one had been detained by matters far greater and people more important than those who waited. Few things irritated Telford more, so he felt a twinge of self-reproach as he hurried into his office through the private entrance, avoiding the waiting area where Donohue kept an engaging but vigilant watch on his visitors.

At his desk Telford pushed a button. On a panel by Donohue, a small green light pulsed.

Seconds later Donohue opened the door. Before he could ask her about his caller, the red-haired woman motioned over her shoulder. "Ms. Orsini," Donohue announced, then stepped aside.

Telford's first impression was of her confidence. The second was of her beauty. A slender woman, perhaps five eight, Telford reckoned, she held herself erect. She walked with a gymnast's poise, a stranger to mincing steps. Her black hair was dusted with a gray rich with highlights. Dark eyebrows boldly punctuated her face, arching over clear, deep blue eyes. High cheekbones and a strong, almost square jaw were softened by full lips and a smile that was convincingly taken up by the rest of her face.

"Kathleen Orsini," she offered, extending her hand. Her hand was warm, the grip firm. She wore a tailored navy suit.

Telford searched her face, looked down at the appointment card on his desk, then to the door. Donohue had disappeared.

"We met in Berlin." Kathleen Orsini watched him for a hint of recognition. "I was in the back of a limousine. On the Strasse Des 17. Juni."

Then Telford saw the flesh-colored tape on her forehead, partially hidden by her hair.

Releasing his hand, she touched the bandage. "Six stitches. Concussion, too. But that was all. I was lucky."

"Please. Sit down." Telford motioned to the sofa. He moved toward a chair, still trying to connect the woman in front of him with the person he'd pulled from the embassy car.

"I'm afraid I got here under false pretenses," she confessed. "I got the security office at State to make the appointment. I tried any number of times to write, but thank-you notes for saving one's life tend to sound either understated or hackneyed."

She looked gravely at him. "Jack Crothers told me how it was. How he tried to pull you back . . ."

Telford felt his face warm. He made an embarrassed gesture of dismissal. "People do things by reflex. It all seems so unreal now." Wanting to deflect any further discussion of him and the night in Berlin, he asked how she'd come to be in Germany.

"Oh—part of the continuing theater of talks with the Germans about keeping American troops there. I commute between Washington and Berlin on a too-frequent basis. We're trying, but I'm afraid Neuhaus has his mind made up. He wants us out. I thought for a while that night he'd gotten around to getting rid of us one at a time."

Telford laughed. "How long've you been doing this?"

"I've pretty much gotten identified as a European specialist. I got into arms control. Geneva, Vienna—I made the circuit. It was a backwater until Gorbachev. Then, with Neuhaus and Letnikov, it's picked up even more." She smiled ruefully. "Too much so, sometimes."

She paused, then gathered herself. "I don't want to take any more of your time." She stood, offering her hand. "Again, I'm very grateful to you. Life's sometimes trying, but it's better than the alternative."

Telford, expecting—wanting—a longer visit, was surprised. He sat for a second, then got to his feet, feeling slightly off balance. Shaking her hand, he hastily launched an improvised probe.

"We all need more hours in the day. I thought I was busy in industry until I came to Langley."

Suddenly he realized how incredibly awkward

and stilted he must appear to her. But unwilling to back down, he lurched on.

"I suppose your husband sees very little of you."

By now they were at the door, which he was holding open for her. Tilting her head ever so slightly, she looked at him, a knowing wrinkle around her eyes. "About as much as your wife sees of you."

Flustered, he blurted, "I'm not married."

Leaving, she smiled. "I know. That's what I meant."

Vladimir Mikhailovich Krotov, sometime lover of Constance Higby and senior-ranking GRU officer in the United States, claimed to be the North American senior correspondent for *Ogonyok,* a weekly literary journal circulated widely in the Soviet Union. The cover was quite good. The FBI and the Agency's CI people knew Krotov was GRU, but they did not know he was the *rezident* —the GRU's senior intelligence officer in the United States.

The Bureau and the Agency had quietly spread the word about Krotov to the Washington media, but the whisper campaign was generally ignored. After all, smiled the Brahmins of the Fourth Estate, the Bureau and the Agency routinely said that about all Soviet journalists. And, as the Brahmins nodded in smug agreement, they needed no warning, for certainly they never had any illusions about their colleagues from Moscow. Moreover, Krotov had a fat expense account, so the National Press Club decided to allow him an associate membership if only to bilk the GRU out of free drinks on thirsty Friday afternoons.

Krotov's Washington beat included Capitol Hill.
The Hill was good pickings for Krotov, either in his
role as journalist or in his profession as a spy.

Congress had liberated itself from the challing
discipline of the old seniority system. No longer did a
few mossbacks like Sam Rayburn or Richard Russell
make America's national security policy in private
White House meetings or in discreet phone calls
with the secretary of state. Now each and every
senator and congressman weighed in on matters
such as Nicaragua, Stealth bombers, and disarmament.

The resulting confusion was awful. The babble
of five hundred and thirty-five competing and often
contradictory voices made it difficult for Krotov and
his media and espionage associates to determine just
where the United States would come down on any
specific issue.

On the other hand, the congressional anarchy
handed Krotov countless opportunities to tap into
and shape the making of American policy. And
agents of influence were as useful as those who had
access to the most closely guarded secrets.

As if this weren't enough, Krotov had even
more going for him. Part of the poison of the Vietnam era was that Congress increasingly viewed the
FBI with ideological distaste. And so the Bureau's
trailing of foreigners onto Capitol Hill came to be
seen as an infringement of the Constitution's separa-
tion of powers. Unsurprisingly, as the Hill was put off
limits to the FBI's counterintelligence agents, it became a rich hunting ground for foreign espionage.
And this explained why Krotov felt relatively at ease
in the Senate office of Joseph Cantabile.

Cantabile studied the Russian. Constance had

introduced them, and Cantabile fell prey to off-and-on suspicions that she had something going with Krotov. There was nothing definite, of course. But just as the dirty pictures would fade from his imagination, Cantabile would catch a glance exchanged between the two of them. Or a touch of the hand. Then Cantabile would have to beat back fresh waves of gut-eating jealousy. Constance looked at and touched many men in those special, intimate ways, he argued with himself. Flirting. It was her nature. She wouldn't—*couldn't*—be fucking them all. *Could* she?

Cantabile's drive for the White House required that he be seen as a serious man of international stature—a man who could deal with the Russians. And that, in turn, required a well-connected Soviet official. After Constance introduced them, Cantabile had put Krotov on a short list of potential contacts. The rumors about Krotov settled the matter. From the briefings he'd gotten on the Intelligence Committee, he knew that the GRU had its own direct—and very secure—communications with the new Soviet leader.

The relationship between Cantabile and Krotov, guarded at first, progressed well. It was helped by Constance Higby, who in her sweaty encounters with Krotov, gave him detailed feedback on how his latest meeting had gone over with Cantabile. Krotov would then make minor adjustments, and the link between the Soviet spy and the American senator would ratchet another notch closer.

"More coffee, Vladimir?" asked Cantabile.

The Russian held a hand over his cup. "No, no. Our doctors are getting to be as bad as yours. That which is pleasurable they now wish to limit or eliminate. I've reached my limit for today."

Cantabile sat in a massive leather chair. Its peacock back flared around him, which, when combined with the high armrests, gave the impression that the senator was granting an audience from a throne. This was reinforced when visitors were put on the sofa opposite him.

The sofa, an inch or two lower than the chair, was obviously of lesser quality, and its front edge tilted forward. Although the rigging of the sofa wasn't visible, it was effective. One continually felt as if he or she were sliding downward onto one's knees. The physical effort to keep from doing so was disconcerting, giving Cantabile the edge he sought over the supplicants his staff paraded before him every day.

Krotov, however, appeared very much in control of things. He held his smile at Cantabile until he judged the American was becoming uneasy. "When last we met, Joseph, we continued our discussions about European stability. As always, I found your views sound. As you recall, you mentioned the idea of exposing President Letnikov to the thinking of American congressional leaders."

Of course I recall, you asshole, Cantabile wanted to reply. That was the whole purpose of that meeting and the meetings before that. He pretended to go through the motions of recall. Furrowing his brow for a moment in concentration, he then nodded in recollection. "Oh. Yes, that. Yes, Vladimir, I think Mr. Letnikov would benefit from a closer relationship with us—the Congress."

Cantabile changed gears into his oily-slick TV evangelist tone. "I know the White House line—that

America can't have a foreign policy made by five hundred and thirty-five members of Congress. And I agree that's a bad way to do business." Then he snapped the trap shut. "But there's a worse way, and that's to think that George Bush is the only person in Washington who has to be dealt with."

He narrowed his eyes and intoned a warning. "Daniel Ortega knew from the start that good relations with Capitol Hill pay off. Your Gorbachev should have taken lessons from him."

Krotov forced himself to smile at the reference to the failed Nicaraguan dictator. Ortega! That clown! Ortega fooled the American Congress, but he couldn't fool his own people. This idiot's vanity was exceeded only by his stupidity! He looks like some comic-opera emperor, sitting in that absurd chair. "I quite agree, Joseph. I know that Yegor Kuz'mich is anxious for a dialogue with Americans on a nuclear-free zone," Krotov soothed, using Letnikov's patronymic to hint at intimacy. "Your point about Ortega is particularly appropriate. President Letnikov would welcome an informal exchange of views with the Congress."

"That sounds easier than it is, Vladimir." Cantabile held up both hands, fingers spread, in a gesture of helplessness. "Congress doesn't have the communications that the White House does."

Cantabile had raised this before. This time Krotov was prepared. He unsnapped the flaps of the exquisite English leather letter case beside him on the sofa. Withdrawing a creamy parchment envelope, he offered it to Cantabile, holding it short, so the senator would have to rise from his chair to take it.

"This describes a trusted channel of communications, Joseph, should you desire to use it."

Cantabile stared at the envelope for a second, expecting Krotov to bend further forward. When the Russian didn't, he suppressed a frown and, to cover his concession, stood. Looking down at Krotov, he took the envelope. Turning it, he saw a red wax seal.

"It is in English," Krotov offered.

"I will read it later, Vladimir." Walking to his desk, Cantabile put the letter on the green blotter pad, then turned to Krotov. "I want you to remember my sincere desire for peace and stability in Europe. I've been the first to support the idea, and all I've gotten for it has been abuse from the White House," he complained with a look of wounded innocence. "Why, they're trying to harm me politically for it. All of a sudden the Republican party in New Mexico has unlimited campaign funds to run somebody against me."

Posture time, Krotov sighed to himself, time to create a little sincerity. He rose and walked to face Cantabile. He put a hand on the senator's shoulder. "Joseph, President Letnikov has much to learn about America, but he knows already of your devotion to peaceful relations between the United States and the Soviet Union. He knows, too, of those whose dark interests drive them to sabotage those relations."

"We must start by pulling our troops out of Germany, Vladimir," Cantabile returned with oily earnestness.

"Yes," Krotov nodded in agreement. "We will do our part. But we need help in overcoming those who would block it."

Cantabile walked to look out the window. The view from Dirksen wasn't as good as that enjoyed by the more senior senators over in Russell. And it certainly wasn't as good as from the Oval Office. He turned, frowning. "You can count on my help, Vladimir." Then, as if to make certain his virtue and patriotism were unquestioned, he added stiffly, "Both our countries need peace."

"Peace." Here Krotov could not resist an impulse to venture into the banal. "Yes, Joseph, we must give peace a chance." His contempt of Cantabile grew as the American nodded vigorously in agreement. It's impossible to overdo it with this idiot, he thought.

Then, confidence surging, Krotov closed in. "One obstacle is the White House's secretiveness. If the two sides would meet in open negotiations, I am certain that progress can be made. But if other talks are any indication, we will be cursed with all sorts of Machiavellian subterfuges." He trailed off wistfully.

Cantabile came back from the window. "Vladimir, Woodrow Wilson said it: 'open covenants of peace, openly arrived at.' He made that promise to Congress over seventy years ago, and those people in the White House have ignored it." He jabbed a finger at the window, in the rough direction of Pennsylvania Avenue.

Here Cantabile leaned forward toward Krotov. Cantabile's hands rested on the desk, the letter between them faintly luminescent in the cone of light from an antique brass banker's lamp. Cantabile took on a tone of earnest desperation. "You may be assured, Vladimir, that as long as I have the power, I will work to assure a peaceful Europe."

Krotov's voice matched Cantabile. "With help

such as yours, Joseph, our nations cannot help but succeed." He had worked hours to choose his next words. They had to be clear enough to make certain that the bribe that was offered was realized as such but could be treated as nothing more than an innocent promise of cooperation.

"Russia and America will advance together. Even before our final goal is reached, there will be victories. Victories of understanding between us. You may be certain that President Letnikov will insure your contributions to peace receive their proper due."

Cantabile, poker-faced, raked over Krotov's message for opportunities and snares. His pulse quickened. Letnikov was offering him the stage! Center stage in Moscow! Joseph Cantabile would come off as a man of substance, a man with a relationship with the new Russian leader. A better relationship than Bush. Better than the president! It was now two years before the elections. Never too early to emerge as a national figure. But, shit, it had to be done just right.

As Cantabile was thinking, Krotov anxiously studied the politician's features in the lamplight. The glistening black eyes were those of a reptile, unblinking, emotionless.

For an instant Krotov worried that he'd gone too far. That he'd lose this one. His hands were tingling, beginning to sweat, and he had to force himself to breathe. It would not go well for him if Cantabile slipped away. He'd be sent back to Russia, and a promising career would be smashed. The room was dead silent except for an occasional traffic noise through the thick stone walls.

Cantabile straightened up, came around the

desk, and took Krotov by the elbow. They walked together to the door. "Give my best to Mr. Letnikov, Vladimir. Tell him he has a partnership in peace with Joe Cantabile."

Having seen Krotov out, Cantabile returned to his office, leaving word with his administrative assistant that he didn't want to be disturbed. At his desk he sat for a moment, turning the envelope this way and that in the light. Save for the red seal, there was nothing to indicate its origin. Reaching into a pocket, he came up with a penknife. He scraped off the seal, the red wax breaking into hard fragments. These he swept off his desk into the wastebasket. No need for the letter opener; the flap had not been glued shut. Freed of the seal, the flap of the envelope opened.

The letter was as Krotov described it. Typed, with penned salutation and signature. The English, though good, had a certain ponderousness about it. All their translations, Cantabile reflected, seem to have been done by piano movers. Cantabile scanned the two short paragraphs once more, then folded the page and replaced it in the envelope.

Cantabile thought first of destroying the letter. But why? It was a private communication to a United States senator, by God. And it said nothing wrong anyway.

From habit he ran his tongue over the flap edge and pressed the envelope closed. The red seal gave Cantabile an idea. From a drawer, he took the ceremonial kit given each senator, consisting of a brass seal of the Senate and three sticks of sealing wax: red, white, and blue. Choosing the blue stick, he lit its wick. Holding it just so, he built a large glob on the back of the envelope, then pressed the seal into it, and, on the edge of the still-warm wax, added his thumbprint. There.

An hour later Joseph Cantabile stepped off the small open subway car at the stop beneath the Dirksen Senate Office Building. Nodding absently to the Capitol policeman's informal salute, he made his way to the elevator bank. Glancing right, then behind him, he saw he was quite alone. Hesitating for a moment, he strode quickly by the elevators, turned down the corridor, took a few more steps to the Blind Man's.

The Blind Man's was empty, except, of course, for the blind man. Tonight, it was the old one, Cantabile noted. The black. Benny. Cantabile scuffed a shoe on the beige asphalt tile. Now

Benny turned, pointing his right ear, the one nearest the noise, toward Cantabile.

Cantabile stood very still, holding his breath. He felt a rush of excitement at the flicker of fear that crossed Benny's face. Old bastard. He thinks somebody—or something's—here. But he isn't quite sure. Those eyes. You could see the yellowed whites where the lids didn't quite close. And the hands! Always busy, touching, reaching—dark crabs darting along the candy bars, arranging the cigarettes just so. Like a cat's whiskers, letting him know what's around him. Where he is. Cantabile let loose his breath.

"Ah, Benny. How goes it tonight?"

Relief came in a smile from the blind man. Working swiftly through his catalog of sounds, he identified the voice. Now certain of himself, he waved. "Slow, Senator Cantabile. Slow."

Cantabile looked over his shoulder, out the door. The corridor was still empty.

"Just some mints, Benny. The Lifesavers."

Benny waited, listening for Cantabile to rustle among the candy bars. Cantabile stood still, taking up a demanding silence. Then, fluttering, Benny's hands picked across the waist-high counter in front of him. The blind man came up with a silvery roll.

"These them, Senator?"

Quickly, quietly, Cantabile moved two steps to Benny's right.

"Yes, Benny."

The soft voice, now oddly menacing and coming from a different direction, startled the old man. Jerking around, he pointed the Lifesavers toward Cantabile.

"Forty cents." He left off the "senator," and he had a hard edge on his voice. Overhead, he could hear the faint hum of the fluorescents.

Cantabile held out a dollar bill so that it barely brushed the fingertips of the blind man's outstretched hand.

Benny had to reach out, missing the bill on the first sweep as Cantabile moved it ever so slightly. On the second pass he found it.

"This a dollar, Senator?" The hardness was gone, replaced by a faintly pleading tone.

Cantabile's pulse lurched and quickened. "No, Benny. It's a five. It's all I have."

Benny took the dollar, and, feeling among the specially folded bills in the till, gave Cantabile four singles and change in return.

Cantabile thanked the blind man. As he left, he pitched the mints into the trash container that stood by the elevator marked Senators Only.

Twelve

Telford called a week after they'd met. Typical of Washington, there were the frustrations of cluttered calendars. At an impasse Telford then pretended to find an overlooked open evening, resolving to duck a dinner at the New Zealand embassy.

On the other end of the line, Kathleen Orsini remarked on the coincidence that she, too, had nothing that night, quickly scratching through a benefit reception for the most recent victims of the most recent South Asia floods.

Three nights later Telford's driver flashed his identification, and a State Department guard waved them down the ramp. State severely limited access to the underground VIP parking and pickup area and had used that access for diplomatic purposes. Once, to show Jimmy Carter's displeasure with Moscow, State resolutely denied Anatoly Dobrynin, the Soviet ambassador, his customary wave-through, putting the Russian through the indignity of having to use a public entrance.

Several minutes passed; then Telford saw Kathleen Orsini step from the elevator and push through the glass doors of the waiting room. Framed by the lights behind her, and wearing a dark fur coat, she seemed taller than he remembered. Quickly he got out to open the car door for her. There were smiled greetings, a clumsy shaking of hands, then a faint clean scent of perfume when her hair brushed his face as she got into the car.

They had a corner table upstairs at the Occidental. There they went through the ritual of first dinners: the intense scrutiny of the menu and wine list and the obligatory chatter about Washington's weather.

Drinks arrived. She raised her glass to him. "To rescuers."

Telford countered, "To those rescued." Then, not wanting to dwell on that night in Berlin, "And to a calmer Germany."

"There's little chance of that," a worried look crossed her face. "Neuhaus's party has held four rallies in the past six days. The last one, in Karlsruhe, was . . . but you know . . ."

Frances Watkins's report had detailed the Karlsruhe rally, and how thousands afterward had streamed through the streets to besiege an American army-supply depot. A skirmish line of riot police had held the mob in an uneasy standoff until a gasoline bomb was flung out of the crowd. The police answered with tear gas; then, when a policeman fell to a blow from a club, his comrades nearest him opened fire with their pistols. Score: three dead, seven wounded.

"Yes," he nodded. "Dietrich Neuhaus has his martyrs."

Through the rest of dinner, they batted their conversation back and forth, strangers in a polite game of catch and toss. As if by accord they avoided the personal. The darkening clouds across Europe occupied them; then, circling ever closer to home, they traded bits of Washington's less wicked gossip. She was refreshingly direct, and he found himself enjoying her biting humor.

Both sensed the break. They were done with an opening display of sample wares, of playing a grown-ups' show-and-tell. One of them would now have to signal an interest in continuing or calling it quits.

Telford moved first. He nudged his plate aside and leaned forward, elbows on the table, one hand loosely cupping his wine glass. "I've had enough of Yegor Letnikov and Dietrich Neuhaus for the evening. What about you? Where did you grow up? What brought you here?"

She hesitated only briefly, then smiled and seemed somehow to relax, a barrier surmounted, a decision made. She told him about a childhood in Palo Alto, sharing a large old house with an older brother and two younger sisters.

"Italian father, Irish mother. Both taught at Stanford. Dad was an astrophysicist, retired now. Mom's still at it—professor of organic chemistry. I came east to school. And wouldn't you know, I ended up at Columbia at the start of the Vietnam protests."

"Were you in them?" Telford asked, remembering his puzzlement, then outrage, over what he still considered an unfathomable attack on American values and on America itself.

"In them?" She laughed with irony. "Looking back on it, I think that's *all* I did."

"I never understood any of that stuff. What did you ever think you'd accomplish?"

"Oh"—she swirled her wine, watching it come

close to the rim, then fall back—"the end of the war, I suppose."

"There was more to it than Vietnam, wasn't there?"

"There was." From nowhere came the face of the young military policeman at the Oakland Army Terminal as she put a flower in the muzzle of his rifle. "There was the excitement. The newness of it. But we never got past the beginnings. We fell in love with the barricades and wanted to stay there."

"You were young," he offered.

"Others weren't—the professors and the preachers. They saw the crowd, jumped in front, and anointed themselves leaders. The wallflowers loved the sixties. It put meaning into their dry little lives."

"Some of them are still at it. What changed you?"

"I saw what 'liberation' brought to South Vietnam—prison camps and boat people. Then the same crowd—the Berrigans, Sloane Coffin, and the rest—began making the noises about Ortega that they made about Ho Chi Minh." She shook her head. "I wasn't going to be fooled twice."

Emotionally breathless, she regarded him for a moment. "It was a different time for you, wasn't it?"

As Telford thought back, a small smile of nostalgia appeared. "Yes. I suppose it was very different. There was a certain resonance. We felt"—he groped for the words—"we were in sync with each other. With the music, with the movies, and with what passed then for television. We played off each other. It was a harmonic time. I sometimes think the fifties didn't die until Dallas. Until sixty-three. I hadn't been back long from Germany before they killed him. . . ."

"They?" She looked at him curiously.

He struggled with an answer. "I don't know why I said that. I *know* it was just that nut Oswald, yet I can't help but feel it was a 'them.' We were never the same after that—after Dallas."

Telford made much of stirring his coffee; then, shifting moods, he gave her a puckish grin. "You came out of the sixties with a talent for investigation. You'd make a good detective."

She frowned in puzzlement.

"You knew I was single." Telford thought he caught a faint blush.

"That! There'd been that profile of you in the papers when you were nominated. It stuck in my mind—there aren't any other bachelors among the president's men."

Telford found himself disappointed that she made so little of it, that she hadn't gone to any special effort.

"You know, you're lucky," he teased. "Unlike the newspapers, the Agency can't dig into Americans' private lives."

"Fair's fair, I suppose." She raised a hand in playful surrender. "No marriages; a close call, once. We both blinked at the same time."

"A while ago?" Telford asked, the answer suddenly important.

She smiled at him. "Long enough."

On reaching her apartment he paused on the sidewalk between the car and the building entry. She turned to face him.

"I just want you to know," he told her, "that that morning in my office, I realized I wanted to see you again. It caught me by surprise. I . . . I suppose that accounts for the clumsy approach."

She studied him, taken by his warmth and openness. Not perfect, she thought, or anywhere near it. But rare. An original.

"We have a decision to make," she told him, nodding toward his car waiting at the curb.

It took him a second or two, but then understanding crossed his face in a smile, and he walked with a nonchalance he didn't feel to the car to send his driver home.

Her body delighted him. Firm thighs, lush breasts, and tight, muscular buttocks responded to the exploring of his hands and mouth.

The full moonlight captured erotic images of her. Kneeling, her mouth full of him. Straddling him, selfish for her own orgasm. Leaning forward to offer her nipples. The back and forth of her hips becoming a frenzied grind as she straightened up, arching her back and screaming silently to the ceiling as she came.

Minutes later, breathless and now beside him, she stroked his erect penis, then moved under him.

"This's for you," she whispered, still hoarse with desire.

He entered her again and began slow, deep thrusts.

"No," he told her, "this is for both of us."

And, long minutes later, it was.

"Are you awake?" came her whisper.

"Mmmnh," Telford answered from the edge of sleep. He searched for her hand and found that she was searching for him.

He rolled over to face her. He could make out her silhouette, the curve of her nose, her lips. "Thinking?" he asked.

"Yes."

"About?"

She laughed, a warm ripple in the dark. "A man's question! What else would a woman be thinking about? The Redskins? Pros and cons of the Twelve Mile Limit?" Another laugh, one even warmer. "About this." She squeezed his hand.

Telford felt the bachelor's alarm, the sensing of an impending trap. Nevertheless, he ventured on, surprised at his own bravery. "Regrets?"

"No—no and yes."

"Yes? What's the yes?" he asked, his ego overriding his caution.

She was silent for a moment, then, mischievously, "Oh. That it was so . . . predictable."

"Predictable?" he asked, astonishment evident. "That stuff in Berlin? That I'd come along? That . . ."

She chortled and reached over and lightly pinched his earlobe. "No, that it was strictly formula: Woman in distress. Knight to the rescue. Bed. There was no chase to it. No sexual tension, as the literary critics would say."

"I thought for a second or two there was a chase."

"Oh? When?"

"At the restaurant. When I kidded you about checking up on me. I was disappointed you hadn't."

She brought his hand up and brushed it with her lips. "I lied."

* * *

She awoke to find him stumbling in the dark. "What's the matter?"

"I—I have to go."

She sat up and turned on a bedside lamp. Her full breasts tempted him to come back to her bed.

"Go? Why?"

He gave her a sheepish look. "I sent the driver back. But the security . . ."

"Security? I didn't see anybody. . . ."

"They were two tables away at the Occidental. They followed us here. They're parked down there." He motioned toward the window and the street below.

"And they're probably freezing," she laughed.

"I might be head of the world's most powerful intelligence agency, but they won't let me spend the night out by myself without permission." He sat on the bed beside her. Putting his hand on her cheek, he leaned forward and kissed her. "I want to see you again. Soon."

At the door he turned. "And I'll get permission."

She smiled back. "If it helps, I'll write a note promising to take good care of you."

Thirteen

Kupperman, in a ragged sweater and faded jeans, gnawed at a stubborn cuticle. Staring unseeing at his scuffed topsiders, he rocked his chair back and forth on its back legs, a slow metronome, pushing off with his feet propped on a cluttered desk. Unable to sleep, he'd showered, shaved, and driven to Fort Meade, Maryland. It was now 3:25 A.M., or as the clock on his desk reminded him, 0825Z—Greenwich time.

Swinging his feet to the floor, he crashed forward out of the chair and stepped over to work the dial on a large wall vault. Inside he found a blue file folder and from it pulled the slip of paper that had caused his insomnia.

TOP SECRET/MYSTIC/CHAUCER
SPECIAL INTELLIGENCE
REQUIREMENT SUPPLEMENT 8-93

Special Handling UP
DOD Directive 32100.34
and USC Section 403

1. (TS) This Special Intelligence Requirement (SIR) supplements standing requirements and is limited to access by those on CHAUCER List A. This SIR may not be

reproduced by any means or transmitted electrically. It may be transferred from your custody only upon written permission of S.G. Rubel, Deputy Director, Central Intelligence Agency.

2. (TS/M/C) The following topics have been designated as national priority issues by the director of Central Intelligence:

A. Relationship between Soviet president Y.K. Letnikov and German chancellor Dietrich Neuhaus. Information preceding succession of Letnikov will be annotated as to date of collection.

B. Dedicated communications (probably voice secure) between offices of Letnikov and Neuhaus. Said communications originated on German side by Bundesnachrichtendienst (BND).

C. Activities of MIELKE, Erich (NMN), German ambassador to USSR; and colonels GOLDBACH, Joachim (MNU), and GAEBLER, Klaus (NMN), Bundeswehr.

D. Existence in USSR of Bundeswehr element under command of GOLDBACH or GAEBLER. Element may be identified as Ostgruppe RABE (East Group RAVEN).

3. (S) CHAUCER working group will meet on Monday, 22 February, in Room 6E524, headquarters.

TOP SECRET/MYSTIC/CHAUCER

Unlike CIA, the National Security Agency was never restricted by law from engaging in any activity. In fact, the basic document by which Harry Truman authorized NSA in 1952 remains secret. NSA's budget far exceeds that of CIA, as does its payroll of over seventy thousand employees. As befitting the world's premier electronic espionage agency, NSA eavesdrops on the communications, private and public, of nations and individuals, of enemies and friends.

Within NSA's sprawling headquarters at Fort Meade, A Group, charged with spying on the Soviet Union, was considered by far the most elite. And in A Group, nobody was better at analysis than Charlie Kupperman.

Kupperman was a member of the CHAUCER core group Sam Rubel had recruited the week before. As such he'd been read into the text of the TABARD message, though he did not know—and didn't want to know—of TABARD's identity. But the full text conveyed speculation, which the SIR did not, about a deeper secret, a shift in the fundamental relationship between Moscow and Berlin. That nagged at Kupperman, making sleep virtually impossible.

Requirements 2B and 2D were squarely NSA's. Even so, Kupperman hadn't expected to score immediately on 2B. If Letnikov had wanted to keep his communications with Neuhaus secret from Gorbachev, it was probably a land-line, perhaps even a fiber-optic circuit. Even with NSA's nearly unlimited assets, fiber optics were a bitch. What frustrated Kupperman was 2D.

Kupperman made the assumption that Raven was a formal military unit of some sort. Given that its commanders had been colonels, that alone presupposed a headquarters. And headquarters made their living by communicating. And damnit, Kupperman cursed, NSA justified its existence by knowing about communications.

He'd run all his traps. The huge Crays in the basement had ground through years of communications tapes and recordings. The whole Soviet electronic net had been gone over—telemetry; X-, S-, L-band radars; army, navy, air force comms; the Soviet National Command Authority. The entire take had been sifted, searching for any clues about Germany, Germans, Ostgruppe Rabe. Result—a goddamn zero, no sleep, and Sam Rubel bound to be on his ass before the day was out. And Sam Rubel was one person you wanted to keep happy.

Pissed off, worried, and sleepy, Kupperman walked out into an institutional cream corridor with scarred but well-polished asphalt tile floors. Entering the darkened lounge, intending to fire up the coffee urn, he flipped on the overhead lights. One complete wall was a map of the Soviet Union, a map Kupperman had seen a thousand or so times before. And as always he stopped to stare at it.

The lines, shades, and tints of the huge map mocked him. Somewhere in those eight million square miles was a bunch of Germans. They were eating, sleeping, and shitting. And they were also talking and moving around. There had to be something in all that—something that had registered on some sensor or another. What was maddening was that the answer was probably in this building. In files, on tape, or perhaps in a computer memory. He looked at the map again. There . . .

The thought was a living thing. Kupperman could feel it blossom, swell, and finally take form. "Ohhh! Oh shit!"

Kupperman spun on his heel and sprinted from the lounge, leaving behind any thoughts of coffee or of Sam Rubel's ass-chewing.

That afternoon Sam Rubel surveyed the table. After Telford gave him the nod, Sam sketched out a series of concentric circles. In the center, at the bull's-eye, the core group. Here everyone knew all there was to know about CHAUCER, except for the operational details such as names of case officers, agents, and sources. The core group had to be large enough and of sufficient authority to tap the many independent domains of the American intelligence community and to reach into the "friendlies"—the intelligence services of countries such as Great Britain or Israel. At the same time it had to be kept as small as possible for security.

Sam noted with satisfaction that all were present. All eleven would soon be bonded together, Sam knew, by their mutual and exclusive awareness of CHAUCER—an Order of the Great Secret. They would argue and rage among themselves, but they would come to look down on outsiders with a subtle but very real disdain. They would become an elite within a select community, an aristocracy of Those Who Knew.

There were the collectors and the analysts. The three collection disciplines—photography, signals, human—were covered by representatives from Defense, NSA, and the Agency's Directorate of Operations. Analysis was generally divided along geographic boundaries, and so Sam had picked Russian and German specialists from the Directorate of

Intelligence and from the Defense Intelligence Agency.

Rubel glanced at the sign-up sheet, made introductions around the table, then saw to the necessary administrative details. After the security and admin officers left, Sam opened his folder and glanced at the SIR. Beneath it was the original of Paul Brandt's report. Two pieces of paper. A slim beginning. He imagined the target: thick files somewhere in Berlin and Moscow; the hundreds of people who knew something—anything—about the world that CHAUCER intended to explore.

He scanned the table again, then rapped his knuckles on the polished wood beside the folder.

"We distributed the requirements. Did any of you do your homework?" He turned to his right.

Stan Bleifeld shook his head. Bleifeld ran the Soviet division of NPIC, the National Photographic Interpretation Center. NPIC occupied a large windowless building in Washington's Navy Yard, where experts dissected photography from the satellites and from now-retired aircraft such as the SR-71s and U-2s. It had been NPIC that discovered Nikita Khrushchev's missiles in Cuba, and thereafter a flow of funds and advances in overhead photography insured NPIC a prominent place in the jostling and elbowing of American intelligence.

Bleifeld had spent his intelligence career in SovDiv. Starting as an order of battle analyst in the early sixties, he'd graduated from hunching over a light table to count tanks to the demanding work on issues of high-level contention in the American government, issues that shaped the relations between Washington and Moscow. From the disputes over the range of the Backfire bomber to the accuracy of the SS-18 Mod 4 ICBM, to the creeping buildup of Soviet missile defenses, Stan Bleifeld's analysis was a rare blend of the imaginative and the accurate.

A tall, gaunt man, Bleifeld captured in one sentence a major shortcoming of photographic intelligence.

"Sam, we don't know what we're looking for." Bleifeld spoke with the expressive gestures of a sculptor, making his hands a bowl, then opening them in supplication.

The KH-series satellites were crowning accomplishments of American technology. KH-8 and -9 were the last of the satellites that ejected their cassettes of exposed film for midair and ocean pickup by a fleet of special aircraft. KH-11 and -12 televised their take, first to a relay satellite, then down to ground stations near Washington, D.C., and Woomera, Australia. Within five years three KH-13s would hang in geosynchronous orbits over twenty-two thousand miles above the Soviet Union, their vast photoplane arrays of optical and electronic sensors providing real-time coverage of an astonishing range of military and civilian activities.

While the satellites drew the interest of outsiders, intelligence professionals around the world recognized them for what they were—cameras. Splendid cameras, but cameras nonetheless. What the professionals admired was the American photointerpreters who figured out what the pictures meant. Over the years NPIC had trained and nurtured a cadre of men and women who knew the nooks and crannies of secret bases, factories, and training areas better than most Americans know their own hometowns.

Sam Rubel next acknowledged DIA's Collins

and gritted his teeth. Sam would have preferred anyone in DIA to Collins. But even the CIA's deputy director couldn't infringe on DIA's prerogatives to select its representatives.

Collins was a man of shimmering emptiness. A meeting scavenger, he contributed nothing of substance, doing so with enthusiasm and vigor by stringing together great clumps of bureaucratic Washington's current clichés.

Collins was in full cry. Rubel let him ramble on and drifted off into a late-afternoon daydream. He tuned back in at the close of the peroration. He did so as Collins, true to the lessons he'd learned at Dale Carnegie, was flailing the empty air in decisive judo chops.

". . . and I maintain that at this point in time we have to keep our internal powder dry, prioritize our efforts, and continue to work in the locus of the centroid."

Finally finished, Collins grandly surveyed the table. There were flat stares while others intensely studied blank writing tablets before them. Sam thought he heard an under-breath groan of contempt, then realized it was his own. Faces began losing their glaze, and there were minute shakings of heads as the group came back to life. Sam met Kupperman's eyes and knew the NSA analyst had something going.

Sam and Kupperman had crossed paths frequently over the years. Kupperman, Sam knew, had more than his share of intelligence and nervous energy. Yet today the NSA analyst had suffered through Collins's bullshit with a minimum of squirming and grimacing. A man sitting with a pat hand. Kupperman confirmed this when, catching

Sam looking at him, he gave Sam a slow, conspiratorial wink.

"NSA? Charlie?"

Kupperman, elbows on the table, consulted his notes. There would be nothing about how they'd nearly struck out. Or how he'd gotten that wild hair early that morning. In addition to being a hotshit analyst, Kupperman was a gamesman, and he would not let a prick like Collins—and hence, all of DIA—know how close NSA had come to a dry hole. Or that he, Kupperman, the best of A Group, ever tossed through a sleepless night fighting self-doubt. Screw that.

And so, Kupperman limbered up to give one of his better performances, delivering with brio the message that, as usual, NSA (and by association, Kupperman) had come through once again. With a studied casualness he addressed Rubel.

"It was awfully short notice, Sam," he began, lowering expectations, setting up for his spike. Kupperman noted with satisfaction the leaden expressions around the table. Oh shit, he thought in kidlike glee, it doesn't get any better than this. He struggled to keep his voice level.

"A train carrying German military forces pulled into Brest Litovsk on eighteen February—last Monday—and left at about oh-one-fifteen Greenwich on twenty February. The train, approximately fifty cars long, was en route to Germany from Kazan, in the Russian SFSR." He opened his hands to the table, showing them empty. "That's all we have for now. But as I said, it was short notice."

Kupperman's bombshell created a tumbling gabble of questions and conjectures. Even Collins saw the significance of it. There was much pummeling of Kupperman's offering and a fruitless exchange on probing for ways to attack and exploit the fact that a train five days before sat on a siding in a Soviet border town. Finally a lull gave Rubel the opportunity to close the meeting down. He sat, thinking, as the room emptied.

"You got a minute?"

Kupperman turned. Sam Rubel stood in the corridor, head cocked toward the door to his office.

It didn't take Kupperman long to explain. ". . . so, then I thought about them—the Germans —how they'd move. Just about everything in the Soviet Union goes by rail. Has to. Lousy road net . . ."

Sam Rubel listened intently. Ordinarily NSA kept its raw take carefully guarded, even from colleagues in the intelligence community, but he and Kupperman went back a long way together and were bound by other, earlier shared confidences. And, too, there was the intriguing complexity of Kupperman. Deeply cynical, he nonetheless took a child's sunny enjoyment in bringing an achievement to someone he knew would appreciate the full dimensions of it. He was now visibly excited, leaning forward toward Sam, his eyes glittering. Daring not to break Kupperman's mood, Sam smiled in encouragement.

". . . checked everything, but none of the military comms gave us anything. But I remembered that the state railway has its own communications systems. . . ."

That morning at Fort Meade, Kupperman had run breathlessly into NSA's operations center. Seating himself at one of the six major console keyboards, he'd logged himself into the QUEST program, giving his secret alphanumeric identification code. QUEST took the parameters he rapped into the keyboard, then began scanning the tapes and files across the vast holdings of NSA.

Minutes later Kupperman frowned at his console. The Crays should have given him an answer by now. He typed a check-status command. The screen told him that the system had him in queue. He'd be tended to in good time, thank you. He frowned again, muttered a fuck-you to the Crays, and entered a priority override. That would put him at the head of the line. It would also put everyone else on hold. Priority overrides were reported right to the top of NSA. The director himself would read about it in his daily update. There would be questions, then explanations. Follow-up memos. Fingers wagged. No matter, Kupperman told himself, you weren't doing a job unless somebody was slightly pissed at you.

". . . the railroaders use a land-line net, see. It's more secure than radio. It's all wire, like one big telephone system. No codes. No scramblers. And anyway, it's not something the KGB's worried about. I mean, the stuff you could get from it normally wouldn't tell you anything."

"Except this time," Sam prompted.

Kupperman rocked back in his chair, giving in to the impulse to hug himself in delight. "Except this time," he laughed in agreement. "The net used to be all land-line. But in one place they replaced an old segment with a radio relay."

Rubel guessed the rest. The intercept had probably been made by one of the JASON satellites. Each JASON flew huge elliptical orbits, coming to within two hundred miles of the south pole. Then, over the arctic, JASON would soar almost twenty-five thousand miles away from earth. In effect this brought JASON and its antennae the size of a football field to a near hover relative to the Soviet Union until it was replaced by one of its brothers. The Soviet railroaders' conversations were safe while in the land-lines, but the radio relay, though only a few miles wide, provided a window through which JASON snatched its prize.

". . . we picked up an exchange between the yard in Brest and a railway supply depot in Sverdlovsk. The guy in Brest kept talking about 'the German train from Kazan.'"

Kupperman digressed, holding two index fingers parallel in illustration: "Russian railroads are wider gauge than the rest of Europe. Brest is one of the places where they change the wheel trucks so trains can go back and forth. Obviously there'd been some fuck-up. Brest didn't have the wheel trucks. Some German officer was raising absolute hell about it. Brest was screaming for help. The stuff finally came in from Sverdlovsk on the nineteenth—last Tuesday—and the krauts got on their way."

Sam Rubel knew Kupperman had finished, by the way the NSA analyst leaned back, waiting, expectant, his fatigue returning to deepen his eyes and pull on his face. Sam said the words of admiration and encouragement, giving them special force as he squeezed Kupperman's shoulder at the door. "You gave us a lead, Charlie. All we need now is a little luck."

Fourteen

Klaus Gaebler wearily rubbed his unshaven face. His eyes were dry, his stomach felt as if it'd been fried. The journey from Kazan had been one bitch-up after another. There'd been no dunnage or tie-down chains on the railcars. You were supposed to provide that, a fat Russian major had told him. As if the small German contingent somehow had its own independent sources of supply within the Soviet Union!

Then at Brest Litovsk, the rail-yard crews hadn't gotten the word about the shipment. That caused a forty-three-hour wait. Gaebler remembered his rage. He had scorned the Russians' offer of a guest house for himself. With his troops he'd shared the iron-hard emergency rations and suffered from the cold. The cold! There'd been no escape from it. One finished freezing on guard duty to then freeze in the unheated sleeping cars. The Russians—a superpower? Gaebler laughed bitterly.

They crossed Poland without incident. When they finally reached the German border at Frankfurt an der Oder, Gaebler heard shouts of joy up and down the train. There was laughter all around, and even a few tears to be furtively wiped away with callused hands. Home! To his surprise Gaebler had found his own eyes misting. The oppressive alienness of Russia had become such a familiar burden that he'd no longer given it any thought. Now, back on German soil, that weight suddenly lifted, and his spirits soared.

Telford fought a sudden nausea. He had suddenly swooped down from over three hundred miles above the earth to an altitude of just two thousand feet.

Or so it seemed.

"That's it," came a voice in his ear, at the same time a glowing green arrow appeared, suspended in midair, dancing and pointing.

Telford sat in what resembled an optometrist's chair. His eyes were pressed into a form-adapting mask. Inside the mask stereoptic images gave Telford the sensation of flying. Two feet away, in a similar chair, Stan Bleifeld saw the same scene.

The pictures were taken days before, at the edge of outer space. A KH-12 satellite telescope focused its images onto an optical plane covered with millions of gallium-arsenide detector elements. Each microscopic detector could register black and white, as well as over twelve hundred shades of gray in between. Every detector's shade sensing was given a binary number by the on-board computer, and the result was transmitted back to earth.

Bleifeld's NPIC was one of the privileged subscribers to the exclusive service provided by the KH-12. Digital data from the satellites were fed from a ground station to NPIC's computers in building 312, a windowless building in the Navy Yard in the slums of southwest Washington.

When queried, the computers recreated the picture on the miniature screens in the face masks, reversing the KH-12 process. The binary numbers for each of the detectors came out of the computer in the form of coded electronic pulses. Each pulse commanded its own microscopic screen dot—pixel in the trade—ordering it to change to one of the twelve hundred shades of gray corresponding to the original picture. Like the much larger dots in newspaper photographs, the pixels formed an image, but an image sharper by several orders of magnitude.

Earlier computer systems served up one still picture at a time. EAGLE-EYE, however, created new terrain images instantaneously. The operator merely moved a joystick, much like a fighter pilot. This told the computer where the operator wished to go. The gargantuan memory would instantly change the number sets to generate a spectacular and sometimes stomach-churning "flight" over the most secret and heavily defended hot spots in the world. Like the rail yard at Brest Litovsk.

The green arrow bobbled along the train. "See, here," Bleifeld explained. "You can see the crews at work, changing the wheels under the railcars."

The small specks resolved into human figures. Telford also could see the difference between the wheel trucks coming off the railcars and the narrower ones going on.

The clarity of the scene below hypnotized Telford. He could easily imagine the workers looking up to see Bleifeld and him above them. Then a question that had been nagging at him broke his concentration. "How'd you happen to get this? Luck? We certainly can't be taking daily pictures of every rail yard in the Soviet Union."

The green arrow flashed off, then the picture. Telford pulled away from the inky blackness of the mask to face Bleifeld leaning toward him in the other chair.

"No," Bleifeld admitted, "we can't be everywhere. But this"—he gestured toward his mask— "this wasn't luck, either. Or at least, not much. You see, the rail yards at Brest are a Priority Alpha eye and double-u target."

Telford nodded in understanding. *I and W*— Indications and Warning—had grown to an intelligence art form. The trauma of Pearl Harbor had forever shaped American intelligence. Before December 1941 the United States saw no need for a national intelligence. Gentlemen, one secretary of state had sonorously and sanctimoniously proclaimed, do not read each other's mail. Pearl Harbor insured that even after the war, American presidents would insist that warning of surprise attacks justified the massive spending necessary to maintain the sprawling intelligence community.

And so, I and W. I and W was concerned with a Soviet surprise attack on the United States or its allies, though considerable attention was also paid to such troublemakers as North Korea. I and W began with detailed studies of how the Soviet Union or any other opponent would most likely go to war. Although ballistic missiles could destroy nations within a matter of minutes, even a garrison state like the Soviet Union was not always ready for war. Certain steps had to be taken. Missile forces brought to maximum alert. National leaders evacuated to command shelters. Food stocks increased. Troops moved from peacetime garrisons. Over the years I and W specialists developed and tested tens of thousands of such indicators.

Next the specialists asked the question, "If these are actions the opposition must take, what sensors can detect them doing it?"

Frequently the answer was nothing. But often enough there would be a well-placed human agent. Or a signals-intercept station of proven reliability. Or a particular spot where a unique and necessary action couldn't be concealed from a prying photography satellite. And that is why each day a KH-12 satellite photographed the rail yards of Brest Litovsk.

"But what makes this a German train?" Telford asked, gesturing again toward the mask.

Bleifeld flipped switches on the control panel of his chair. "Let's go back. I'll show you."

Once again Telford had the eerie sensation of unaided flight. There was the train and the now-familiar rail yard.

Suddenly he was plummeting toward the earth. The train cars were tilting crazily this way, then that, reminding him of gunport photos he'd seen of a torpedo plane attack on a ship at sea. Though he knew Bleifeld was rotating the images through the computer presentation, he was still struggling to orient himself as he zoomed toward the train as if flying a few feet above the ground. Involuntarily his fingers locked the armrest, pulling up to avert colliding with a large railcar to his immediate front.

At the last second everything froze. "I brought us down to look at this." In front of Telford was a large slab-sided vehicle with multiple wheels. Bleifeld continued. "It's a standard Soviet item of issue. Communications van. Only thing that's uncovered that we can see." Bleifeld made an adjustment, bringing the van side closer and into sharp focus. "Given Kupperman's intercept about a German train and the human-source report, we figure this pretty well identifies our target," Bleifeld remarked dryly.

Telford saw it at once—the black raven. And with it he felt a chill of premonition.

Later Telford sat over coffee in Bleifeld's office. Like the rest of the building, the original windows had been bricked up. To compensate for the lack of natural light, they'd added extra banks of fluorescents. Bleifeld had then spent a weekend with a paint roller and several gallons of nongovernment light peach paint, trying to soften the resulting glare. Around the walls were enlargements of photographs known throughout the intelligence community.

Telford was taken by the photograph behind Bleifeld's desk and stepped closer to study it.

"Summer of 1960," Bleifeld explained. "*Discoverer* mission fourteen. It was the first satellite picture we got of a Soviet ICBM on its pad. That was before they began putting them in silos."

What Bleifeld didn't say was that he, Bleifeld, had discovered the launch site as a junior analyst, going through old signals reports and World War II maps. He'd pestered his superiors until they finally gave in and included the suspected location as one of the targets for *Discoverer* 14. And there it was.

Telford turned, heavy china mug in hand, and moved to one of two battered easy chairs. "What's next, Stan? Where're you going to go?"

Bleifeld scratched the back of one large-knuckled hand and stared thoughtfully into middle distance. Then he focused on Telford. "Got time for a lesson?"

Telford nodded. The time he didn't have, given his hectic schedule, but he judged this would be worth Donohue's brief sulking and frantic juggling.

"We have that photography of the train only because of a tip-off from NSA and because the rail yards at Brest Litovsk were a preplanned target. Most people think that because the KH-12 can see a silver dollar from three hundred miles up, that we can see everything in the Soviet Union."

"And we can't," prompted Telford.

"No we can't," Bleifeld repeated. "They call the satellite program 'Keyhole.' And that's what it is. It's like peeking through a keyhole. We can see a little bit very well. But when it comes to seeing a *lot*, we don't do very well at all. Look at Krasnoyarsk."

Telford nodded. The Soviet star-wars radar at Krasnoyarsk had been built and tested before the Americans even knew it existed.

"Big as it was and sitting right in the open, it was still hard for us to find," Bleifeld continued. "We need some low-cost wide-area search birds up there. A constellation of them. When they spot suspicious activities, they cue in the high-resolution sensors like KH-12."

The rangy man pulled a face. "And the Soviets don't help us. They've got what we call a CC and D program. Cover, concealment, and deception. It's a sophisticated system that tracks all our satellites and provides warning so the Sovs can avoid detection. They do everything they can to work at night or under cover of bad weather."

Bleifeld stopped abruptly, a flush coloring his cheeks. "I owe you an apology, Mr. Telford. I was giving you the new-boy lecture. I forgot about Astronetics."

"It's Steven," Telford was quick to say, already liking Bleifeld. "And we were mainly in the sigint satellites and airplane business. I never paid much attention to photography. I just assumed that the KH-12 had a search capability." Telford took a sip of his coffee. "But what now?"

Bleifeld frowned in concentration. "There are things we know." He ticked off the points on his fingers. "Ostgruppe Rabe is a German military outfit. The communications vans can tell us a lot. So far they tell us that Raven's a field unit. We know it's been in the USSR—in Kazan. We can estimate troop strength from the number of sleeping cars. It's got to find a home somewhere in Germany.

"And what we know gives us other things to look for. New requirements." Bleifeld interlocked the fingers of both hands, squeezing until the knuckles whitened.

Telford was distracted by a small framed sign on the coffee table: "Espionage is practiced occasionally by spies—and constantly by neighbors."

". . . have KH-12 take a look at Kazan. We don't have any file pictures of the place. We should look, too, at the German rail yards, maneuver areas, and barracks. We'll be searching for those comm vans. I suspect NSA will get back into the act, too."

"Care to hazard a guess about that unit?" Telford asked.

"Hell, I don't even bet on the Redskins." Bleifeld shook his head, lips pressed primly into a thin line. "No. No, I wouldn't. I've been at this game too long for that." Unconsciously taking on a tone he saved for newcomers to 312, Bleifeld admonished,

"You start guessing, even for fun, and it gets to be a habit. I say what I think the evidence shows. Nothing more."

"And that is?"

Bleifeld rapped off his points. "It's a German outfit that has Russian comm equipment. It's called Ostgruppe Rabe and has been on a train inside the USSR. It's probably headed back into Germany."

Finished with his staccato recital, his face softened. He shrugged, hands open palm upward—empty.

"Aside from that, Steven, we don't know squat."

Gaebler had made arrangements for the train to be put under guard at the military railhead at Fürstenwalde. Ostgruppe Rabe would stand down for twenty-four hours before unloading their equipment to move by road to Königsbrück. Gaebler saw to it that there would be plenty of good food, hot showers, and clean bedding for his men. He gave a small belch and patted the pockets of his dirty parka for an antacid tablet. He too ached for a full stomach and clean sheets. Instead he was here in the commandant's office under the unblinking scrutiny of Felix Ehren.

The commandant had introduced Gaebler, then left, only too eager to be out of the small room. Ehren, unsmiling, had not offered to shake hands but instead took the absent commandant's armchair behind a littered desk. Seated, he continued his appraisal of Gaebler, who was still standing.

"We expected you days ago."

Gaebler bristled. Part of it was the man's arrogance; another was that he was a politician. Germany had been blessed with the best soldiers in the world and cursed with the worst politicans. The soldiers had never betrayed Germany. He calmed himself. After all, the somber man before him hadn't levied an accusation. It had been a clinical observation. As if he'd said the world was round.

Gaebler responded in kind. "The reasons were reported."

Ehren took this in, while continuing to weigh Gaebler. As if finally finished with his analysis, he then motioned to a nearby chair. "Please sit, colonel." There was another pause. "Do you know who I am?"

Again the curious flatness. Other men would ask a question like that to establish their superiority. This one sought only to define a spatial relationship between two impersonal elements within some grander plan. See here, Ehren was saying, let us understand precisely where we are. My position is neither superior nor inferior to yours. Merely different. And you and I, Colonel Klaus Gaebler, must understand those differences.

"You report directly to the chancellor. To Dietrich Neuhaus." Gaebler never put much stock in subtlety. The core of soldiering was precise communication. Letting the other fellow know exactly what was going on. Nonetheless, he picked his next words carefully. Let's see how sharp this fellow Ehren is. "I know also that all activities of Ostgruppe Rabe come to your attention."

Ehren's face was unfathomable. He answered Gaebler, then, in a measured tone. "Yes, reports. I read them all. But they do not give me the full dimensions of you. Of your men. Your accomplish-

ments. Your capabilities. For that I must see you.
And in so doing deprive you of much-deserved rest."

Very much as one equal to another, Ehren
sought Gaebler's contribution to a mutual enter-
prise. "It is cold outside, but better than the stuffi-
ness in here. If you will show me your train—explain
the equipment as we walk—I will satisfy my curiosity, and you will be able to be rid of me sooner." He
got up from the chair, shouldered into a heavy overcoat, and motioned to the door. "After you, Colonel."

Followed at a discreet distance by one of
Ehren's aides and a senior noncommissioned officer
of Ostgruppe Rabe, the two trudged along the heavily guarded siding. The long train was composed of
boxcars interspersed with long flatcars, their cargo
shrouded under dirty canvas tarpaulins.

Gaebler showed Ehren the command and communications vans, six-wheeled cross-country vehicles, able to traverse the roughest terrain without
damaging their exquisite electronics.

"We have both inertial and satellite navigation
systems," Gaebler explained. Pointing to the top of
one van, "In three minutes, we can mount the satellite dish that will provide thirty-seven communications channels. The same antenna takes care of
survey data. Inside of eleven minutes we know our
position within half a meter."

"What happens if there are no satellites?"

"We take positioning data from our inertial systems. Ring-laser gyroscopes give us an accuracy of
one meter. Not as good as the satellite fixes, but
adequate."

Ehren examined the flatcar, walking down the

length of it. Apparently finding it satisfactory, he turned to Gaebler. "And where is the rest?"

Gaebler waved a gloved hand. "There. Between the security cars." The two walked in silence along the tracks until they came to two boxcars distinguished from others in the train only by the guards.

Four men patrolled in pairs on each side of the tracks. While the security of the rest of the train had been turned over to local troops, on these cars it was Gaebler's men who stood two-hour watches, alert, suspicious, their weapons loaded and at the ready. As much as he'd wanted all his men completely off duty, this was the one security task Gaebler would not entrust to anyone but troops from Ostgruppe Rabe.

There was a clashing metallic sound, a rifle bolt slamming home.

"Halten Sie."

A sentry challenged them, his AKS-74 assault rifle carried so as to be able to sweep across them in seconds. His partner was positioned to cover Gaebler and Ehren from a different angle.

Gaebler scanned the nearby rooftop of a repair shed. Yes, there he was, the hidden sting in the guard force. Gaebler wondered if Ehren knew they were in the scope of an SVD sniper rifle. Probably wouldn't turn a hair, Gaebler thought, remembering Ehren in the commandant's office.

"Wait here," Gaebler instructed.

Ehren stood and watched Gaebler stride to the first guard, who, recognizing his colonel, slung his rifle over his shoulder and gave a field soldier's familiar salute, rounding off the sharp corners prescribed by regulations. Gaebler turned and waved Ehren up.

"In here?" Ehren pointed to the car to their front. Without waiting for an answer Ehren made a sliding gesture. "Have him open it up. I wish to see them." No more first among equals. This was definitely an order.

Gaebler nodded to the nearer guard, who strode to the boxcar. From his jacket he took a pair of heavy pliers and worked to cut through the steel banding and seals on the door. That done, the soldier strained against the door. At first, jammed with ice, it refused to move. Then, with a crackling sound, the door grudgingly gave way, dry rollers screeching in protest. A black space of perhaps a meter yawned, a dark opening into the boxcar. The guard, having done as he'd been told, stepped back, incuriously watching his colonel and the blocky stranger in the heavy overcoat.

Standing together at the edge of the open door, Gaebler watched with interest as Ehren assessed the problem before him. The sloping gravel rail bed, combined with the height of the boxcar, put the threshold of the doorway just under armpit level. Ehren glanced right, then left. There were no built-in rungs, no nearby crates. Ehren clearly wanted to climb into the car. What was not clear was how it would be done.

Gaebler glanced at the guard. A grizzled sergeant, the man had the studiously detached and respectful—but secretly delighted—expression of enlisted men who see their superiors get themselves into a mess. Gaebler saw the sergeant's eyes suddenly open in surprise. Turning quickly, he saw the last of Ehren's arms only vault into the boxcar.

On his feet Ehren stood in the open doorway. He stood close to the edge. Gaebler had only to look a certain way, and Ehren would extend a hand. Now Gaebler felt the sergeant's eyes on him. Cursing himself, Ehren, and the sergeant, he put his hands on the threshold and, taking a deep breath, swung up. Lights exploded behind his eyes as his trailing knee clipped the edge of the boxcar. He ignored the sharp pain, moving to his feet with a pretension of agility.

Ehren's back was already to him. "Only ten in this large car? It could easily carry more."

"For safety," Gaebler explained. "In case of an accident, a fire. There is little chance of a full-scale detonation. But for safety we do not load each car to capacity."

"And the total, then?"

"One hundred in this shipment."

Ehren nodded. He walked around the nearest container. It was a gray green horizontal steel drum, nearly two meters in diameter, one end fastened with twelve heavy snap latches.

"Each container is slightly pressurized," Gaebler offered. "The air inside is humidity controlled. We unfasten the snap latches, and everything rolls out on shock-mounted tracks."

"How long does the process take?"

Gaebler considered. "With a trained crew perhaps as little as fifteen minutes. Certainly not more than twenty. There are only a few tests to be performed. . . ."

Ehren grunted in understanding. He turned. "I have seen enough, Colonel Gaebler. I must get back to Berlin."

The two men jumped down from the car, and

Gaebler gave the waiting guard a signal to close and secure the door. He and Ehren trudged back along the rail bed, their footsteps grinding the gravel under the dirty snow. From somewhere in the yard came the crashing noise of railway cars being coupled.

Ehren broke the silence. "You have done well, Colonel Gaebler." He gave out praise with precise economy.

Gaebler nodded to indicate he'd heard. But now, with Ehren about to leave, his mind raced to questions that had come to him in Russia. The curiosity of the past months finally overcame his caution. Ehren, as one who reported only to Neuhaus, was one who would know.

"There are questions, Comrade Ehren. Questions I have about all this."

The two men stopped. Ehren stared impassively at Gaebler. It was impossible to read his face, Gaebler thought.

"You may ask, Colonel." Ehren's voice was guarded.

"This operation—Ostgruppe Rabe—it is obviously more than a simple modernization of our military forces." Gaebler waved back at the boxcar they'd entered, now being shut and sealed again. Gaebler paused to frame the rest of the question.

Ehren, thinking the officer was finished, asked, "So what does Germany have in mind for these weapons? Is that it, Colonel?"

"No, Herr Ehren. I can think of any number of uses for them," he said, concealing his distaste. "What I cannot understand is the Russians."

"How so?" Ehren began walking again, toward the waiting car.

"They have always kept such things under their own control. Very strict control. They have even limited our research. What arrangements will be made for the Russians to establish their command over these weapons?"

Ehren's eyes were on the ground as they walked. Then he looked at Gaebler steadily for a moment. Gaebler had begun to think he'd not get an answer when Ehren pursed his lips. "Ostgruppe Rabe, Colonel Gaebler, represents a new relationship between Germany and the Soviet Union. You and your men—this train—is one move in a more complex strategy. A strategy in which Berlin and Moscow are partners."

They reached Ehren's car. The aide hurried around them to open the rear door.

Gaebler was still turning Ehren's words over as the stocky man got into the car. The aide, unhappy that the conversation was not yet over, stood holding the door, shifting from foot to foot.

"You frown, Colonel. My answer doesn't meet with your approval?" Ehren asked with a touch of irony.

"I am still puzzled," Gaebler admitted. "Mikhail Gorbachev was in power when Ostgruppe Rabe was formed. It does not seem to fit that he would have approved of such a move in light of the disarmament treaties with the Americans."

Ehren gathered his overcoat around him and shifted to settle himself in the backseat. He looked up to Gaebler, his eyes now almost black. "Chancellor Neuhaus's understanding was not with Gorbachev, Colonel. It was with Yegor Letnikov."

Gaebler took a moment to consider this. As he did so, one implication after another successively battered him. Whatever the agreement with Letnikov, it was reached while Gorbachev was in power. That, in turn, meant that Neuhaus knew that Letnikov would try to overthrow Gorbachev. Moreover, that Ostgruppe Rabe had been kept secret from Gorbachev was possible only if Letnikov had also gotten to the Russian generals.

Gaebler knew that Ostgruppe Rabe was special. In his wildest fantasies he never would have put it in the center of an international power play such as this. He breathed deeply and reached for another antacid tablet—but then made himself wait until he was unobserved.

As the aide closed the door, Ehren gave a salute, touching his index finger to his eyebrow. He held the salute as if by doing so he would hold Gaebler's attention. "You should know, my good colonel, that the understanding between Dietrich Neuhaus and Yegor Letnikov is an understanding between partners." Ehren paused for emphasis, forming his words precisely. "Equal partners." A locomotive whistle gave a short, grating screech. "Our chancellor insisted on full custody of these weapons on principle. We are, after all, a sovereign nation."

Ehren dropped the salute. "Auf Wiedersehen, Colonel. Get some hot food and a good night's sleep."

Gaebler returned Ehren's salute and started to walk back down the track.

"Oh—Colonel . . ."

Gaebler spun around.

Ehren had a sardonic smile on his lips. He pointed to the knee Gaebler had scraped at the boxcar. "Be sure to have someone take a look at your leg."

Fifteen

Visitors to the White House Situation Room are usually surprised by its small size. It is a basement room perhaps twenty feet by ten. The floor is covered with a medium blue short-napped wool carpet. Seals of the military services and CIA adorn blond oak wall panels that can be moved aside to display maps, chalkboards, and video screens.

In the center of the room is a conference table seating no more than eight people, ten at most. Jimmy Carter had banished the ashtrays, and they had not returned. The cut-glass bowls that had held Ronald Reagan's Jellie Bellies had been refilled with decreasing regularity until they now stood empty.

Telford looked at the glass bowls. They'll probably disappear altogether one of these days, he mused. He sat to George Bush's right. On Bush's left was Harry Scott, who had replaced Brent Scowcroft at the National Security Council. Scott, a solid silver-haired man, was the honest broker for national security issues. Like his predecessors, he saw to it that State, Defense, and CIA got a hearing; that George Bush would know of dissenting views without being unnecessarily brought in as an arbiter or referee.

Across from the three were Rubel, Kupperman, and Bleifeld.

Rubel began, tersely defining CHAUCER and describing its origins with Brandt's initial report. Sam and Telford's eyes met briefly, and Sam felt a flash of guilt pass between the two of them. The killing had come up again as Sam and Telford drove down from Langley. Again both reluctantly concluded that their first inclination had been correct, that telling Bush would force him to choose between risking Wolf or becoming an accessory to hiding the act from Congress.

Kupperman explained the JASON satellite intercept of the Soviet railroad transmissions. Bleifeld segued in, passing the president enlargements of the yard at Brest Litovsk. Bush examined the photographs, then gave them to Scott.

Bleifeld waited until Scott looked up. "We targeted the maneuver areas north of Kazan." He rapped a large-knuckled finger on a map board on the table in front of Bush. Kazan was marked with a large orange dot, as was Brest Litovsk. "We had to run several KH-12 missions—cloud cover made for bad viewing." He shook his head. "We found nothing. We could see fresh vehicle tracks all over the place, recently closed latrines, that kind of thing. But no signature items and no troops in the field for training, German or otherwise."

Bleifeld sorted through the photo enlargements and came up with one showing the large communications van with the raven insignia. With a small telescoping metal pointer, he tapped the top of the van. "We did a little better with subsequent analysis of the Brest Litovsk material. We measured the antennae on the communications vans and passed the information back to NSA." He nodded to Kupperman.

The wiry NSA analyst picked up without pause. "The dimensions of the antenna gave us the frequency bands Raven uses—or used—in their communications. We searched our library tapes to find everything that worked those frequencies. Everything inside the USSR, that is. Next we took that information and ran a second sort. That came up with transmissions in the Kazan area over the last six months.

"We then did a traffic analysis of the Kazan transmissions. They showed . . ."

"Excuse me," interrupted Scott. "Traffic analysis?"

This was the fault line of many Washington briefings: the simple question whose answer could cause a landslide of epic proportions, burying the original message under a jumble of technobabble. Fortunately Kupperman was good at explaining the arcane.

"Imagine tracing all the phone calls in a small town. You can't eavesdrop on *what's* being said. But you do know *when* and *how often* each call is made. And you know who's calling whom. We can do that with radio communications, too. Even if we can't break the codes, the pattern of the transmissions— the traffic—can identify the kind of military unit. We can tell if it's an infantry or tank outfit on the move or a headquarters or supply company in a fixed garrison."

Scott nodded.

"Once we establish a pattern, we can ask the computers to give us the dates and locations of similar patterns." Kupperman's finger traced a circle around Germany on the map board. "We found nothing here. Nothing in our files. Nothing in current transmissions. By now Raven is probably somewhere back in Germany, all right. But It hasn't used its comm gear. It may be that they're still setting up after getting back from the USSR."

From the corner of his eye, Kupperman saw Bleifeld begin the smallest frown of disapproval. And so for Bleifeld, not Bush, Kupperman quickly added, "But that's only conjecture."

Kupperman ran his finger east. "We did find, Mr. President, the same pattern of transmissions elsewhere in the USSR."

Bush, sensitive to nuances of intelligence briefers' techniques, cocked his head.

Kupperman jabbed an area northeast of Leningrad, south of the White Sea port of Arkhangelsk. "Here. Here, in Plesetsk."

"Historical activity?" Bush probed. "Or current?"

"Both, Mr. President."

"Both?" asked Scott.

Kupperman nodded. "Yes. We show activity that began in Plesetsk in December. Our source says Raven left Germany in October. That would have given Raven two months for travel, orientation, housekeeping, and equipment issue. The Plesetsk activity broke off. That same activity soon resumed in Kazan. That could be connected with Raven's move from Plesetsk to Kazan. The Kazan activity ceased when Raven moved to Brest Litovsk and returned to Germany."

"You mentioned current activity in Plesetsk," Bush reminded him.

"Yes, Mr. President. Shortly after Raven left

Plesetsk for Kazan, an identical pattern came on the air. It's still operating."

Bush sat silently, looking first at Kupperman, then at Bleifeld and Rubel. Still without a word he got up and walked to the Silex and poured himself a cup of black coffee. Returning to his seat, he turned to Telford.

"Steven, sum it up. Where are we?"

"First, there's what we know for certain," Telford began. "Neuhaus was getting money from the Russians to run against Heinemann. Neuhaus is elected. A major plank in his campaign is to get American troops out of Germany. Letnikov overthrows Gorbachev. Then he comes out for a treaty with the Germans. The Letnikov treaty also calls for our troops to get out of Germany.

"Now for those things that are less certain. We have a single uncorroborated report from a high-level source with excellent access. He tells us that Letnikov was in some sort of conspiratorial relationship with Neuhaus before he became chancellor. Our source points to two manifestations of that relationship: the secret communications link and Ostgruppe Rabe—Raven—both of which he says were kept secret from Gorbachev.

"Then NSA comes up with an intercept about a German train." Telford motioned toward Kupperman. "This caused us to check Brest Litovsk photography. NPIC identified a likely shipment as part of Raven. And from what we've heard today, NSA has indications that a unit similar to Raven is active inside the USSR."

Telford searched the president's face and found no sign of dissent or question. "That's it, Mr. President."

Bush pursed his lips thoughtfully, then asked Telford, "Where now?"

"We have to find out about Raven and its companion. All we know is that it's some sort of military unit. The specific kind of unit could tell us a lot about this relationship between Neuhaus and Letnikov."

"I see," Bush nodded. "How do you propose to go about it?"

Telford didn't hesitate. "We'll work our German source, Mr. President. But you know how that is, it could be some time—or never—before he gains access to what we need. Overhead photography could also do the trick. But we have no idea as to where Raven is in Germany.

"So if we're going to identify Raven, our best bet is to identify its twin—we know where that is—Plesetsk. And that leaves us no choice but an overflight."

Sam Rubel watched the president and his national security adviser. Bush was calm and thoughtful while Scott's eyes widened.

"Why an overflight?" Scott asked. "Why can't the KH-12 do the job?"

Telford motioned to Rubel. "Stan?"

From his folder Stan Bleifeld produced a clear acetate overlay that he fitted to the map board. A series of overlapping spiraling traces made a belt around the earth.

"These are paths a satellite makes over the earth," Stan motioned to the map. "That is, a satellite that flies over the north and south poles. What we call a ninety-degree orbit." He removed the overlay and replaced it with another. The traces were similar, except that they did not reach as far north or south. "This is the diagram of the KH-12. It flies an orbit of fifty-five degrees inclination."

"Why doesn't it fly the ninety-degree orbit?" asked Scott.

"Because we have to launch all our KH-12s from Cape Canaveral, and you can't go into polar orbit from the cape. The best we can get from there is the fifty-five-degree orbit."

Scott peered at the map. "So this white space in the USSR . . ."

". . . is everything the KH-12 can't see," finished Bleifeld.

Fully a third of the Soviet Union was denied to the KH-12's probing lens.

"And that includes Plesetsk," murmured Scott.

"A few points about Plesetsk and Kazan, Mr. President," Sam Rubel offered. "Plesetsk is a large Soviet military restricted zone. Although it's cold as hell, the Sovs have expanded their operations there because it's almost impossible for us to photograph."

Bush frowned in concentration. "I remember that about Plesetsk. And Kazan?"

"You have to go back pretty far for Kazan, but there's an interesting parallel. It was at Kazan that Stalin helped Hitler avoid the Versailles Treaty rearmament ban."

Bush's frown deepened.

"Kazan," Telford explained, "was a secret training area for the German army."

Sam Rubel adroitly wheeled his car through the evening traffic, crossing the Teddy Roosevelt Bridge, then turning north on the parkway toward the Agency. Oncoming headlights briefly illumi-

nated the car's interior, then left darkness broken
only by the green glow of the dashboard.

"The president," Sam asked. "What did he say
about notifying Congress?"

Steven Telford recalled the careful conversation with Bush. The president had stayed for a moment at Telford's request after the others had left
the Situation Room. "Full notification. We brief both
the Senate and House committees. But only on the
mission itself. We don't divulge anything about
Raven—no specifics. Not yet. We justify the mission
on the grounds that we suspect something's going on
in the area we can't cover with the KH-12."

The glare of a passing car made Telford's face a
mask of dark, sunken eyes. "Another thing, Sam.
The president wants me to notify Cantabile in person."

Rubel gave a bitter laugh. "I don't envy you."

"I don't know," Telford mused. "It just might be
very interesting."

Dark clouds scudded over a dismal landscape of
ragged dunes—huge mounds of damp paper, scrap
metal, rotted food, and discarded clothing. Two men
stood shoulder to shoulder, silent, heads bowed.

"And this is where he found it?" asked the one
in the black overcoat.

The uniformed policeman nodded, looking
from the body partially covered with garbage, to the
dump attendant slouched a few paces away, a thin,
runny-nosed old man dressed in tattered green coveralls and patched knee-high rubber boots.

Lothar Kelch, inspector third rank, Criminal
Police Department of the Ministry of Interior, hud-

dled deeper into his wool coat. At least the cold served a purpose. Had it been warmer, the smell would have been much worse. The garbage alone would have been bad enough. He looked at the ravaged body, then a swift, furtive movement caught his eye.

"Rats," grunted the policeman. "The place is crawling with them."

At the same time Kelch caught the sweet stench of decomposing flesh. He fought a spasm of nausea, clenching his fists inside his pockets and breathing deeply. "Preliminary search?"

The policeman held a plastic bag in his gloved hand. "A wallet. Identity card. Several keys. Eighty marks and some change."

Kelch circled the corpse, taking care to watch his footing in the refuse. "Use another bag," he ordered the policeman. He motioned to the ravaged corpse. "Get a sample of the stuff around him. Forget the food. Papers, trash—that sort of thing."

The policeman hesitated, unfolded another bag, then beckoned to the dump keeper, who fearfully hobbled forward. The policeman gave him the bag, then directed the collection, cursing the old man for his slowness.

Kelch walked away to get a different perspective. Still looking at the corpse, he shouted to the policeman. "A name? There is a name to"—he pointed to the ground—"to this?"

The policeman fumbled in his bag and came up with the identity card. "Yes," he answered against the wind. "Weihs. Manfred Weihs."

Sixteen

Ruth Donohue buzzed in to Telford. "Senator McCary called," she announced.

Telford reached for his phone.

"He's already on his way out," Donohue told him. "He was quite insistent. Said he had to see you."

Ten minutes later Frank McCary rushed into Telford's office.

McCary, obviously anxious, declined Telford's offer of coffee with a shake of his head. "We've got to talk." He made it almost a command.

The two men moved to the sofa. McCary put a worn leather briefcase on the coffee table before them, then turned to face Telford. "First, a short story." He glanced at his watch. "My staffer on the Intelligence Committee's a bright guy. Name's Gibson, Kyle Gibson.

"Last week Kyle tells me that he had to escort a Russian to see Joe Cantabile. Krotov—a journalist." McCary gave journalist a sarcastic inflection and continued. "While they're waiting for Cantabile, Kyle sees the Russian pull out an envelope. No address on the outside. Heavy yellowish paper. Had a red seal on the back."

McCary leaned toward Telford, checking his watch as he did so. He began to talk faster. "Russian's in there five, maybe ten minutes. When the Russian comes out, Kyle walks him down to the horseshoe drive at the Hart Building."

Telford shrugged. "We know Krotov. He's not a journalist, but there's nothing we can do about him going to the Hill. . . ."

"Damnit, Steven, that's not it. Let me finish." McCary interrupted, now even more impatient.

"That afternoon Kyle sees Cantabile go into the Intelligence Committee members' reading room. It's a vaulted area, off-limits to staff. It's set aside for the members to lock away their private notes, memos, that kind of thing." McCary waved a hand in explanation. "Anyway, Cantabile is carrying the same envelope. Now, though, it has a blue seal on the back. Joe is in the reading room for no more than a minute or two. Then he comes out. Without the envelope."

McCary again looked at his watch. His breath was now coming noticeably faster. "This morning, Steven, I was in the reading room. Joe was there, too. He got a call from his office. The majority leader wanted Joe to go down to the White House with him. That caught Joe off guard. He left his personal safe open. A lot of us do that all the time—the reading room itself's secure. The only reason we have individual safes is to keep the other members from snooping."

Telford winced. He sensed what was coming.

McCary, catching the expression on Telford's face, dropped his eyes, pretending a shame he didn't feel. "And so I snooped. The letter was there. Right on top."

Telford nodded. It had been a good tale. It was

useful to know that some kind of communication had passed between Krotov and Cantabile.

Telford, believing that was the end of it, was thinking ahead to a contentious budget meeting later that day when McCary unzipped the briefcase and pulled out a large brown manila folder. Holding it upside down, he gave a shake, and a smaller envelope slid onto the coffee table. It was a creamy parchment, fastened by blue wax seal.

For the third time McCary looked at his watch. "They'll be at the White House for another two hours. I gotta get it back before then."

Telford stared at the envelope for long seconds, seconds when neither man seemed to breathe. He looked up to find McCary watching him expectantly. Telford went to his desk, picked up a telephone, and dialed a number. After a cryptic conversation he hung up.

"We can handle it. Do you want to wait here?"

McCary shook his head. "I'm in this far, I might as well see how you guys go about it."

Sesu Nagata knew paper. The men of his father's family, both the branches in America as well as those in Japan, were masters of origami, the folding of paper. The men of Nagata were of a long line of samurai. To these warriors, origami was not an idle pastime of women and children. Rather, it was an ultimate Zen discipline of the self, and the mastery of paper applied as much to the warrior as to the artist. When Sesu was three, his father introduced him to the art, teaching his little fingers to do the simple folds, then the more complex ones, always beginning with immaculately clean hands, sitting on a mat before an *ozen*, the low Japanese table.

Nagata met Telford and McCary in the anteroom to his workshop. After a brief introduction Telford passed over the large manila envelope. Nagata took the envelope, then, giving an almost imperceptible bow, turned and went into his workshop, closing the door behind him.

"Hell," McCary complained, "I wanted to watch."

"He works alone." Telford took McCary's arm. "This way."

Another door opened onto a short stairway, which led to a small soundproof gallery where one could peer over Nagata's shoulder through one-way glass panels. Above the glass were television monitors that could give close-ups of Nagata's hands.

The workroom walls and ceiling were painted a flat black. Precisely in the center of the room was the *ozen*, a perfect white square perhaps three feet on a side. Around the table were straw mats. The simple furnishings created a deceptively sparse impression of the room. Overhead, hidden on electrically operated booms in the ceiling, were ultraviolet, infrared, white, and various-colored lights, as well as high-resolution Polaroid and still-frame cameras.

Nagata carefully laid out his equipment on two longer, darker tables that angled like wings from the right and left sides of the *ozen*.

"It's in the order he'll use it," Telford explained.

Nagata made minute rearrangements; then, satisfied, he slid the Cantabile envelope out of the manila folder and onto his white worktable. Never moving his eyes from the envelope, Nagata raised a waiting hand. There was a distant machine-whir and a light boom lowered squarely into Nagata's hand, whereupon he directed an intense baby spotlight down onto the work surface.

The Cantabile envelope seemed to glow. Nagata turned it this way, then that, then shook it to see if the contents had been glued in place, a common tradecraft trap. Repeating the examination under ultraviolet light, he then laid the envelope back on the table, seal up.

Another whir, and another boom descended, this one carrying a Leica IIIC camera. Making the necessary adjustments, Nagata squeezed the cable release three times. He unloaded the Leica and put the film canister in a vacuum carrier tube to be whisked to the Agency darkrooms for priority processing. For insurance he took three more pictures with the Polaroid.

Nagata carefully nudged the letter back into the center of the table with wooden tongs and sat back on his ankles studying it.

"For God's sake, Steven. We aren't gonna have time," McCary whispered in anguish. "That thing's not going to open itself through meditation."

Telford, too, shared McCary's impatience but said nothing, putting a hand over and squeezing McCary's forearm.

Nagata was not meditating. He was contemplating the envelope. Paper, ink, glue, and wax. The elements of the fortress before him. He would not assault it, battering down its defenses by brute force. Rather, he would enter like the fog, seeking the smallest openings, flowing through them. Accomplishing all through being nothing.

He decanted eight drops of mineral oil into a

tiny petri dish and with a fine sable brush applied a thin coat over the face of the seal, taking care that none got on the paper. Turning to the long equipment table, he stirred two grams of Albastone powder into distilled water with a tongue depressor. His voice came over the speaker in the gallery, startling McCary. "I am looking for a consistency that will fill the features of the seal but will stay within the waxed boundary." McCary realized that Nagata was talking into a recorder for files, much as a pathologist described an autopsy.

Nagata used another tongue depressor to put the Albastone mix into the depression of Cantabile's seal, building a plaster mold. Satisfied with his work, he brought down a small infrared lamp and turned it onto the damp plaster for less than a minute.

Switching the lamp off, he probed the now-hard plaster. Before removing the mold from the seal, Nagata made two tiny pencil marks on the mold opposite the lines made by the flaps of the envelope in order to orient the seal when he replaced it. Down came the Polaroid for another series of pictures. The mold lifted cleanly off the seal. Nagata placed the mold face down in the petri dish containing the mineral oil.

From the left equipment table, he unrolled a length of aluminum foil, which he wrapped around the envelope, leaving only the blue wax seal exposed.

"What's that for?" McCary asked, whispering as if to avoid disturbing Nagata.

"To keep from scorching the paper," Telford answered. "Watch."

The infrared lamp was down again, Nagata focusing its heat on the seal. When the wax softened, he pushed it up from the edges, using the flat end of a manicurist's orange stick. Soon the wax formed a ball that Nagata picked up and set aside. He stripped the aluminum foil from the envelope.

His disembodied voice came over the speaker. "I am going to use a dry opening. The envelope is made of a hard paper—of a kind that glue does not penetrate." Thus Nagata had discarded the options of either using a chemical or steam process. The dry opening is the simplest but requires an exquisite sense of touch and manual dexterity.

Nagata carved his dry opening tools from a cache of ivory piano keys he'd accumulated on forays to junkyards and antique stores. Ivory was better than wood because it could be made extremely smooth and fashioned into more intricate shapes. This particular tool's rectangular handle showed its musical origins, but the other end of the key curved into a flat, pointed hook.

Left hand holding the envelope firmly against the tabletop, Nagata inserted the point under the flap at the opening at the end of the envelope. He then gently rocked the tool while sawing it in a back-and-forth motion. Even on the television monitors, his hand movements were barely perceptible. The object was to work the ivory sliver to part the glue seam without disturbing the paper of either the flap or the body of the envelope.

Nagata bent forward over the envelope, head cocked to one side, straining to hear the slightest sound of a fiber parting. Finally, ten minutes later, he sat upright on his crossed ankles, straightening his back. Resting a moment, he pressed the envelope to the table, reached in with a pair of flat-faced wood tongs, and carefully slid out the letter. Down came the Leica and the Polaroid.

The letter's contents recorded, Nagata carefully but swiftly retraced his steps. He examined the dry mucilage. One spot was thin. On it he brushed a minute amount of 101-X, a neutral glue. Over the original glue Nagata rolled a dampened cotton swab. Then he carefully folded the flap closed, insuring he matched the faint line caused by the first sealing.

Nagata next studied the Polaroids he'd taken of the original seal, noting its general shape and placement over the envelope flap. He fashioned another aluminum foil mask for the envelope. Making a small sucking sound over his teeth, he took the plaster mold out of the petri dish and wiped off the excess mineral oil. He placed the ball of blue wax on the envelope back, consulted the Polaroid photo once more, then played the infrared lamp until the wax was well softened. Lining up his penciled guide marks on the mold, he pressed it into the warm wax.

Two minutes later, the wax now cool, Nagata removed the mold. Under a bright halogen light, he inspected the seal to make certain no bits of plaster remained. Satisfied with his work, he looked up toward the gallery with the modestly satisfied look of the warrior who'd passed through the defenses of the enemy with the invisibility of a ghost.

"Son of a bitch," muttered McCary in admiration. "Guy coulda been one helluva brain surgeon." He watched as the small Japanese spray-misted a white blotter, then laid it on the envelope. "What's he doing now?" he asked, a note of alarm at the thought of yet more work to be done just when he'd thought the whole thing was over. The digital clock overhead showed McCary had less than thirty minutes left.

There was a hissing, a soft pop of air, and a sound of metal striking padded metal as the vacuum system disgorged a message tube.

Telford twisted open the tube and removed a single sheet of paper. He looked at the anxious McCary. "Nagata's going to run a warm iron over the envelope," Telford explained. "To work out any small wrinkles around the seal. Be finished in less than a minute. You'll have a plain car escort back to the Hill." He waved the paper at McCary with an ironic smile. "You might be interested in the Honorable Joseph Cantabile's correspondence."

McCary, still apprehensive, grabbed roughly at the paper. As he read it, disbelief crossed his face, crowding aside his concern about the time. McCary whispered bits of the letter. ". . . greet you in the name of peace and justice . . . journalist friend Vladimir Krotov . . ."

McCary, scowling, threw the paper onto the desk as if he'd found filth on his hands. "Looks like Joe's setting himself up to go into business. Gonna be his own secretary of state. And the good journalist Krotov is going to be his messenger." He pointed to the paper. "No wonder Joe kept that. Not every good American politician gets a personal invitation to communicate directly with Yegor Letnikov."

In the car Kathleen Orsini leaned across and gave Telford a brief, brushing kiss. After she pulled away, they hesitated, looking at each other in smiling silence, then came together again, this time with passion. They abruptly broke when someone in a car behind tapped their horn.

"Your security?" She laughed breathlessly, sliding to her side of the car.

"No," Telford motioned to the exit of the State Department garage. "They're out there."

"This is a treat, the director of Central Intelligence picking me up, and driving his own car, yet."

"I thought women were impressed by cars with drivers."

"Depends on the driver." She laughed again. "Now, where's dinner?"

"My secret."

Fifteen minutes later they turned down a winding drive to an isolated cluster of town homes in a quiet North Arlington neighborhood. Kathleen saw the security car pull into a garage in the adjoining house.

At the door Telford worked the security-system buttons. "Dinner at home," Telford announced, holding the door open for her.

There was a sound, and a large cat bounded into the foyer. "My roommate. Kathleen Orsini, meet Bear."

Telford led her into a large kitchen. On either side of a large fireplace, French doors opened onto a deck overlooking a park. The wall behind the large Vulcan range was exposed brick, and the remaining two walls were floor-to-ceiling bookcases. Two well-used easy chairs faced a small sofa; end tables were a friendly litter of books and periodicals. Bear walked to a corner near one of the French doors, sat down, and fixed Telford with a waiting stare.

Telford fed the cat, then poured two beers. He and Kathleen chattered about the latest Washington scandal while he dived into the refrigerator, waving aside her offer to help. He'd had a catering service bring over a rack of lamb along with the accompanying small vegetables. He checked the oven temperature, slid in the roasting pan, then set a timer. Finishing making the salad, he saw Kathleen was browsing along the bookcases. Coming up behind her, he kissed her gently on the neck.

"I've missed you," he said hoarsely. "I worry about you when you're away. Especially in Germany."

She turned and was in his arms. They kissed, tenderly at first, then with growing desire. She dropped the book she'd been reading, wrapping both arms around his neck. He ran his hands down from her waist over her buttocks, kneading them hungrily.

"Not here," she whispered.

They clung to each other, somehow managing the stairs, leaving a trail of tangled clothes to his bed. He sat on the edge of the bed and finished undressing her. Reaching around, he undid her bra. Her breasts before him, he circled the hardening nipples with his tongue, then drew one, then the other, into his mouth while his hands caressed and explored her buttocks and thighs.

Moaning, she bent forward, fastening her teeth on the joining of his neck and shoulder, snuggling a hand under his armpit. Telford ran his hand up her thigh, sending a finger to rim her vagina.

She gave an explosive gasp, pulling away to stand upright before him. "There. Keep rubbing. There."

Transfixed, she began to quiver, and he again took a nipple into his mouth, this time roughly, giving hard, sucking nips as she bucked into a wild orgasm, his fingers busy all the while, circling, nudging, rubbing.

She moved onto the bed; then, stroking his erection, she threw a leg over, mounting him, rocking slowly at first, then faster as they both began working together. She smiled crazily in triumph as she felt him begin his powerful thrusts, but abruptly she lost focus as she came again.

They lay exhausted in each others arms, legs entwined, his mouth near her ear. "I smell something."

"Mmmmmh," she responded dreamily, "we just made . . ."

"No, it's not that. . . ."

"Oh my God! It's the lamb!" she finished, sitting bolt upright. Their naked dash to the kitchen failed to rescue the lamb.

Later, in a pair of worn jeans and plaid wool shirt, Telford consigned the charred remains to the garbage can out in the garage. Dinner that night was phone-in pizza eaten on the floor in front of the fire and washed down with a rough Chianti.

With a second glass of wine in hand, Telford stared into the fire as if hypnotized by the guttering flames.

Kathleen, nearly lost in one of his old flannel robes, snuggled closer and reached up to tweak his earlobe. "You're a thousand miles away."

Unsmiling, Telford looked at her for long seconds. Having made a decision, he bent, kissed the tip of her nose, and began telling her of McCary's visit and the Letnikov letter.

Long before he'd finished, she had pulled away

from him and sat, arms hugging her knees, concentrating on his story.

". . . and tomorrow I've got to see him—Cantabile. We've got to run an operation, and I've got to tell him about it."

"Does the president know about the letter from Letnikov?"

Telford put his hand on the back of her neck. "No, not yet. When you get down to it, that's all it is —a letter from Letnikov to a United States senator. Cantabile hasn't answered it. Even if he has, who's to say he's done anything wrong?"

"All the same," Kathleen shook her head, "I'd be careful about what you tell him."

Telford nodded in agreement. Bear, curled up on the hearth in front of them, stretched out, gave a huge yawn, then rolled over and continued his nap.

"I can't understand him—Cantabile," Telford mused. "Here we have in front of us a prime example of the unpredictability of Moscow. Gorby's in, and everything's sweetness and light. Then, zap!" Telford snapped his fingers. "He's out. Just like that. And now we have Letnikov and Neuhaus, who seem to be heading back into the heart of darkness. Yet Cantabile seems blind to it all."

Looking into the fire, Kathleen absentmindedly twisted a strand of hair through her fingers. "We all build facades. Cantabile's got his. He doesn't want to recognize how Letnikov's changed things, because if he did, it'd destroy the world that he's comfortable with—the world he thinks he understands.

"Think of everything we've ignored because the answers could bring chaos. Who's really satisfied about the Kennedys? Why did your agency's investigation of King's assassination end so abruptly? What about the attempt on the pope? Or the death of Zia in Pakistan?

"We don't follow up because we're afraid of what we might find. We're like the wife who ignores the lipstick on her husband's shirts because she knows if she says something about it, she'll have to face much nastier things."

"So we stick our heads in the sand," Telford said. "But if enough people work at the illusion, really work at it, can't it hold together?"

"That's what I thought in the sixties," Kathleen replied. "But mirrors and blue smoke don't last forever. All our pretense couldn't make it different, make it go away. Vietnam was a grand illusion. The hawks believed helicopters and American troops could win the war, and the doves believed the Vietcong were agrarian reformers. None of it ever was or ever could be."

"So there're things people don't want to know about Letnikov and Neuhaus. Where does that leave me?"

She gave him a small, tight smile. "What is it that's carved in the lobby at Langley? 'Ye shall know the truth, and the truth shall make you free'?"

Seventeen

Guenther Ferner, administrative director of the BND, regarded Lothar Kelch with pig-eyed suspicion.

"You say there is a problem with this case?" With a pencil Ferner poked warily at the Weihs folder on his desk, as if by touching it he might soil his hands or cause an explosion.

Kelch wearily shifted from one foot to the other. This fat prick Ferner would never offer him a seat. Ferner was a hack who got along by getting along. To Ferner getting embroiled in interministry disputes was a calamity of the first order.

"Yes, there is a problem," Lothar sighed. "As I explained in my memorandum, the dead man, Manfred Weihs, was one of yours—a member of the BND. In my investigation of the circumstances surrounding Weihs's death, I am encountering resistance from your ministry."

Ferner's eyes widened. "Resistance? How?"

"Access to certain records."

Ferner's frown deepened. He dropped his hands into his lap to put more distance between himself and the threatening file. "We cannot open our records to everyone, Inspector. Even to the police. I am certain you understand the needs of security. . . ."

"I understand fully," Kelch interrupted, "but we have a responsibility to investigate criminal matters, especially murder."

Ferner's round face took on a crafty smile. "But Inspector, no criminality has yet been proved."

"A young man is found in a garbage dump, and what remains of his head appears to have been crushed. I should presume . . ."

Ferner's little eyes gleamed. He sat back in his chair, making a tent of his fingers, pronouncing pompously, "Just so, Inspector. Presume. You are presuming. If the Ministry of Interior wishes access to the most sensitive files of the BND, there must be the proper papers."

It was the end of yet another twelve-hour day, and Kelch's feet hurt badly. Dinner tonight would be greasy sausages and cabbage. The bed would be lumpy, and he would not sleep because of the non-stop fighting of the couple next door. Why should he leave this fat bastard in peace?

"Yes, Herr Generalmajor. At all costs the proper papers." He pulled his briefcase into his lap and thrust his hand inside. "I brought the authorizations from our ministry. If you still have objections, I have prepared a request denial for your signature."

"Signature?" Ferner looked at the file, eyes wide, his earlier fears now confirmed.

"Yes," Kelch answered, beginning to enjoy himself. "In the event that you believe the BND should continue to deny me the information I require, you can sign this denial. I shall convey it to my superiors."

Kelch savored Ferner's discomfort. He, Lothar

Kelch, would not be the only one to miss sleep tonight.

"Section C of the national criminal code requires a formal denial of access to evidence in cases such as this." He leaned forward and laid out the papers.

Ferner sat frozen, staring at the legal-size documents. There might later be recriminations. Accusations. And there would be his signature! He thought of demotion. Of the loss of privileges—the shopping discounts, the special medical care, the private school for his children.

"Can't you . . ." He looked pleadingly at Kelch.

Kelch shook his head in mock humility. "I'm sorry, Herr Generalmajor. If you cannot assist us because of security, the papers must be signed." He pointed to the open folder, drawing Ferner's attention to it again. "They must be signed either by you or by your superior. The law is quite clear."

Ferner felt faint. He had been making discreet inquiries about leaving this grim place behind. The Ministry for Foreign Trade offered an alluring prospect. A good Neuhaus loyalist might inveigle something over there as long as he didn't get caught in a nasty squabble with someone like this Kelch. Or get in trouble with his superiors here. To take these papers in to have his boss sign them would be as bad as signing them himself. It would be recognized as a responsibility-dodging maneuver on his part.

"Ah, yes." He put on a smile for Kelch. "I understand, Inspector. There is no need for these papers. I will make certain you have the information you need."

Guenther Ferner pushed the file away and

breathed a sigh of relief. The problem was solved: this Kelch could grub around all he wanted on this sordid murder case, and Ferner's boss, Rudolf Wolf, would not have to be bothered about such an inconsequential matter.

Eighteen

The High Desert's dry lake bed was a ghostly white under unblinking stars and a quarter moon. Stark against the whiteness, a dark airplane's cooling engines made hollow popping sounds of shrinking metal. Noiselessly a plume of alkali dust swirled toward the plane.

A solitary figure waited for the jeep. The open vehicle had not fully stopped when he swung into the front passenger seat.

"Where the hell is this, Telford?"

Telford slipped the jeep into gear, tires making a crisp whisper. Leaving the headlights off, he set a course toward a faint green light in a black huddle of buildings a mile distant.

"They didn't tell you?"

"Tell me? Christ! I got on the plane at Andrews four hours ago and got off here—wherever that is—and nobody said jack-shit to me. Hell, I don't even know what direction we flew. The damn thing had the windows covered over. Like flying inside a tin can."

Telford laughed. Through the complaints he knew Frank McCary was enjoying himself. He'd called McCary, asked him to spare a day. It's something you have to see, he'd told McCary, refusing to give any details over the phone.

"It's Edwards Air Force Base."

"The test place?"

Telford nodded. Edwards—where men tested themselves and machines; flight records and smudges on the desert floor were testaments to their courage and, some might say, craziness. Sixty miles northeast of Los Angeles, the isolated Mojave base was ideal for secret flight tests because they could be hidden among the constant hubbub of other experimental activity.

In seconds Telford summarized the Brandt report, the finding of Raven, and Bush's approval of an overflight. "The president insisted I tell Cantabile personally."

"Did you tell him about that report? About the German unit, Raven?"

"No. Just that we had to see what was going on in northern Russia, where the satellites couldn't cover."

"It's going to be a four-wall day when he finds out about you folks flyin' me out here." McCary waved at the desert.

"Cantabile told me he was scheduled to speak in New York tonight, so there wasn't any sense inviting him."

"No matter. He's still gonna be pissed."

They reached a darkened guard shack. Telford flicked the headlights on, then off. A figure came from the shack and took Telford's coded identification card.

McCary gave up waiting for an explanation. "Steven, none of this tells me just what the hell you and I are doing here."

"I came because I didn't want to sit this out in Washington."

"This? This what?"

"The overflight," Telford explained. "The mission's on. It's tonight." Telford looked at his watch. "In about an hour and a half. And that's why you're here. If Cantabile couldn't come, I wanted to have one member of the committee along."

The guard returned with Telford's ID card. To their front the chain-link gate silently rolled open. Telford gunned the jeep forward. Two hundred yards later they pulled into a parking place by the darkened hangar.

The two men got out and, stiff legged from the cold, walked to a small door in the side of the huge building. Telford pressed his card against a scanner, then held the door open for McCary.

Stepping out of the darkness, McCary was assaulted by the silver white glare. His mouth opened a half second after his eyes.

"Jesus, Joseph, and Mary!" He stood stupefied, staring in disbelief.

Telford felt his heart pound. He remembered a beginning amid overflowing ashtrays and Styrofoam cups half-filled with cold, acid-laced coffee. Seven years ago the Air Force came to him at Astronetics with a "do it yesterday" priority to replace America's best spy plane, the SR-71 Blackbird.

The Blackbird had been built in the early sixties and could photograph one hundred thousand square miles in less than an hour. Though the manta-shaped Blackbird's speed (over twenty-two hundred miles per hour) and altitude (above eighty-five thousand feet) put it beyond reach of any other airplane in the world, it had become increasingly vulnerable to sophisticated missile interceptors. The Air Force still needed a manned aircraft to complement satellites, and Telford beat out Lockheed's fabled Skunk Works for the contract.

Telford and others had long believed that there were other ways to fly into space than on top of the costly and fragile vertical launch rockets used since Yuri Gagarin and John Glenn. Revolutionary materials and advanced propulsion techniques, they reasoned, made it possible to build an airplane that could take off from a runway and fly straight into earth orbit without boosters or staged rocket systems.

The problem, of course, had been money. But Air-Force directors of covert programs could be generous, and that generosity led Telford to sketch a dartlike plane on a pad of quadrille paper during an all-night session with his top engineers.

Later, when he'd first seen the fuselage taking shape in the supporting tooling at Palmdale, he nearly wept in the pride of his creation. Carbon-composite skin, fiber-optic controls, and advanced sensors made a living thing as much as did flesh and blood.

"It's called *Ariel*," he whispered.

The eye could no more focus on *Ariel* than it could fasten on the vastness of outer space. Its black matte finish and flowing lines drew all light into its depths, imprisoning everything, reflecting nothing. Though the size of a small airliner, the first impression of *Ariel* was of a slender needle, straining forward on its tricycle landing gear. The small delta wing at the end of the long fuselage struck one as a designer's afterthought, as did the swelling of the aft belly that wrapped around its engine.

"God, it's big."

"It's the fuel," Telford explained. "Liquid hydrogen. We need a lot of it. The engine's the real secret. Rocketdyne design. Cross between rockets and jets. Not as powerful as a full-fledged rocket engine, but then, we don't need to carry liquid oxygen, either."

They walked to the front of the big plane and stopped by the nose gear. Telford pointed up. "Quartz ports for the cameras. In back of them are the skin antennae for the SAR."

"SAR?" McCary gave a wry, self-mocking smile.

"Synthetic aperture radar. Very high resolution. Can give us detailed pictures in the dark and through clouds or smoke."

Stepping out from under the plane, McCary and Telford stopped and looked down the length of the fuselage toward the tail.

"Small wings."

"Big enough. Above Mach one the fuselage generates more lift than the wings."

McCary continued to stare at the plane in awe. "I knew we were building something, but I didn't know we'd put it into orbit."

"We've taken it up when the Soviets have been distracted elsewhere—tracking launches of the Shuttle, that kind of thing. But this is the first operational mission."

McCary turned to him, disbelief on his face. "Don't you need more test flights. . . ."

"We can test forever. But we've done the testing we absolutely need to do for this—one pass over the Soviet Union, then down again."

"But over the Soviet Union? Won't they interpret that as a hostile act? There'll be all kinds of people saying we should have notified Moscow."

"Why should we? *Ariel*'s a spacecraft, the same as the Shuttle."

McCary shook his head. "But, Steven, the Shuttle flights are public knowledge. This . . ."

"*Ariel*'s a spacecraft, Frank," Telford repeated, "and we aren't going to start asking Moscow for permission to fly out there. Come on." Telford unzipped his battered leather jacket and motioned toward a small door. "Suit-up room for the crew."

The room glowed with a blue white light. Frank McCary would remember being struck by the total lack of shadows or glare. In the center of the room, three technicians in white coveralls huddled around a large object. Stepping closer, McCary saw a figure in a space suit, fishbowl helmet and all, in a tilted support frame that let the person inside the suit rest while giving the techs the access they needed to the life-support system.

"One?" McCary's face registered his surprise.

The technicians ignored the two visitors and continued with their tests, one noting instructions from a list displayed on a computer screen, the other two checking and double-checking each connection on the suit.

"Just one? For that big plane?"

Telford nodded, watching the technicians. "Just one. As I said, most of the plane is fuel. You add people, and the weight requirements go up exponentially. And *Ariel*'s not designed for sustained operations in space. It's a recce bird—up and over.

High and fast. One man can handle the flying. The sensors take care of themselves."

The senior technician signaled his satisfaction. The two others stood on the dais with the space-suited figure and lifted off the helmet, carefully putting it into a foam-lined carrying box.

The figure raised a hand from the extended armrest. "I'd join you, gentlemen, but as you can see, I'm somewhat indisposed. Come on up."

Telford introduced Frank McCary to Ira Crawford. McCary stepped closer to Crawford.

"I was tellin' Steven here"—McCary jerked a thumb to Telford—"that that airplane seems to be a big piece of work for one man."

Crawford gave a lazy, right-stuff grin. "Depends on who the man is, Senator. It might be too much for a bomber puke, but not for a fighter pilot."

"I didn't know you were Air Force, I thought you . . ."

"Were Agency?" Crawford finished. "Neither." He rolled his eyes to Telford. "This guy lured me out of the Air Force."

"Good test pilots are hard to find," Telford joined in. "Ira's still at Astronetics."

McCary judged Crawford's age to be near his own. "You flew in Nam?"

Crawford's eyes shifted to middistance, suddenly seeing the towering thunderheads over the Red River Delta.

"Yeah." It came softly.

"When?"

"Seventy to seventy-three."

"Long tour for a pilot."

"Didn't have any choice. I was a guest at the Hanoi Hilton."

Except for the techs stowing away their test equipment, the small room was dead still.

Crawford cocked his head, then asked for the countersign of their generation. "You there, Senator?"

McCary drew himself up, giving a small smile. "Yeah. Only twelve months, though—different kind of cage."

"Army?"

"Yeah. The First Horse."

"Officer?"

"No. Grunt, line infantry. First of the Seventh Cavalry."

Telford was struck with the bond that so quickly locked the two men together. He'd seen it before among those who had known war twenty years ago in Southeast Asia. Whatever they thought of the war itself and the politicians who started it, they carried with them the pride that they'd been there—that they'd endured. It was a pride that would forever mark them from those who had not gone.

"My brother was Air Force," McCary offered quietly.

"Pilot?"

"Yeah. One-oh-fives out of Udorn."

Crawford looked at McCary with sudden understanding. "He didn't make it, did he?"

McCary shook his head. He remembered the day they'd come to the farm, the two men in uniform with the sad, deferential voices that broke his father's heart. The next day Frank McCary had dropped out of college and enlisted in the Army.

"I don't know. His plane went down over Thud Ridge. They never found any bodies."

For the first time Telford saw the silver bracelet on McCary's right wrist.

McCary stood erect, shutting out Vietnam yet again. He pointed over his shoulder toward the hangar where *Ariel* waited. "Doesn't it bother you to take that thing into orbit by yourself?"

"We've been out there alone before." There it was again—the pilot's easy confidence that he could master any situation but the last one, and that one he would meet with studied nonchalance.

A chirping electronic tone, and the techs came back, one carrying a small cooling unit. "My keepers," Crawford grunted. "See you guys later."

Telford and McCary stepped away. Telford glanced at his watch. "We've got another flight to catch, Frank."

"Flight? What do you mean? Aren't we going to watch this thing?"

"We're going to watch it, but not from here." Telford zipped his jacket against the desert chill outside. "It's forty-five minutes to Sunnyvale, to the Satellite Control Facility. If we stayed here, all we could see is the takeoff and the landing. At Sunnyvale we'll see the whole show."

In the jeep heading toward the plane, McCary was silent, his thoughts on the meeting with Crawford. Telford filled him in on the pilot's background: Air Force Academy, test pilot training at Pax River and Edwards, Ph.D. in aeronautical engineering at Rensselaer.

"Must have been tough for him, getting into the Air Force Academy," McCary mused.

"You mean, because he's black?" asked Telford, suddenly aware and tense.

"Black?" McCary laughed. "What's that got to do with anything? No. His size. Big. He's gotta be near the max limits. That guy doesn't get into airplanes, he puts them on. Even something like *Ariel*."

Nineteen

A few minutes after Frank McCary took off from Andrews Air Force Base to meet Steven Telford, Joseph Cantabile was on a late-afternoon New York shuttle out of Washington National to LaGuardia. There a limousine belonging to Constance Higby's Foundation for International Relations met him.

As the featured dinner speaker, Cantabile delivered a stem-winder in which he painted the Soviet Union as sinking ever more deeply into an economic mire of its own making. While excoriating the Soviet bureaucracy for continued abuse of human rights, Cantabile described Yegor Letnikov as a daring visionary "who wishes to rid Europe of its nightmare." After an interminable after-dinner session over cognac with the foundation's advisory board, Cantabile followed Constance to her suite in the Plaza.

She was impatient to get the obligatory sex out of the way, but the liquor, the heavy meal, and the lateness of the hour worked against her. At last, however, Cantabile flopped over onto his back and lay beached, gulping air in rattling gasps. Coming back from the bathroom, she wrapped herself in a white silk robe and sat on Cantabile's side of the bed. He would soon drift off to sleep, but he liked to talk—

ramble—about the daily skirmishes on the Hill; battles, to hear him tell it, that he always won. As he began, she lit a cigarette and with her free hand massaged his temples.

"What?" She was stubbing out the cigarette and, caught by surprise, her voice cracked.

"Telford," repeated a groggy and spent Cantabile. "Smug bastard. Going to fly over Russia. . . ."

"Telford's going to Russia?"

Desperate now for sleep, Cantabile shook his head in the pillow. "No," he mumbled irritably. "Spy plane. F'r pichers."

"Pictures? Why?"

"Fugger woudn' tell me," came Cantabile's last slurred reply.

Constance Higby forced herself to wait ten minutes. Then, using the telephone in the bathroom, she called a number Vladimir had her memorize.

Twenty

At engine start Ira Crawford felt a faint growling rumble along his spine, buttocks, and thighs. *Ariel*'s engine was a tapered combustion chamber open at both ends, the smaller of which pointed to the front of the plane. Through this inlet air was mixed with hydrogen, and the mixture burned at nearly six thousand degrees Fahrenheit, producing a controlled and continuous explosion, which, venting out the rear, pushed *Ariel* forward.

Unlike conventional jet engines, *Ariel*'s combustion chamber could change shape. This enabled it to perform as a jet power plant at lower speeds, allowing *Ariel* to take off from a runway, thus making a potential spaceport of any airfield that could handle commercial airliners. *Ariel* and its successors would pave the way for man's future in space, freeing explorers from the costly and vulnerable vertical launch complexes at Kennedy and Vandenberg.

Ira Crawford eased the throttles forward. *Ariel*'s cockpit was configured like a fighter, with a control stick rather than the wheel and yoke of bombers and cargo aircraft. He began the takeoff roll. Runway 17 was over seven miles long, but he planned to take only about ten thousand feet. Even that wasn't needed, but Crawford wasn't a man to horse an airplane into the sky. At one hundred seventy miles per hour, Crawford eased back ever so slightly on the stick. *Ariel* reached for the black sky and the stars.

Three hundred miles away Telford and McCary sat hunched forward in the glassed-in command balcony of the Satellite Control Facility in Sunnyvale, just south of San Francisco.

The map before them flickered, and a stream of red dots marked a huge circle, one that swung north out of Edwards, crossed into Canada at the juncture of Washington State and Idaho, then turned east. Passing over western Canada, the dots marched back into the States by way of Thunder Bay and Lake Superior. The circle's eastward limit touched Chicago, then arched west again, over Arkansas, Texas, then New Mexico and Arizona. From Edwards the dots were connecting at a rapid rate, becoming a solid line of glowing blue.

"I thought we were going over Russia."

Telford settled back in his chair, eyes still on the large map. "We are. This is the run-up to make certain everything's working." In the upper right of the screen, a digital clock counted up from zero, registering the elapsed time of *Ariel*'s flight.

McCary made a rapid calculation on a pad of paper. "Christ! That's gotta be at least five thousand miles. . . ."

"Six," corrected Telford.

"How long's it gonna take him to fly it?"

"That's a continuous two-G turn he's making. He'll get to Mach fifteen in the vicinity of one hundred twenty thousand feet. If everything checks out, he'll take it up to Mach twenty-five, shut off his engine, and transfer into orbit. The whole thing'll take about forty minutes."

In awe McCary stared at the map, where the glowing blue line was a sharp incision into Oregon.

Telford nudged him. "Come on. Time for a cook's tour." He motioned to the map. "Nothing's going to be happening for a while."

Passing rapidly through Mach 1—the speed of sound—the *Ariel*'s engine began to change shape. Within the inferno of the combustion chamber, the cone-shaped hydrogen spray unit moved forward, choking the air inlet. This made the incoming air flow ever more rapidly as it entered the chamber, much as a thumb held over the end of a garden hose causes the water to spray faster.

Approaching Mach 12, Crawford danced his fingertips across buttons set into the joystick. Instantly, as if suspended in space before him, the heads-up display reported on q—the dynamic pressure created as *Ariel* fought the resistance of the earth's atmosphere. If q dropped below one thousand pounds per square foot, air-flow turbulence inside the engine would rob it of its efficiency. Above two thousand pounds per square foot, *Ariel*'s skin would heat to catastrophic temperatures.

He grunted to himself in satisfaction: q was just under sixteen hundred. By all rights heating should be within limits, too. Nonetheless, Crawford tapped a different combination on the joystick buttons. He scanned the multicolored outline of *Ariel* projected before him, paying attention first to the nose and wing leading edges.

The temperature was just above fifteen hundred degrees Kelvin—more than twenty-three hundred degrees Fahrenheit. Crawford knew *Ariel* as well as any of the engineers. He knew the exquisite designing that had gone into foiling soakback—the insidious infiltration of heat from the outer skin along structural members, and into the cockpit—heat that could turn his tiny compartment into a crematorium. He knew, too, that just inside the nose and wing leading edges ran arteries of liquid hydrogen that cooled *Ariel*'s carbon-carbon skin, using the additional heat energy thus gained to wrest even more thrust from the fiery engine.

He knew all this. But it was a daylight knowledge, a knowledge of engineers; it did not ward off the nights of fear, of waking drenched from a primal nightmare of hell.

Passing over Cape Girardeau, Missouri, Crawford again went through the displays. It was as if *Ariel* was as eager as he for the flight—there were none of the eccentricities he'd come to expect from the temperamental thoroughbred. The small frown muscles around his mouth relaxed, and he found himself humming a bar of James Taylor's "Fire and Rain." This ought to be a piece of cake.

Just outside Moscow, Colonel General Pyotr Gladkov fought off the temptation to demand another update. He had to have green lights beside the *antisputnik* segment of the status board, and he had to have them soon.

Gladkov glanced at the recalcitrant status lights, then gave in to his temptation. He barked for his aide to get the antisatellite force commanders onto PVO's guarded command net for a conference call.

The aide, one Lieutenant Redliks, a Latvian, knew the old man was getting into an ass-scorching mood, and so he got the hell out of the immediate area to make things happen. Which is why he tore into the communications center to get the old man's three subordinates on the line as soon as possible.

Around headquarters the lower ranks universally regarded Redliks as a bully. And so, when the lieutenant began shouting and storming, Signals Sergeant Kolkov did what most sergeants would do: he did *precisely* what the lieutenant ordered—and no more. Had Redliks been less disliked (and perhaps a true Russian), Kolkov might have asked the lieutenant if he wanted the connections on the land-lines—which were secure—or on the microwave channels—which were faster, but much less secure. But Redliks was a prick and a Latvian to boot, and so Kolkov gave him the microwave hookup.

Telford and McCary had just returned to the command balcony from their tour of the Satellite Control Facility when a red light flashed on the control panels in front of each of the six high-backed chairs. An Air Force colonel in a crisp blue uniform picked up a telephone, listened intently, then hung up.

"NSA reports increased comms activity between PVO command center at Sharapovo and entities at Tyuratam, Dushanbe, and Pushkino."

McCary caught Telford's concern. "What's PVO? What're those places? Shara . . ."

"PVO is an acronym for their air defense forces. The major control center is in Sharapovo—the one they've been expanding to handle their defense against ballistic missiles."

"You mean the Russian 'star wars'?"

Telford nodded. "Pushkino's the headquarters for the GALOSH and GAZELLE interceptor missiles and battle-management radars for the Moscow Defense."

"What about the other places?"

"Moscow claims Dushanbe's a scientific facility for satellite tracking. But it's got high-energy lasers, and the fact that it's tied in with PVO indicates it has some military purpose. And Tyuratam is . . ."

As if on cue the yellow light in the deep south of Russia changed to red.

The Air Force colonel swiveled his chair around to Telford and McCary. The artificial lighting bleached the colonel's face, turning his lips almost blue. "CIA reports evidence of pending launch at Tyuratam."

Telford looked at the clock and guessed the information had come from a KH-12. The big satellite's sun-synchronous orbit would place it over southern Russia about now. But by the time the KH-12 got over Tyuratam again to confirm its sighting, it would be almost an hour and a half later—*Ariel*'s mission would be over. One way or another.

On Tyuratam's launch pad 3-A, ground crews surrounded the gantry for the ten-story-tall SL-11 launch vehicle, tending to the readying of the liquid-fueled rocket. Two kilometers away, on 5-K, the frantic activity was repeated.

Pyotr Gladkov snapped the wooden pencil in two. Redliks, standing prudently two steps to the rear, saw the general's neck muscles bulge over his collar. The conference call wasn't satisfactory. Not at all satisfactory. The commander at Tyuratam tried to stick to the standard three-hour reaction time for launching the SL-11s.

Gladkov would have none of it. He reminded Tyuratam that this operation was ordered by Ligachev himself. When Tyuratam whined about safety regulations, Gladkov flew into a rage over the ass-covering maneuver. He roared a short Russian expression that, roughly translated, told the Tyuratam commander to fuck the regulations.

Gladkov looked at the clock. Almost noon. If the Americans were indeed going to try something, he should know about it soon.

In Sunnyvale, Telford and McCary watched *Ariel*'s track, completing nearly a full circle over San Diego.

Telford pointed. "He's coming out of the turn." The blue line was moving noticeably faster. Twenty-seven miles above Lake Tahoe, *Ariel* passed Mach 20.

"Ira?" Telford asked into the telephone.

"Here, Steven."

Telford was surprised at the clarity. Crawford could have been next door, instead of crossing the Canadian border.

"You've got the intel?"

"Roger." The voice was laconic with a faint electronic burr as the crypto devices coded and decoded the down link from *Ariel*.

"You understand there's nothing definite—increased comms from their air-defense people and indications of a possible launch at Tyuratam."

"Roger."

Telford felt a sliver of panic. Crawford's flat voice was a trackless void so lacking in expression that Telford couldn't judge how Crawford had interpreted the information about Tyuratam. Telford was troubled that he might have understated the threat. He desperately wanted to see Crawford's face—to read a narrowing of the eyes, a downturn of the mouth, an attitude of the head.

Trying again, Telford cleared his throat. "But it could be that somehow they've detected you. That they're waiting."

Again the metallic "Roger." Nothing more.

"Ira . . ."

The voice came again, this time richer, more human. "Steven, it's your call. Not mine. You know what's at stake here. I don't. You make the decision. I'll fly the mission."

Ten seconds to transfer orbit. The blue line was streaking across the map. Once more Telford was trapped in the vise of events, boxed into choosing the least bad of very awful alternatives.

"Ira?"

"Roger, Steven."

McCary saw indecision flicker across Telford's face.

"It's a go, Ira."

There was no pause. The voice was level, even. "Roger, Steven."

"Ira?"

"Roger?"

"Godspeed, Ira."

Engine shutdown came, and with it a buoyant surge as earth's gravity was neutralized. Ira Crawford scanned his instruments again. It would be a

smooth entry into orbit. He checked the computer
event log. He would fire *Ariel*'s engine briefly to
smooth out his orbit at an altitude of one hundred
fifty miles—just as he entered Soviet airspace. To his
front and just below him, he saw the dark curve of
the earth's edge change lightninglike from orange
to scarlet, then to a glistening, brilliant silver as he
began his flight into day.

An insistent buzzer drew Gladkov's attention to
the early warning display. On the Pacific coast,
nearly four thousand miles away, the over-the-hori-
zon radar at Komsomolsk was reporting a fast
mover. The Russian fidgeted as the OTH radar made
another probe. The computers needed two, prefera-
bly three, sightings, each at different times, to project a most likely path for the object.

Seconds later the buzzer sounded again. The
computers were generating the expected trajectory.
Before Gladkov's eyes segments superimposed
themselves over a map of the Soviet Union. Gladkov
and Steven Telford would have found it ironic that
both operations centers used a bright blue for the
trace of *Ariel*.

"Speed and altitude?"

Instantly the large screen answered Gladkov.
He nodded. It was the American, all right. The numbers fit a hypersonic aircraft in orbit. He allowed
himself a moment of grudging admiration. It's a
good thing, he reflected, that the Americans' foreign
policy doesn't match their technical sophistication.
Another light. An early-warning radar on the Kola
Peninsula was confirming the Komsomolsk sighting.

* * *

On board *Ariel* the ALQ-208 electronic warfare suite was coping with the Soviet radars. Earlier at Edwards, Ira Crawford and a team of CIA and Air Force intelligence and mission specialists had carefully plotted the course across the Soviet Union, taking into account PVO's radars and weaponry. Drawing on encyclopedic knowledge gained by decades of probing the intricate webs of Soviet defenses, they had foreseen the likelihood of detection by the long-range OTH radar at Komsomolsk and the older radars dubbed HEN HOUSES in NATO parlance.

The ALQ-208's brain was a computer Crawford christened Hal, after the machine in Arthur C. Clarke's *2001*. Like his famous namesake Hal could communicate by synthetic speech with Crawford and ground mission controllers. Right now Hal was busy feeding his own particular brand of electronic snake oil to Colonel General Gladkov and PVO.

Hal's antennae, embedded in *Ariel*'s skin, picked up the Soviet radar pulses and fed them into the world's fastest digital-signal processors, capable of performing chores at a speed of over one hundred forty million instructions a second. Hal analyzed the structure of the Soviet radar waves, then manufactured and broadcast a counterfeit response to the waiting PVO receiving antennae. All this was done in eleven nanoseconds—eleven-millionths of a second.

Hal's twisted signals spoofed the Soviet radars and computers, making them believe that they were receiving the reflections of the signals they had earlier transmitted. In actuality Hal had altered the signal strength so that the returning radar "echo" showed Gladkov a track that was almost a hundred miles east of the route taken by *Ariel* and Ira Crawford.

"TWO RADAR LOCK-ONS NEUTRALIZED, IRA," reported Hal.

"Next threat, Hal?" Crawford asked.

"L-PAR AT GREMICHA IN RANGE IN OH-ONE-NINE SECONDS, IRA."

The large-phased array radar at Gremicha was completed in 1989. There were seven other L-PARs in the Soviet Union, the most famous of which had been at Krasnoyarsk, a radar the Soviets finally admitted had been a violation of the 1972 Antiballistic Missile Treaty. Together the eight L-PARs were the nervous system of the Soviet star-wars system, forming an overlapping trip wire to detect and track incoming American ballistic missile warheads.

Theoretically Gremicha could also follow a target such as *Ariel.* But, claimed the same experts, Hal and the ALQ-208 theoretically could thwart Gremicha's sophisticated circuitry and computer algorithms.

Theoretically.

Pyotr Gladkov felt his face flush. Moscow was calling every few seconds, it seemed. When would Tyuratam be ready? When would Tyuratam be ready? For years the wise men in the Kremlin had shorted the budget for the *antisputnik* program. With just a little more funding, they could have had an interceptor that was quicker off the mark. But oh, no! They squeezed every ruble till it bled; then, when Letnikov got his steam up, they took on looks of injured innocence and passed the trouble down to PVO and, of course, to Colonel General Pyotr Gladkov.

The board showed the American's course over the Soviet Union, and on it the computers calculated the last possible intercept point. The killer vehicle had to meet the American nearly head-on. With the American crossing from northeast to southwest, the engagement had to take place before the American got to Chagoda, north of Moscow. After that, Gladkov thought with growing trepidation, the killer vehicle would be chasing the American, an impossible race to win, given the American's greater speed. And the cursed lights from Tyuratam still mocked him. When would they be ready?

At Sunnyvale, Telford and Frank McCary, not talking, sat sipping coffee, fatigue washing expression from their faces. On the display board *Ariel*'s path touched a pink fan extended from the Kola Peninsula.

"Gremicha L-PAR with intermittent lock-on Xray three." The anonymous intercom voice reflected the growing stress stalking the floor of mission control.

"IRA, GREMICHA SCANNING US."
"Status?"

Hal assessed the situation. *Ariel* was giving the Soviet radar fits. Unlike the low-frequency radars, this one was unable to get a steady lock-on because of *Ariel*'s many stealth features. Before Hal was the question of whether he should actively counter

Gremicha's fitful attempts or do nothing, letting the passive stealth measures confound the radar. Considering the parameters given him by the mission specialists, Hal decided to zap Gremicha. The whole decision process, leisurely by Hal's standards, had taken eight-millionths of a second.

"INITIATING ACTIVE SPOOFING OF GRE-MICHA, IRA."

At the same time Ira Crawford made certain the cameras and imaging radars were ready. They would be over Plesetsk in less than two minutes.

One, then two, green lights flashed.

It seemed to Pyotr Gladkov that they did so reluctantly, Tyuratam obstinately opposing him to the last. The predicted intercept point was inching toward Chagoda. Time was bearing down on him. His chest tightened. It was as if he were breathing against shrinking steel bands. If he requested permission to fire, the delay in transmitting his request up to Letnikov could well let the American escape. But the blame would fall on Pyotr Gladkov, not on delays in Moscow.

Gladkov leaned closer to the microphone, struggling to keep his voice from trembling. "Order Tyuratam to fire at once. Both interceptors. Notify Moscow that interceptors have lifted off and are headed toward the target."

He straightened up, suddenly calm. If Moscow had any reservations, he could order an in-flight destruct. He watched the lights signaling a dual launch at the space center. He then saw, for the first time, a companion display, one that reported on the Soviet ICBM fleet. Thirty RS-20s, the monster missiles the

Americans called the SS-18, had been brought to a higher level of alert. Before returning to his problem of the American plane, he thought briefly of his wife and his daughter and wondered if he would ever see them again.

Far out in space, twenty-two thousand miles above the Indian Ocean, a Defense Support Program satellite's Schmidt telescope caught the double flare of the SL-11s lifting off from Tyuratam. As programmed the DSP satellite infrared sensors then began taking readings each eight seconds. Thirty-two seconds later the azimuths of the two Soviet missiles had been calculated and flashed to ground stations in Australia, Spain, and the United States. And, obviously, to the Satellite Control Facility in Sunnyvale, California.

The big board was showing three traces. One, arcing from upper right to lower left, the familiar glowing blue of *Ariel*. Parallel to this was a lighter blue line—the phantom path of *Ariel* created by Hal. Coming up from lower right toward upper left was a series of bright red arrows, the SL-11s.

"The ASATs," McCary asked in a rough whisper. "How do they work?"

Telford grimly watched the progressing arrows. "SL-eleven second stage puts the warhead into rough orbit, then falls away. Warhead has a radar sensor." Here Telford faced McCary, holding up both fists, bringing them toward each other. "Once it locks on the target, it maneuvers closer with vernier rockets. When it gets in the target's path, it explodes." He suddenly opened one fist, fingers splayed, pointing to the other still-closed fist. "Sends thousands of steel pellets out."

"Jesus Christ," swore McCary. "Ira's a sitting duck."

"Not at all," he pointed to the two blue traces. "The radar sensors on the warheads aren't as powerful or as sophisticated as the ground-based systems, and we have those spoofed." He said it with a confidence he didn't feel.

McCary nodded but said nothing.

In seconds *Ariel's* photo cameras and imaging radars scoured the hundreds of square miles of the Plesetsk military reservation. As quickly, the results were translated into coded pulses and up-linked by Ku-band transmitters to a tracking and data relay satellite in a higher orbit. The TDRS bird then relayed the take to the same ground stations that supported the KH-12.

A three-note tone-and-light sequence told Ira Crawford he'd gotten what he'd been sent for. The flush of triumph flashed quickly. Now to get his ass out of here.

"Intercept in twenty seconds, General."

Pyotr Gladkov said nothing, transfixed by the two lines rapidly rushing to intersection.

The lines met and—nothing! No bloom of explosion—nothing! Among the disciplined control crews below, there was a stir of confusion and restlessness.

Lieutenant Redliks was astounded. The lines

had met and were now continuing on their rapidly separating ways.

"The interceptors didn't work," he exclaimed.

Gladkov had been earlier puzzled by the course of the American plane. It did not overfly the most obvious reconnaissance targets. Why, for example, did the charts show the plane flying so far to the east of the experimental center at Plesetsk? And why, having missed the target, hadn't the *antisputnik* warheads destroyed themselves? Unless . . . "Continue the engagement," he snapped. "This may not be over."

Crawford's threat display showed twenty seconds to intercept. Perspiration broke out on his face; his arms were suddenly weak. The Soviet ASATs hadn't been spoofed. They were still coming!

"Interceptor status, Hal."

"INTERCEPTOR RADARS NEUTRALIZED, IRA." The voice had a reproachful copper sound. "THREAT ELIMINATED."

Crawford fought the panic rising sour in his throat. Think, goddamnit! If the interceptor radars were spoofed, then their guidance had to be working on something else. Hal had been told—programmed—that the interceptors worked off radar guidance. If Hal knew the radar guidance was jammed, then by all rights the interceptors were no longer a threat. But the interceptors were still coming. Guided by something other than radar. And Hal was wrong.

Thirteen seconds to intercept.

Ira Crawford lifted a red cover and flipped the switch for emergency ignition, then jammed the throttles full forward with such force that he thought for an instant he'd sheared the thick steel levers.

Nine miles away and closing at a speed of almost thirty thousand miles an hour, the backup infrared seekers on the interceptors registered the massive heat plume of *Ariel*'s engine. Instantaneously the interceptors' computers recycled, calculating a new kill point to achieve the optimum pattern for their steel-pellet warheads. Given the sudden increase in strength of the heat source, the computers believed they were closer to *Ariel* than they indeed were and so commanded immediate detonation.

"Intercept completed, General."
Curiously sad, Gladkov watched the first, then the second warhead blossom on the screen. Around him there were subdued murmurs and smiles. On the floor there were boisterous shouts of victory.

At Sunnyvale time and motion were frozen. On the mission screen the dual explosions had superimposed a large red blot over the blue line of *Ariel*'s path. Mission specialists stared in disbelief at the screen; others, stunned, slumped at their consoles. One, a great hulk of a man, wept onto the shoulder of his neighbor.

Telford stood, eyes closed, thumb and forefinger pinched at the bridge of his nose, head bowed. McCary, standing beside him, reached for Telford's shoulder while looking in shock at the screen.

And so it was McCary who first saw it, followed almost immediately by a small blond woman on the floor, who began screaming at the top of her lungs and pointing to the blue line, now emerging from the red cloud, moving steadily, bravely, to the south-west, toward the larger blue of the Mediterranean.

Twenty-one

Sam Rubel's call canceled Telford's plans to return to Edwards for Crawford's touchdown. Instead Telford and McCary, still jubilant over the mission, sped east in Telford's plane. Fatigue overcame their excitement, and both men quickly fell asleep before their plane cleared the Bay Area.

Rubel and Kupperman met them planeside at Andrews Air Force Base. It would be a bright Washington day, the low winter sun was already taking the edge off the morning chill. Telford's sedan, sandwiched between lead and chase cars, made its way toward Washington.

Rubel spoke first: "We're going straight to the Navy Yard. Stan's got something to show you."

Telford yawned, rubbing a knuckle into a still-sleepy eye. "Come on, Sam, don't keep us waiting."

"It'll keep," Rubel insisted. He nodded to Kupperman. "Charlie's got some preliminaries that might be interesting."

Kupperman, in the front seat beside Rubel, turned to Telford and McCary. The NSA analyst's eyes were red-rimmed, and he was badly in need of a shave and sleep.

"We fed much of the mission analysis to you at

Sunnyvale," Kupperman began. "So you got most of what we picked up during the overflight.

"You'll remember we reported increased PVO activity from Sharapovo *before Ariel* left the United States?"

Telford and McCary both nodded.

"Alone it wouldn't have meant much," Kupperman continued. "But after the mission, I had our RADINT people go over the OTH activity. . . ."

"Too many acronyms too early in the morning," McCary pleaded. "English, please."

"RADINT: radiation intelligence," Kupperman explained. "OTH: over the horizon—that's a kind of warning radar the Sovs have. Ordinarily the OTH radars are aimed at picking up ballistic missiles we'd fire over the pole at the USSR. The American warheads would come in at a much higher altitude than *Ariel*. Yet the OTH radar at Komsomolsk tracked *Ariel*."

"Meaning?" asked McCary.

"Meaning the Sovs had to make extensive adjustments to their OTH radars to find *Ariel*. And our RADINT guys have evidence those adjustments were being made about the same time *Ariel* was taking off."

"They knew we were coming," McCary whispered.

Bleifeld stood on a dais in the small curtained briefing room. To his right a podium on which he'd arranged several sheets of handwritten notes. On his left an easel on which a blue cloth covered a large panel perhaps five feet square.

Without preamble he flipped the cloth back

over the top of the easel. With a pointer he tapped the panel. "We're still processing the take from *Ariel*. This is the best we have now, but it'll do."

The black-and-white picture was free of the grainy effect of older enlargement processes, thanks to computer enhancement. Even so, Bleifeld saw that Telford and the senator were having trouble puzzling it out.

He drew the pointer across the panel. "This is a road through the restricted zone northeast of Plesetsk." Moving the pointer along the road, he stopped at an object near overhanging tree limbs. "Here we see a Moskva military vehicle."

Now understanding the scale and references, Telford nodded. In the center of the picture, on either side of the road, were clearings that closer inspection revealed to be protected by earthen berms.

Bleifeld pointed to the smaller area north of the road. "Here we see two control and communications vehicles. Note they're covered with camouflage netting. See the antennae here"—he tapped the photograph—"and here."

Several large black lines snaked across the road to the other clearing, where they linked three long multiwheeled vehicles. The last vehicle in the serial had erected a tube almost as large as the vehicle itself.

"These are the cables from the control vehicles to the tels, transporter-erector-launchers." Bleifeld's voice was crisp and professorial.

"Launchers?" interrupted McCary. "Launchers for what?"

Bleifeld's face had a haunted look. "Missiles, Congressman. What we call the SS-22. Range about nine hundred kilometers—roughly five hundred fifty miles," he answered. "If this outfit is the twin to Raven—and we believe it is—then Yegor Letnikov's furnishing the Germans with missiles that can reach London and Paris."

Waiting for his car at the west wing entrance, Telford glumly reviewed his meeting with the president. It hadn't gone well. George Bush had listened in grim silence as Telford summarized the results of the *Ariel* mission. The president had wanted to know why, and Telford hadn't been able to tell him.

The president's question would spur the secret legions of Washington's Sovietologists to great intellectual battles over this conjecture or that hypothesis. In the search for the why of Letnikov's missiles, lights would burn late and dinners would grow cold. Eventually the media would get wind of it, and hundreds more would join in the chase. It would become the question of the day, a question to which no one in Washington had the answer.

Leaving the president, he had called for an immediate appointment with Cantabile. When Bush had mentioned briefing congressional leaders, Telford took the opportunity to tell him about the Letnikov letter. The president was not pleased as Telford explained his decision to open it but agreed with Telford's plan to meet with Cantabile.

"These, Mr. Telford, could be anyone's missiles." Senator Joseph Cantabile gestured to the eight-by-ten glossy on his desk. "Why should anyone believe they belong to the Germans?"

Is he playing devil's advocate? Or is he pumping me? Telford wondered. "Because, Senator, previous German activities tipped us off. We didn't fly over Plesetsk on a hunch. We had evidence from other sources."

"Such as?"

"The usual kind of thing," Telford dodged. "Signal intercepts, satellite photography."

"That's not very specific, Mr. Telford."

Telford again fended off Cantabile. "I don't know all the details of our collection efforts myself. But I'm certain that when the time comes to make all this public, we'll have a good case."

"Public?" Cantabile leaned forward, now even more interested. Though still a handsome man, age and alcohol were taking their toll, his face on the slope to puffiness, a jaundiced yellow lurking just below the tan. "Public? When might that be?"

"I don't know. That's the president's call. But I can't imagine he's going to allow that"—Telford pointed to the picture—"to fester for very long."

In the shuttered library Constance Higby refilled Joseph Cantabile's glass, then stood by the fireside bar.

"Have you discussed this with Vladimir?"

"No," answered a distraught Cantabile. "Why should I? After all I've done—the crap I've put up with from the right-wingers—Moscow goes and pulls some shit like this." On the coffee table the *Ariel* photo was an embarrassing witness to Soviet ingratitude, and worse, to the gullibility of Joseph Cantabile, chairman of the Senate Select Committee on Intelligence.

Settling beside him on the morocco leather sofa, Constance selected a cigarette from a silver-filigreed box. She fumbled with a massive jade table lighter, Cantabile oblivious to her struggle.

"Look, Joe, there's a lot to this you haven't considered."

"Such as?" he asked irritably.

"Such as who gains if you take the position that the Russians fucked you."

"What do you mean?"

She exhaled a long, feathery plume. "If you take the line that this is some sinister move by the Kremlin, it undercuts you and all you've worked for."

Understanding worked across Cantabile's face. He downed his cognac. "Yes, I'd look like a fool."

"Don't forget the movement, too, Joe. They look to you as a voice of reason, a leader for peace, for disarmament. If you let this align you with Bush, they'll dump you. They'll find somebody else."

Cantabile's eyes grew wide at that. He'd seen others stumble. The plagiarists, the womanizers who dug their graves with their dicks, the tellers of racist jokes on press buses. He saw the crowds find new champions in the short space of an evening news broadcast. Derision, then worse, ignominy—the wages of sin in American politics.

"But I'm between a rock and a hard place," Cantabile complained.

"Not necessarily. You ought to raise this with Letnikov."

The thought stunned Cantabile. "Letnikov?"

Constance smiled patiently. "Joe, this is an opportunity! You've got the opening. Letnikov told you he wanted a direct dialogue with you as a leader in Congress. Take him up on it! Put yourself in the middle—the honest broker—that sort of thing. Letnikov didn't do this in a vacuum. He must have his reasons. If you leave it to the White House, though, they'll distort everything to make Bush look good. You could be the one person who could contribute some sort of balance, a rational perspective.

"But you've got to take the initiative," she continued, eyes now flashing with excitement. "If you aren't a part of this when it hits the newspapers, it'll be strictly between the White House and the Kremlin. You'll be sitting on the sidelines, Joe."

Joseph Cantabile wasn't thinking about sidelines. He already saw himself in it—The Great Game! Krotov had hinted at an early Letnikov initiative. From there Cantabile imagined a summit where a place of honor might be found for a prominent American statesman. A man such as Joseph Cantabile. His heart pounded, and he tossed off another cognac. The frantic shuttling between Moscow and Washington. The breathless press conferences on the Hill.

The *New York Times* calling for the Nobel Peace Prize!

He heard the gushing praise at the convention, the cheers. Oh shit, it'd be wonderful! To stand there under the spotlights, the falling balloons, arms raised to the tumult on the floor. He'd kick the Republicans' asses in the campaign, and on election night a Cantabile landslide would rumble west across the continent!

Constance was now close to him, her breasts

firm against his arm, her hand exploring the dimensions of his erection.

He scarcely felt her insistent, stroking fingers. The fucking White House! He'd have the fucking White House!

Twenty-two

"And which is the man you saw on the stairs?" Lothar Kelch asked.

The old woman impatiently jabbed a gnarled finger at the fifth picture from the end. The fingernail was cracked and indelibly grease-stained. The picture was of Manfred Weihs.

The trash collected from the dump near Weihs's body yielded various documents from the Metropol. And in one of Weihs's pockets, they'd found a single key, separate from others on a key ring. That key opened room 507 of the hotel. Kelch's men had begun questioning the help assigned to the fifth floor and found the old woman at once.

"Tell me about seeing this man."

"I've told the others. Many times." There was a hint of defiance, even belligerence.

Her records showed that she'd gone through the hell of the fall of Berlin in forty-five. She wasn't frightened of the police or impressed with him. This one, Kelch told himself, is a tough old bird.

"I know you have. Please indulge me." He put a faint pleading in his voice. "The people we get these days . . ." He made a gesture of helpless frustration, luring her into a conspiracy against the young. "You are an important witness, and it is vital that I hear these things from you directly." Kelch picked up a telephone and ordered tea to be brought in.

Mollified, the old woman told again how Weihs and his woman—his *Schatz*—had knocked her down and how, barely getting to her feet, she'd been trampled by another man who obviously was chasing Weihs.

"The woman. She stayed with the man?"

"No. She went into the corridor on the second floor. The man continued down. The other man chased him."

"You've seen the woman before?"

"No," the old woman sniffed, "but I've seen her kind."

Kelch took another photograph from an envelope. It was the composite likeness the old woman had worked over with the police artist.

"And this is the other man? The one who did the chasing?"

The old woman nodded emphatically.

"You're certain? He went by you so quickly. . . ."

The old woman rolled her eyes in exasperation. "Of course, I'm certain. I saw the fellow twice, you know."

Stunned, Kelch flipped quickly through the interrogation reports. "Twice? It says nothing here . . ."

She tilted her chin up in triumph, her eyes squinting shrewdly. "Your young men didn't ask me. They only asked . . ."

Kelch couldn't conceal his excitement. "There! You see why two old heads are better than all those young ones." He pretended to join in her gloating.

"Now tell me," he waved the composite of Paul Brandt. "When did you first see this one?"

Busying himself signing a sheaf of documents, Rudolf Wolf gave Lothar Kelch a look one gave a yipping dog or a pesky child.

Kelch did not change expression. You can always spot the officious ones, he reflected. They worked at their desk in their suit coats. Not a hair out of place. Probably tucks his undershirt into his shorts.

Wolf carefully inserted his fountain pen into a holder, folded his hands in the center of the blue desk blotter, and riveted Kelch with a severe look.

"General Ferner tells me that you are engaged in some—ah—some investigation?"

He makes it sound like we're out picking up dog droppings, Kelch thought. I suppose we do clean up the shit. This one's obviously angry at Ferner for involving him.

In reality Wolf had had to force himself to feign indifference when Ferner told him about the investigation and the detective named Kelch. He let two sleepless nights pass before having Ferner summon the homicide inspector.

Wolf consulted a slip of paper. "Yes, an investigation into the death of . . ."

"The *murder*, Herr Generalleutenant," Kelch corrected Wolf. "The murder of one Manfred Weihs." Without waiting for an invitation, Kelch sat. He could not be arrogant, for one did not trifle with a deputy minister, particularly a deputy minister of the BND. On the other hand, if he was too deferential, the arrogant Wolf would roll over him.

Wolf stared icily at Kelch. "However you would have it, Inspector, please be brief. I'm a busy man, and I haven't all day."

Kelch sketched the case with the sparse precision of the professional policeman: the finding of the body, the tracing of Weihs to the hotel, the fat chambermaid's identification of Weihs, and her description of Weihs's suspected assailant.

"So you have a place, a witness, and a suspect, Inspector—an unidentified suspect. Is that all?"

Kelch hesitated, suddenly uncertain. What was it in Wolf's voice that bothered him?

"There is a certain connection, also," Kelch continued. "In Weihs's possession was a key. To room five-oh-seven. That room is permanently reserved for the BND. As a place for discreet meetings, Generalmajor Ferner tells me."

"This Weihs. Was he seen in the room?"

Was Wolf just a bit too quick on that? That something in his voice—concern? Was that it? Was the man worried?

"No, no he wasn't. But the man who chased him—and perhaps killed him—that man was seen in the vicinity of room five-oh-seven earlier that day."

Wolf had not moved. He sat as a statue, his hands on the blotter, fingers interlaced. "That is not much of a connection, Inspector Kalch."

Kelch gave Wolf a long look. "Kelch." He paused for emphasis, then continued. "You're correct. It is not. But it provides me a hypothesis. I am working on the assumption that Weihs's murder was the result of a meeting gone bad. A meeting in room five-oh-seven."

"A meeting?"

"Yes. A meeting between Weihs and the man who chased him."

Kelch detected Wolf's relief—a softening around the mouth and eyes, a minute slump of the shoulders and back. "Between Weihs and his killer?"

"That is the assumption."

"But why?"

Kelch shrugged. "Again, I don't know. Your man Weihs had access to information some would pay dearly for. That cannot be ruled out."

"Weihs?" Wolf almost smiled. "Killed because he was selling secrets?" He sat as if deep in thought. Finally: "As much as I do not want to believe something like that would be going on in the ministry, Inspector, you will find that we will cooperate with you fully." Wolf pushed a button. Instantly the door to his office opened, his secretary stood waiting to escort Kelch out. "Remember, Inspector, this could be a matter of highest sensitivity. I wish to be kept fully informed." Wolf nodded to the departing Kelch. "Fully informed."

For the second time Yegor Letnikov read the translation, occasionally glancing at the original: the letter from Senator Joseph Cantabile. Finally he pushed the paper away and took off his gold wire reading glasses.

"It seems that the Honorable Joseph Cantabile wishes an explanation for the German missiles."

Boris Chernov folded his copy of the translation and pointed to the *Ariel* photograph that accompanied the letter. "This could be trouble."

Letnikov saw the worried look on the GRU chief's face. "Not at all: think about a two-headed tactic. We show a reasonable face to this Cantabile fellow and the American audience he commands. At the same time we continue our course with Neuhaus, helping him stand up to Paris and London. 'Look,' we tell Europe, 'the Americans are losing their hard edge. Who will protect you now? Make the best deal with us, we will tell them. Be reasonable. Side with us for your safety and protection. The Americans are a force of the past.'"

Letnikov laughed. "No, Comrade Chairman, you owe your people in Washington my congratulations. The good Senator Cantabile may well be precisely what we need."

Brandt parked two blocks from the huge television tower, then walked north along the Prenzlauerallee. As before, the meeting would take place over the lunch hour. This time, however, Brandt made the arrangements. He was confident that it would be as secure as such a meeting could be.

One car at the taxi stand displayed a not-for-hire sign. Its driver was busy under the hood. Walking by, Brandt saw on the front seat a socket wrench and screwdriver with a red handle. He was not being followed. Now he needed one more signal.

Turning left, he walked into a small park a block off the boulevard. The second bench on the right side of the path from the Belforterstrasse entrance was taken by two old women, bundled in shawls and rough wool coats against the north wind, pensioners luxuriating in the sudden clearing of the overcast.

Brandt took the bench opposite. He glanced at his watch. Ten minutes. And these old women would stay as long as the pale sun reluctantly warmed their upturned faces. They dozed motionless, turtles on a warm rock.

Eight minutes.

Brandt cleared his throat. "It is good to see the sun."

As one, the women opened their eyes, blinking at Brandt, first in confusion, then with the baleful suspicion of the old.

Before they could close their eyes again, Brandt continued. "You are fortunate to be able to be here when so many are getting in the line at the grocer." Brandt waved toward the boulevard.

Both women jerked as if shocked. "Grocer?" asked one, fishing in the pocket of her coat, coming out with a net shopping bag.

"I think it was oranges."

Without a word the old women scurried off toward the boulevard.

From where he sat, Brandt could now see the confirmation signal: a silver thumbtack in the edge of the bench seat. Stretching, he got up and walked quickly from the park.

Five minutes later Brandt found the apartment building. The key was taped beneath the stairwell railing on the fourth floor. Brandt turned and went down to the third floor.

"I do not like this place."

"Our people arranged it, Herr Generalleutenant." Brandt looked at Wolf with reproach. "Professionals. We won't be interrupted."

Wolf's eyes narrowed. He would not take this from the American. "They found the body almost immediately."

"You said that day that he was one of yours."

Wolf acknowledged slowly. "There have been—

ah—repercussions." Wolf went on to describe Kelch's visit. "A despicable little man. Dressed like a ragpicker. A born snooper."

Brandt probed for the details, first about Manfred Weihs, then about Lothar Kelch. Finally satisfied, Brandt went to a table nearby and opened a bottle of mineral water. Pouring two glasses, he handed one to Wolf.

Giving a curt nod of thanks, Wolf took a large, gulping drink, then fixed Brandt with an inquiring look. "Our Russian friends. They were upset about your spy plane. Over Plesetsk. I assume it had something to do with Ostgruppe Rabe."

Brandt looked steadily at the German. A good opener, Brandt admitted. Enticing. Brandt wanted to find out how well connected Wolf was with the Soviets, but he wasn't going to spill how much the Agency knew in order to find out.

"Yes. It had something to do with *Ostgruppe Rabe.*"

"And there is something else, Herr Bancroft. The Russians have a photograph that the spy plane took." Wolf paused for effect. "Your security, it seems, remains a sieve." His lips curled in contempt. "I hope you can better protect your human sources."

Though stunned, Brandt mounted a counterattack. "There's no one on your tail, Wolf. Do you imagine they'd let you run if you'd been blown? I'll take care of you if you take care of me. Now, damnit, tell me what you've got on Raven."

Hatred flashed across the German's face, then as quickly was replaced by resignation. For the next thirty minutes, Wolf talked, Brandt interrupting only for minor clarifications. After Brandt and Wolf left the apartment, the security team from Berlin Station would disarm the self-destruct mechanism on the recorders and retrieve the tapes. Through a dead-drop Brandt would have a copy by nightfall. The originals would be pouched to Langley.

Wolf finished, and after several questions Brandt was satisfied that he'd gotten all the German had on Raven.

Brandt tried a new tack. "Our friend Neuhaus seems to be doing well."

"He should. He's got his opposition intimidated. No one dares raise their head."

"What is the tie between Ostgruppe Rabe and Neuhaus?"

Wolf thought, frowning in concentration. "I don't know. Not for certain."

"Your guess, then."

The German paused again. "Certainly there is a relationship. Ostgruppe Rabe and whatever your spy plane found in Plesetsk will somehow play a part in Neuhaus's negotiations with the Russians." Wolf shook his head. "But there is nothing . . ."

"What about Felix Ehren's organization? It handles both the political connections to Neuhaus as well as the . . . the Ostgruppe Rabe."

Wolf gave a sly smile. The American had nearly mentioned something in addition to Rabe. Perhaps what they found at Plesetsk. "Ehren has built a wall around his operations. One must have special security clearances." Wolf shrugged in helplessness.

"And you don't have those clearances?"

Wolf shook his head. "No." Wolf watched Brandt take that in, then dangled another tantalizing tidbit in front of the American. "But I know the compartments Ehren has established—the kinds of clearances."

Determined not to seem eager, Brandt waited silently, without expression.

Realizing he'd get nothing from Brandt, Wolf began. "There are three general categories. First, there is THOR. Those in Ehren's organization who have this clearance are mostly military. I can only assume these are members of Ostgruppe Rabe. The second category is BALDER. These people have been seconded from our covert-operations organizations. These are probably engaged in supporting Herr Neuhaus."

"And the third?"

"Ah, yes. The third. It has an intriguing code name: MIMIR." Wolf spelled it out. "This is the most restrictive category. Only a few people besides Ehren have a MIMIR clearance."

"You know nothing about the clearance?"

Wolf hesitated. "No. Again, nothing specific. Yet . . ."

"Yet?"

"The code name. It comes from a list we reserve for a very special clearance."

"Special? How?"

"These are clearances," Wolf explained, "that we apply to information that we are not to share with the Russians."

Brandt considered this, then carefully framed his next question. "And you have no way to penetrate Ehren's organization?"

Wolf shook his head.

A thought occurred to Brandt, one he needed first to work out with Langley. "Perhaps, Herr Generalleutenant, Manfred Weihs can help us."

Twenty-three

The knock came precisely at twelve past the hour. Brandt crossed the room and peered through the judas hole. Telford was standing back so his face was clear under the hallway light. Even so, it was with apprehension that Brandt slid back the bolt and opened the door.

Telford brushed by him. As quickly, Brandt shut and bolted the door.

Brandt's motions were familiar—the tilt of the head, the listening a second or so for an outside noise, the back-and-forth twist of the doorknob. Telford recalled them; scraps from a time of trust and knowing sides.

"You're all right?"

"Yes. I suppose so." Brandt's grip was tentative, and he seemed eager to drop Telford's hand. A silver carafe of coffee waited on a small table.

Immediately after the meeting with Wolf, Brandt had used the emergency procedures to contact Washington control. Later that morning a flight from Berlin to New York. A rental car under an assumed name, and the four-hour drive to Washington. From a roadside booth in Delaware, Brandt called control for the hotel where reservations had been made under yet another name.

Pouring coffee, Brandt nodded to the window. "Control seems to be suffering from a rare fit of good humor." Almost directly across the street was the Soviet embassy, where, even in the fading light, one could still clearly see the large hammer-and-sickle banner.

"Sam will be here shortly. You asked . . ."

"There's a photograph." Brandt began his accusation abruptly. "The GRU has it. It's from the Plesetsk overflight."

Brandt studied Telford's face, waiting for an explanation, hoping there was one.

"It was a barium tracer."

There was a slight relaxation of Brandt's features. "Who?"

"A senator. Cantabile—on the Intelligence Committee."

"He's efficient—the picture showed up in record time."

"We also wanted Moscow to know we knew about the missiles," Telford added, eager to ease Brandt's concern.

"So they know we know about the missiles. And now you know about this senator." Brandt put the cup and saucer down gently, without a sound. For a long time he looked down at the Soviet embassy. By the main entrance, under an awning, a driver stood waiting by his car, smoking. "What is it that any of us know?"

"Less and less." Telford stood beside him, watching the man at the embassy.

"There was a time when we were certain, remember?"

"We knew them, and we knew ourselves," Telford agreed. "We knew the dividing line."

"Dividing line? Between what?"

"Them and us. A simple choice between slavery or freedom."

"Freedom." Brandt said it bitterly. "What about the freedom to let people live?"

Down below the man at the embassy flicked his cigarette out into the rain-wet street.

"There was no other way. Logic—reason . . ."

"It wasn't reason. It was a parody of reason. I should have walked out of there."

"If you had . . ."

"You're going to say that if I had let that kid live, we'd be standing on the brink. Something like that."

"Yes. Something like that."

"The Aztecs made human sacrifices, too. To keep their world from falling apart." Brandt turned to Telford, taking him by the elbow. "Who's to say? Weihs might have gone back to his desk and kept his mouth shut. Or we could have bought the kid off." He dropped his hand. "Even if Weihs had blown it for us, are you going to tell me we couldn't have fixed things up further down the line?"

Telford regarded Brandt for a long moment. "At the farm. You said you'd know when it was time to quit."

Telford's words brought to Brandt the haunting trace of Elise's laughter, the blues and whites of a special day in the sun. He felt the hollow aching of loneliness.

He said nothing but looked steadily at Telford, waiting.

"Well? Is it, Paul? Is it time to quit?"

Brandt shrugged. "I'm here, aren't I?" He searched Telford's face. "It isn't you," he assured

Telford, "it's this thing we're caught up in. As long as I'm in this, I couldn't ask for better company."

"I didn't do well on the S-Bahn platform that night."

Brandt laughed a young man's laugh, as if remembering a friend caught in a misfiring prank. "We weren't there to take on the Warsaw Pact. We were supposed to run."

"Still . . ."

A rapping came at the door.

"Wait." Brandt stopped Telford. "Before Sam comes: at the farm—you kept the coin, our recognition signal. I think it embarrassed you."

Telford nodded.

"It shouldn't have." Brandt picked his half of the fifty-pfennig coin from a pocket and flipped it into the air. Both men followed the quick trace of silver, Brandt catching it with a smile and a wink on his way to answer the door.

"Can we start with your cable on Raven?" Sam Rubel asked, beginning an hour's probing to fill out Brandt's report on the latest information from Wolf.

Sam sketched the analysis of the *Ariel* mission, then followed up with the questions that remained open—questions only a human source could answer.

Telford summed up with a wry smile. "We know all the facts and none of the reasons."

"Ehren's carefully hidden them," Brandt replied. He explained the security barriers. "I'm convinced the whole thing comes together in MIMIR—that's the only security compartment that excludes the Soviets. The other two—THOR and BALDER—have to do with the missiles and covert operations. They're shot through with Russians, straight military and GRU."

"What could they have in mind? What are they hiding from the Russians?"

"I don't know." Brandt's face was lined with fatigue and frustration. He shook his head in exasperation. "It may be that the MIMIR compartment's nothing more than some administrative device—a clearance for the paymasters, clerks, and supply specialists.

"But it nags at me, Steven." Brandt looked at his hands and, finding no answer there, looked up at Telford. "There's the fact that Neuhaus and Letnikov conspired against Gorbachev. We assume that Neuhaus was the junior partner simply because East Germany was for so long a client state—a stooge—for the Soviet Union. We're no longer dealing with a divided Germany. Or one that's tied to a bunch of alliances. What if Neuhaus has something up his sleeve and he's using Letnikov to get it?"

"We've got no proof," Sam Rubel interjected softly.

"No, no we haven't," Brandt admitted. "But this isn't a courtroom, Sam. You know that. If we wait until we have an ironclad case in hand, it may be too late. And anyway, I'm not proposing we do anything drastic."

"What is it, then?" asked Telford.

"Cantabile. Are you certain that the stuff you're feeding him is all he's got access to?"

"How do you mean?"

"He's on the Intelligence Committee. The story you're trying to feed the Kremlin through him might be contradicted by other information. Are you monitoring him? His connection with Moscow?"

Sam Rubel looked at his feet.

"No," said Telford. "We're not. We only . . ."

"My God! This guy could be funneling them everything including the kitchen sink. And we don't have the watchers on him?"

"No, Paul, we don't," Telford admitted, trying to avoid confrontation. "Any more than we could control any member of Congress, or anybody who has a security clearance. We . . ."

"But we *know* Cantabile's working for them!" Brandt protested. "We're running a risk, and it's my neck that's out there."

"Paul, your argument's with me," Sam Rubel interrupted. He nodded toward Telford. "Steven here was all for bringing charges against Cantabile, or at least having the president go to the Senate majority leader, but I talked him out of it. We can't put a U.S. senator on ice based on what we have—no judge would listen to us."

"But taps—mail cover . . ." Brandt protested.

Rubel shook his head. "There's not even enough to get approval for that. Even if we could, there'd still be a risk, you know that."

Brandt listened, saying nothing, his face an impenetrable mask. Finally he nodded. "I don't suppose I have any choice. I just need to know you"—he gestured to Rubel and Telford—"that you're watching my backside as best you can."

"We are, Paul," Telford said with emotion. "You've got to believe that."

"You go back," Sam Rubel asked. "Then what?"

Brandt didn't hesitate: "We penetrate the MI-MIR compartment."

"And how do we do that?"

Brandt gave a small smile. "We dispatch the good Senator Cantabile to carry out a little mission for us."

* * *

Alone, dwarfed by the huge ornate office, Rudolf Wolf sat before a large desk. He fought down the sour acid taste that lapped at the back of his throat and clenched his hands in his lap to hide their fearful palsy.

Fifteen minutes ago three brutish thugs had burst unannounced into his office. One carried Wolf's hat and coat. The lead jerked his head toward the door. "You are wanted at the Staatsrat." Their abruptness and rude manner stunned him. Surprise, then anger, were quickly followed by alarm. Ruffians, even from Dietrich Neuhaus's office, didn't talk to a deputy minister in such a fashion. Unless, of course, that deputy minister was in very deep trouble.

The drive to Pankow had been in fearsome, brooding silence, the heavy dark sedan hurtling like a devil beast through the deserted Berlin streets. Wolf knew that he'd been found out; that after torture and interrogation, painful death waited for him. He remembered the KGB film in basic training. How a traitor, screaming and crying, had sawed his wrists against the wire that bound him to the iron frame, trying to kill himself before he was slowly fed into the maw of a roaring furnace.

"Good of you to come, Herr Generalleutenant Wolf."

Still certain of his death, Wolf turned as if drugged. He registered the dark hair, the high forehead, and desperately searched for a name. The man was . . . was . . .

"Felix Ehren," the man offered, moving behind the massive desk.

Seated, Ehren studied Wolf for seemingly endless minutes. The office was hushed. Somewhere outside, Wolf knew, life went on. He suddenly was overcome with a desperate, clutching envy for all the innocents who occupied themselves with the trivia of living—sex, eating and drinking, savoring petty victories and minor triumphs—the little amusements and distractions that filled waking hours. That tide of life flowed without him, rushing water around a cold stone. Here—now—in this place—none of that existed. From here only the cells, the beatings, the oven.

"Forgive the urgency, General, but the chancellor himself needs your immediate assistance."

It took a second or two for Wolf to realize that he, Wolf, was not the object of Ehren's concern. They hadn't found him out! Something was going on of great political sensitivity, and it was as a deputy minister of the BND—not as an American spy—that he was brought here.

"You are feeling well, General?" asked Felix Ehren. "You seem rather pale."

"It is perhaps a cold coming on, Herr Ehren. Nothing more." Wolf now was almost giddy with relief. He would have to watch it, he warned himself. Ehren didn't survive in this position by being a fool or unobservant. "How may I be of service?"

Ehren opened a drawer and from it withdrew a sheet of telex flimsy. "This is a personal message from Yegor Letnikov. Chancellor Neuhaus received it less than two hours ago."

Wolf was impressed by Ehren's matter-of-fact manner. Wolf had never before seen a direct communication between chiefs of state, and here Ehren treated it as if it were a common occurrence.

". . . Letnikov summarizes information given to him by the GRU. One of their sources—presumably in Washington—reports that the CIA has penetrated the BND."

Wolf caught his breath, and he began to plummet back into despair. He cleared his throat. "Such claims are common," he protested.

Ehren's face was flat and expressionless. His black eyes stayed on Wolf. "The Russians say that the BND source tipped the Americans to the missile units in training at Plesetsk, General. That this source was the basis for the American spy-plane mission."

Wolf struggled to breath. "If that is all we have to go on, Herr Ehren . . ."

"No, fortunately, it is not." Ehren looked again at the flimsy. "The GRU says that this information was obtained from the CIA director himself. The CIA director—Telford—described the source as being a low-level clerk in the BND. And the implication was that this person is no longer furnishing information to the Americans."

A second powerful wave of relief washed over Wolf, a palpable lifting of tension and fear. He thought of Brandt. That bastard! Wolf knew nothing, of course, of Brandt's meeting with Telford, or of Telford's subsequent misleading of Joseph Cantabile. Wolf knew, however, that all this somehow was Brandt's doing. Brandt hadn't shared his plans with him. That may have added to Brandt's security, but it damned near caused Wolf a coronary.

"Let us grant that the Russians are correct, Herr Ehren. Your operation is strictly compartmented. Clerks, even those in the BND, do not pick up a document to read about these missiles of yours."

Ehren waited for Wolf to continue.

"We must consider the possibility that the clerk in question had someone—a contact—within your organization. . . ."

Ehren erupted. "Impossible!"

Wolf, having successfully provoked the man, was now more confident. "It may only be an outside chance, Herr Ehren. Nonetheless, as a prudent man, certainly you . . ."

Ehren frowned in capitulation. "Yes, yes, General. One has to consider that possibility." Ehren knew where Wolf was leading and obviously did not like it. But he briskly picked up again. "Obviously this is a matter of extreme sensitivity. The chancellor must assure Letnikov that we have taken care of this. . . ." Ehren pointed to the paper. "And at the same time, we cannot—absolutely cannot—compromise our security."

Wolf nodded. Ehren had revealed more than he'd intended. Ehren wanted the presumed leak to the Americans blocked off without the investigation revealing anything to the Russians. Wolf recounted Kelch's investigation. "We can pursue this, Herr Ehren, only if we have access to your organization."

"But the clerk—this Weihs—he is dead."

"Yes. But his source is probably still in place," Wolf countered, making the most of the opportunity to solidify and embellish the figment of Weihs's treason. "And the Americans may well have kept someone in the wings to replace Weihs."

Ehren did not challenge this. Once the slightest possibility of breached security was raised, it could be suicide to oppose the bloodhounds, even for Felix Ehren. "I understand, General." He leaned forward over the desk. "You shall have your access. But it must be limited. I cannot have every safe and drawer opened by legions of your snoops."

"You don't have to fear that," Wolf smiled. "I can assure you and the chancellor that we can do the job with very few people. With very few, very capable people."

Twenty-four

The Globe and Mail (Toronto)

SOVIET UNION SENDS NUCLEAR WEAPONS TO GERMANY

Barricada (Havana)

MOSCOW REAFFIRMS SOLIDARITY WITH BERLIN
Castro Hails Soviet Resolution

The New York Times

GERMAN CHANCELLOR ACCEPTS NUCLEAR MISSILES
Needed to Balance French, British Weapons, Neuhaus Claims
by Judith Muller

Berlin—Chancellor Dietrich Neuhaus dismissed concerns about Soviet-provided nuclear missiles, saying that they "only partially balanced French and British missiles aimed at Germany."

"The French and British have themselves to thank for this," Neuhaus said today in a brief interchange with Western journalists. Neuhaus described his "Herculean efforts to engage Paris and London in disarmament talks." These talks failed, Neuhaus claimed, because of "French arrogance and British ignorance."

Soviet president Letnikov, in a live interview carried by Radio Moscow, said that the missile shipment was "a prudent measure" taken in response to threats "from the growing nuclear arsenals of France and Great Britain," whom he called "shadow accomplices of the United States."

In Washington, Frank Gaffney, director of the Center for Security Policy, a respected think tank, described the missiles as being of a range as to be "able to hold all of France and much of Great Britain at risk, but of little threat to the Soviet Union."

While President Bush is preparing a statement, respected congressional leaders are urging immediate action.

On the television show *Face the Nation*, Senator Joseph Cantabile, influential chairman of the Senate Intelligence Committee, called for the United States to "do its share" to reduce tensions in Europe. "The Cold War is long over," Senator Cantabile said. "We should fold our tents and bring our boys home. American soldiers no longer have a mission in Europe. Their presence there adds to the current unrest."

The senator referred to "traditional Russian fears of encirclement" as a "regrettable though understandable cause of Mr. Letnikov's concern." Cantabile called for "a greater commitment to the peace process" on the part of the White House and announced emergency hearings on the Bush administration's European policy.

At a press conference after the broadcast, Senator Cantabile clarified his remarks. "If we are concerned about German missiles, think of Chancellor Neuhaus's view from Berlin as he looks out on French and British nuclear weapons probably targeted at Germany and the persistent efforts of the Bush administration to keep American troops on German soil."

"Bastard!" Kathleen Orsini pitched the newspaper to the floor.

"Which one?" Steven Telford asked with a mocking smile. "Theirs or ours?" He put another log on the fire and shrugged. "What do you expect? Cantabile's been pretty imaginative in alibiing for the Kremlin."

"Well, nothing's wrong with Letnikov's timing. He made the announcement before Bush could bring it up at the UN. And he did it in time for the Sunday papers and talk shows. Who says the Russians don't enjoy freedom of the press? They do—ours."

Telford sat on the sofa beside her, put his arm over her shoulders, and looked into the fire.

"They've gotten good at PR," Telford admitted. "It's nothing like the good old days with Nikita banging his shoe at the UN. They were going to unveil the missiles in Germany whether we did it or not—part of their carrot-and-stick act to get us out of Europe and browbeat the French and British. We

made them rush it. Now we'll see if it does us any
good."

"Letnikov's making you the heavy, Mr. President." Harry Scott, the national security adviser,
passed two pages of editorial cartoons to a grim-
faced George Bush. "Not the deepest intellectual
content, but they show the spin the European papers are putting on this."

In the center of the page, a caricature of George
Bush stood in the prow of a rowboat in the manner
of Washington crossing the Delaware. La Mettrie,
the French president, and Britain's Prime Minister
Hill were pulling at the oars. The boat, headed to a
shore marked European Peace was filled with tanks,
jet fighters, and artillery pieces.

"How is it," the president asked, "that it's Ligachev who puts the missiles in Germany, but it's me
who ends up as the greatest threat to European
peace since Genghis Khan?"

Telford frowned. "Berlin Station reported this
morning that a German poll has Neuhaus picking up
a twenty-two-point jump in his approval rating."

Bush shook his head. His own standing in the
polls was rapidly eroding with events in Europe. And
along with that erosion, he was beginning to learn
just how debilitating political defections could be.

"We aren't getting much help from some of our
friends on the Hill," Bush commented dryly. "Advance press on Cantabile's hearings has it that he'll
be out to prove we've provoked the peace-loving
Mr. Letnikov, and that everything'll be all right if I
just get out of the way."

The president took off his glasses, massaged his

eyelids, and gave in to a yawn. "Long hours," he explained sheepishly. Then, looking at Telford, "You and your people did a good job on the missile thing, Steven. I want to send a letter out to them—a special thanks." Bush crossed his legs and resettled his glasses. "I guess the Agency's part in all this is mostly over. State and the Pentagon'll take over and try to figure out what a Germany with nukes will mean."

Telford raised a hand. "I'm not certain, Mr. President, that it is mostly over for us." He outlined Wolf's discovery and penetration of the MIMIR compartment, the one segment of the Ehren organization kept secret from the Soviets. "Our source came up with a list of the Germans who have a MIMIR clearance," Telford explained, "and our biography-analysis people have done a scrub on them."

"And?"

"And, Mr. President, the list consists of over six hundred scientists and engineers. We checked their technical specialties and the overall composition of the MIMIR list—to figure out just what they'd do as a group."

Bush's head was cocked attentively. Harry Scott leaned forward in his chair.

"MIMIR is a collection of the best missile people in Germany."

"Not surprising," Scott interjected, "when you look at the SS-22s."

"That's what we thought at first," Telford came back quickly, "but these aren't the kinds of people you'd call in to maintain something the Sovs gave you off the shelf. There are designers. Fabrication engineers. We spotted some in the MIMIR organization who helped Khadafi put together the long-range missiles we found in Libya and later in Syria."

"What does it mean, Steven?"

Telford shook his head. "We don't know, Mr. President. Not yet. But we need to find out. And the only way we can do that is to talk with some of the MIMIR people."

"And you'll do that—how?"

"We're working on something. Our guy"—Telford, even in the Oval Office would not use Brandt's name—"in Berlin is putting something together. . . ."

Twenty-five

Brandt followed the lieutenant, their footsteps echoing over the gray marble of the long corridor. The rough wool collar of the German uniform had rubbed Brandt's neck raw, and now his sweat was eating at the flesh. Brandt moved as if in a nightmare, his every sense telling him it was impossible that he could be inside BND headquarters.

He and Wolf had settled on their target, one Heinz Rentner. A missile engineer, Rentner was high enough on the MIMIR list to have good access to a wide range of information; low enough to be a plausible suspect as an accomplice to Manfred Weihs. Last night Wolf had had Rentner taken in. Today, making use of the uniform and credentials supplied by Wolf, Paul Brandt had become an officer in the service of German intelligence.

At the end of the corridor, the two stepped into a waiting elevator operated by a thin-faced private who had learned not to see officers. Anyway, these were small beer—a headquarters lieutenant and a nondescript lieutenant colonel. The car dropped with an angry jolt, its cable reels screeching.

The elevator door ground open onto another corridor, one faced with rough stone, its low ceiling strung with mesh-guarded bulbs whose feeble yel-

low light scarcely touched the moisture-slicked
floor. The universal signature of prisons assaulted
Brandt, a pervasive stench of urine and disinfectant.
Suddenly the lieutenant stopped before a rust-
rimmed metal door.

"In here, Colonel."

He swung the door open for Brandt.

"*Guten Tag*, Colonel. You are in time for the
afternoon performance." Rudolf Wolf spoke with
more than his accustomed arrogance. Brandt made
a hurried survey. He couldn't see the microphones
but assumed they were there. Wolf gestured to a
chair. The lieutenant saluted, spun on his heel, and
departed, closing the door behind him.

The interrogation room was a small dark cube
crowded with a table and three chairs, two of which
sat to one side of the table. The third chair, a massive
ugly thing of blotched teak, faced the table from a
distance of perhaps two feet. It was bolted to the
floor.

Wolf proceeded, talking to Brandt and to the
hidden microphones. "The procedure, Colonel
Bruckner, is as follows. Our suspect, Heinz Rentner,
is the prisoner of the Ministry of Defense. The ministry permits us to interrogate him here, but after
each interrogation he must be returned to their custody."

Brandt read the meaning in Wolf's eyes. Ehren
hadn't given Wolf a free hand. He nodded his understanding. Wolf pressed a buzzer on the table.

Rentner was pushed into the room with a sound
of chains. Stumbling disheveled and wide-eyed, he
was a manikin of fear. The guard, a squat, brutish
woman, jerked Rentner into the chair, roughly
twisting him back and forth as she snapped his man-

acles and ankle irons to eyebolts on the chair back and legs. Momentarily oblivious to Brandt and Wolf, she stood back, hands on hips, looking at the pinioned Rentner, her eyes glittering, a smile playing on her lips. Then with a curt nod to Wolf, she left.

The heavy metal door closed with a sound of finality, sending a shock wave of damp air across the small room. Rentner sagged in the chair, chin on his chest. A great flap of hair hung to one side of his head. Brandt realized Rentner used it to cover his baldness.

Wolf's voice cracked like a whip. "You are a spy, Rentner."

The engineer's head came up at that, his watery blue eyes dulled with pain and confusion.

"No," he croaked. "I am no . . ."

Brandt interrupted, using a quiet, reasonable tone. "Tell us, Rentner, how you came to know Manfred Weihs."

Rentner shook his head weakly in despair. "I know of no Manfred Weihs."

"Liar!" Wolf shouted.

"Perhaps, General, Herr Rentner knows Weihs by another name," suggested Brandt.

Rentner's eyes fastened with a small gleam of hope on Brandt, then turned to Wolf in fearful anticipation.

Reluctantly, slowly, Wolf considered this. "Perhaps." Then, with a glare at Rentner, Wolf opened a thick file before him. "Perhaps," Wolf repeated. "But there is the matter of his statement."

Brandt raised a cautionary hand. "Let me, General." Then Brandt turned to Rentner. "There are certain vague areas, Herr Rentner. Vague areas in your initial statement."

"There are penalties," Wolf menaced, "severe penalties, for concealing information from the state."

Rentner looked at Brandt, imploring deliverance.

Brandt, elbows on the table, leaned forward. "Herr Rentner. We must have a more complete accounting of certain parts of your life." Here Brandt rolled his eyes meaningfully toward Wolf. "You and I know, Herr Rentner, that there are facts of great importance that even innocent people can possess without realizing that importance. We need your assistance in developing some of those facts. Will you help us?"

Rentner's eyes darted to Wolf, then back to Brandt. He nodded.

For the next twenty minutes, Brandt and Wolf questioned the engineer, not about his work for Ehren, but of an earlier time, when Rentner had secretly worked on a missile project in Syria. Each question got a longer, more detailed answer. Rentner seemed to fill out as he gained confidence and sat straighter in the chair.

Brandt nudged Wolf with his knee. The German general searched into the file and came up with three typed sheets stapled together.

"Very satisfactory, Rentner," Wolf grudgingly allowed. He frowned toward Brandt as if in pique at having lost a wager. "Your cooperation has been noted." Rentner seemed relieved, almost relaxed. "And now, Rentner, the next area of concern—the details of your work in the MIMIR project."

Rentner tensed, now wary, guarded. "I've told your people everything I . . ."

Wolf lunged out of his chair, seemingly restrained only by the table from getting at Rentner. His face flushed in anger, the veins standing out on his neck.

"You've told us shit, Rentner." Wolf crushed the statement and flung the papers in Rentner's face. He slapped the tabletop for the buzzer.

Immediately the metal door crashed open. The female guard hurtled into the room with a bestial smile splitting her coarse, flat face.

"Take him," Wolf shouted. "Show this scum how to cooperate." As the woman began working enthusiastically on the manacles, Wolf snarled at the petrified Rentner, "She is going to instruct you, Herr Engineer, a very important lesson: everything you know belongs to the state. And, Herr Engineer," Wolf hissed in hatred and contempt, "in this place, in this room, I am the state."

Rentner doubled over in the chair, kept only by his manacled arms from pitching forward onto the floor. Deep cramps convulsed him. They put a de-layed emetic in his food, Brandt realized. Rentner was now retching onto his lap. The guard stood back, grimacing in disgust.

Brandt cleared his throat and addressed Wolf deferentially. "Herr Rentner obviously is not well, General. He may be more cooperative if . . ."

Wolf stared coldly at Brandt. "He has had every opportunity to—as you say, Colonel—'cooperate.' " Brandt said nothing but waited. Rentner's eyes were now desperate. Wolf sighed, then motioned to the guard. "We'll be outside in the corridor. Clean this—this spy up. Do it quickly. Then come get us."

Outside, Wolf lit a cigarette.

"You're playing it pretty goddamn rough," Brandt whispered.

Wolf took a deep drag from the cigarette and blew a rich blue cloud toward the ceiling. "We're not playing, Colonel Bruckner. We're not playing."

A few minutes later they returned to the room. Rentner had been sponged off, but the place still stank of vomit. Wolf ironed out Rentner's crumpled statement, running his hands over the paper on the table.

"Now, Rentner, let us begin. You describe your place in the MIMIR organization as 'engineer.' What, precisely, are your duties?"

Rentner, still hesitant, looked beseechingly to Brandt. Brandt gave a small nod.

"I was—um—in production."

"Production? Specifics, Rentner," Wolf demanded, his voice ominous.

"Propulsion integration."

"Integration?" Brandt asked softly.

"Yes." Rentner took on a professorial tone. "One cannot merely strap the Soviet guidance units and warheads to our propulsion stages. Integration is the engineering of a fit."

"What propul—?" Wolf started to ask.

Rentner thinks we know something we don't, Brandt thought. Quickly he interrupted Wolf. "Tell us, Herr Rentner—how did it begin?" Brandt urged.

"A number of us who'd worked on the Syrian project were gathered together and told of a new project. To adapt the propulsion units we'd used in the Middle East to a new missile."

"So long to make a mere modification?"

Rentner drew himself up. "It was not that easy, Colonel. Or simple. The Russian missile had but one stage. Ours required three."

Brandt played the good student. "Ah, yes.

Three stages. For greater range. And that, in turn, would require a guidance system with greater precision than for shorter ranges."

Rentner nodded in agreement.

Brandt smiled encouragingly. "And just what was the increase in range, Herr Rentner?"

Rentner didn't hesitate. If he lost the good will of this one, the other would surely kill him. "The original Russian weapon had a range just over nine hundred kilometers. Ours is eleven thousand."

With Brandt's encouragement the engineer told of clandestine test firings in Africa, of the design modifications required, and the final production runs of the advanced propulsion systems. After fifteen minutes Rentner began to get into such technical details as specific impulse and guidance updating.

"And this is the information you gave to the spy Weihs?" Wolf's voice, grating, harsh, came as a slap to Rentner. The engineer looked at Brandt, first with dismay, then with the bitterness of the betrayed.

Minutes later, in Wolf's office, the German waved aside Brandt's attack. "He could have told you no more," Wolf contended. "He might—might —know that the Russians were kept in the dark. But he couldn't have told you *why*. He is only an engineer. He does what he is told. He is a good witness to what he has done. Anything more, and you're asking for guesses."

Brandt frowned and admitted to himself that Wolf was right. Brandt sat looking at the patches of light on the carpet from the late-afternoon sun. Then he asked Wolf: "You must return Rentner to the Ministry of Defense for custody?" The German nodded. "Can we get him out again?"

Wolf considered this. "Yes. Perhaps so. Yes. I can make a case that follow-up interrogation is required. But only once can I do this. Beyond that, we need evidence of his collusion with Weihs."

Brandt again fell silent.

"You have some plan, Colonel Bruckner?" Wolf asked with irony.

"No. Not now." Brandt stood to leave. "Not yet. But soon, I think."

Twenty-six

As soon as Sam Rubel deciphered Paul Brandt's summary, he called Telford's office, only to be told that Telford was in a budget meeting. Sam swore under his breath and told Ruth Donohue to interrupt and to "get his ass down here in one big hurry." Sam then turned to deciphering the body of the long message. Before he was finished, Telford came into the communications center and paced until Rubel pushed back from the code machine. Without a word Sam handed over the clear text.

Telford scanned the five pages, then read them more carefully, unconsciously rocking back and forth on the edge of his chair. Finished, he handed the message back to Sam and sat lost in thought.

A somber Telford finally looked up. "It's never any good, is it, Sam?"

Without waiting for Sam's answer, Telford stood. "I'll have Donohue call the White House. What is it they say about bad news—it doesn't improve with age?"

It was at the kitchen table in the White House family quarters that George Bush gave it a name journalists later headlined. "It's a con job."

The president sat, hands jammed deeply in his

bathrobe pockets. "I imagine it got under way sometime after reunification. Neuhaus probably approached Letnikov. Offered him a sanctuary where he could organize a coup against Gorbachev. In the process Neuhaus persuaded Letnikov that the missiles could give Neuhaus a lever to demand the French and British get rid of their nuclear weapons. And, of course, Neuhaus added to the bargain that he'd get the American troops out of Germany. Then he and Letnikov would split Europe between themselves."

"Stalin and Hitler thought they could do it, too," Sam Rubel offered, caught up in the president's speculation. Telford heard the hard note in Rubel's voice and saw that Sam was running his fingers over the seared flesh on the back of his left hand.

The president nodded. "And Letnikov probably had it in mind that sooner or later he'd dump Neuhaus. But Neuhaus had his own plans. He'd take the nuclear warheads off the short-range missiles he got from the Russians and put them on his own missiles —missiles that can reach anywhere in the Soviet Union."

"Or the United States," Telford added.

"So Germany could have a hundred fifty, maybe two hundred, missiles," Scott, the national security adviser ventured. "It's not many, compared to the Soviets—or us."

"Enough, Harry," the president countered dryly. "Two hundred intercontinental nuclear missiles would guarantee that neither we nor the Soviets would try anything rash. Neuhaus would probably make them mobile. They could be easily hidden—Germany's only a little smaller than California."

"They'd also give Neuhaus breathing space to build more," Sam Rubel continued.

"So Dietrich Neuhaus wants a Fourth Reich." The president shuddered, recalling a long-ago war, then looked at the three faces around the oak table. "How do we stop him?"

Leaving the silent group, George Bush went to the Silex and returned with a pot of hot coffee and refilled the cups.

It was Telford who spoke first. "The missiles. We have to keep Neuhaus from getting them operational. Once he does, he'll be in the driver's seat."

"Can't we just tell the Russians?" asked Scott. "They could stop the second shipment of missiles and nukes from coming in from Plesetsk and they could . . ."

The president shook his head. "I don't know that Letnikov would believe us. We have no proof." Bush turned to Telford. "You're right, Steven. The missile scam is the key. We have to expose Neuhaus. And it has to be convincing."

Harry Scott asked quietly, "What do you have in mind, Mr. President?"

"Imagine a press conference." The president smiled, himself imagining the scene. "One at which I introduce two German defectors who tell their stories—the head of their counterintelligence and a missile scientist."

The president looked steadily at Telford. "That German general—Wolf. And the missile fellow. Get them out of Germany, Steven. I want them by day after tomorrow."

* * *

Four hours after leaving the president, Telford and Sam Rubel sat alone in the director's conference room. Around them were notepads, paper twists, and scattered pencils, the debris of the meeting to coordinate what Agency hands called "an extraction"—a secret mission to bring Wolf, Rentner, and Brandt out of Germany.

True to form, quarreling erupted over shares in the mission. Special-operations representatives of the military services each sought a leading role for their parent organizations. A florid Air Force general with a potbelly argued for an Entebbe-type pickup: a C-130 cargo aircraft would put down at an abandoned German airfield, disgorge a commando team for "local security," and fly off under F-16 fighter escort.

The general was interrupted by an intense admiral, who frantically waved his hand at Telford. Navy SEALs, the admiral offered, would infiltrate swimmers into Germany along the Baltic Sea coast. They would meet Brandt's people and carry them via rubber boat to a small sub in Mecklenburg Bay.

Telford then looked down the table to the Army representative, a colonel whose uniform was starkly bare of the fruit salad of campaign ribbons worn by his colleagues. A spare, grizzled man with close-cropped hair, the colonel wore only the blue-and-silver Combat Infantryman's Badge and the parachutist's wings of the American and Vietnamese armies, quiet statements of proficiency in a violent profession.

Telford had recognized the colonel, who went to the wall map. "Your people get out of Berlin. Have them make for the Elbe River." He swept a hand westward across the map. "We'll pick them up

by helicopter and bring them into France." And
with that the colonel sat down.

The simplicity of the proposal and the colonel's
assurance caused a momentary hush. Then came the
haggling from the Air Force and Navy. The general
and the admiral had to bring *something* back for
their services—some part in the operation. Couldn't
the Navy furnish the pilots for the Army helicopters,
asked the admiral. There ought to be fighter cover
flown by the Air Force, protested the general.

Telford had listened, then rapped them into silence. "This is how it's going to be," he began, and
talked quietly for a few minutes, then adjourned the
meeting.

Sam Rubel regarded Telford with a glint of admiration. "You know, you avoided a disaster here."
He gestured at the now-empty room, a deserted
battlefield. "If you hadn't stopped it, each of those
guys would have gone back to the Pentagon with a
piece of the action. That kind of crap gave us the
Desert One mess when we tried to rescue the hostages in Iran. And it gummed up Grenada, too."

Telford, drawing on his relationship with the
president, had ended the interservice squabbling.
The detailed planning and running of the operation,
he declared, would take place inside Germany, and
the only people involved would be those from Berlin
Station and the army's top-secret European Special
Operations Group, people who were most familiar
with the problems to be faced. There would be no
micromanaging by hordes of kibitzers thousands of
miles away.

Telford, secretly pleased, shrugged modestly.
"When you cable Berlin to set up the operations

center, ask Frances Watkins to find me a place to stay."

Sam's eyes widened. "You going over?" Sam was now scribbling furiously.

"Yes. Might as well be where it's going to happen."

"You can be out of here in an hour." He was already thinking of the logistics required for the dash across the Atlantic. He looked up from his notes. "Ah, Steven. Isn't Kathleen . . ."

Telford smiled. "Yeah. She's there, too. Been there a week." A week, and it seems like months, Telford thought. He wondered how much his missing her had to do with his decision to go to Germany, then gave up, deciding he'd have gone anyway; but her being there did make the prospect more attractive.

At the doorway to his office, Telford stopped. "By the way, who was that fellow from Defense Intelligence Agency?"

Sam shook his head, puzzled.

"The one," Telford explained, "who kept asking all the self-serving questions. Seemed more concerned about Congress than the mission. Pompous fellow. Silver hair, red face."

Sam laughed derisively. "Oh. That's Collins. A DIA basket case. If he isn't covering his own ass, he's figuring out how to stick it up someone else's. An empty suit, nobody to worry about."

"No. She's not here." The charwoman from the Metropol leaned forward, her head nearly against the one-way glass. Lothar Kelch sat at her side. They looked onto a small floodlit stage on which seven women stood in various states of anger, fear, and self-consciousness.

The missing woman nagged at Kelch. She had been with Weihs before the old woman had seen them in flight down the stairwell. Although it was probably a straightforward case of Weihs's contact killing him, Kelch wanted to know what Weihs's companion had seen.

"I'm tired, Inspector."

"Patience. There are just two more groups."

The old woman grunted. "Two more *tonight*, you mean."

Kelch smiled. He and the old woman had gotten along well. At the third session of lineups, she'd brought a small battered cardboard box of marzipan. The two of them shared the sweet confections over cups of coffee Kelch brewed on a burner in his office. "I can't bring them all in at one time. Our lonely businessmen would have no one to help them pass the cold nights."

The old woman gave an earthy laugh. "I told you she wasn't a nice girl."

Kelch nodded. He'd checked Weihs's background. No women friends of long standing, and nothing currently going on. And so he'd started the roundup of prostitutes. The next group was coming on the stage. Kelch was eyeing a particularly provocative redhead when the old woman clutched his arm.

"There. The third one from the left." The old woman pointed to a thin, hard-looking blond. Through the loudspeaker Kelch had the matron turn the woman this way, then that.

The old woman nodded emphatically. "It's her. I'm certain."

* * *

The two huddled into their heavy coats and watched a stiff north wind beat the mud gray Potomac into dirty whitecaps. High water had littered the sidewalk with trash, leaves, and other river leavings. On the roadway behind them, an occasional car crept by; otherwise West Potomac Park was empty and still.

"I don't see why we had to come here," Constance Higby complained.

"To talk, damn it," Joseph Cantabile barked.

Constance came back sharply. "We could have talked someplace warmer, Joe, and don't get snotty with me."

Cantabile gritted his teeth. "Goddamn it, Constance, this is important, and it's something I'm not going to talk about inside."

She looked at him in waspish silence.

"A man came to my office this morning. Collins. Defense Intelligence Agency. An egotistical shit. Did nothing the first ten minutes but give me a bunch of crap about how he thought intelligence ought to work more closely with Congress. Dumb fuck used 'well-oiled team' every other sentence."

Constance listened with patience to Cantabile's preamble. He's having trouble getting to the point, she was thinking, and so nearly missed it when Cantabile's voice dropped to a whisper.

". . . Collins claims the Agency's getting ready to run a covert operation. One the president hopes will break Letnikov's relations with Neuhaus."

Searching for the implications of Cantabile's revelation, Constance frowned in concentration.

"Why did this man come to you? Are you certain it's not a trap of some sort?"

Cantabile shook his head. "No. He did it to suck up to me. He's that sort. If they were setting me up, they wouldn't use such a turkey."

"What is it, then?"

"What's what?"

Constance took on her "you dumb shit" look. "What could Bush possibly do that would turn things around in Germany?"

"I don't know," Cantabile shrugged. "Collins has been cut out of the high-level stuff. He only knows that it depends on some operation to get some people out of Germany."

"Did he tell you the details?"

"Yes. Excruciating detail. I thought he'd never quit."

Constance was silent for long moments, then: "Well, Joe. This brings you to the brink, doesn't it?"

Cantabile nodded morosely. "If there's no treaty, if there's no troop pullout, I won't be moving into the White House."

Across the Potomac came the roar of a jet taking off from National Airport. Cantabile tracked the plane until it disappeared into the overcast.

"It can still happen." Constance slipped her arm around his, moving closer to him.

"How do you mean?"

"You could warn Letnikov."

Cantabile had been thinking the same thing. He burned with the confused shame of one caught in some darkly intimate forbidden act.

Unnoticing, Constance continued. "You could talk with Vladimir . . ."

Cantabile sought shelter in anger. "Talk with

Vladimir," he mimicked Constance. "Maybe I should climb into bed with him, too. Does he swing both ways? You ought to know."

Constance's eyes grew wide with surprise, then narrowed again. "Why the accusations, Joe? You don't own me."

"It's not an accusation, Constance." His anger left him as suddenly as it had flared. "No accusations. Call it an accounting. A coming to terms with you. I knew about Vladimir. I also know you told him about that spy-plane mission."

"Does it bother you?"

Constance watched him consider this. He suddenly seems so old, she thought.

Finally Cantabile spoke: "No, that's what's frightening—none of it bothers me." He looked at her sadly. "It would have once, you know." It was suddenly important to him—very important—that she believe him. No, that wasn't right. It was important that he believe himself.

She was silent, and he saw a flat hardness about her eyes.

He turned again to the river, toward Alexandria and around the bend, Mount Vernon. "Cantabile's law of politics: ambition drives out integrity and honor. Now all that's left to me is the ambition. That's why it doesn't bother me to share your cunt or my country's secrets with our Russian friend Vladimir."

She spun him around to face her. Her lips curled in fury, and she spat her words at him. "Cut the melodrama, Joe. It's too goddamn late to be playing the raped virgin."

Her face softened, and she took another tack. "Don't forget—those bastards in the White House aren't goody-two-shoes. They're playing hardball with this, too." Her voice became anxious, urging. "Can't you see, Joe? The Republicans know you're their major competition next year. They're out to get you. That's what's behind this attempt to sabotage the German treaty. They know what it'll do to you."

Incapable of sustained self-reproach, Cantabile once again escaped into the comfortable world of political competition, a world of games for the grown; an exciting world of move and countermove, of jockeying for edges and advantages. As he did, a small smile of cunning flickered at the corners of his mouth.

Seeing this, Constance pressed on, bringing her face closer to him. "Think of how it could be," she urged. "Berlin—worldwide television. You and Letnikov." Her eyes glittered. "A new order in Europe! And the history books will show that it was Joseph Cantabile who made it happen."

Cantabile's smile was now wider, and he scarcely heard her. The Potomac was replaced by a packed Potsdamerplatz, and he looked out on tens of thousands of worshiping faces from the same place where Jack Kennedy had declared that he, too, was a Berliner.

And the crowds cheered. And cheered.

Brandt called her from a pay booth on the Ku'damm. Their meeting had been guarded—both were self-consciously formal. They had walked through the Tiergarten for the better part of an hour, Brandt talking, Elise listening carefully, interrupting only occasionally to ask a question.

Afterwards he'd been the one to suggest the Corsican's place, and to his surprise she took his arm, her hand nestling in the bend of his elbow. The Corsican had greeted them, remembering their table, and Brandt filled the first part of the meal with talk of banking and German politics. The restaurant had been their favorite—a small, smoky place, paneled in dark oak, where regulars sopped up the thick, peppery vegetable soup with heavy crusts of black bread.

The plates cleared, Elise looked at him with frank, gray eyes. "There's something I want you to know, Paul. I love you."

Brandt was perplexed, confused. "Then why did you leave?"

Elise tipped her wineglass, bringing the raw Algerian wine just to the edge. "I could have stayed if I hadn't come to love you. But love is demanding, don't you see?"

"You should have told me. Earlier."

Faintly, over the sounds of the restaurant, came bits of Piaf's "Milord." It was a raucous song of a time thirty years before, when, late at night, he and Telford would stop here before going home.

She looked at him sadly. "It wasn't a matter of me telling you. If the saying of the words was all, I would have told you long ago."

"Then what is it?" he asked, not wanting to hear, because the hearing of it would bring a finality he wanted to avoid.

"It would make no difference. Me telling you. Whether you knew or not."

"I still don't understand."

"I came to love you in spite of myself—in spite of us. We knew from the start what there was between us; that we couldn't give ourselves to each other. Not completely."

Brandt began to voice a protest.

Elise reached across the table and put her hand over his. "Don't, Paul. Don't. Answer me this. Can you tell me you love me? Can you tell me that we can leave here—leave Berlin—never to return? That we can leave tomorrow? That we could have a life together?" She tilted her head, waiting for him.

Brandt looked at her, thinking about how it could have been had they met thirty years ago. He was now—what?—fifty-two. He'd spent those years —*his* years—as if somewhere in Langley someone would finally tote up things and decide enough was enough. He'd been foolish, of course. They'd run him until he dropped. There was always something more. When would it be his turn?

He paid. They gathered their coats and stepped out into the night. The cold mist muffled the neon signs and robbed her face of color. She walked to the cab at curbside.

Brandt touched her elbow, and she turned toward him before getting in the cab. "I do love you, Elise. I can tell you that."

She touched his cheek, then kissed him lightly. "But you are not free, are you?" She lifted a hand in a gesture of helplessness.

Not wanting her to answer, Brandt took her by the shoulders, his fingers pressing into her. "This one thing. When it's done, will you be here?"

She kissed him again, again lightly. Twisting slightly to be free of him, she stepped back to enter the cab. As she got in, she hesitated, facing him. He could see her tears. "I don't know, Paul. I don't know."

* * *

Vladimir Krotov made a show of studying his notes. They weren't needed, but they were a useful stage prop. He looked up to Joseph Cantabile, who was well into his fifth gin.

"So all we actually know is that this operation will take place after dark tomorrow; that American helicopters will pick up three persons and take them into France. Are you certain there's not more? Something to help us? Germany's a large country. Isn't there any indication . . ."

"No, damn it," cursed Cantabile in a slurring mumble. His eyes were those of a wild man—darting, desperate, bloodshot eyes. "You've gotten all I have."

The Russian folded the elegant leather notebook. He looked at the drunken senator with contempt. Time for repairs, he thought. He began with a soft, earnest voice. "Let us be clear about this, Joseph. We are in a partnership. A partnership to bring about a less dangerous world. In any partnership each of us contributes in our own way." He slipped the notebook into his breast pocket. "You have done your part. Now we will do ours."

Seeing Cantabile out, Krotov stood quietly for a moment after closing the door. He would return to the embassy, encipher his report in the security of the *rezidentura,* and get it off to the Aquarium by satellite.

Pale afternoon light came through the apartment windows. On the glass coffee table, the ice in Cantabile's drink had melted. The American poet— what was his name?—Dickey? Yes, Dickey. Dickey had written a good line—one that applied to Joseph

Cantabile. Something about "we have all been in rooms we cannot die in."

Krotov smiled as he heard the technicians in the adjacent apartment noisily rewinding the video recorders.

Twenty-seven

The U.S. Army's 227th Attack Regiment took up much of the former Luftwaffe base at Hanau. The way the strategists originally planned it, the 227th's armed helicopters were to have blunted the massive tank attack that never came across the old East German border only sixty miles away.

To be ready, the 227th flew day and night, through years of the worst weather the continent could muster. Their proficiency was one of the last strands of deterrence that for decades kept the Soviet tanks from grinding through the Fulda Gap. Although destined to return soon to America, the regiment's round-the-clock flying still served another purpose. It masked a helicopter detachment of the European Special Operations Group, a detachment whose whispered name was Task Force Viper.

Viper was commanded by Lieutenant Colonel Jack Wilhelm, a great bear of a man who stood by a large map, pointer nearly swallowed in a massive hand. Wilhelm swatted the pointer against the map.

"This is Operation Skyhook. We'll go in with two OH-58 Deltas."

"Two? Just two helicopters?"

Challenged, Wilhelm stood for a moment, looking at Steven Telford. "Two," came the unequivocal response. "If two won't make it, twenty wouldn't, either." He paused a moment for emphasis. "I'll be flying the lead." His eyes locked with Telford. I'm a no-nonsense son of a bitch, the eyes said. It's important that you know that.

Tension built between the two men. Wilhelm rocked slightly. Once back, then forward again. From somewhere above the underground bunker came the faint sound of a helicopter turbine running up.

Finally Telford gave a nod and a friendly smile. "Go on, Colonel. I'm with you."

Wilhelm returned the smile, and there was a relief signaled by small noises—a cough, a chair scraping the concrete floor. "As Ms. Watkins explained," Wilhelm motioned to Frances, sitting next to Telford, "we analyzed a number of possible pickup zones."

Telford knew that Brandt, after consulting with Wolf, had transmitted to Berlin Station the coordinates of isolated areas they could reach from Berlin. Wilhelm, working with Frances, had chosen those most easily reached by his helicopters.

"This is the best." The pointer tapped an oval traced in black marking pencil on a clear plastic overlay.

Seventy miles from Berlin, perhaps much more, Telford estimated, driving the dark back roads of the Altmark region. Once Brandt and Wolf got the scientist into a car, there would be no turning back. They had to get out of Germany.

"What's the backup?" He looked first at Frances Watkins, then at Wilhelm.

Frances seemed uncomprehending. Wilhelm muttered something about a standby helicopter team.

"No. I mean an alternative way out. If the helicopter extraction doesn't work at all. If you can't get into any of those pickup zones. Or they can't get to them."

Frances Watkins and Wilhelm exchanged glances. Frances broke the silence. "As far as our getting them out of Germany, Steven, this is it. If this doesn't work, they're on their own."

Yegor Letnikov read the GRU report from Washington. The Russian leader's face was blank, his eyes unblinking. Finally Letnikov put the paper aside.

"What do you make of this, Comrade Chernov?" he asked, intently watching the GRU chief's face.

Chernov got the worried, intense look of a dim student wrestling with a trick question. "Make of it? I . . . ah . . . that is . . ." he blundered, Letnikov's stony expression panicking him. "Why . . . it . . . it must be another American provocation. They are getting . . . getting panicky." Chernov clung to the theme onto which he'd stumbled. "Yes, they are attempting to provoke us."

Letnikov's eyes narrowed. "What of Cantabile's claim that Bush hopes this operation will disrupt our relations with Germany?"

Settled now, Chernov gave a sneer of contempt. "We have them. It is the hope of a desperate man."

Letnikov scrutinized Chernov's face for a hint of duplicity, for a glint of treasonous knowledge. He saw nothing. Yet his unease persisted. Were they—the great unknown "they"—becoming uneasy about his relations with Germany?

There had been nothing direct, of course. Just small things. There seemed to be more emphasis in recent television programming on German atrocities during the Great Patriotic War. And then there had been the funeral of Marshal Leonov. The old man had been a forgotten vegetable in a Black Sea sanatorium for the past fifteen years. Yet at his funeral ceremony, every speech scored the treachery of Adolf Hitler and Leonov's heroism in stopping the German panzers at the gates of Moscow. Small things, indeed. But often they were the only warnings one had.

"What? What was it, Comrade Chernov?"

"I asked about the report. Do you want me to notify the general staff?"

Letnikov thought for a moment. Though stupid, Chernov was right. Bush could do nothing to stop the treaty or the departure of American troops. No sense giving his hidden opponents grist for their mills.

"No, Comrade Chernov. This is a minor thing. Our military has no need for this information, and I do not wish to risk compromising our good friend Senator Cantabile."

Paul Brandt inspected the radio one last time, slipped it into the false compartment of the large leather briefcase, then put on the heavy overcoat that concealed his uniform. At the door he took a look around the apartment, then went out into the dark hallway.

Twenty minutes later he flashed his false credentials and drove into the basement garage at BND headquarters on Normannenstrasse.

Rudolf Wolf stood at the window, watching Berlin's lights come on. He turned as his secretary shut the door behind Brandt. The German's face was pinched and tight.

"Taking a last look at Berlin." He motioned to the lights below.

"It had to come sometime."

"Oh?" Wolf challenged.

"We can't last forever at this, you and I. Sooner or later we all have to cut and run. It's the knowing when that's important."

Wolf stood still. His face softened, and he nodded slightly. Then, perhaps in embarrassment, he coughed, straightened his tunic with a jerk, and rapped an order into the intercom.

"They gave you no trouble?" Brandt asked.

"No. As long as the proper papers were signed, of course. There are certain advantages to living in a disciplined society."

"Especially if one is at the top."

Wolf ignored the jibe and motioned to the intercom. "They're bringing him up now from the holding cell."

A cricket chirping caught Wolf's attention. He frowned and picked up his telephone. The frown deepened into a scowl as he listened. "Who?" he asked. Then, "No, no. It is not possible today. A messenger will deliver them tomorrow."

He hung up, obviously shaken. "That was our external liaison office," he gasped. "The Ministry of the Interior just called them. It seems that one of their investigators desires photographs of all BND officers stationed in Berlin. Because of the sensitivity, external liaison called me. The investigator, of course, is our good friend Kelch."

Fifteen minutes later they were in the garage. Rentner had been brought in by two guards whom Wolf had dismissed. Handcuffed, frightened, and still bruised from his beatings, the missile scientist had meekly accompanied Wolf and Brandt to the small elevator in Wolf's outer office.

The car was a glossy black Mercedes. As Brandt opened the heavy back door for Rentner, he saw the thick greenish tint of the glass. "Armored?"

Wolf nodded. "The state is concerned for the well-being of its servants. Just a moment." Wolf reached into his tunic and came out with a leather kit, which he put on the roof of the car. From it he withdrew a hypodermic needle.

"Hold him," Wolf motioned to Rentner.

For the first time the scientist showed alarm. Brandt hooked one arm around Rentner's neck and with his free hand grabbed the man's manacled wrists while immobilizing him against the car.

"It will be an uneventful ride, Herr Rentner. You may as well catch up on your sleep." Wolf plunged the needle through Rentner's trouser leg into his thigh. There was a momentary stiffening; then Rentner went limp.

"It ought to be good for several hours," Wolf noted with satisfaction. "There's no sense in having him able to cause us trouble."

Brandt managed the unconscious Rentner into the rear of the car, then turned on Wolf. "Listen, damn it. We didn't talk about that little touch. You don't know what that stuff can do to him." He motioned to the hypodermic still in Wolf's hand.

Wolf jerked his head to the car. "There's no time to discuss medical malpractice. You drive. I'll mind our patient."

Less than ten minutes after Wolf and Brandt left BND headquarters, Lothar Kelch stood in Felix Ehren's office.

"Why, Inspector Kelch, do you insist on this?" Ehren waved a document.

"Because I have reason to believe that Rudolf Wolf may be implicated in the killing of Manfred Weihs." There was a pause as Kelch reconsidered. "No, Herr Ehren. Because I have reason to believe that Wolf *is* implicated in the killing."

Ehren looked at the document again. An extraordinary request for the immediate arrest of a deputy minister of the BND. It had been brought by dispatch rider to Neuhaus's offices, where the duty officer had at once referred it to Ehren. Ehren, on reading it, had then summoned Kelch.

The stocky German motioned to Kelch. "Sit, Inspector. And talk."

Ehren listened, his dark brown eyes never leaving Kelch's face. For his part Kelch took Ehren over the high points of the investigation—the charwoman and her identification of the prostitute; the grilling of the thin, attractive blond, and her description of the men she'd seen when Weihs opened the hotel-room door.

"And this woman—this prostitute—identified Rudolf Wolf?"

Kelch nodded. "Yes. From a photograph. I had trouble getting it, you see. . . ."

"And the other man? The one that chased her and Weihs? She identified him?"

Kelch, still absorbed in the difficulty of getting the BND photographs, was slow to answer. Finally, "No—no, she couldn't. We have a composite drawing she agreed was a good likeness. . . ."

Ehren studied the man before him, sorting through the implications of what he'd been told. Wolf had been in on the killing from the start. He then used Weihs's murder to fasten onto Rentner, who was at this moment in Wolf's hands. And this third man, Weihs's killer. Ehren's breathing stopped as he added the last piece—the report from Moscow GRU that the Americans would attempt tonight to cross the border to pick up three persons and spirit them out of Germany.

The GRU source said the Americans hoped to stop the treaty. Now he knew how they would do it! And for a split second, Felix Ehren reveled in his sole possession of this knowledge, enjoying the tumultuous feeling of vast power it gave him. Then, as quickly, Ehren was sobered by the predicament in which he and the unwitting Dietrich Neuhaus now found themselves.

He tossed the warrant aside. "We don't need this. We shall close on Wolf like this." He clapped his hands together.

Kelch pulled a worried face. "I'm afraid it won't be as easy as that, Herr Ehren. In the search for the photographs—the BND photographs—one of my assistants called directly to BND headquarters. That was just over an hour ago. I've just checked—Wolf's gone, and the prisoner Rentner with him."

* * *

Paul Brandt's first message came through. He and Wolf were at the Schönefelderkreuz, the interchange on the outskirts of Berlin, where they would then take the autobahn west toward Helmstedt. An operations officer had made a blue mark at the highway junction, beside it writing the time in neat, precise figures. Wilhelm glanced at the large digital clock over the map board, then gestured to Telford, jerking a thumb toward the ceiling.

The two men left the underground bunker and walked in the semidarkness toward a low arched combat hangar. A damp breeze carried the oil smell of aviation fuel and the metal sounds of men working on machines. For a moment neither spoke.

Wilhelm stopped and faced Telford. "The fellow on the radio. I saw your face when he called in. He means something to you, doesn't he? Something special."

Telford nodded. "He saved my life once. I would have been dead thirty years ago."

Telford made as if to continue walking, but Wilhelm stood rooted. "I want to know about this," Wilhelm insisted. "How important it is." When Wilhelm saw Telford hesitate, the big man pointed to the hangar and the dark figures standing by their helicopters. "They're young. None of them would ask you. They'd go out there—just on your say-so."

"And that's not good enough for you?" It was only faintly a question.

Wilhelm studied the ground, where he was scuffing a boot toe into the earth, then looked up at Telford. "It would have been once. But I've seen it before. The politicians send us out to die for something that's a big fucking deal, and then after it's over, the big fucking deal isn't so big anymore, and all that's left is a stack of full body bags."

Wilhelm remembered the tropical heat and heard the awful sounds of the dying. "It doesn't so much matter about me. But if I'm going to tell them that getting your people out is something they might have to die for, I want to know it's worth it.

"So tell me, Mr. DCI." Wilhelm reached out with one large hand, wrapping it around Telford's biceps. "Is this worth it?"

Telford heard scraps of grab-ass laughter from Wilhelm's crews. It was the jumpy banter of nervous kids before a championship game. The pressure on his arm was strong and reassuring, but at the same time ominous.

He looked for a long time into Wilhelm's eyes. He thought of mobs and a burning automobile in Berlin, of Ira Crawford's photographs of the nuclear missiles. He remembered other photographs, older ones of walking skeletons and gas chambers.

"Yes, Jack," he said quietly. "It's worth it."

Ten minutes later the Viper flight of two OH-58Ds headed northeast, skimming the countryside to avoid German radars.

At the same time, seventy miles to the southwest, an ungainly single-seat jet managed a kitelike takeoff from Ramstein Air Force base. The TR-1 clawed for altitude and set out on a northerly course that would parallel the border of France and Germany.

And at headquarters, Fourth Allied Tactical Air Force, the American commander called for a no-notice air-defense exercise. As squawking Klaxons scrambled interceptor crews, the American commander made certain that a NATO exercise notification was properly transmitted to the Soviet military liaison mission offices in Frankfurt.

"What time is it?"

Paul Brandt glanced at the dashboard clock. "Nineteen-fifty. About an hour to Burg."

The big Mercedes was an E-30, the autobahn connecting Berlin to Helmstedt. It was now quite dark, and the traffic was sparse. Brandt noted that most of the oncoming lights were those of heavy trucks. The plan was to take the autobahn as far as Burg, then head north along farm roads to one of the rendezvous points on the east bank of the Elbe.

"I am worried about that Kelch fellow." Wolf's voice came from the back of the car, disembodied, sepulchral.

"We'll be in France before he gets moving."

"But you don't know him. He's one of those ferretlike people who only cares about getting the goods on someone. Sleep, food—nothing matters except sorting through others' dirty laundry. And the dirtier, the better."

Brandt checked the rear- and side-view mirrors again.

"You may be right, Herr Generalleutenant." Brandt thrust a thumb over his shoulder.

Wolf muttered a curse. The darkness behind the car was pierced by a powerful white beam. On either side of the glare were two flashing blue lights.

Brandt tapped the brake, and the big car began to slow.

"What are you doing that for?"

"If we speed up, he can stay back there behind us. I want him alongside."

The motorcycle was gaining. Brandt could see light glinting on the helmet of the dark rider. He began to edge the Mercedes toward the wide shoulder of the autobahn. The motorcycle was at Brandt's left rear fender. Brandt's hands were suddenly slippery on the steering wheel. Looking over, Brandt saw the rider, perhaps ten feet away, now parallel to the front window. The rider was motioning to the roadside.

Jamming his foot on the accelerator, Brandt pulled the wheel to the left. Tires screeched and shock absorbers protested. Over his left shoulder Brandt saw the motorcyclist slow and veer, struggling to keep balance. The light wobbled, lay over, then righted itself.

"You missed him!" Wolf's voice carried an edge of recrimination.

Brandt heard splattering noises and felt the car shudder ever so slightly.

"He's shooting at us!" cried Wolf.

The rear window was pocked by two bullets that had flattened against the armored glass. If the Mercedes was properly done up, Brandt thought, the gas tank was probably shielded by something like Kevlar, and the tires could run flat for at least a hundred miles.

"Get the radio on." Brandt gave Wolf the main and alternate frequencies for the single-sideband transceiver. The speedometer was registering one hundred eighty—almost one hundred ten miles an hour. Another splattering sound, and a third crater appeared on the rear window.

Wolf was now cursing steadily. Brandt heard the metallic sound of the German's pistol chambering a round and felt a sudden draft on his neck. "Damn it, Rudolf. Don't shoot!"

"But . . ."

"All you'll do is scare him off. I need him close."

The motorcycle was centered in the rearview mirror. About fifty feet back Brandt estimated. The autobahn ahead was straight and deserted, glistening with a light slick of rain.

"Hold on," Brandt ordered as he simultaneously slammed the brakes and wrenched the steering wheel hard left.

The massive Mercedes immediately went into a stomach-twisting skid. Wolf shouted in surprise. Maps, a flashlight, and other car junk flew crazily about. Brandt felt the car begin a lurching roll to his right. Just as the left front tire was breaking contact with the pavement, he tapped the accelerator and straightened the steering wheel. The Mercedes was now sliding sideways down the highway at eighty miles an hour in what Brandt's instructor at the Farm would call a rather sloppy four-wheel drift.

The motorcyclist, his speed unchecked, found himself racing into the Mercedes, suddenly a wall of steel across the highway in front of him. He knew it would do no good to brake. Instead he swerved toward the rear of the car, hoping to pass behind it. He begged the rear of the car to swing slower—pleading for the few critical feet of open space he needed. He gunned the big cycle and began a small smile of triumph as his front wheel cleared the Mercedes's left rear bumper.

The smile was still on his lips as the right corner of the car came around and caught his left leg. With incredible force the motorcycle spun to the left, crashing into the pavement, its fuel immediately catching fire. The rider, as yet uninjured, flew forward over the handlebars. Two seconds later his neck was the first to go, snapping with the impact of hitting the concrete at almost one hundred miles an hour. After that the shattered limbs and ruptured organs didn't matter.

Brandt turned into the skid and accelerated, straightening out the car. Wolf leaned forward, excited. "Good driving!" He clapped Brandt on the shoulder. In his mirror Brandt saw a crumpled doll lying in the glare of the burning motorcycle and recoiled from the German's hand.

Sixty thousand feet above Norway, the TR-1 spy plane found the coded beacon of Paul Brandt's radio. The TR-1's northerly course, combined with its speed and altitude, insured that the computer was able to triangulate Brandt's location with a high degree of precision. As it did so, the information was instantaneously encrypted and down-linked to tightly guarded command posts and, of course, to the underground operations center where Steven Telford watched Brandt's progress.

The operations officer told Steven Telford what he already knew—that something had gone wrong. "Sir, they've left the autobahn and they're heading north." The young woman marked the change on the map overlay.

"They've run into something," whispered Frances Watkins.

Telford sat transfixed, staring at the latest blue arrow, now pointed straight to the medieval city of Brandenburg.

Twenty-eight

Wolf insisted on the Brandenburg exit, though Brandt had wanted to take a smaller road even if it meant a few more minutes' exposure on the autobahn. The road to Brandenburg was too well traveled for Brandt's liking. German police were efficient, and even now, he guessed, roadblocks would be going up in Brandenburg, five miles ahead.

The headlights cut a tunnel through the pitch black countryside. Only occasionally could Brandt make out hints of hedges and the borders of plowed fields along the roadside. Beside him Wolf was peering intently into the night ahead, his face ghostly in the dashboard lights.

"There," the German snapped. "Ahead on the left. That road. Take it."

Brandt braked violently, barely managing to make the turn. The big car lurched and bounced on the rough farm road. "What the hell . . ."

"Slow down and dim your lights! There will be a large shed—there! On the right. Turn off your lights and pull around back."

Brandt stopped the car but left the engine running. His hand closed around the cold metal of the pistol he'd kept on the seat beside him, and he turned to face Wolf. "An explanation. And make it goddamn fast."

Wolf gave a brittle laugh. "Basic tradecraft, my American friend. You were taught as I—a wise man makes contingency plans in this line of work. This car served us well." He motioned to the shed. "But from here, we need alternate transportation."

Brandt hesitated, then switched off the engine. "Where—what is this?"

"A training camp." Wolf got out of the car. "My office has a person here. He has made the arrangements and seen to security."

The German made for the large shed and was at the door when Brandt caught up with him. "What about Rentner?"

Wolf looked at his watch. "Another injection ought to keep him . . ."

A dazzling beam blinded the two men.

"Stand still, the both of you."

Freezing, Brandt could make out a dark figure behind the large battery lantern.

"Schumann? Is that you?" asked Wolf.

"Ja, Herr Generalleutenant."

"The meaning of this, Schumann—what is the meaning of this?" Wolf demanded, his voice stiff with authority.

"I have received"—Schumann, momentarily shaken, fumbled for an answer—"there are orders. Recent orders . . ." He trailed off.

It's no longer a police matter, Brandt thought. The BND's gotten into this, too.

Wolf started toward the light. "Schumann, I insist that you . . ."

The lantern wavered ever so slightly as Schumann cocked his pistol. The metal sound carried in the night. Wolf continued walking.

"Stop, General. Stop there."

Schumann did not threaten. And that made Wolf stop.

At that moment, just behind Schumann, Rentner stirred in the car, groaning loudly. When the lantern swung reflexively, Brandt made a sprinting dive, aiming to the left of the lantern.

His momentum crushed Schumann against the Mercedes. He felt the German bringing the pistol around. Desperately Brandt sought the man's arm. Schumann's mouth was against Brandt's face, and Brandt could smell a hot, sour breath of cabbage and wurst. Schumann twisted against Brandt, trying to sink his teeth into Brandt's jaw, while Brandt clawed blindly at the bulge of Shumann's neck, searching for the carotid artery.

An electric charge exploded within Brandt, sending a massive wave of pain rolling upward, paralyzing him with its sheer intensity. Losing his grip on Schumann, Brandt crumpled to the ground. He looked up into the muzzle of Schumann's pistol.

Flame split the night, and crashing sound waves beat against Brandt's chest. The lantern dropped, smashing on the ground.

Wolf stood over the two figures, his pistol resting on his thigh.

"It is the trouble of age," he rasped, breathing hard. "Our balls lose their usefulness and retain their vulnerability." He holstered his pistol and extended a hand to Brandt.

Brandt ignored Wolf and struggled painfully to his feet. Unsteady, he gathered himself as Wolf checked Schumann's body. Having played well his small part, Rentner had slipped back into unconsciousness, curled up on the car's backseat.

Felix Ehren knew the lower ranks called the operations room *die Börse*. And it did resemble a stock exchange. The small circular floor was surrounded by terraced rows of desks and communications stations, each of these with a clear view of the floor and various status displays.

Tonight Dietrich Neuhaus presided from a large black leather armchair in the center of the floor. Before him colored pushpins studded a map of the area approximately fifty miles north and south of the Helmstedt autobahn. Felix Ehren sat beside Neuhaus in a straight wood chair next to a bank of telephones.

"The green pins show their path," explained Ehren. "The first is where the motorcyclist came upon them, here, on the autobahn near the Lehnin exit. He was killed shortly after reporting in."

"And the second?" Neuhaus asked.

"Route one-oh-two to Brandenburg. Yesterday Wolf ordered a vehicle to be held in readiness at a BND training camp."

"And they did it?" an incredulous Neuhaus asked.

"He was not under suspicion at the time. Orders from deputy ministers aren't questioned," Ehren commented dryly.

"But didn't we have people waiting for them?"

"They arrived too late. Wolf and his companion killed one man who apparently tried to stop them. They left Wolf's car and got away minutes ahead of us."

"We *do* know what they're driving?" Neuhaus asked sarcastically.

"Yes. We've just found out from the BND." Ehren took a breath before delivering the bad news. "It is a Bundeswehr command car. I assume they also have appropriate uniforms and credentials."

Neuhaus, frowning, closed his eyes for long moments, then opened them, unblinking, to stare at Ehren. "Two spies, Felix, either accomplished or very lucky spies, heading to a rendezvous with American helicopters."

Neuhaus struggled with his rage, then spoke slowly, clearly enunciating each word. "Felix, close down the border. Close it down completely."

Ehren looked at the map. "The Americans . . ."

"Tell the Americans it is a police matter—that we are looking for criminals. We are establishing an emergency zone." Neuhaus rose partially out of his chair, face filled with anger and fear. He pointed a trembling finger at Ehren. "Tell the Americans anything, Felix, but stop those spies."

Ehren turned to the telephones. Within minutes standby interceptors were airborne from their bases at Dassau, Güstrow, and Eggersdorf. Surface-to-air missile units began coming up in status, and two of Germany's elite commando battalions reported to their helicopters.

General Vasily Yarymovych shifted in his chair, stubbed the remains of his cigarette into a nearby ashtray, and turned to an aide.

"Let us see what is going on in NATO."

Beside him an air force colonel punched buttons and rapped terse commands into a lip mike. Before Yarymovych and the colonel, colors blurred dizzily on a huge screen, then resolved themselves into a map of Western Europe. On the map, lights marked every major military unit in NATO. The lights semaphored NATO activity; their color and frequency of flashing was a code easily read by Yarymovych.

This was Sharapovo, the Soviet military holy of holies. American intelligence called it the Soviet National Command Authority. Eighteen miles south of Moscow and half a mile below the ground, Sharapovo was the primary command center from which the Politburo would direct the next war.

The colonel consulted the computer screen. "The air defense exercise continues. Otherwise all is normal."

Yarymovych continued to stare at the map. "There is an unusual amount of activity in Germany." It wasn't like it used to be, Yarymovych reflected. When there was a Warsaw Pact worthy of the name, you'd at least know what was going on in East Germany. Now you had to worry about the Germans *and* the Americans. The playing field was getting crowded, especially when you added in the British and French, who were also going their own way. Perhaps a treaty with the Germans *might* make things easier, Yarymovych thought. But that's not going to help tonight.

Again the colonel worked the computer. The screen soon displayed the status of what little Sharapovo knew of Germany's military forces.

Yarymovych grimaced. "That doesn't tell me much. I could as well read that out of *Pravda.*"

The colonel made desperate sounds into his lip

mike, then listened to the response through his headset. He turned to Yarymovych. "They've called up their Northern Air Defense Division," he reported to Yarymovych. "First-level interceptors are airborne. Their surface-to-air units are at battle stations in the sector directly west of Berlin. There is also some ground-forces activity, but we have no detailed information yet."

"Query Berlin." There were communications links with the Germans, but Yarymovych held out little hope of clarification. The Germans, Russia's about-to-be allies, Yarymovych thought sourly, were stiff-necked pricks. Reunification just got more of the pricks together.

Minutes later the colonel turned to Yarymovych. "They're not saying much—just that it's an internal matter."

Yarymovych grabbed the headset and microphone. What he got from his German counterpart was as vague. And so he forged the first link in a chain of ever-worsening events—he acted on the best information he had at hand. Perhaps it wasn't a NATO exercise. The Germans might be up to something.

Frowning, Yarymovych studied the map. Red lines defined a number of wedges radiating from Moscow. Each wedge was a *Teatr Voennykh Deistvii,* a geographical concept meaning theater of military operations. The Western TVD encompassed southern Norway to Spain.

There were seven levels of alert, ranging from the present peacetime level seven, to level one—all-out war. On his own authority, Yarymovych could move from level seven to level five. He thought for a moment, and here the instinct for bureaucratic survival came into play.

If Moscow was caught napping, it would be Vasily Yarymovych who'd be the scapegoat. Yarymovych had before him the recent lesson of the American spy plane: Colonel General Gladkov's career had been ruined after the *antisputnik* people botched that one. He shrugged and ordered the Western TVD to level six. It was a shift of only one level. A prudent move. And it couldn't hurt anything.

They'd had no choice but to go through the middle of Brandenburg. Brandt, at the wheel of the Gaz, was now familiar with the jeeplike vehicle's handling and took the narrow cobblestone streets with ease.

Wolf peered though the windshield, continuously fidgeting with the AKS assault rifle in his lap. Rentner, jackknifed into the rear seat, though occasionally groaning, was still unconscious.

"Slow down," Wolf directed. "The square is up ahead. From there, Route One west."

Brandt brought the Gaz to a crawl and nosed into the central square. He craned forward. The *Rathaus*—the town hall—anchored one end of the long square, a Gothic church the other.

"Route One passes to the left of the church."

"You mean, through the roadblock?"

Wolf's head snapped forward. At the end of the square, sawhorse barriers had been thrown up, red flares on the pavement marking a single-lane approach to a control point.

Wolf frowned. "This is a Bundeswehr vehicle. We are in uniform, and our credentials are . . ."

"So are the guys they've stopped." Brandt pointed to a light truck at the roadblock. Its occupants, a handful of German soldiers, were milling about while the police were going through the vehicle.

"They'd have a few questions about our friend, here." Brandt motioned to the comatose Rentner.

"There is no other way," exclaimed Wolf. "Not if we're to get to the helicopters before daylight."

Brandt studied the activity at the roadblock, almost one hundred yards away. He switched off the lights. "They haven't seen us here. We'll wait."

"But . . ."

"We'll wait, Herr Generalleutnant, and then we'll see how good you are with that." Brandt pointed to the assault rifle gripped in Wolf's hands.

After clearing the army truck through, the four policemen retreated to a portable shelter to escape the cold. As they did so, Brandt eased the Gaz into gear. Rounding the fountain, he picked up speed, aiming straight for the flares.

The last policeman entering the shelter door heard the sound of the engine and screeching tires. At that moment Brandt switched the headlights on high beam and hit the accelerator. The policeman realized that the vehicle wasn't going to stop. He shouted a warning as he tried to bring up his submachine gun and scramble for a clear field of fire.

"You'll kill us," screamed Wolf.

"Shut up and shoot, goddamnit!"

The policeman with the submachine gun was blocking the exit to the shelter. His comrades pushed by, causing his first burst to spray far to Brandt's left.

"Shoot, Wolf!"

Wolf opened fire with the unfamiliar weapon, the first rounds jittering high across the facade of the church. Compensating, the next burst ripped into the shelter, by now only yards away. Brandt saw the first policeman go down. A solid body-hit, judging from the way the man was hurled backward.

The command car hit the wooden barricades with a crashing noise of bending metal and shattering glass. The windshield on Wolf's side was now in shards on the German general's lap. Wolf himself was leaning out the side of the command car, emptying the AKS magazine at the cowering survivors.

"They'll be after us in no time." Wolf's breath came in ragged gasps.

"It won't be as easy as all that."

"You've got to call now."

"We've got at least twenty minutes before we're near the first possible pickup zone. We call now, and the helicopters will have to wait for us."

"So?" asked Wolf, anxiously. "What is wrong with that?"

"We're already in danger. No sense in exposing them as well."

Wolf cursed. "If we have to wait for the helicopters, we may never get out."

"We'll get out, Wolf. But I'm not going to call for the helicopters until we need them."

In *die Börse*, Felix Ehren jabbed another green pin into the map. "They got through a control point here," he motioned to Neuhaus, "here in Brandenburg."

" 'Got through'!" Neuhaus shouted, voice rising. " 'Got through'? How did they manage to do that? They pass by as if they are strolling through the park." Neuhaus's rage hushed the operations center. "Get them, Felix. Whatever you do, get them."

Ehren looked at the map. Route One west led to the flatlands along the Elbe. Wolf and his companion had to know that time was against them. Where would the helicopters land? Route One connected Brandenburg to Genthin. They'd never risk another town. South of Route 1 was the Havel Canal. They could only turn north!

Ehren summoned the senior army and air force operations officers.

Telford considered the map. They were out of Brandenburg, again heading west, paralleling the autobahn.

"No call yet?" he asked the operations officer.

She shook her head. "I don't expect anything for five, maybe ten minutes, unless . . ." She cut off to listen to her headset.

The operations officer turned to Telford. Her eyes carried her concern. "TR-one reports heavy and intense ground activity along Route One."

On the board red arrows were being plotted, one east from Genthin, another west from Brandenburg—between them, the small blue arrow that was Paul Brandt.

* * *

Flight leader Lieutenant Franz Bosselmann checked his fuel. Twenty more minutes—twenty-five at most—then back to Güstrow. Probably another refueling and yet another mission. Berlin was putting them through it tonight.

He saw his wingman in the dark sky, a darker shape, slightly behind and above him. Only minutes before, Berlin control had commanded them to engage any aircraft in the Magdeburg-Salzwedel sector that was not positively identified as friendly. When Berlin warned of helicopters, Franz had laughed into his oxygen mask. On patrol at seventeen thousand feet at near Mach 1, he didn't relish the thought of going down on the deck in the dark for a damned eggbeater.

"Attention, flight nine. Unidentified aircraft bearing oh-seven-six-oh. Range thirty kilometers."

Berlin control hadn't finished transmitting before Franz flipped on the J-band search radar and activated his infrared search/track sensors. He was now sweeping the skies within fifty miles. Two blips suddenly appeared on his screen. Range twenty-eight miles. Franz reported radar lock-on to control and as he did so, he armed his two R-23T air-to-air missiles.

In *die Börse*, Franz's targets matched the traces of two NATO aircraft—fast-movers, not helicopters. Their flight path, unless changed, would soon carry them into the newly declared emergency area.

Franz could not fire without control permission. The senior colonel watched the two pairs of aircraft —four blips on his screen—approaching each other on a head-on course. His fingers raced over his keyboard. Instantly the computer generated the expected intercept point for Franz's missiles. The electronic cross danced along the border of the emergency area, then crossed it.

The senior colonel looked up. Felix Ehren nodded.

"Flight nine, you are free to engage."

Franz heard the disembodied voice, then went smoothly and quickly through the familiar motions. Range to intercept was now less than fourteen miles. Missile one, then missile two, signaled seeker lockon. Both missiles had found the heat plume of a moving aircraft within the search limits set by Franz's radar. Range now twelve miles—maximum range of the missiles.

In the underground bunker in Hanau, activity at the plotting board picked up.

"Something's popped," whispered Frances Watkins.

The operations officer turned to Telford. "We have reports of air action vicinity Schöningen." Marks were appearing on the board just south of the autobahn at Helmstedt. "German aircraft have fired on a patrol of American F-16s."

The operations officer's voice was calm and clear. She listened for another moment, then turned to Telford.

"Your man's reporting in. He's asking for pickup at an alternate location. We're calling it PZ Julia. Their ETA is fifteen minutes."

Telford looked at the plotting board. The rendezvous—pickup zone Julia—was just west of a German village with the improbable name of Zabakuck.

The operations officer was staring at him, her lips compressed. Finally she broke into Telford's thoughts. "Sir. ETA at Julia is now fourteen minutes. Do we send Viper in?"

The red arrows were now inches away from the blue marks that were Paul Brandt. Farther away—perhaps half a foot—other marks that told of an encounter in the night skies of Germany. On a dark field some two hundred miles to the north, Wilhelm and two black helicopters waited for his word.

The White House situation room was sour with the smell of frayed nerves and overheated coffee. At one end of the long table, Sam Rubel jotted notes onto a pad, a gray secure phone cradled between his shoulder and ear. He hung up and looked to the president.

"That was Hanau. Steven's given the word for them to go in."

The president, casually dressed in an open-necked polo shirt and navy blue windbreaker, nodded, then turned back to Harry Scott.

". . . we don't know, Mr. President," Scott was saying. "Our guy's defensive avionics warned him of a missile launch—probably a heat-seeker like an AA-7. He reported it, and then we lost him."

"We don't know where it happened?" asked the president. "Our side of that emergency zone or theirs?"

Scott shook his head. "It'll take analysis of the radar tapes, and that could be hours."

The president searched the map board and status displays for a handhold, for anything firm. He turned back to Scott.

"What is it the chiefs want?"

Scott had just gotten off the phone with the

chairman of the Joint Chiefs of Staff. "To move up to DEFCON four. DIA says that Sharapovo's cranked up to level six in the Western TVD."

Bush considered this. DEFCON was like a ladder, the lowest rung being five. At each rung more preparations were taken for war; preparations necessary to prevent being taken by surprise. Yet avoiding surprise—a purely defensive move—could be mistaken by a suspicious enemy as a step toward a sudden attack.

"What brought the Russians up?" Bush asked.

"We don't know that, either. CINCSAC wants to put ten B-1s on airborne alert."

Bush swiveled. Scott knew the pressure this put on the president: the United States had not flown battle-ready bombers with nuclear weapons in their bays for nearly thirty years. To do so now could send a potentially ambiguous signal to the Kremlin—that deadly American retaliatory forces would survive any surprise attack—or that the Americans were preparing an attack of their own.

The president shook his head. "No. No airborne alert—not yet. Increase to DEFCON four, but the bombers stay on the ground."

Bush tilted his chair back and looked again at the silent map and display lights, pulling pensively at his lower lip. No matter how many satellites or spies, it's always the same—when you've got to make the decisions is when you have the least information. He rocked forward.

"Harry, get Mr. Letnikov on the horn. We've got some talking to do."

* * *

Never more than fifty feet above the ground, the two OH-58Ds flew eastward, skirting hilltops and dropping into valleys. Wilhelm soon saw the night glow of Magdeburg in the south. Coming out, they would fly even closer to the city: they would skim along the Mitteland Canal, hoping that the German antiaircraft guns hadn't been redeployed since last week's update.

Overhead and to the rear of Wilhelm, the OH-58D's mast-mounted sight gave the small helicopter an unmatched ability to fly and fight. Above the whirling rotor blades, a round beach-ball head rested on a long, shoulderless neck. Two mismatching lens made up the eyes, giving the mast-mounted sight a friendly if somewhat surreal personality. Wilhelm had long ago abandoned the government nomenclature for the sight and joined with his crews in using its nickname.

"ET's laser?" Wilhelm asked by intercom to Ted Deming, his observer-gunner in the left seat.

Deming gave a thumbs-up.

ET's right eye was an advanced forward-looking infrared sensor. Its thermal images, combined with the night-vision goggles Wilhelm and Deming wore, turned the night into day. Behind the larger left eye was an all-light level television camera that could do skin-pore close-ups through fog, smoke, or battlefield haze, and do them from more than five miles away. Below the eyes—ET's chin—was the long-range laser designator Wilhelm asked about.

The chronometer seemed to be racing. Less than six minutes to PZ Julia. Plenty of hostile air around, but that didn't concern him. Wilhelm knew from countless hours of mock combat against friendly jets that fast-movers had a hell of a time finding helicopters flitting in the ground clutter of scarch radars. It was the stuff below that was worrisome—the ZSU-23 guns or the hand-held SAMs.

Wilhelm pushed a switch on his control stick. The display screen flickered, and a map appeared of the area around Julia. Stationary symbols showed the village of Zabakuck, and to the west PZ Julia. To the south a tiny circle flickered—Brandt's location as relayed from the direction finders on the TR-1. On either side of the circle, flashing triangles —the bad guys.

Brandt swore. The odor of gasoline was stronger.

"What's the matter?" asked Wolf.

"We must have taken a hit in the gas tank."

"How bad is it?"

Brandt rapped the gauge. The needle quivered at empty. "Can't tell. How much farther?"

"Four, perhaps five, kilometers." Wolf motioned at the road before them. "Just over this hill we turn north. Then there is a branch. We go left to Zabakuck."

Cresting the hill, Brandt could see the road junction just ahead. Then he and Wolf saw the approaching lights strung out before them, perhaps a mile away.

"A convoy!" shouted Wolf.

Brandt accelerated. "Radio on."

"Are you certain you . . ."

There was a flickering from the lead lights.

"I'm not worried about them finding us. They've already done that."

The shooting from the convoy was high and off

to Brandt's left, the bullets hitting the trees along
the roadside. The Gaz was now full out, racing head-
long into the approaching convoy.

Brandt's transmission came just as Viper flight
was clearing the small village of Mützel, less than
three miles from the road junction. Deming
switched to the television.

"That's our guys." Wilhelm's cursor pointed to
the Gaz, which had just made the road junction and
was turning north.

Deming soon found the front of the pursuing
convoy. At lead was an eight-wheeled BTR-70, an
amphibious personnel carrier. Someone's after the
Gaz, he thought, seeing the muzzle flashes of the
BTR's heavy machine gun.

Wilhelm pressed a button, and a flashing trian-
gle was superimposed over the BTR image. Deming
passed the cue to ET. Instantly ET's laser zipped an
invisible beam onto the flat armor deck of the BTR,
just behind the machine-gun turret. Wilhelm could
maneuver as he wished, but until told otherwise, ET
would keep the laser beam locked onto the BTR,
now a mile and a half away and gaining on the Gaz.

"Viper Two, this is Viper Six," Wilhelm called to
his wingman. "I have ET laser lock. Engage ASAP."

Viper Two had no ET. The weight saved went
to carrying a rack of four Hellfire missiles. Viper
Two's pilot had armed the Hellfires on lift-off. The
stubby missiles's autopilots were warmed up. Now
their seeker heads began their search, sweeping a
quadrant right and left of the path of flight. Within a
fraction of a second, all four Hellfires reported finding ET's laser beam.

"Viper Two launch one."

Over the roar of rotors and engines, Wilhelm heard the dull crumping explosion of the launch. Through his smoked visor, he followed the bright trail of the Hellfire motor. At this range, he thought, it ought to burn almost all the way into the target.

The Hellfire detonated precisely on the turret ring. Its heavy shaped charge created a lance of white hot molten metal that cut through the armor and torched into the troop compartment. Twelve infantrymen, the driver, and the gunner were instantly killed by the ricocheting shrapnel as ruptured fuel lines turned the BTR into a funeral pyre.

Dietrich Neuhaus stood before the huge map. His lips were pulled back in a grimace of lust and excitement. He would get the spies and the American helicopters as well!

The arrows converged just north of Route 1. No more dodging! He knew where they were. And they would not get away.

Neuhaus turned to his generals. "Saturate this area," he drew the long pointer across the plastic surface of the map. "Here—from Rossdorf to—here, Altenkitsche and Zabakuck."

Within minutes, a flight of forty helicopters lifted off from Potsdam with the assault elements of two commando battalions. On the Baltic island of Rugen, a company of the elite Willi Saenger Parachute Battalion loaded into An-26s. *Die Börse* controllers pulled out all stops and began vectoring all available aircraft into the Magdoburg Salzwedel sector, even those from bases as far south as the Czechoslovak border.

Amid the disciplined hubbub, Neuhaus stood transfixed at the map, staring at the road to Zabakuck.

With the convoy chasing Brandt stopped briefly by the exploding BTR, Jack Wilhelm circled Zabakuck and was in approach to PZ Julia when he crossed the road just north of the tiny village.

"Oh, shit," he muttered to himself, and keyed his transmitter.

Two hundred miles away Steven Telford answered. "Go ahead, Viper Six." Telford waited, hearing only an electronic wind in his headset.

In Hanau, Telford had been monitoring the radio traffic between Wilhelm and Brandt. The map could no longer show what was going on in the few square miles that was rapidly becoming a battlefield. Wilhelm had seconds before switched to the exclusive channel connecting him with Telford.

"Ah, Roger, Home Plate," came Wilhelm's voice. *"Our man is approximately two miles from Julia. He's in a squeeze play. They're boxing him in, north and south."*

"Can you pick him up on the road?"

Wilhelm saw the dark forest just below his helicopter skids.

"Negative. Too many trees. No approach."

Telford's hands were slippery with sweat, and a remembered terror clutched at him. He keyed his mike. "Viper Six, can our man make it to Julia for pickup?"

The rush of static, like some otherworld wind, filled the operations room. Then, at last, Wilhelm's voice came, strained and wavering. *"It's going to be close."*

Telford sat back, haunted by a premonition of plans going very badly wrong, remembering ghosts of Challenger's voices from a long-ago Florida sky.

Twenty-nine

Wilhelm called up the tactical display. In the center of the screen was Zabakuck and the narrow north-south road through the dense forest. Brandt was racing toward the village from the south, hoping to make PZ Julia before the German pincer closed on him. A large convoy was approaching Zabakuck from the north, and the convoy to the south, having gotten itself back into order, was in hot pursuit.

Darting just above the trees a mile to the west, Viper flight paralleled the road, hiding behind a low ridge. Three times Wilhelm bobbed only high enough to let ET scan the road. Infrared and television gave Wilhelm the lineup of the northern convoy, his next target, and what he saw wasn't encouraging. Five BTRs, carrying up to eighty troops, were bad enough, but there were also two ZSU-23-4s. Vicious, self-propelled antiaircraft guns, each ZSU could pour out a thousand explosive slugs a minute.

With an ease born of hundreds of hours of practice, Viper flight slipped into position. Both OH-58s at a hover, Wilhelm eased up until ET barely cleared the ridge line. Viper Two, three hundred yards away and almost on the ground, was completely out of sight from any observer on the road.

ET scanned the convoy. Wilhelm swung the cursor to a BTR at point on the convoy. As he did so, he made a mental note that a ZSU was just behind the armored carrier. ET's laser locked on, illuminating a spot just above the front drive wheel.

A Hellfire on Viper Two roared into the night. Clearing the ridge line, the missile's seeker sought and found the laser's telltale mark. The Hellfire continued gaining altitude until its computer angled it over to dive on the armored vehicle.

The flare of the exploding missile momentarily blanked Wilhelm's display. Before the screen cleared, ET had slewed to and locked on the ZSU.

Inside the armored hull of the ZSU, the radar observer frantically searched his acquisition screen. Nothing. The BTR's ammunition was now exploding, and the ZSU crew felt the claustrophobic desperation of men who fight encased in steel.

Two hundred meters behind the burning BTR, the convoy commander, an infantry *Oberleutenant,* struggled to regain control of his troops. When the BTR had been hit, they'd gone into their drill: out of the carriers and into hasty perimeter-defense positions. Berlin control had just countermanded that— Berlin wanted them moving at all costs.

The lieutenant heard the ZSUs, first one, then the other. Firing, then traversing. Firing, traversing again. They hadn't found a target; they were shooting blind down likely avenues of enemy attack, their yellow tracers grazing the treetops along the road.

A shock wave rocked the lieutenant's command vehicle. The lead ZSU was enveloped in flames, its four guns firing a last defiant burst before a second and massive explosion tore through its ammunition stores.

In a fleeting instant the faces of the BTR and ZSU crews passed before the lieutenant. Men—good men—*his* men. He raged against the unseen helicopters lurking somewhere in the night.

Franz Bosselmann didn't need his radar or infrared search sensors—the stricken convoy was a fiery beacon just north of Zabakuck. His stomach lurched as he rolled into a steep dive. Inverted, he saw Viper Two's third Hellfire launch, the missile lighting up the side of the helicopter.

"VIPER TWO!"

Wilhelm shouted again, knowing as he did so that Viper Two was the fireball that lit the ridge in a harsh magnesium flash. Before the light had dimmed, he threw his helicopter into a hard left bank. Over his right shoulder he saw a stream of twenty-three-millimeter tracers. Deming was busy at his console as Wilhelm spun them into an even tighter turn.

Pulling out of his dive, Bosselmann cleared the ridge by scant inches. He'd bagged the one helicopter with his cannon, and in the glare he'd spotted the second one. He would have to pull maximum Gs to get back for another firing run. He whipped the stick into his stomach and kicked the right rudder bar.

As the MiG climbed up to the right, the OH-58 was completing its turn, a spin on its axis that brought the Stinger missile into line with the jet fighter's exhaust plume.

As soon as he heard the warbling tone of seeker lock-on, Deming pickled the Stinger.

Bosselmann's MiG exploded as Brandt and Wolf

topped a low rise. The fireball appeared to be nearly overhead, adding to the conflagration of the burning convoy several miles ahead. Small arms fire crackled, and shock waves from explosions rocked their vehicle. The road into Zabakuck looked like hell itself.

Brandt braked to a quick stop and got on the radio. Calling several times for Viper flight, he heard a high-pitched caterwauling tone, rapidly shifting in volume: German jamming. He tossed the now-useless radio onto the seat and eased the Gaz into gear.

"We're not going to Zabakuck?" Wolf's voice had a hysteric edge to it.

"No. The way is blocked. They will have the town."

"We're not going to Zabakuck," Wolf repeated the pronouncement of his own death sentence.

Brandt looked at Wolf, attracted by a movement and a snicking sound. Wolf's automatic was pointed at him, Wolf's teeth bared and clenched.

"What the hell are you doing . . ."

"You've held two cards over me—the threat of exposing me as a spy and the promise of getting me out. You've played the first. Now you must get me out. We are going to Zabakuck—to the helicopters." Wolf jerked his head in the direction of the road.

"But the helicopters . . ."

"Drive!" Wolf jammed the cold steel of the muzzle against Brandt's temple. "We can't waste any more time!"

Brandt floored the Gaz; then, without warning, stood on the brakes. Wolf crashed heavily into the dashboard, and before he could recover, Brandt had twisted the pistol from his hand and flung it out the window.

"Goddamn you, Wolf! Sit still and shut up!"

Now overcome with fear, Wolf cringed against the door, his face in his hands.

For an instant Brandt studied the road ahead, then started up. Fifty yards later he saw it, a small road to the right that would lead him east of Zabakuck.

Little more than a logging trail, the road twisted and turned, making its way up a small hill. Several times Brandt glanced warily at Wolf, but the German kept to the far side of the Gaz, frozen, staring fixedly through the shattered windshield down the narrow lane.

"I'm stopping here for just a moment," Brandt explained, taking pains to appear calm.

Brandt aimed a small flashlight down the road, blinking, then waiting; blinking, then waiting. On the third repetition two short and two long flashes came in answer. He eased the command car ahead.

Passing where the light had come from, Brandt saw two men in camouflaged battle dress trotting onto the road from the nearby trees.

"We're almost there," he told the seemingly unhearing Wolf.

The road opened onto a clearing on the hilltop. A great black shadow hulked near the far tree line. Not until he was almost on it could Brandt make out the large drooping rotor blades. As the Gaz pulled alongside, he recognized it as an Mi-24 and saw the large red star just aft of the rocket pod.

Brandt got out and motioned Wolf to do the same. From the darkness three men came to carry Rentner to the helicopter.

"I'm sure you would have preferred the United States," Brandt said, now relaxed, almost casual.

"But one must be flexible. Don't you agree, General?"

Vasily Yarymovych got word that Letnikov was on his way to Sharapovo. He glanced at the chronometer. The secret subway from the Kremlin would take about half an hour. The communications technicians had tested the link to Washington; both audio and video channels were working well. It would be the first time Letnikov and Bush used the new "hot line," the original being a clumsy teletype that was slow and vulnerable to intercepts. This latest version had been thoroughly vetted during construction by the KGB and swarms of American inspectors.

Communications attended to, the Soviet general turned to force status. The crucial element here were the three hundred RS-20s. Each carrying ten thermonuclear warheads, they were accurate enough to destroy the American Minuteman ballistic missiles in their hardened underground silos. They could, that is, if they were ready for instant firing.

But unlike the American missiles, the RS-20s could not be kept indefinitely at high-alert levels because of the relatively short operational life of their complicated electronics and guidance systems. Yarymovych's problem this morning was whether to bring the RS-20s up or to leave them dormant. The former would ensure that they could be used immediately if Letnikov and the Defense Council so ordered them; it would also put the Americans on guard.

On the other hand, if he left the RS-20s dormant, the missiles might be vulnerable to attack by the American submarine-launched missiles. Yarymovych picked up his green telephone and ordered a report on the number and position of American ballistic missile submarines in port and those at sea.

God, he looks awful, Kathleen Orsini thought. Steven Telford, chin nearly on his chest, sat slumped over a mug of coffee. His eyes told of bone-weariness; deep furrows framed his mouth. Accompanied by a Station officer, Kathleen had flown to Hanau from Berlin. There she and a dispirited Telford boarded the Gulfstream and were soon heading west.

Telford haltingly described the hours at Hanau; the repeated attempts to contact Brandt; Wilhelm's escape into France; the call to Bush to tell him of the mission's failure. He finished, wrapping his hands around the mug as if to warm them.

"I was—was helpless." He filled the words with self-reproach. "I sat there listening to it all falling apart." He looked at Kathleen, unable to grant himself understanding, unwilling to ask it of her. "I just sat there," he said bitterly.

She wanted to pull his face into her breasts, to enfold him, protect him from the torment. She fought the urge to touch him.

"What could you have done, Steven?"

He looked up, unable to answer her.

"Did you think that somehow you could keep everything on track all by yourself?"

Telford regarded her silently for long moments, then shook his head. "No. No, but . . ."

"If there were things beyond your control," she persisted, "why do you feel responsible? Didn't you do the best you could?"

"I did the best I could. But you see," he explained, "I'm still responsible."

"How? Why?"

"Because," he said quietly, "I'm the director of Central Intelligence. I was given a mission by the president. I was in charge. The mission failed. It is as simple as that."

"What now?" she asked, wanting to know about the next hours and, she suddenly realized, about the rest of their lives.

Telford, understanding, squeezed her hand. "For now? For now, back to Washington."

James Blair, secretary of defense, sat in the balcony overlooking a sprawl of desk officers, communications specialists, and status boards in the Pentagon's National Military Command Center.

Blair found it endlessly amazing that in seconds he could see the location of every major American and allied military unit, or satellite photographs of the clandestine Soviet germ warfare laboratories in Sverdlovsk, or a count of the number of Rumanian T-62 tanks in the Drăgănești Olt repair depot.

This place is seductive, Blair thought. Sit here long enough, and you come to believe that it's the center of the universe; that from it all can be known, everything can be controlled.

This evening the Honorable James Blair knew that wasn't so. Conflicting reports had been coming in from DIA, NSA, and the Agency about Operation Skyhook and what the military called the collateral damage. Only fifteen minutes ago was it finally determined that the Germans had, indeed, downed an American F-16.

Most alarming was the warlike posture rapidly being attained by Soviet tactical units in their Western TVD. On the ground nearly every armored division was preparing to move into field formations.

Blair's review of the Soviet armor situation was interrupted by another board blinking a harsh warning red. Yet another Delta IV ballistic missile sub had just put out to sea from the Guba Zapadnaya Litsa fiord on the Kola Peninsula. Blair fumbled for a cigarette, fired it up, and took a deep drag.

The Delta IV carried the new SS-N-23 Mod 2 missile. The Mod 2, fired on a depressed trajectory, could drastically reduce warning time at SAC's bomber bases. The B-1s would get off in time, but the slower B-52s would be sitting ducks.

Blair did his doomsday arithmetic: each Delta IV carried sixteen missiles. Each missile had ten warheads. He scanned the status boards again. Yes—eight Deltas now deployed—over twelve hundred thermonuclear weapons.

NMCC could tell him what it saw. It was what it *didn't* see that worried Blair. He looked at the Delta deployments again, then at SAC's array of bombers and missiles. He took another drag from his cigarette and reached for the telephone.

Harry Scott put the telephone aside amid piles of messages and reports. "Mr. President, Jim Blair's recommending that we flush the MXs and begin airborne alert of the bombers."

Sam Rubel was a silent but observant witness to

the discussion between George Bush and his national security advisor. The MXs were the problem.

Fifty of the big ten-warhead missiles had been adapted to be launched from trains. Normally the missile trains remained in seven above-ground garrisons spread across the center of the continent. To evade Soviet satellite targeting, the trains needed at least two hours to spread out and lose themselves on the vast American rail net. Once they did this, they'd be as difficult to hit as submarines but would retain the considerable advantage of instant communications that the subs lacked.

Deep in discussion, the president and Scott were interrupted by a uniformed navy chief petty officer. The president asked a question or two, and the chief pointed to the wall clock.

"It's Letnikov," Bush explained. He gathered his notes and followed the chief to the communications studio next door. The studio was scarcely large enough for the president and two technicians; those in the situation room would follow the exchange through wall-mounted monitors.

Sam watched Bush settle himself in the straight wood chair behind a small desk. Behind Bush was the American flag. The studio was painted a soft blue.

An ear-splitting squawk of static came over the loudspeaker; then the left screen showed a Soviet flag. A shadow passed as Yegor Letnikov came on screen, settled himself in a chair, and stared stolidly into the camera.

"You wished to speak, Mr. President."

The translator was damn good, Sam Rubel observed. Letnikov's Russian was immediately followed by a soft-neutral voice with an American accent.

"Yes. I am concerned that certain events in Germany are creating dangerous tensions between the United States and the Soviet Union."

Rubel glanced at Scott. Scott approved. Bush had been explicit without pointing fingers. Rubel noticed Bush had avoided calling Letnikov "president."

"I, too, am concerned, Mr. President. We see numerous provocations by your Strategic Air Command, by your missile submarines."

Bush tilted his head slightly, taking on a quizzical look. I raise Germany, and he comes back with SAC. He's dodging, Bush thought.

"These are defensive precautions. But we take them because of what is happening in Germany. I suggest we focus on Germany. . . ."

Letnikov's Russian was a gutteral staccato, and the translator's voice picked up the harsh tone. "What is happening in Germany, Mr. President, is an example of American adventurism—a game being played by your cowboys."

The president suppressed a flash of anger. "I am not here to exchange accusations. It is important that you have certain information about the situation in Germany—information that bears on the activities of Dietrich Neuhaus."

Letnikov sat expressionless as Bush quickly sketched what the Americans knew of East Group Raven.

So far unremarkable, save for a testimony to the efficiency of American intelligence. Quite good, Letnikov thought, if only we were as proficient. Thinking Bush had finished, Letnikov started to speak, but before he could, Bush continued, and it was then that a cold fear swept through Letnikov.

"There are other things we know. Things about your relationship with Dietrich Neuhaus and the plans the two of you have made together."

Yegor Letnikov's understanding of English, while not fluent, was good, and so he frantically jammed the button in the arm of his chair well before the American translator began. From here on his translator was cut out of the circuit as well as Sharapovo's monitoring and recording machines.

"Go on, Mr. President."

Bush noticed immediately that Letnikov had spoken in English and knew then that the two of them were now on quite different grounds.

"We know that before Mikhail Gorbachev was overthrown, you and Neuhaus had established a secret communications channel. It was through this channel that you agreed to provide secret military assistance."

"We have talked of this." Letnikov tossed his head in dismissal.

"Yes," Bush countered quickly, "but it was this same channel through which Neuhaus supported you and helped you plan to unseat Gorbachev."

Bush thought he saw Letnikov flinch; just the slightest recoil.

"You have no proof."

The president continued, quietly relentless, speaking slowly to be certain Letnikov understood. "Did you know that Neuhaus intends to double-cross you? Do you know that he has taken the warheads from the short-range missiles you have given him and will put them on long-range missiles? That he intends to use those missiles to build a world military power—a Fourth Reich?"

Bush waited a heartbeat, then asked very deliberately: "Do you know these things, Yegor Kuz'mich Letnikov? Do your comrades on the Politburo know these things?"

In the Situation Room Sam Rubel saw a brief, last picture of Letnikov—a man thoroughly frightened, staring out of the television monitor—then the screen went blank.

Scott turned away from his telephone as a grim George Bush returned to the Situation Room. "It's Blair again. He wants to flush the MXs and put the bombers on airborne alert. He says the Russians are bringing up their SS-18s."

In a windowless room in the KGB's modernistic concrete-and-glass building off the Moscow ring motorway, Gregori Romanov, now chief of the First Chief Directorate, pushed his chair back from the screen. The technician in the control room gave a thumbs-up—they'd recorded the Bush-Letnikov exchange from start to finish.

Romanov sat stunned. The American president's allegations were explosive—but still only allegations. To wait to see if Bush was telling the truth would be to wait to see if Neuhaus unveiled his missiles. And by that time it would be too late.

He watched unseeing as the technician retrieved the master tape and made copies. There ought to be steps that could be taken without arousing suspicion. Romanov remembered that Sharapovo was bringing up the forces of the Western TVD. An association clicked. He bolted forward to the telephone to call his close friend, the chief of the Border Guards Directorate.

At cruising altitude, when the noise of the big helicopter's turbines faded, Rudolf Wolf leaned forward on the nylon troop seat. Paul Brandt, seeing this, did the same. The two men's faces were but inches apart.

"When did you go over?" Wolf asked.

"Go over?" Brandt's eyes were cold. "I didn't go over, Wolf. I made a"—A separate peace, he almost said, realizing it himself for the first time—"a certain . . . arrangement."

"An arrangement with the Russians?"

Still stunned by this revelation, this sudden understanding of himself, Brandt felt wrapped in a sense of comforting serenity. No, Brandt wanted to say, I finally made an arrangement with myself.

"With the KGB," he answered Wolf. "With their Berlin *rezident*."

Wolf appraised Brandt through slitted eyes. "You made the arrangement with the Russians because you did not trust your own people."

Brandt said nothing but looked at him steadily.

"That was it, wasn't it?" Wolf persisted. "You did not trust your own people."

Brandt measured Wolf, making adjustments for a final image of the man.

"Trust?" Brandt smiled bitterly. "We're spies, Wolf. We don't know trust. Deceit and deception are the tools of our trade. But they turn against us in the night. We know there is deceit and deception in the things we do, and so we imagine it in the things others do. The games we play with others, others play with us."

Brandt shifted away to look into the darkness beaten by the rotors overhead.

Wolf tugged insistently at Brandt's sleeve.

"What will happen to me?"

Brandt struggled with his anger and contempt. "You—and Rentner here—will go on to Moscow. For a short time you'll be the celebrities among the other espionage expatriates in the Philby colony. Then you'll settle into a routine job somewhere— research, something like that."

"And you?"

"They no longer need me. You and our friend there are the prizes." Brandt jerked his head to Rentner, bound on the floor of the helicopter, watched over by two *spetznaz* sergeants.

The helicopter's pitch changed, and with it came a noticeable loss in altitude. One of the *spetznaz* slid open the large troop door. Just below Brandt saw Spandau. They were heading southeast, descending into the Grünewald, the large forest south of Charlottenburg.

The Mi-24 touched down with a light bumping motion. The *spetznaz* by the door made hurried motions at Brandt, pointing to the forest outside.

Freeing himself from the seat, Brandt squeezed by Wolf and jumped to the ground. The helicopter was already lifting as he straightened up. For a frozen second he and Wolf faced each other through the still-open doorway. He thought for an instant to wave but instead turned to make his way into the city.

* * *

At NSA in Fort Meade, two Flash-Immediates superimposed themselves on Kupperman's computer screen. They were preliminary reports, both from A Group. Taking a few minutes to call one of the analysts for clarification, he next dialed Sam Rubel on the priority gray line.

"Is he certain?" The president asked, obviously shocked. "Tanks moving on Moscow? Russian tanks?"

Sam Rubel nodded. "It was a satellite intercept. NSA didn't have any trouble with it—the Russians weren't even encrypting their traffic—everything was transmitted in the clear."

"And the airline business?"

"From an intercept station in Norway. They picked up the Aeroflot order to ground all flights. It's been confirmed by DIA's port-watcher program."

Scott interrupted. "State's got an open line with Embassy Moscow. A twenty-four-hour curfew's been slapped on. Those tanks—they're in Red Square. Our attaché says they're from one of the KGB's guards divisions—not the Red Army."

Five minutes later Radio Moscow's normal programming went off the air. There followed an uninterrupted broadcast of classical music.

War was brought even closer by a fragment of nickel ore no larger than a child's fist—the messenger of an unnamed planet's death countless thousands of years before. At thirty thousand miles an hour, it ripped through the solar panels and ex-

ploded with the force of a small bomb in the guts of
the eighteen-ton satellite.

Sam Rubel held the telephone away from his
ear. His voice was hoarse with tension. "Mr. President. It's Langley. We've lost a KH-12."

Time was momentarily frozen in the situation
room.

"How did it happen?" Bush asked, already an-
ticipating the answer.

Sam shook his head. "We don't know. It's just
gone."

"Like that?"

"Yes, sir. Like that."

"Where?"

"Over Novosibirsk—Siberia."

"Did the Russians do it?"

"We don't know," Rubel replied. "We just don't
know."

"Is this the only one? There haven't been any
others?"

"It's the only one." Rubel barely kept himself
from saying, "So far."

Bush nodded grimly.

Sam Rubel knew what was on the president's
mind. If the Soviets blinded satellites like the KH-12,
this would deprive the Americans of explicit warning and hamper a retaliatory strike. The experts had
long theorized that this would signal the onslaught
of a massive rain of Soviet nuclear warheads. From
this the experts built intricate response decision
trees: do this with the bombers, that with the
ICBMs, and order the subs to . . . But the experts
weren't sitting in the situation room this night.

"Tell Blair to flush the MX trains." George Bush's voice was steady and certain. "And tell him to get the bombers airborne."

Standing pools of water disappeared, flashed into steam from the B-1's four afterburners. The first sleek bomber had barely broken free of the ground before another began its takeoff roll. The B-1s, some forty in all, would separate, meet with their tankers, then begin to hold in great orbits, pacing the lonely skies above Canada and the Atlantic. Spread over thousands of cubic miles, forty crews waited for the word to drop to two hundred feet to begin their screaming runs into the Soviet Union at nearly the speed of sound.

Near Little Rock, Arkansas, Lieutenant Colonel Patricia Warren watched the communications and systems checks play out. In four hours her train with two MX missiles would be near Muskogee, Oklahoma. She ran through her initial targeting orders. Her twenty nuclear warheads were aimed at the Soviet SS-18 missile silos at Uzhur. She wondered if the SS-18s would still be there.

"Mr. President, it's time to leave."

"Leave?" Bush asked Harry Scott. "What're you talking about?"

"KNEECAP, Mr. President. The alternate command post."

KNEECAP, a special Boeing 747, sat on ready alert a few miles from the White House at Andrews Air Force Base. It would whisk the president out of endangered Washington and serve as an airborne seat of government until landing at a secret airstrip in the Rockies. From KNEECAP a president could maintain contact with the Joint Chiefs of Staff and military commanders around the world, to include the commander in chief of the Strategic Air Command. From KNEECAP a president could bring America into a nuclear war.

Bush was pensive. "I'm not going, Harry. Have them get the vice president or the speaker of the house. I'm staying here."

"But Mr. President . . ." Scott began a protest.

Crossing the Situation Room at a quick walk, the chief petty officer from communications thrust a note before the president. Bush read it, then looked up.

"Hot line. This time it's Moscow calling."

George Bush stood for a moment beside the chair, attempting to stretch out his cramped back. The monitor before him was blank.

There another blare of static, and the monitor showed the Soviet flag. Off-camera voices in Russian came through the loudspeaker. Bush picked up the earphone through which he would get the English translation. A weary president fumbled with the earphone wiring, waving off the proffered hand of the navy chief.

Bush was still standing when a small movement on the screen caught his eye. A man's back showed on camera; the man turned and sat. A familiar face looked out of the monitor.

"You seem surprised, Mr. President. You expected someone else?" Mikhail Gorbachev's smile was almost roguish.

George Bush recovered quickly. "As a matter of fact, I did. I . . . I assume you are . . ."

Gorbachev nodded. "I am the president," he said without bravado.

"Things are not going well between us."

Gorbachev sighed deeply. "That is so. Yegor Letnikov quite naturally kept his affair with Neuhaus a secret from the Politburo. Our military, knowing nothing about it either, did not comprehend what was happening in Germany, and so . . ." Gorbachev shrugged. "I have ordered a stand down in the military alert, Mr. President. I assume . . ."

"We are," Bush finished for him. "Even now my people are seeing to it."

Sam Rubel was already on the immediate-access line to CIA's operations center and NATO task force, and he saw Scott deep in conversation, most probably with Blair at the Pentagon.

"I take it that you know what caused this?" asked the president.

"A recording was made of your conversation with Yegor Letnikov, Mr. President. From that I gathered the outlines of his stupidity."

"I'm surprised that my words carry so much weight."

Again the roguish smile. "With me? Why of course they do, Mr. President. But others had to be convinced as well. It is fortunate that we had corroborating evidence in the form of one of Neuhaus's scientists. I understand we owe a considerable debt of gratitude to your intelligence operatives."

"It did not work out the way we planned."

"No?" Another shrug. "Such things rarely do. But we have a saying about all's well . . ."

"I believe we have something similar. What will happen to Mr. Letnikov?"

Gorbachev's mouth tightened. "That is a matter of Party discipline, Mr. President."

"There is another matter, President Gorbachev, that requires your attention."

"Oh?"

"Dietrich Neuhaus."

Gorbachev's brow furrowed, then he nodded in understanding. "Let us discuss that, Mr. President."

Sam Rubel's call came as they were over the English Channel. Kathleen Orsini saw a smile on Telford's face as he came out of the communications cabin. The Gulfstream was now banking sharply.

"Gorbachev's back in. Apparently a KGB coup. Sam says the Russians have Rentner and Wolf. The military alert's over."

"And Brandt?"

Telford's smile vanished. "I don't know. That's why we're going back."

"Back?"

"To Berlin."

They were met by the American consul, a fussy little man who led them past the airport customs down a back hall toward a waiting car. One instant Telford was aware of Kathleen beside him; the next, she was gone.

Spinning around, he saw her transfixed, looking into an open doorway. Inside, a round, bald man in suspenders and shirtsleeves, his lunch of bread and sausage now forgotten on his desk, sat staring at a television screen.

"Look," she pointed to the television set, "it's Gorbachev."

The German ignored the three Americans who crowded into his office. All four soon were totally absorbed by the Soviet leader.

Through a German translator Gorbachev explained the collusion between Dietrich Neuhaus and Yegor Letnikov that resulted in Gorbachev's overthrow. Letnikov's treaty with Germany, Gorbachev continued, was not intended to assure the security of either Germany or Russia but, rather, was a first step toward a renewed assault on stability in Europe.

"Jesus H. Christ," muttered the American consul.

The camera view widened. On Gorbachev's left was Rudolf Wolf; to his right the missile scientist Rentner. First Wolf, then Rentner, outlined Neuhaus's plan to betray Letnikov.

Over the television Telford could hear a swell of astonished voices in the public waiting room of the airport just over the office's partition.

"And finally," Gorbachev was saying, "there is the matter of manipulation of political events in Germany."

The screen flashed, and a montage of news clips first showed the torchlight rallies of Dietrich Neuhaus, then fastened on a close-up of the shouting demagogue, eyes maniacally wide, ropy veins bulging in his neck.

The image of Neuhaus still on the screen, Gorbachev's voice-over continued. "This man was used by the Letnikov conspirators, paid by them, and directed by them to deliver Germany and its citizens into the hands of a warlike clique."

In the small office Kathleen and Steven were startled when the German suddenly pounded his fist on his desk and began cursing the image of Dietrich Neuhaus. Outside, from the public waiting areas, came the swelling uproar of angry shouts.

"Come on," Telford pulled at Kathleen's elbow. "That's the sound of a score on the way to being settled. Let's find Brandt."

Brandt's apartment, as if keeping itself for his return, seemed to reproach Kathleen and Steven for their intrusion. And at the restaurant the old Corsican stared blankly, then shook his head at Telford's questions.

Outside the restaurant Telford and Kathleen walked slowly to the car the consul had put at their disposal. They paid no attention to the black BMW that pulled to the curb just ahead of them. From the car a tall, conservatively dressed man in his forties approached them, buttoning a dark overcoat.

"Mr. Telford, Ms. Orsini. I am Gregori Romanov. I was en route to Washington when we were told you diverted here."

Though taken aback, Telford dimly recognized the name. "You are . . ."

"The formal title is Chief of the First Chief Directorate of the KGB. I am responsible for all clandestine operations abroad." Romanov gave a small bow. "It is good to stretch my legs. May I walk you to your car?"

Telford nodded his assent, and they moved off slowly.

Romanov offered Telford a small package. "I am to deliver this to you on very explicit orders from President Gorbachev himself."

Tolford's surprise and wariness were evident.

"It does not tick, Mr. Telford," Romanov enjoyed his joke. "I believe you will find it very useful."

The avenue beside them was thick with army and police vehicles, and they stood watching the crowd gathering around the Bundestag.

"I understand a special session's been called," Romanov explained. "I should imagine Neuhaus's party will be voted out. The wagering is that Helmut Kohl will be back."

They took a few more steps, then Romanov spoke again: "You should know that Paul Brandt is alive and safe."

"Safe? Where?" asked Telford, a sharp note in his voice.

Kathleen moved closer to Telford, who reached out to find her hand.

Romanov smiled. "Not with us, I assure you. I have no doubt he'll ultimately show up when he decides to." The Russian arched an eyebrow. "He can enjoy a well-deserved rest on that Basel account that our General Wolf now no longer needs. Meanwhile, he is on his own—somewhat so."

"Somewhat so?"

"He is with a woman. An Elise Jacob."

"Jacob?"

"Yes. Apparently they developed a relationship neither you nor I knew about."

Telford searched the Russian's face.

Romanov had an ironic look. "There is a certain

symmetry to all this." He waved his hand toward the distant Brandenburg Gate.

"How do you mean?" asked Telford.

Romanov laughed. "You and I both have lost our best operatives in Berlin. You see, Elise Jacob was my *rezident* here."

Epilogue

"Come in, Joe," said Frank McCary, opening the door wide.

Joseph Cantabile stepped into the hideaway, taken, as most were, with the imposing grandeur of the Washington Monument framed in the window to his right.

"You know Steven Tolford." McCary gestured to the other end of the long room.

Cantabile's head swiveled, scenery forgotten. It was the politician's reflex: the smile went on, and the hand went out.

Telford stood somberly, ignoring Cantabile's hand.

Cantabile dropped his hand, flushing first with embarrassment, then anger. "Here to rub in your victory, Telford? You damned well better not gloat yet. The Agency's going to have some answering to do. . . ."

"Joe," Frank McCary interrupted, "you're right. The Agency's going to come up for the hearings, all right. But you won't be here."

Eyes wide, incredulous, Cantabile worked his mouth before the sound came out. "Not be here? What in hell are you talking about?"

"He's talking about this, Senator." Telford held

up a video cassette. "The KGB found it in the GRU files after Gorbachev returned to power."

Telford stepped to the console and slipped the cassette into the VCR, pushed a button, and the screen glowed. The three men stood silently watching as the screen flickered once, twice, then showed a room distorted through a fish-eye lens. At the bottom of the screen, numbers began to run, a clock superimposed over the picture.

"That's you, Joe," McCary gestured to the screen, where Cantabile was standing at a bar, mixing a drink.

"And the other one is Vladimir Krotov," Telford added. "What the rest of this tape shows is something most people would call treason."

The Washington Post

SENATE LEADER RESIGNS

Joseph Cantabile, a respected leader in the U.S. Senate, today resigned, citing reasons of personal health. This surprising development . . .

The Los Angeles Times
STARS SUPPORT OF SPEECH RIGHTS

Hollywood's best and brightest gathered last night at the Beverly Wilshire to support freedom of speech, and, in the words of the hostess, Constance Higby, "to protest the repressive policies of the Bush administration."

Ms. Higby, founder of ActPac, a bipartisan political action committee, said that the affair began when the State Department refused an entry visa for Enrique Valdez, Cuban minister for information.

"It is a travesty that this country would deny Mr. Valdez his freedom of speech," Ms. Higby said. Mr. Valdez was scheduled to speak at ActPac's annual fundraising gala.

Ms. Higby denied that the State Department action will hamper ActPac. "ActPac will continue to seek out the best of the nation's progressive political talent to run for national office," she said.

Time magazine:

MILESTONES

MARRIED. CIA Director Steven Telford and State Department arms negotiator Kathleen Orsini; in a private ceremony in the Senate hideaway office of Oklahoma Democrat Frank McCary. Telford, rumored to have played a major role in Mikhail Gorbachev's return to power, is picked by many insiders to be a new and promising contender for the Republican presidential nomination.

ABOUT THE AUTHOR

ROBERT ANDREWS, a former CIA officer and Green Beret, was most recently the national security adviser to a prominent United States Senator. He is now a senior executive in a major aerospace corporation and lives in Washington, D.C., with his wife, B.J.